I0541148

REPUTATION

REPUTATION

Ekaterine Nikas

little FOX

Long Beach

Copyright © 2014 by Ekaterine Nikas
Cover illustration by Donald Terlinden

All rights reserved. This book, or parts thereof, may not be
reproduced in any form without permission.

Published by Little FOX
PO Box 90191
Long Beach, CA 90809

ISBN: 0989189333
ISBN-13: 978-0989189330

This book is lovingly dedicated to my mother Susan.

Chapter 1

Devon, January 6, 1813

He is quite a devilish rake and actually kidnapped a poor girl—or was it two?"

Jane had been deep in a brown study and had heard little of her sister's whispered commentary on the various gentlefolk entering Farthingsgate's candlelit ballroom. Now she looked about, startled. "Who—" she began to ask, but there was no one to address her question to. Letty had moved off to speak with Squire Elton and his family. Her sister looked back over her shoulder and flashed Jane a reproving look. Letty was punishing her for not paying proper heed to her gossip, but it was also certain that her sister knew exactly the dramatic effect she had achieved by making such a pronouncement and then moving on.

Jane scanned the latest arrivals searching for the gentleman in question. She could not, at first, find any man under fifty in the group, let alone one who looked as if he could be the Lothario of Letty's description. Then her gaze traveled farther into the ballroom and she saw an unfamiliar gentleman dancing with her sister-in-law, Catherine. He was tall, though not as tall as Ryde, Jane's giant of a brother. His profile was handsome enough, but not anything out of the common way. His hair—though it glinted golden in the candlelight—was a bit shaggy compared to the precise cut Bevin, her late husband, had always insisted on. His clothes were neat, but not ostentatious, and he danced with the tight, controlled grace of a military man.

Could this be Letty's rake? While the gentleman was perhaps attractive enough to endanger a few maiden hearts, neither his manner nor his behavior seemed in any way remarkable. Of course, Jane was perhaps not the best judge of how remarkable or unremarkable a rake would appear. Her late father, known to the *ton* by the unfortunate sobriquet "Wild Ryde," had never seemed either as wild or as terrible as his reputation made him out to be.

Letty picked this moment to gaze back and note Jane's scrutiny of the stranger. She gave a slow and deliberate nod and then had the impudence to wink. Jane's lips tightened in irritation. Letty thought her tittle-tattle a fine joke, but behind every amusing *on-dit* there was a real person whose error or folly or heartache was being trumpeted to all the world. Sometimes people deserved such treatment; often they did not.

Jane's high-mindedness did not last long, however. Curiosity—and the appeal of further distraction from her own melancholy thoughts—got the better of her, and she turned back to observe the mysterious gentleman and Catherine proceeding down the line of dancers. The music was jaunty, and the dancers seemed in good spirits, especially Catherine. Her partner looked grave, almost wary, but when Catherine bestowed one of her sunny smiles upon him, his mouth almost relaxed into a grin.

The figure had reached the point where the gentlemen circled the ladies. The mysterious gentleman circled Catherine, and Jane had a clear view of his superfine-clad back. Her breath caught. Now that, she had to admit, was remarkable. His dark blue coat was expertly tailored to show off impossibly broad shoulders tapering down to a slim waist and powerful hips. For a moment, Jane pictured the contrast with Bevin's slight form, imagining the stranger without his coat. Then the thought of how disloyal such imaginings were washed over her, and, even though she now knew that her late husband deserved no such loyalty, she felt her cheeks heat with shame.

Perhaps God, too, disapproved her thoughts, for the mysterious gentleman made another turn in the figure and then looked straight at her. Jane had not noticed, during her study of the man, just how close the dance was bringing him. Now he stood a mere arm's length away from her. Close-up, he was more handsome than he had appeared at a distance, despite the small scars above his right eyebrow and near his mouth, and his eyes were alight with an intelligence that made the heat in her cheeks spread across her entire face. He inclined his head slightly and flashed her a quizzical smile. Heaven help her! Did he guess what she had just been thinking? Mortified to think he might, she turned away.

"Jane!"

Schooling her features in what she hoped would pass as a neutral expression, Jane turned toward her brother, who had come up behind her. "Yes, Ryde?"

He frowned down at her. "Well, what have I done?"

"Pardon?"

"What have I done to place me in your black books? You only call me 'Ryde' when you are angry with me."

"Do not be ridiculous. I am merely being polite. We are in public. Why should I not call you by your title?"

"Because you aren't Maria to stand on such ceremony. I begin to think Catherine was right to be fretting about you. Are you enjoying the Twelfth Night festivities?"

"Of course. Dinner was lovely, the shawl you and Catherine gave me is beautiful, and the ball," she paused and made a small gesture with her hand, "is obviously a great success."

"Then why aren't you dancing?"

"Because no gentleman has yet asked me," she snapped, her tone sharper than she intended. Seeing her brother's look of startled chagrin, she added more gently: "In any case, there are few enough gentlemen willing to dance, Drew. I would not deprive the young ladies of the neighborhood of any of their gallants. They have matches to make. I do not."

"My dear, you have been out of your black for nearly six months now. I know you still grieve, but—"

"Do I?" she replied bitterly.

"Janie?"

This time her brother's startled look irritated rather than soothed her raw feelings, but this was not the place or time to speak of her hurt, especially when its cause was so depressingly hackneyed. Eager to divert her own thoughts almost as much as her brother's questions,

Jane made a gesture toward her sister-in-law, "Why aren't you dancing with your lady wife?"

He flashed Jane a searching look. Then he accepted the change of subject with a slight lift of his shoulders. "Maria has decreed that I cannot monopolize the hostess. I am to be allowed two waltzes and a minuet. That is all." As he said the words, his gaze strayed toward Catherine, a smile tugging at his lips. The affection in that look gave Jane a pang of envy.

"You do not seem to mind overmuch. Are you not worried that she is currently standing up with a gentleman Letty has pronounced a 'devilish rake?'"

He laughed. It was a deep contented sound full of complacence. "Do not be silly, Jane."

"You used to worry about such things!"

"I used to be a fool who had no notion of the true state of my beloved's heart. I hope I am wiser now."

What was she doing? Of course, her brother had nothing to fear. Catherine loved Andrew with an intensity that was clear to anyone who caught a glimpse of them together. As for Drew... her besotted brother could not even speak his wife's name without grinning like a mooncalf. Jane reached out and seized both his hands in hers. "Forgive me, Drew! I am being a fool—a sad, bitter, cynical fool. Please ignore me."

"Janie, what the devil is wrong? You must tell me what is weighing on your spirits so heavily. Catherine warned me that something was amiss, but I—blast! They are headed this way. Our talk will have to wait, my dear, but talk we shall. Understood, sister mine?"

Jane gave a reluctant nod.

Her brother turned to greet his wife as the mysterious gentleman escorted her back to him. The gentleman made his bow. "Thank you, Lady Ryde, for a most pleasant dance."

Catherine smiled. "Mr. Winston, you know my husband the marquess."

Her brother inclined his head and the gentleman nodded. "Lord Ryde."

"And this is my husband's dear sister, Lady Jane Brawley."

The gentleman turned to meet Jane's gaze. "A pleasure, Lady Jane," he murmured dutifully, though she could detect no pleasure in his tone. It was as stiff as his suddenly rigid spine.

"Jane, allow me to introduce Mr. Anthony Winston. Mr. Winston is our newest neighbor. He has rented Rosington until Michaelmas."

"Welcome to the neighborhood, Mr. Winston," Jane murmured in return.

Catherine, seemingly insensible to the tension in the air, continued cheerfully, "Mr. Winston, I am sure Jane would enjoy standing up for a dance with you as much as I did."

Something tightened still further in Mr. Winston's expression, but he bowed and said politely, "Lady Jane, if you would do me the honor?"

Dancing with this suddenly fierce-looking stranger was the last thing Jane wanted to do, but rake or not, she could not humiliate him by refusing him after Catherine had basically ordered the man to dance with her. "Of course, sir," she replied, taking the arm extended to her. Only when they were out on the floor did she realize the next dance was to be a waltz. As Mr. Winston took her gloved hand in his and placed his other warm hand at her waist, it suddenly occurred to her that she had never waltzed with anyone but Bevin. The thought was enough to send her into a panic.

The music started, and he began twirling her in graceful circles across the floor. Her agitation slowly subsided, or rather transmuted into something less frantic but more painful: longing. He was a lovely dancer, and she enjoyed the feel of his strong arms around her and the sensation of being held so close to his broad chest. The lilting rhythm of the music at once soothed her and made her want to weep. It was Twelfth Night, she was dancing with a stranger, and nothing was right with the world. She wanted to be loved and cherished as her sisters were, as Catherine was, as she had once thought herself to be.

Suddenly Mr. Winston drew her closer and leaned near enough to speak into her ear. "Lady Jane, your dislike of my company is obvious, but could you please attempt the semblance of cordiality or at least glance my way on occasion so that the entire neighborhood does not believe I have offered you some unforgivable insult?"

Startled, Jane looked up directly into his green eyes. For a moment she saw a tumult of emotion in them; then all went still, like a becalmed sea, and she could make out nothing but a normal gentleman's irritation at being ignored.

For a moment, Jane wavered. It would be easy to lie. What could it possibly matter to this gentleman with the opaque eyes why she had treated him with such incivility? Yet she was suddenly sure that it did matter to him. *Intensely.* And, somehow, the fact that he did care made it impossible for her not to offer him the truth. "Sir, forgive me," she said quietly. "It is not your company that pains me, but my own sad thoughts. I am a widow, you see, and this is the first time I have danced with a gentleman since my mourning was over."

She paused, expecting him to offer her the usual polite sympathy for her true, if incomplete, statement. But he did not. Instead, he watched her face intently—his hand on her waist tightening as they continued their spinning progress—and waited for her to continue.

When the silence had drawn on beyond what she could bear, Jane reluctantly added, "The truth is, sir, that I do enjoy dancing with you. Indeed, I think I enjoy it more than I ever enjoyed dancing with any-one, even my late husband." She paused, searching for moisture in her suddenly dry mouth. The intentness of his gaze as he watched her was having an odd effect on her, making her strangely breathless. "But you see, you are reputed to be a rake, and I am a lady whose heart has been broken, and—and dancing with you is quite wonderful, but also quite terrible, because it reminds me of what I have lost and what I will never have." She finished in a rush, stupefied by her disastrous candor to this handsome stranger. Lord in heaven, what was wrong with her?

She could not imagine what he must think of her after this extraor-dinary avowal, but though she longed to run off and hide in a corner, she forced herself to keep her head high as they whirled through the last measures of the waltz.

His green eyes were no longer opaque, but dark and full of feeling. "You do not balk at your fences, do you, Lady Jane?" he said with surprisingly gentleness.

She regarded him for a long moment in silence. "No. I merely have a terrible tendency to rush them." She bit her lip. "Mr. Winston, I do beg you will forget my nonsense?"

The music had come to a stop, but still he stood there, holding her in his arms. "And if I do not wish to?"

"Sir, the dance has ended."

"Has it?"

"Yes, and in another moment we will become the focus of attention."

"And are you a lady who cares so much what people think?" The sudden intensity of his tone sent shivers across her skin.

She looked up into his eyes one last time. She wanted to deny it, to deny anything to remain as she was for a few moments longer. But she was Wild Ryde's daughter, and she knew too well the price to be paid for flouting society's opinion. "I fear I am," she said in a whisper.

"Very well, my lady," he said, his voice suddenly emptied of all the feeling that had thrilled her just moments earlier, "I will return you to your brother."

Mr. Anthony Winston joined the throng heading for the dining room to partake of Twelfth Night cake. He was grateful not to have to take another turn around the ballroom, ignoring the covert glances thrown his way by clumps of whispering ladies. He was even more grateful for the temporary suspension of the dancing. His thoughts were still focused on Lady Jane Brawley. Even if that were not the case, it was unlikely he would find another lady willing to do him the honor of a dance. Tales about him had clearly burned through the room with the speed and efficiency of a wildfire. Every chaperone in the place was eyeing him as if he were a fox among the chickens. He had but to begin to walk in the direction of a maiden lady, and her mother or aunt or sister would hurry the girl to some other part of the room, out of his way.

It was not surprising really. Indeed, he was used to it. In London, he never danced or even approached a lady who was not either married or a widow. But it was worrying that it was already happening here, in this new neighborhood, when he had only just arrived. Naively, he had hoped to find a brief respite here from the tattle. How in the world was he to help Georgiana, if he was labeled a pariah from the start?

He unclenched his jaw, inclined his head, and smiled at an old trout bustling by him to claim her cake. He had been introduced to the woman when he had first arrived, before the news of his reputation had made the rounds of the assembled matrons. Then she had simpered and fawned over him, no doubt eyeing him as a possible match for her empty-headed niece. Now she looked thunder at his effrontery in greeting her and muttered under her breath about the decline in morals in the younger generation.

Anthony gazed past her retreating back to where Lady Jane stood waiting with her three sisters, their husbands, Lord and Lady Ryde, and Lady Ryde's young brother, the Earl of Trenwich, for the butler to cut the cake—or rather, cakes. Due to the large number of guests, four large Twelfth Night cakes decorated with crowns and white pastillage were displayed on a large gleaming table decorated with evergreen garlands in the old-fashioned style. On either side of the cakes were large silver bowls full of punch, and next to one of the punch bowls was, strangely, a hat.

Most of Lord Ryde's family seemed to be enjoying the Twelfth Night revelry, but Lady Jane did not. She did not seem interested in the cutting of the cake or curious to learn who would find the bean and pea. Instead, she gazed rather wistfully at an ugly sprig of green bedecked in ribbon and hanging from the ceiling above a small doorway to her right. Anthony was reminded of his first sight of her, as he had entered Farthingsgate's fine ballroom and spotted her standing with one of her sisters, the dark haired one, who had been prattling in her ear. He had thought Lady Jane pretty, but not particularly memorable, until he'd followed her gaze and realized that she was not, as he had supposed by her sister's animated commentary, watching the entering guests but instead staring at a rather ugly wall sconce to the left of the doorway. For a moment, an unfamiliar chuckle had burbled in his throat. Then he had noticed the lady's melancholy expression and the bowed line of her pretty shoulders, and all desire to laugh had fled.

The butler finished his ministrations, and Lord Ryde gave the signal for the footmen to begin distributing cake and punch to the guests. Lady Ryde whispered something into her lord's ear that made him laugh and hand her the hat by the punchbowl with a flourish. She took the hat and flashed her husband such a warm smile of affection in return that Anthony felt his shoulders tighten in envy. Lord Ryde was a lucky man. In Anthony's experience, high-born wives of the *ton* rarely expressed open affection—let alone such warm feeling—toward their husbands. Anthony's gaze moved on to Lord Ryde's sisters. They, too, seemed unfashionably fond of their respective spouses—even the prim and proper blonde one, Lady Maria. Several times during the evening, Anthony had caught her casting warm glances toward her husband when she thought no one was looking. He wondered what the St. John family secret was for domestic bliss. They all seemed so happy—all except the one figure standing apart at the end of the row.

Anthony wished she would look his way.

Earlier, when he had been dancing with his hostess, he had turned to find Lady Jane standing quite near. She had been gazing directly at him, her blue eyes filled with open admiration. It had not been a flirtatious look. Its openness had been entirely unintentional. Indeed, she had started a little when their eyes had met, and a wave of pretty color had washed over her face. Yet that look had quite bowled him over, so much so that he forgot to be wary. He had smiled at her, and she—she had turned her back on him.

Since the debacle of Regina Hepworth, he had grown accustomed to receiving the cut direct from many in the *ton*, even friends of long standing, but somehow receiving it from this stranger had stung deeply. When his hostess had urged him to invite the lady to dance, he had done so reluctantly. Lady Jane, too, had seemed hesitant. Yet, somehow, when they began to dance, holding her in his arms felt surprisingly right and natural. So natural that he had grown frustrated when her gaze remained fixed on his cravat. He reproached her for her discourtesy, and she finally looked up, looking almost startled by his scold, and for a moment he was knocked off balance. Her blue eyes were large and beautiful and full of hurt. He kept dancing—holding on to her—trying to get his feet back underneath him, but she started to speak, and all he could do was listen and hang on even tighter, as she spoke with an honesty that both terrified and enthralled him.

A passing footman offered Anthony cake and a glass of punch. He accepted them distractedly, watching as Lady Ryde gathered up the married sisters, the contented ones, and carried them off on some secret enterprise involving the hat, leaving poor Lady Jane to stand alone. She, too, held a plate of cake, but she did not even look at it. He took a step forward, then stopped. It was not his business to draw her out of her melancholy. She cast another wistful—no, mournful—look at that damn sprig of green. He took a few more steps forward, but stopped a second time, as Lord Ryde, with the young earl in tow, moved to her side and engaged her in conversation. Then the marquess led his young brother-in-law across the room and Anthony could bear it no longer.

He crossed to where she stood alone behind the vast table.

"Lady Jane?" he said, his tone more tentative than he would have wished.

She turned. "Mr. Winston." She greeted him with a smile even more tentative than his tone.

"Have you discovered it yet?"

"Sir?"

"The prize pea in your cake."

She looked down at the plate in her hand. "I have not yet begun my exploration."

"Then it is high time you made a start."

"With four whole cakes to hide it in, the odds are very poor that it is in my one small slice."

He shook his head. "On the contrary. I am positive it is there. You had best take a bite."

"I do not know why you should be so sure."

"I am certain, because on this Twelfth Night I will have no other queen."

She stared at him, her smile suddenly emerging like the sun from behind a cloud. "That is nonsense, you know."

"Indeed it is," Lady Ryde remarked, coming up behind them unexpectedly. "I have been informed by no less an authority than my brother Carlton that peas and beans are quite *passé*. Of course, so are many of our decorations, but he has been willing to turn a blind eye to those if I will accommodate him on tonight's entertainment. To that point, please pick a character." She thrust the hat, now full of curling strips of paper, at him.

He reached into the hat and took one.

Lady Ryde looked sternly at her sister-in-law. "Now you, Jane."

Lady Jane did so, and read the script on the paper out loud. *"Frederica Flirt?"*

Lady Ryde laughed. "And you, Mr. Winston?"

Anthony looked down at the scrap of paper in his hand. He said drily, "Apparently I am to be Jack Flash."

"Excellent. Now the two of you go with Alex – I am sorry, Mr. Winston. Allow me to introduce another of my husband's sisters: Lady Alex Alderston. She will show you to your costumes."

The charades were a great success. The guests laughed and clapped and shouted out guesses as to identities with robust good humor. At first, Anthony worried Lady Jane would be too subdued to enter into the spirit of the playacting comfortably, but after donning a red silk gown that her sister had provided her with, she had greeted him in his borrowed military kit with a mischievous smile and a snap of her fan. He had offered her his arm and they had paraded back to the ballroom, she winking at the gentlemen and he leering at the ladies, both of them in high good humor.

Anthony had, at first, been highly self-conscious to be strutting about as Jack Flash, a military dandy with high collar points and a roving eye, but strangely, playing the role with exaggerated brio and for obvious comic effect, he found his neighbors eyeing him more benignly. It was as if the ridiculousness of the role made the tales of his past seem ridiculous as well.

Lady Jane also played her role broadly, and Anthony was both amused and slightly startled to see how convincingly she played Frederica Flirt, the lovely coquette. This Lady Jane, with her saucy smiles and laughing eyes, was quite a different woman from the melancholy lady he had danced with earlier. After their identities had been shouted out and their parading turn about the room was officially over, Anthony was irritated when he was robbed of her company by a young buck who asked her to dance. Determined to ask her to dance himself during the next set, Anthony retreated to the sidelines to watch the others. His hostess appeared at his side.

"Well done, sir," Lady Ryde congratulated him. "You made an excellent Jack Flash."

He smiled at her. "Thank you, ma'am. I must say, I had misgivings about playing that particular role, but it seems to have gone better than I expected."

She nodded. "People do not mean to be unkind. It is just that they sometimes forget to judge a person's character for themselves, and instead rely too much on the reports of others."

He flashed her a sharp look. Had Lady Ryde purposely offered him the hat when that particular strip of paper was on top? "Lady Jane seems to be enjoying her role as Frederica Flirt," he remarked speculatively.

She gazed in Lady Jane's direction with a fond expression. "It is good for her to be reminded that she is still young, and there is still joy in the world."

He stared at his hostess. "Lady Ryde, you leave me speechless."

She grinned. "Why sir, I didn't think Jack Flash could ever be that!"

He chuckled. "My lady, thank you for inviting me to join tonight's festivities. It has been a pleasant and unexpected evening."

"The festivities are not over. After the next dance, there will be a parade under the mistletoe."

"Mistletoe?" Anthony had a vague memory of an aged uncle talking about the joys of catching a pretty girl under the mistletoe and stealing a kiss.

"Another Christmas celebration my brother assures me is quite antiquated. However, my husband insists it is a St. John family tradition."

As if on cue, Lord Ryde swept toward them and claimed his wife for the minuet. Anthony rushed to Lady Jane and made her an exaggerated bow. "Miss Flirt, may I have this dance?"

For a moment, Lady Jane's sky blue eyes regarded him shyly. Then she took his proffered arm and playfully tapped his wrist with her fan. "La, sir, I thought you would never ask." The dance passed pleasantly and much too quickly, and after it was over, Anthony led Lady Jane over to where the couples were lining up for the parade back to the dining room. Lord and Lady Ryde took their place at the beginning of the line. He and Lady Jane were three couples behind them. The line moved forward amidst laughter and excited chuckles. The ladies eyed their escorts from behind lowered lashes and the gentlemen flashed wolfish grins in return. Anthony glanced sideways at Lady Jane, wondering if she regretted dancing with him, since now she would be partnered with him under the mistletoe. But to his great relief, she smiled a rather dazzling smile at him.

As they entered the dining room, Anthony realized that Lord and Lady Ryde were headed toward the doorway hung with the ugly sprig of green. As the marquess led his lady into the doorway, he wrapped his long arms around her, leaned his tall head down, and kissed her while the room erupted in cheers and shouts. To Anthony's surprise, the kiss lasted for a long time, and when the couple finally parted, Lord Ryde, who had a rather wide grin on his face, wished everyone a very happy new year.

Now Lord Ryde's dark-haired sister, Lady Charlotte, and her husband, Mr. Crawford stepped forward. They, too, shared a lengthy embrace. Then came Lady Alex and her husband, followed by Lady

Maria and her husband. Finally, Anthony and Lady Jane stepped forward. He wondered what in the world he had been thinking to get himself into such a situation. The eyes of everyone in the room were on him. He was the rake and outsider about to kiss the sister of the master of the house. Despite the enthusiastic embracing of the married couples, he was entitled to no such freedom, and he wondered if there was any sort of kiss he could give Lady Jane that his audience would consider chaste enough.

Then she looked up at him and he noticed a suspicious glitter in her eyes and a faint hurt quiver near the edges of her mouth. Curse his hesitation! She thought he didn't want her. Forgetting his audience, forgetting his reputation, forgetting even that his host would likely pull a horsewhip out and thrash him for what he was about to do, Anthony leaned forward and pressed his mouth to Lady Jane's soft lips.

He meant his kiss to be a gentle salute, a token of his esteem, a chaste demonstration of her appeal, but he had not reckoned on the alchemy of her touch. When he cupped her face in his hands, the velvet of her skin sent waves of desire spilling down his limbs. When he kissed her, the heat of her mouth sent a spark of fire arcing down his chest. When he deepened the kiss and wrapped his arms around her and pulled her close, he felt as if the very earth beneath his feet had slipped away. And when he belatedly realized the kiss had gone on too long and pulled away from the taste of her and the sweet intermingling of their breath, he felt as if there was no air left in the world for him to breathe.

He stared down at her in wonder.

She stared back at him, her sky blue eyes huge and wary and infinitely beautiful.

Damn, he thought. *I'm lost.*

Chapter 2

Jane woke the next morning to find unexpected sunshine spilling into her bedchamber. She had slept late. The curtains were pulled back, and a fire burned in the grate. She thought of the stranger who had danced with her and kissed her beneath the mistletoe, and she bounded out of bed, brimming with energy and excitement for the new day. She poured water into the basin and splashed her face eagerly, drying it with a soft towel. Then other memories trickled back. She recalled her last day in London and the package from Bevin's man of business.

Her happiness fled.

She sank into the chair before the fire and tucked her feet up underneath her. She poured some chocolate and wrapped her hands around the comforting warmth of her cup. She could not continue to wallow in her misery. She must *do* something about the problem Bevin had left so ignominiously in her lap. What did it matter if her inclination was to turn her back and hide? She had more pride than that, and—she hoped—more conscience. Still, it was difficult to contemplate action, when she could not act alone. She would have to tell Andrew. He already suspected something was wrong. It would be best to tell him everything and get it over with. She sighed. At least her tale would distract him from his anger at Mr. Winston.

Her protective brother had seemed quite tolerant of the gentleman earlier in the evening, even after Mr. Winston and Jane had danced together and paraded together as Frederica Flirt and Jack Flash. That had surprised her, because her brother usually had little patience for rakes. But Catherine had clearly taken a liking to the gentleman and perhaps had soothed Andrew's concerns. However, there had been nothing her kind sister-in-law could do to appease Andrew after that kiss.

Without thought, Jane reached up and touched her lips. *Lord, what a kiss.*

At first, she had thought Mr. Winston reluctant to embrace her at all. She had been nervous about the prospect of being kissed for the first time in a year-and-a-half—and by a stranger. Then she'd looked up into his green eyes and seen a man debating with himself over some unwelcome task. That had been a blow. She had been startled by the strength of her disappointment. She had almost burst into tears. He had seen her distress, and his gentle mouth had descended to hers.

At least, it had seemed gentle, in that first sweet caress of his lips. Then something had changed. Perhaps her melancholy had betrayed her; perhaps her loneliness had fired her need too high. Mr. Winston's kiss had deepened, and his arms had enfolded her, and she had felt herself spinning around in a different sort of dance. She had forgotten who she was, who he was. All she had wanted to do to shoot up like a firework into the night sky.

Jane took a shuddering gulp of air and lifted her cup with unsteady hands to take a sip of her chocolate.

When he had withdrawn his touch, she had stood there a moment, sinking back to earth with her eyes closed. She had opened them to find him looking down at her, his green eyes dark and turbulent. Then she noticed the silence. The room was absolutely still. She turned slowly to see the crowd of merrymakers staring at them. A few nervous titters broke out, and Mr. Winston, the angle of his jaw suddenly drawn as tightly as a bow, took her arm and led her through the doorway, away from the other couples and the crowd but towards her brother's fiery gaze.

Jane set down her cup, unfolded her legs, rose to her feet, and slowly crossed to the bellpull to summon her maid to help her dress. It was no use cowering here in her room. She had to face the day—and her brother—eventually. Best to get it over with as quickly as she could.

‍🐍

Despite her resolution, Jane decided to make a detour to the breakfast room before going in search of her brother. She was extremely hungry this morning, which perhaps was not a surprise. She had eaten very little all week. To her dismay, however, as she approached the breakfast room she heard the sound of raised voices.

"Dearest, don't you think you are perhaps overreacting? After all, it was a single kiss under the mistletoe in a room full of people."

"Confound it, Cat, you heard Maria! He has already kidnapped two women! I'll not have him making my sister a third!"

"Andrew—"

"No! I'm writing to Barrett today. There must be a way to break the lease. Jane will be with us until spring. I don't want him anywhere near her. I want him gone as quickly as possible!"

"But, my dear, is that quite fair to poor Mr. Winston? He has only just moved in."

"'Poor Mr. Winston indeed!" her brother erupted. "Dammit, Cat! You and your rakes! Why don't you start a society!" Her sister-in-law murmured a reply, which had some sort of soothing effect on him, for he replied in a much quieter tone: "My dear, my mind is made up."

Jane stared at the closed breakfast room door in chagrin. She drew herself up, ready to march in and deliver her brother the scold he deserved for thinking her so incapable of dealing with Mr. Winston that he would disrupt the poor man's life and chase him from the neighborhood. Of course, according to Maria and Letty, Mr. Winston was not a man to be pitied in any way, but rather a villain to be excoriated. However, the gentleman's character was not the issue. The issue was whether her family thought her capable of dealing with the rascal on her own. Jane was a widow, for heaven's sake, not some green girl ready to have her head turned by some fumbling embrace.

Not that there had been anything fumbling about Mr. Winston's kiss.

Jane's cheeks grew hot. She pressed her palms against them to cool them. She opened the door slowly, seeking to regain her righteous anger, but instead she felt a wistful longing to find Jack Flash upon her arm. Then she came to a tense and abrupt halt. She had noticed, without really thinking about it, that the breakfast room had grown quiet, but she had been too distracted to wonder at the reason. Now the reason was apparent. Catherine sat on Andrew's lap, his arms around her waist, her hands cupping his face, sharing a kiss so intimate and engrossing that neither had noticed her entrance. Jane tiptoed back out of the room. *Blast this house full of lovebirds!*

Feeling suddenly very tired, she turned and made her way to the main drawing room. However, it was already occupied by Alex, Godfrey, and the twins. On a normal day, Jane would have enjoyed the company of her quiet sister and clever brother-in-law and two adorable nephews, but today the sight of their happy, contented family was like a small knife twisted in the wound of her unhappiness. She turned and did not enter.

She met Letty and George coming down the stairs. "Jane, would you like to join us?" Letty asked brightly. "We are going for a picnic while the day is still fine."

George nodded cheerfully. "Your brother vows there will be snow before sundown, but I think he is just trying to put a damper on our fun."

Jane demurred politely. She hurried toward her room, but did not reach it before encountering Maria, sneaking surreptitiously out of the nursery, her infant daughter in her arms. "Oh, Jane. I just wanted to check on Ada. The nurse told me that she passed a difficult night."

"It is all right, Maria," Jane said, casting an envious glance at her niece's small pink face and bright eyes. "It is quite unexceptional for a mother to want to hold and cherish her little babe."

Maria flashed her a grateful smile. Ada made a cooing sound and waved both her hands in the air. Jane stared down at the perfection of those tiny fingers and felt an ache in her throat. Maria flashed a besotted glance at her daughter and murmured, "She is beautiful, isn't she?"

Jane nodded mutely, patted her sister's arm, and fled.

She had planned to remain in her bedchamber until her emotions calmed, but the minute she returned to her room, Jane was beset by restlessness. Perhaps George and Letty were right. It would be good to escape the house for a while and enjoy the unusual January sunshine. She changed into a warm walking dress, nankeen half-boots, and her brown pelisse. She also put on her new velvet bonnet, for, while the sun shone, she could hear the wind rippling past her window.

At first, she walked without thinking, enjoying the crisp air on her skin and the peace of being alone in the austere beauty of the winter landscape. After a while, however, she realized she was headed toward Rosington. Catherine's old home was seven miles from Farthingsgate, so there was no danger she would inadvertently intrude on Mr. Winston's privacy, but it was unnerving to find that her instinct had been to head straight in his direction.

She walked a considerable distance contemplating the puzzle Mr. Winston presented. She had refused to let either Letty or Maria see it, but she had been shocked and deeply troubled to hear the details of his sordid past. Their tales of depraved behavior contrasted starkly with the courteous and kind gentleman she had spent time with the night before. How could she possibly reconcile the two images—the two men they represented? She wanted to be able to, if not respect the man Mr. Winston truly was, at least accept him. Last night she had liked him, even more than liked him. She could not bear it if in the cold light of day she was forced to despise him.

Suddenly, Jane broke from her abstracted thoughts to realize she no longer had a sense of where she was or how far she had come from Farthingsgate. She was at least four or five miles away, for she had been traversing the western fields for some time. But the sunshine was gone. Dark, lowering clouds were rolling in to blot out the sky, scudding in from the west with a frightening rapidity. The air was much colder. She needed to get a better view, but she was on low ground and the field she was traversing was tucked into a fold of earth that made it impossible to see more than a half-mile in any direction. She hurried forward. There was higher ground ahead.

She walked and walked and finally reached a long stone wall. She clambered up the rough-hewn stile to the top of the wall and turned in a slow circle, searching for some familiar landmark. Finally, she spotted one: old Bagshot's cottage. The wind was blowing harder now, and the clouds were pushing downwards as if grown so heavy that they desired to squat upon the ground. She knew the way home now, but she would have to hurry.

She began to climb down the stile. Suddenly, a strong gust of wind knocked her off-balance. She pressed down with her right foot, trying to steady herself, but the stone was slick and her boot slipped. Her foot bent at an angle it was never meant to. She tumbled to the ground, pain from her ankle engulfing her with a sickening lurch. For a moment, she could not move, only gasp with the effort not to swoon. At last, the pounding waves of dizziness receded, but it took longer for her stomach to settle. She lifted her head and looked about. She had not fallen far and seemed to be in a heap at the bottom of the stile. She started to sit up, but the motion forced her to shift the position of her right foot. Fiery waves of pain and nausea surged through her again.

Devil take it, what was she to do now?

Jane gulped more cold air and then began moving her body upright with agonizing slowness. When she had managed to sit up, she looked about for something, anything she could use as a prop to help her to stand. The stile itself was just out of reach. Her fingers were only tantalizing inches from the solid steps, but those inches might have been miles for all the good they did her. She looked about her for a branch or stick, but she was surrounded by barren earth and nothing more. The nearest tree was fifty feet away, and there was not even a twig within her reach.

She looked about her in disbelief. There had to be some way for her to get up, but she could think of nothing. She would have to wait for someone to come looking for her. And, of course, they would. And they would find her. It would take a while, maybe a long while, but in the end, she would be back at Farthingsgate, sitting before a nice fire with her family fussing over her, wanting to hear of her adventure.

Things really aren't so black, she assured herself.

And she had almost convinced herself of it.

Until the first snowflake fell on her nose.

Chapter 3

Please, Georgiana!" Anthony exclaimed in frustration. "The sun is shining. Let me take you out for a ride. Some fresh air will do you good."

"It is all too much commotion to put everyone to. I am sure you will have a much more pleasant ride on your own. I am not the best company these days."

Anthony knelt by his sister's rolling chair. "You are good enough company for me."

She flashed a tremulous smile at him. "Perhaps another day."

Anthony sighed. "Very well, my dear. Shall I wheel you over to the window so that you can at least look out at the sunshine?"

Georgiana nodded and said wistfully, "And perhaps you could tell me about the ball and the Twelfth Night cake and all the fine ladies you met last night?"

Anthony was not sure he was ready to go over the events of the previous night in the privacy of his own thoughts let alone out loud, but he forced himself to smile. "Of course. I will be happy to tell you of my adventures." He rose to his feet and rolled her chair to the window. "I met many pretty ladies and even acquired a secret identity."

"Goodness, Anthony!" his sister exclaimed, with the first real animation he had seen in her face all day. "It sounds quite a tale!"

He picked up a chair, placed it next to her, and sat down. "It is, dear sister. It is."

Georgiana enjoyed his storytelling. She was full of questions and wanted several retellings of favorite details about the cakes and the gowns and the characters they had played for charades. He had even fetched his old regimental coat and sword and done an imitation of Jack Flash for her that had made her laugh and clap her hands. It had been a long time since he had seen his sister laugh, and her high spirits and animation had lasted through lunch, causing his own spirits to lift. She had grown tired by the end of lunch, and when he had carried her upstairs to her bed to await the ministrations of her maid, she had given him a hug and murmured in his ear, "Thank you, dear brother, for cheering my day."

He returned downstairs with a lighter heart and a desire for fresh air. He was in no mood to go for a ride without her, so he set off for a walk through Rosington's park. He liked Rosington. There was something comforting and friendly about the place. In a surprisingly short time, however, he was past its pretty park and headed out toward the farms, his legs striding at a hectic pace and still not keeping up with his racing thoughts.

The sun had disappeared and dark clouds were surging in from the west. The wind was blowing harder, and the temperature was dropping, but somehow Anthony did not mind. The approaching storm seemed to match his plummeting mood.

He had not told Georgiana about Lady Jane. He had not told her about their shared dances or her enchanting turn as Frederica Flirt or her trip with him beneath the mistletoe. He had not even mentioned her as one of the ladies present or described her gown and hair. He was not sure why. Perhaps it was because no single detail about her could be separated from the painful whole.

You are reputed to be a rake, and I am a lady whose heart has been broken.

It was an agonizing but concise summary of why all the fanciful dreams he had taken to bed with him last night had popped like soap bubbles in the light of day. He wondered at her broken heart. It was possible bereavement had caused her sorrow. She seemed the sort of lady who would love truly and mourn deeply. Yet he sensed it was not fate, but a gentleman who had broken her heart. He felt a sudden flaring anger. How could any man granted access to her heart not treat it with the utmost care? He grimaced. What the hell was wrong with him? He was beginning to think like a cursed poet.

Suddenly, a snowflake blew into his eye. Then another hit his cheek. Soon the air was swirling with them. Anthony spun around, realizing he'd been so lost in thought he hadn't kept track of which way he had come. He was not even sure he was still on Rosington land. It would be ironic indeed if he had trespassed onto Lord Ryde's estate while daydreaming about Lord Ryde's blue-eyed sister.

The snow was starting to fall faster now. Anthony looked for signs in the sky to give him some sense of direction, but the grey, swollen clouds had completely swallowed the sun, and the wind kept shifting and blowing from first one direction and then another. With a shrug of his shoulders, Anthony turned and started walking in the direction he hoped would lead him back home.

He had trudged along for some time when he noticed something odd on the ground up ahead. The light had grown so dim that he could make out little except that there was a brownish shadow—too large to be a rock or a clod of dirt—in the path ahead. Anthony wondered if it might be an animal of some sort, one obviously too dim of brain to seek shelter from the snow. As he drew closer, he realized with a shock that it was not an animal at all, but a person sitting on the ground. Was the fellow injured? Drunk? Whatever the case, if he remained out in this weather much longer he would end up dead.

Anthony hurried forward. He soon realized it was not some peasant farmer who sat there, but a woman—a lady, judging by the cut of her coat and velvet of her bonnet. She was facing away from him, so he could not discern if she was young or old. He could not understand why she just sat there as the snow swirled around her shoulders and settled in a fine white dust all down her back. He began to run.

"Madam! You there!" he shouted with all his might. The wind threw his words back in his face. He tried again. "Madam! You, there! *Madam!*"

Finally she heard him. Her head turned, but she was no owl and could not swing her face around far enough to see him. He called again, increasing the speed of his racing legs. *Devil take her! Why did she not turn her body instead of just her head?* Better yet, why did she not just rise to her feet? Then it occurred to him that perhaps she was incapable of rising. Perhaps she was a cripple like his poor Georgiana.

Gasping, he ran faster still. He finally reached her and sank to his knees in front of her. Struggling for breath, he rasped, "Madam—we must—get you—out of this—snow." He began to swipe at the flakes coating his face and blurring his vision. Then he caught a glimpse of her face, and his arm fell limply to his side.

"Lady Jane?"

"Oh, Mr. Winston!" she cried. "You have no idea how happy I am to see you!"

He lifted her up into his arms, and after her first loud yelp of pain Jane managed to keep mostly silent, burrowing her face into the collar of his greatcoat to muffle the small sobs she could not suppress. They agreed that both Rosington and Farthingsgate were too far away, so she directed him toward Jacob Bagshot's small cottage, but even that was not near enough.

He was already weary and—though he carried her tightly to him with a steely strength she could feel through the wet wool of his coat—the snow was now thick enough on the ground that he had to take great wading steps and fight his way forward against the howling wind. She wrapped her arms tightly around his neck and tried to shift her weight against him to make the work of carrying her as easy as possible, but she was still a virtual millstone around his neck. As they made their painfully slow progress toward Bagshot's cottage, she could hear his hard breathing and feel the increasingly jagged rise and fall of his broad chest as he struggled to carry her. She did not dare express her regret to him about being such a burden, however, for she knew he could not spare the breath to answer.

Finally, they arrived at the small cottage. She begged him to set her down on the threshold and catch his breath, but he refused, shifting her in his arms so he could hold her with one arm and pound on the door with the other. But despite the noise, no one came. Finally, in desperation, he tried twisting the knob. To their surprise, the door swung open.

They advanced slowly into the dark house, and Mr. Winston let out a gasping curse when he barked his shin on a piece of furniture. Fortunately, it turned out to be a chair, so he lowered her into it and sank to his knees, gasping, on the floor. Jane's eyes were adjusting to the dimness of the room. She reached out and put a gloved hand on his shoulder. He looked up at her. His breathing was beginning to slow, but his chest still heaved.

Jane pressed her lips together, fighting back tears. When she was sure she could control her voice, she said simply, "Thank you, Mr. Winston."

To her surprise, he grinned at her, a boyish, lopsided grin that made her stomach do a flip. "We made it! Devil take it, I was beginning to wonder if we would." He reached up and covered her hand with his own and patted it. "Now we need some heat—and light." He rose to his feet and crossed to the dimly visible fireplace. There was a flint on the small mantle and tinder and a neat stack of logs to the left of the grate. He soon had a warm fire going and placed several lighted candlesticks around the room to fill it with a cheerful glow.

He took off his gloves, hat, greatcoat and top coat and laid them on the floor to dry before the fire. He came to stand next to her, and she could see that even his waistcoat and shirt were soaked through, and his fair hair clung in damp curls around his face. "Now, how long were you out there in that cold?"

"I d-d-do not know," she said. Oddly, now that the room was beginning to warm, she was feeling much colder. "It s-s-seemed like f-f-forever."

He reached down and began untying the strings of her bonnet. "We will have to get these wet things off of you."

"I c-c-can do that f-f-for myself."

"Shhhhh," he said, batting away her hands. "You're shaking too much. It will be easier for me to do it."

"I d-d-don't know why I feel so c-c-cold now, but not b-b-before."

"Don't use up your strength speaking." He lifted her bonnet off and placed it on the floor. "It's a good sign—the trembling. It means your body is waking up again. It wants you to be warm. Before, when you were sitting in the snow, it had given up. That's how men freeze to death without ever really knowing it."

He began undoing the cord fastenings of her sodden pelisse. Nervously she watched his nimble fingers. Suddenly, he stopped and shook his head. "It will be impossible to remove the thing entirely while you are seated. Wait a moment. I will see if I can find a blanket." He took one of the candlesticks and left the room. He returned after only a few minutes with his arms full. "Your Bagshot is a neat and orderly man. I found two blankets and a clean, dry shirt."

"I am g-g-glad you will be able to ch-change out of those wet things."

"The shirt is for you, my lady, not me."

She stared at him, speechless.

"This is no time for modesty. You will never get warm with those freezing, wet clothes on. You will have to take off every sodden stitch."

She gasped and then clamped her lips together in regret. He was right. She should not reproach him for speaking the truth.

"You will have the shirt to put on—and the blankets."

She resolutely said nothing, just bowed her head in acceptance.

He tipped up her chin so her gaze would meet his. "We are not going to be able to get those wet clothes off of you sitting down. You will have to be standing up." He drew a deep breath. "So I am going to lift you up. When I do, I want you to put your weight down on your one good foot and hold on to me. Understood?"

She nodded.

"That is *all* you are going to do. Your task is to remain upright and not fall. That is your *only* task. I will remove your clothes." Red spots of color suddenly appeared in his fair cheeks. "You are not to fuss with fastenings or buttons or tapes."

Without thinking, Jane brought her hands up to her cheeks in mortification.

Gently he pulled them back down again. "Listen to me, Lady Jane. As I said before, this is not the time for modesty. Close your eyes, if you like. Pretend I am your maid."

She gave a faintly hysterical giggle at this notion.

"You need not be embarrassed," he insisted. "To be blunt—to a gentleman, the naked female form is basically the same, no matter the woman."

Now that is a lowering notion, Jane thought. *Did Bevin think the same? Is that why he found me so—replaceable?* She felt her eyes fill with tears.

"Please, Lady Jane!" Mr. Winston's voice caused her sad thoughts to recede. "I wish you to be safe. You will need to keep a firm hold on me to maintain your balance. I do not want to risk you falling and injuring yourself further. Will you do as I say?"

"Y-y-yes, Mr. Winston."

The tension in his face relaxed, and he pressed a sudden kiss on her forehead. "Very well then. Shall we begin?"

Chapter 4

She was upright and—for the moment, at least—balanced. Her breathing, however, was ragged. He had hurt her, shifting her, and he would not soon forget that first wrenching cry of pain and the valiantly suppressed gasps that followed. Her grip on his waist was firm. He had removed his wet waistcoat and shirt and stripped off her sodden gloves so her hands could warm on his skin while she endured this undressing. Her fingers were pale but not discolored, and he prayed she had escaped frostbite. He would have to make an inspection of her extremities later. For now, he took reassurance from the strength in those beautiful fingers and focused on the task at hand.

He had already undone all the fastenings of her cursedly thin and sodden pelisse, but even with her upright and it pulled entirely open, slipping the thing off was another matter. The wet sleeves of her coat seemed bound up in the wet sleeves of her dress in an exasperating tangle, and only the thought that she would need them both in the morning kept him from ripping the cloth in two.

After several long minutes of frustrating toil, the coat was finally off. Removing her dress was a little easier. The fastenings were far greater in number and more difficult to undo, but once the dress was open, the wet fabric of the sleeves pulled free from Lady Jane's arms. The wet fabric of the skirt was tangled in the sodden linen of her shift, but this was less a puzzle than the coat, for he could undo this

Gordean knot by simply dragging the dress down and away from the shift in one mighty tug.

Unfortunately, the tug also pulled Lady Jane backwards, and he was barely able to throw his arms around her and catch her before she tumbled to the floor. For a moment, he held her too close—so close he could feel the rise and fall of her breathing and the sweet press of her breasts against his chest. Then he came to his senses and loosened his hold, allowing her to push away and steady herself with her grip on his waist.

He wished he could steady himself as easily. With clumsy fingers whose trembling he hoped she did not notice, he began untying her stays. Just as he had nearly finished, his fingers slipped and brushed against a nipple. She gasped. "Forgive me," he muttered, yanking fiercely at the knotted ribbon that had made him seem so inept. *Damnation!* He was trying to remain in control; instead, he felt like a green, awkward boy bumbling his way through an unintended seduction.

Desperate now to be done with this, he pulled loose the drawstring at the neck of her shift and pushed the straps down off her chilled shoulders. The sodden shift cascaded to the floor. Her eyes were tightly closed, so for one long, guilty moment he let his gaze drop. Oh, he was being sorely punished for his lie to her about all women being equivalent. Feeling as if he had just made the greatest error of his life, he seized the dry shirt and yanked it down over her head.

Her eyes opened, full of relief.

He did not feel so lucky. The shirt did nothing for *his* piece of mind. Not when the damned thing barely came down past the middle of her thighs. Not when the cursed droop of the overlong sleeves and too broad shoulders made her look both devastatingly fetching and entirely vulnerable. Not when the image of her *without* the shirt was burned into his memory and would no doubt haunt his dreams for the rest of his benighted existence.

He sighed.

He picked up one of the blankets and draped it around her like a hooded cloak. Then he lifted her up in his arms and set her gently back down in Mr. Bagshot's overstuffed chair, tucking the blanket tightly around her like a woolen cocoon. "Better?" he asked.

"Much. The trembling has … almost stopped." She paused and then said in a more subdued tone, "Though I do f-feel quite humiliated — "

He tensed.

"—to be bundled up like this, as if I were a swaddled b-babe."

He chuckled in relief. "Do not fear. No man with a pulse could mistake you for an infant. Even in swaddling clothes, the telltale signs of your womanhood are quite evident."

She blushed.

He was relieved to see some color in her cheeks, but he suspected a blushing Lady Jane was more than he could handle at the moment. To distract himself, he gathered up her wet clothes and set them before the fire. Then he took the other blanket with him into the kitchen and used the privacy there to slip out of his damp small clothes and breeches. He tied the blanket round his waist and carried his clothes in to dry next to Lady Jane's.

He realized he needed further occupation. Thinking of her injured ankle, he settled on another task and went in search of what was needed. Underneath Mr. Bagshot's bed he found a small chest. Near the window he found a worn oval rug. He carried his treasures downstairs and set them down near Lady Jane's chair, fashioning a makeshift Ottoman upon which to elevate her leg. But when he looked at her injured foot, he blanched.

He had already removed one sodden boot, the one on her good foot, the one that did not matter. But he had delayed removing the other, because the process of shifting her had already caused her so much pain. Now he realized that had been a grave error. Perhaps it was an effect of the warming room or her improved circulation or the time spent on her feet, but her injured ankle was now badly swollen, and Anthony wondered if he would be able to remove her boot at all.

He sat down on the makeshift Ottoman and lifted her good leg onto it. Then he slowly lifted her bad leg onto his lap, watching her face for signs of the pain he knew he must be causing her. He bent to take a closer look at the fastenings of her boot.

He began the simplest way, by untying the laces. But even with the laces not just undone, but completely removed, there was no give. He tried angling the boot this way and that, flinching at the looks of agony that crossed her face. "Curse it," he snapped, "I do not mind if you cry out. I am sorry I must hurt you so." But it was soon clear that no matter how much he pained her prying at the boot, the damned thing was not about to budge.

He swore long and fluently and with all his pent-up frustration. What a cursed day—no, night. There was no light coming through the cottage's small windows anymore. Outside there was only darkness and snow and howling wind. He looked at her face, ready to offer an apology for his execrable language, but to his surprise there was no censure in her expression. No doubt he had offered so many outrages to her propriety and her person in the last hour that the indignity to her ears was of no significance. But what had he done to deserve that look of kind sympathy she bestowed on him instead?

"I am sorry to be such a burden to you," she said softly.

The words, and the apologetic tone with which she said them, made him want to swear again—even more lengthily and fluently.

Instead, he carefully set her legs aside, rose to his feet, and strode to the kitchen before he could utter some heartfelt folly that would embarrass them both.

Jane gazed about the room and waited impatiently for Mr. Winston to return. The place was beginning to feel quite cozy. She was grateful for the heat of the fire, the golden glow of the candles, the feel of the stiff, dry shirt on her skin, and the rough warmth of the wool that enfolded her. But she missed the company of her rescuer.

From the next room, she heard the clatter of yet another drawer being opened and then slammed shut.

She supposed she should be cowering in fear to be stranded in this lonely cottage with a hardened rake. After all, she had no ability to escape his attentions and nothing to provide her modesty but an over-large shirt and a patched wool blanket. Yet, she felt no fear of Mr. Winston—none at all. Perhaps it was because he had saved her. Perhaps it was because she was a fool. Still, she felt sure there was kindness in the man and, despite his reputation, a core of honor. Indeed, she suspected the only danger to her virtue lay in her own increasingly heated feelings.

She glanced to where their clothes lay drying by the fire, and her mind was suddenly filled with the memory of him turned away from her, unbuttoning his sodden waistcoat and crossing his arms above his head to pull off the wet linen of his shirt. She had nearly swooned at the rippling beauty of his naked back, but her mood had sobered when he had turned, and she had seen the long scar running from his right shoulder to his ribs.

Then he had crossed to her and pulled her painfully to her feet. He had placed her hands on his waist and told her to hold onto him. She had still been reeling with pain from the jostling of her injured ankle, but she had done as he asked. The warm silk of his skin and the feel of his hard muscles had completely driven away even the memory of her pain, but it had also set her heart to pounding and her breath to rasping in short, ragged gulps.

She wondered if there was something wrong with her.

She did not understand how she could feel such physical passion for this stranger, such lust—to use the mortifying but absolutely true word—when she had never experienced such a thing with her late husband. She had loved Bevin. She had admired him. She had reveled in being his wife. But she had never felt this feverish desperation for his touch.

There was a sound behind her. She turned. Mr. Winston had returned from his explorations of Mr. Bagshot's kitchen, but his appearance startled her. His expression was fierce, and there was a knife in his hand. For a moment, she felt a flutter of trepidation. With his bare chest, and the blanket slung low on his hips, and the knife held grimly in his hand, he looked wild and untamed, like a Saxon prince about to go to war. But the two of them were alone in this small house. So with whom, exactly, did Mr. Winston intend to battle?

Not whom. *What.*

Once more he resumed his seat on the footstool he had fashioned for her, and once more he placed her leg on his lap. Despite the bleak look he flashed her before aiming his baleful glare at her injured foot, she found her greatest anxiety centered not on the knife he held so tightly in his hand, but on the debauched impulse she felt to slip her good foot beneath the blanket and tickle his thigh with her toes.

"I fear, Lady Jane, that I will have to cut the blasted thing off," he muttered grimly.

"My foot?" she squeaked.

"*The boot!*" he growled. "I know it will be difficult, but please do not move suddenly, even if my movements hurt your ankle. I do not wish to nick you with the blade."

That sobered her. All impulse for tickling vanished, and her attention became as fixed on her injured foot as his was. He pulled the top of her boot as far away from her ankle as he could get it and pushed the point of the knife through the soaked leather. The violence of the motion hurt, but she balled her hands into fists and forced herself not to flinch. Finally, the knife was through and he began carefully sawing away, one strip of leather at a time. As each strip came loose, he would brace her foot and then pull the strip free, flinging it to the floor with a curse. It was a laborious process, but finally the entire top half of the boot was gone. The bottom half was now little more than a slipper. Mr. Winston eased it off and flung it across the room into the fire.

Jane tried to flex her liberated foot. Pain seared through it and she found it almost impossible to wiggle her cold, wet toes.

Mr. Winston cupped her foot in the warmth of his hand. He began running his fingers over it, gently probing her throbbing ankle. His face seemed to relax. "I do not feel anything amiss with the bone. I think it is a bad sprain, not a break." He touched her toes. "They feel cursedly cold." He slowly ran his fingers along each one, his expression abstracted. Then to her utter shock, he repeated the process with his lips. Torn between a desire to snatch her aching foot away and an even stronger one to close her eyes and purr, she remained rigidly still.

"I'm sorry, my lady, but my lips, at this point, are a great deal more sensitive than my fingers. I want to make sure that everything is warming up properly and you haven't suffered frostbite."

"Oh," she murmured faintly.

Apparently satisfied with his inspection, he placed her sore, cold foot against his warm, hard stomach. The heat felt glorious, as did the soft matted tickle of the golden hairs that traced their way up his belly from below the blanket. He checked the toes of her other foot and then set that foot, too, to warm against his skin.

Then he started on her fingers.

No wonder he is such a successful rake, she thought, feeling a bit faint. *He has me completely in his thrall, and he is not even trying!*

She took a deep, steadying breath when he was done with her hands. "So," she said as lightly as she could manage, "I have escaped serious damage?"

"I still need to check your face and ears."

"Surely not, Mr. Winston! Everything feels fine." But when she looked into his face, she could tell from the obdurate set of his mouth that he was determined.

"Your face and ears were the most exposed, and you still have too little color in your cheeks for my comfort." He rose to his feet and came to stand over her. He gently pushed back the wet hair curling over her left ear. Jane braced herself for his touch, but she still felt lightheaded, almost dizzy, when his warm lips brushed down the entire curve of her ear in one delicate motion. Then to her surprise, he cupped his hands around her ear and blew softly into his hands. His breath eddied and swirled around her ear, warming it, but also sending butterfly tingles down her belly. "Only one thing more," he added, his voice low. "Forgive me." Before she could demand to know what there was to forgive, his lips moved down and closed on her earlobe, sucking it into the hot moisture of his mouth.

To her utter mortification, she yelped. She could not help it. *He is doing this to warm you,* she told herself sternly. *There is nothing more to it than that. Be still.*

But it was difficult.

The only thing that saved her was that he did not move. Did not even seem to breathe. He held her earlobe in the heat of his mouth for nearly a minute, then suddenly released it and jerked his head away.

"Now the right ear, my lady."

Jane did better keeping her composure this time—outwardly. Inwardly, anticipation made the sensation more intense, and she had to use every ounce of her will not to emit a small moan.

"Your face, my lady," he said in short, clipped tones.

Setting back her shoulders, Jane lifted up her face obediently, trying not to meet his eyes. He leaned forward and his lips swept across her forehead like a parent checking a child for fever. Jane's shoulders relaxed a bit.

Too soon.

His mouth moved lower, brushing soft, methodical lines across her cheeks. Her breath caught, and then she made the mistake of meeting his gaze. To her surprise, he looked as abashed as she felt. For both their sakes, she closed her eyes.

"Noses are the most vulnerable," he said.

Her eyes snapped back open. "Goodness no, sir! You cannot be serious." But there was no humor in his face. Reluctantly, she lifted her head still more, thrusting her nose forward like the prow of a ship. She closed her eyes and clamped her lips tightly shut so she would not be tempted to giggle at the ridiculousness of her situation. Yet when his mouth shifted, and his lips skimmed up one side and down the other, all urge to laugh disappeared. She was startled by how sensitive her skin felt there and how charged his touch. Once more, he cupped his hands and blew into them. This time she could breathe in his warm breath, and she felt faintly intoxicated by it. She sank down a bit, relaxing back into the chair.

Then she felt his tongue caressing the tip of her nose. *Good God in heaven! He was* licking *her.* She closed her eyes and held her breath and realized to her everlasting shame that she liked the sensation. And when he stopped and drew away, she felt both cold and forlorn. She opened her eyes and watched him from behind her lashes. He was staring down at his hands. He did not seem interested in inspecting her chin, and he had studiously avoided her mouth. Seized by a flare of temper that he could overset her in such a myriad of ways, she felt a sudden need to prove that she could overset *him.* "I take it, sir, that my lips are quite immune to the depredations of the weather?"

He made a sound that was close enough to a groan to satisfy her. Then he leaned forward and touched one finger lightly to her mouth. He traced his finger around her lips, then replaced his finger with his mouth, then his mouth with his tongue, tracing the outlines of her mouth over and over again until she wanted to spiral down into his warmth and never come out again.

His hands mesmerized her as well. At first his touches were tentative, gentle, light. Then he pushed back the blanket and began running his fingers across the stiff fabric of the shirt she wore, tracing the curves of her body as he had traced her mouth.

Too late, Jane realized she had miscalculated badly.

As he slowly pushed her back into the chair and covered her with his body, she realized that she had counted on being able to stop things from going too far by appealing to his honor. But the problem wasn't his honor. The problem was her not wanting to ask him to stop.

Suddenly, with a gasp, he pulled away from her. He stumbled to his feet and turned away. He did not say anything. All she could hear were his great panting breaths.

She sat up and pulled the blanket tightly around her. It was as if there was a great silent wall between them, and, eventually, she did not even have the sound of his labored breathing to assure her he had not turned to stone. "Mr. Winston?" she whispered. There was no answer. "Mr. Winston?" she said again, more insistently.

He would not turn. In a harsh, low voice he spat out a single syllable. *"Yes?"*

"Thank you," she said simply. "Thank you for saving us both."

Chapter 5

oo small.

The damned cottage was too small. He had slept in shepherd's huts in Portugal—mere lattices of sticks covered with clods of earth and perhaps a hide or two—that had felt more spacious than this accursed house.

Anthony paced desperately around the tiny kitchen as if he were a sentry trying to keep sleep at bay. He thought of the room upstairs. There would be a few more square feet of pacing room up there. Then he shook his head. There was also a bed, and his imagination was far too quick to provide an image of Lady Jane in that bed for it to provide him any sort of escape.

She had actually thanked him.

He had nearly taken her right there in that cramped, stupid chair. And she had *thanked* him for his restraint in not actually carrying the folly through. *For saving us both.*

Dammit to hell.

It was possible he had saved her. It was quite certain he had not saved himself. Even now he had to resist the urge to try again. It would mean he had to turn deaf to conscience, dumb to honor, and blind to the hurt he would see in those sky blue eyes, yet still he was tempted. It was why he was hiding in this damn, tiny room. He wished there was some firewood in here. And an axe. He would dearly love to chop something in two.

"Mr. Winston?" Her soft voice drifted into the room. "Would you come here, please?"

Anthony glared up at the ceiling. "God, have you no mercy?"

But the good Lord did not respond to Anthony's prayer.

"Mr. Winston?" Her tone was pleading.

A defeated man, Anthony squared his shoulders. "Yes, Lady Jane. I am coming."

         ॐ

She was still wrapped up tightly in her blanket, though she no longer looked swaddled. It was more like she had braced herself for battle, and the blanket was her shield.

Does that make me the enemy? Anthony wondered.

She made a gesture with her hand toward a place on the floor by her chair. "Sir, do you think that you might sit, and that we might talk?" The invitation was made with all the grace of a duchess asking him to tea. Gravely, he crossed to the spot she had indicated. He sat, cross-legged, tucking his own blanket neatly about his legs, so he would not appear so wild. He looked up and regarded her, suddenly grateful she had summoned him. At least, she did not look as if she hated him. "I heard you pacing," she said.

"I—I had a great deal on my mind."

She nodded. "I, too. Indeed, I have spent the past half-hour thinking very hard. I have been trying to understand, you see—"

"How I could behave in such a *rakish* manner?" he snapped, startled by the obvious bitterness in his tone.

"No," she said softly, but with a force that caught his attention. "No, Mr. Winston, you misapprehend me. What I have been trying to tease out is *my* behavior, not yours. I know you will not credit it, but normally I am not a wanton woman. I—"

Anthony's heart began thumping in his chest. "Do not call yourself such a thing!" he exclaimed hotly. "I am to blame—not you. I imposed myself on you. I—"

"Oh, Mr. Winston, please!" She sounded on the verge of tears.

"Please, Lady Jane, do not cry!"

"I will try, if you, in turn, will leave off with your gallant lies."

Anthony stared at her. "I do not know what you mean."

"Then let us deal with the central issue first." Her eyes still shimmered with unshed tears, but the set of her mouth was determined. "A half-hour ago you tried to lie with me." He opened his mouth to exclaim, but she held up her hand, and he clamped it shut again. "It almost happened, but you decided it was not right, and we stopped. Is that not correct?"

Stunned by her blunt words, Anthony could only nod mutely.

"And when you were kissing me and when you were … caressing me, if I had asked you to stop at anytime, you would have done so. Is that not also true?"

"Of course!"

"And did I ask you to stop?

"No. But—"

"Mr. Winston, surely you can see! I did not ask you to stop, because I did not *want* you to stop. If we had consummated our union, it would have been a catastrophe for us both, but my desire for you burned every bit as strongly as yours did for me!"

Anthony was glad he was seated firmly on the floor, else he might have worried about keeping his balance, for he felt oddly giddy.

My desire for you burned every bit as strongly as yours did for me!

He supposed, in the very deepest part of his mind, he had *hoped* it might be so. She had seemed so warm to him—so sweet and yielding. Yet he could not quite believe it was true. It seemed too much to ask. For a moment, he was tempted to spring to his feet and carry her up-stairs to that little bed, so he could show her just how much her caring meant to him. Then he remembered the other part of her astounding statement, and his soaring spirits crashed.

If we had consummated our union, it would have been a catastrophe.

He had forgotten. She was a lady with a broken heart, and he was a rake.

"You know, Mr. Winston," she said, breaking into his black thoughts. "When I was outside today, sitting in the snow, there was a moment when I gave up, when I decided no one was going to find me in time. When I thought I was going to die."

He wanted her to stop. It frightened him to think of how easily he could have missed her in that field. But he did not want her to know how much it bothered him, so he said nothing, just pressed his clenched fists into the floor until they ached.

"When that moment came, and I thought I was at the end, I realized I had only two regrets."

He had to know. "What were they?"

"The first was that I have no child," her voice was sorrowful. "When my husband lived, I wanted a baby very badly."

"My—Lady Jane, I am sorry." He wished he had the right to comfort her. For a moment, he imagined her with a baby in her lap. He blinked his eyes. "And the other?"

Her expression softened. "That I would never get to kiss you a second time."

This time he did surge to his feet, but after a few faltering steps he came to a stop.

"Oh, Mr. Winston," she said, holding her hand out to him. He crossed to take it, gripping it tightly. "You saved my life! I will always cherish you for that. And everything that has happened in this little cottage," she looked around the room, "it is precious to me, too. As for what has passed between us—" She tipped her chin up at him in a fashion that he suspected was meant to look defiant, but only succeeded in looking adorably wistful. "I do not regret *any* of it. I hope that, perhaps, I can persuade you not to regret it, either."

Dumbfounded, he stared at her, unable to think of a single thing to say that he would not regret for the rest of his days.

"I know that for a gentleman—" She stopped, her cheeks suffusing with pink. "I know that—" Again, she stopped.

"Yes, Lady Jane?"

Her whole face was now bright red. "That such an abrupt halt—such an interruption to activities—can be—can be—"

He suddenly realized what she was trying to say. Laughter—rude, bawdy, wholly inappropriate laughter—began roaring up his chest. He erupted in a great guffaw that made Lady Jane jump in her chair. She stared at him.

"You have been w-w-well informed, my lady. Sometimes the halts can b-b-be excruciating!" For a moment, he thought he had offended her beyond all forgiveness.

Then the corner of her mouth twitched and she enquired mildly, "Since you seem in such high spirits, sir, may I presume that you have recovered from *our* halt?"

His own cheeks suddenly flamed hot. "Yes, my lady."

"Then may we please be friends?" She held out her other hand to him.

For a moment, he felt a flattening wave of disappointment. Then he took her other hand, raised it to his lips, and dropped a chaste kiss upon it. Being friends with Lady Jane was better than being nothing to Lady Jane at all.

They were finally settled for the night, Lady Jane in her chair and he on the floor below her. She had fretted about his ability to sleep on the hard floor and had suggested that he sleep upstairs in Mr. Bagshot's bed. He had assured her firmly that he preferred being close to the fire. The truth was that he preferred being close to *her*, but he thought it wiser not to say so.

"But how will you manage to sleep a wink down there? It looks so hard and cold."

Anthony was quite certain he was not going to sleep a wink no matter where he slept, but he wanted her to stop worrying and sleep a little herself. "Trust me, Lady Jane, I have slept on worse. When you are a soldier, you learn to catch your sleep where you can. Any surface can be comfortable when you are tired enough."

"So, you *are* a military man. I thought you must be."

"*Was* a military man. I resigned my commission a year-and-a-half ago."

"Is that how you got this?" she said, suddenly reaching down and tracing a finger along his scar.

His breath caught at her touch.

"I am sorry," she said, blushing. "That was quite rude of me."

He shook his head. "You need not apologize."

"It must have been a terrible wound," she said, sounding genuinely distressed. "How did it happen?"

He grimaced. "I was pulled from my horse. I managed to avoid being shot, but turned to find a bayonet slicing down at me. Fortunately, my collarbone limited the depth of the thrust, but you are right. It was a near run thing."

Her eyes widened in gratifying dismay. "You mean you might have died?"

He gave a small shrug. "Everyone expected me to, but I decided to defy expectations."

She threw her arms around his neck and hugged him tightly. "Oh, I am so glad that you did."

He smiled, touched. "Thank you, my lady."

She seemed to recall herself then. She sat back in her chair and settled her hands demurely in her lap.

"Now, my lady, will you please try to sleep?"

She assured him that she would, and the room grew quiet, with only the crackling of the fire to keep him company. He glanced at her frequently. Her eyes were closed, but her breathing did not change. He wondered if she drowsed or not.

He was almost beginning to feel drowsy himself, when suddenly her eyes opened. "Mr. Winston, are you asleep?"

He chuckled. "And how could I answer you if I were?"

"May I ask you something?"

"Of course."

"Earlier, when you were trying to reassure me about changing out of my wet things, you said that, to a gentleman, all women—when they were —"

"I remember!" he interrupted hastily.

"Is it really true?"

He hesitated a moment, then said, "No, Lady Jane. Not in the least. Indeed, it is probably the greatest lie I ever told in all my life."

"Oh." How could a single syllable sound so dejected?

"My lady, you would prefer it were the truth?"

"It is only that I thought ... perhaps it would explain ... "

"Explain what?"

She was silent.

Something made him ask, "Lady Jane, who broke your heart?"

She stared down at her hands. "My husband."

"So. You loved him." He had not meant for his tone to be so sharp. Fortunately, she did not seem to notice.

"Yes," she affirmed softly. There was a long pause. "But he had a mistress."

Anthony's hands clenched. He unclenched them and said in a neutral tone, "Some men have a great need for ... variety. It does not mean that he did not care for you."

"She was his mistress before we married and continued so until the day he died. If anyone was the variety, it was I."

This time he could not keep the anger out of his voice. *"Then he was a misbegotten fool!"*

She almost smiled. "Thank you, Mr. Winston. That was kindly said."

He reached up and squeezed her hand. "It is the simple truth."

For a moment, she squeezed his hand in return. Then she loosed her hold and settled back in her chair. "Now I must let you get your sleep."

"Lady Jane—"

"Yes, Mr. Winston?"

"Nothing. Sleep well."

He turned on his side, with his back to her, and stared moodily into the fire. For several long minutes there was silence. Then he heard her whisper behind him, "Mr. Winston, do *you* have a great need for variety?"

"If I am with the right woman, Lady Jane, no. I have no need for it at all."

He had not meant to sleep, but suddenly he was in the middle of his old nightmare.

There was a crashing sound, and a woman fell on top of him. He stared at her in horror. Her face was different, somehow—more dear to him, and he was terrified about what he would find when he pulled open the collar of her shirt. But there was no blood. Her neck was mercifully whole. Trembling, he closed his eyes in relief and pulled her close, pressing his face against her breast so he could listen to the reassuring beat of her heart.

"Mr. Winston! You must wake!"

The voice recalled him to something he had forgotten. How could he have forgotten? What sort of monster was he? His eyes snapped open, and he shook her. "The babe! Where is the babe? Curse it! Tell me that you have found him!"

"Mr. Winston, please! You are dreaming! Please! You must wake!"

Dazed, he looked about him. The room was wrong—too big, too neat, too untouched. He looked at the woman lying on his chest. She was wrong, too. Her skin was too pale, her hair too light a brown, her eyes were not staring and lifeless, but alive and full of feeling—and they were blue, not black.

With a groan he realized where he was, who *she* was. "Lady Jane, my apologies," he said, struggling to steady his voice while his lungs still heaved. "Did I pull you from your chair?"

She stared down at him, her blue eyes wide and full of concern. "Oh, no, Mr. Winston. It was my fault. You were having a dream—a nightmare—and you sounded so distressed, I was desperate to wake you. I leaned over too far, trying to give you a shake, and I fear I tipped over."

"I hope you were not hurt by your fall?"

"Not at all. You took the brunt. I thought it would wake you, but you were still trapped in it." Her voice quavered suddenly, and her eyes glittered.

"I seem to recall," he said tensely, "that is, I have a memory, of . . . shaking you."

"It was nothing," she insisted, "hardly more than a jostle. I am fine. It is you—oh, sir! What in God's heaven were you dreaming?" The tears were actually starting to fall now. One slipped off her lashes and landed on his cheek.

He reached up and wiped another away. "Nothing worthy of these," he said. Feeling a tightness in his throat, he rolled carefully sideways so as not to jostle her poor ankle further, eased her off of him, and rose to his feet. "I greatly regret that I interrupted your slumbers, my lady," he said, lifting her up and setting her back on her chair. "But I hope you will try to get a little more rest."

She nodded mutely, her eyes fixed on his face. Unable to endure her continued scrutiny, he turned away and stared unseeing into the dying fire. *Two days.* He had only known her for two short days—a miserably miniscule period of time to completely forfeit his heart. How could he possibly be so head over heels in such a short time?

Suddenly the state of the fire penetrated his befogged brain. Damnation! He had not been frugal enough in his tending. The fire was down to nothing but ashes, and there were only a few stray pieces of wood left to feed the thing. He crossed to the grate, using the poker to spread the ashes into a thinner layer and revive the few remaining embers. He added the last few small logs that remained.

"Lady Jane?" he said, turning to face her.

She was still regarding him steadily.

"I fear I have bungled the fire. It will not last much longer. At first light, I can go and search for Mr. Bagshot's woodpile, but until then it will grow quite cold in here. I—" For a moment, he stopped, too abashed to ask it of her. Then he remembered all he had put her through this evening and realized this was unlikely to be her greatest grievance. "I think we shall have to share our heat. We can lie next to each other on the floor, or, if you would be more comfortable, I can hold you on my lap in the chair."

"As long as it does not entail any more inspections for frostbite, I am willing."

He felt as if his whole face was washed in fire. "Ma'am," he said stiffly. "I shall not set a finger out of place, I assure you. I will swear an oath on it, if you wish."

She regarded him with eyes full of remorse. "Please forgive me, Mr. Winston! It was a failed jest, nothing more. I will be happy to bundle with you on the floor, in the chair, wherever. There is no need for oaths. If you think we need it to keep warm, I believe you. Dear sir, do you not know? I trust your judgment. I trust *you*. Completely!"

He stared at her. No woman had ever expressed such faith in him. Not the green maidens who reveled in his reputation, but scampered away from his polluting touch before he could actually know them. Not the experienced matrons and widows who expected him to play Don Juan, but never remained around long enough to actually know him. Not the three ladies who had cost him so dearly, but did not deem him worth a backwards glance. Not even his dear sister, who refused to believe his assurances that he would care for her always; instead seeming to secretly fear he would turn out to be the same callous, dishonorable lout that society proclaimed him.

"My lady," he said, with the fervency of a man swearing a lifetime oath of fealty, "I will strive in all things to justify your faith in me."

Chapter 6

*J*ane woke, wondering why her bed felt so hard. Then, with far greater surprise, she wondered at the feel of a man holding her close. It could not be Bevin, she thought groggily. Bevin was lost to her. Then her eyes focused on the steely muscles of the arm embracing her and the softly curling hair running along it that even in the faint grey morning light glowed golden, and she remembered.

Mr. Winston.

He had been right about the fire and about the temperature of the room. He had set her right near the grate, with what was left of the fire's warmth beating on her face and hands, and with him spooning her back. She had actually been warm and content. But the fire was only cold ash now, and the air in the small room was frosty. She thought of his poor back, bare and uncovered in this icy cold. She had offered him her blanket to drape over his shoulders, but he had refused, insisting the shirt she wore was too short to keep her adequately warm, even in the circle of his arms. That the shirt was also insufficient to provide a proper barrier to their bundling had doubtless also been in his thoughts.

She smiled. For a rake, Mr. Winston was a man with surprisingly chivalrous impulses. He began to stir against her blanketed back. She tensed, fearing another nightmare, but he only settled against her more tightly, and then snuggled his face into her neck.

"Sweetheart," he murmured.

For a long while, Jane was as still as a statue, loathe to move or even breathe too deeply lest he wake. The poor man needed his sleep, and truth be told, she needed this embrace. It made her feel safe and warm and cared for. She knew that once he woke things would be different. He would bustle about, putting on his damp clothes, stomping off in search of firewood, patting her hand and bidding her farewell, setting off for Rosington to seek help and a carriage to return her to her brother's attentive care.

And their idyll would be over. The thought was enough to make her cry.

His breathing deepened. Trusting that he had slipped back into a deeper sleep, she nestled into him, pulling his arm more tightly around her, so she could gently rub the silky skin on the inside of his arm against her cheek. He made a sleepy, contented sound and moved his arm still further, his hand coming up and cupping her breast.

She tried not to start, though the sensation sent a thousand fluttering butterflies chasing through her. She struggled to regain her composure and wondered how many other women had experienced the joy of lying encircled in this man's arms.

Sadly, she feared that it was, in all probability, a most prodigious number.

Suddenly, Jane heard the sound of voices in the field outside. Heart racing, she pulled on his arm. "Sir," she exclaimed in a low voice, "you must wake!" She felt him stirring, but the voices were nearing quickly—too quickly. *"Mr. Winston,"* she called more urgently, *"you must get up! Someone is coming!"*

She felt him jerk awake, but he, too, obviously needed a little time to orient himself. He noticed the position of his hand and snatched it away; he heard the voices and tensed; she could feel his heart's sudden thumping against her back.

There was loud pounding on the front door. She felt him start to rise, then stop. "Lady Jane," he murmured under his breath. "I do not wish to send you rolling into the grate. Let me ease my arm from beneath you—"

But it was too late. The knob turned with a wrenching twist and the door slammed open into the wall.

Jane looked up into the furious face of her brother standing on the threshold.

Anthony had been enjoying such a pleasant dream. Lady Jane had been perched on his knee, and he had been nuzzling her neck and holding her breast and whispering endearments in her ear, and she had been telling him how she had just come to the edifying realization that she loved him.

Then the real Lady Jane shook him awake, and he realized that he actually was nuzzling her neck and holding her breast. Abashed, he withdrew the offending hand and untangled his face from the wonderful scent of her hair. Only belatedly did he hear the voices outside and understand the real reason she had so urgently urged him awake.

He tried to rise to his feet, but realized he could only do so by rolling her aside like a discarded bed cover. He tried to maneuver his arm out from under her, but had only managed it halfway when the Marquess of Ryde slammed into the cottage, followed by three men. For a moment, time stood still—as it always does before a battle. Arm pinned by Lady Jane's suddenly white-faced form, Anthony could only stare back at the murderous-looking lord, wishing he were upright, wishing he were properly clothed, wishing he could spare more attention to the lady beneath him who was suddenly so silent and still.

But time and tide wait for no man.

The furious lord strode menacingly forward. Anthony locked eyes with him and would not yield. He gestured with his chin at the three men at Lord Ryde's back, gazing open-mouthed into the cottage, ogling them both. The marquess, who had obviously forgotten the men's presence, turned with a scowl.

"*Out!*" Lord Ryde barked.

The men scuttled backwards as Ryde advanced on them and slammed the cottage door shut in their faces. Anthony took advantage of the brief distraction to disengage his arm and give Lady Jane a quick squeeze of encouragement. Then he surged to his feet and planted himself directly between her and Lord Ryde

"*Sir, leave us,*" Ryde commanded, each syllable as pointed and menacing as a knife. "I wish to speak to my sister—alone."

"No, sir, I will not."

The marquess's mouth opened, then shut; his jaw worked furiously. "*By God, you will!*"

Anthony did not bother speaking again. He just shook his head. He had to absorb the brunt of the other man's anger, before the marquess inadvertently unleashed the full force of his fury on his sister. Again, Anthony locked eyes with him.

Lord Ryde took another step forward. "I tell you sir, get out!"

Again, Anthony shook his head. "Your sister has been through an ordeal. I will not abandon her so that you may rail at her in the full heat of your ill-considered passion."

That brought the marquess up short. For a moment, Anthony hoped he would see reason. But Ryde simply moved sideways and demanded of his sister, "Jane, are you hurt?"

Anthony sensed the barely controlled violence in the other man's voice and knew exactly what the marquess meant by the question, but it was clear Lady Jane did not. She took her brother's inquiry at face value. "Not seriously hurt, no," she said in a small voice. "My ankle is injured, but Mr. Winston is convinced it is only a bad sprain and not a break."

"Devil take your ankle!" Lord Ryde expostulated. "Dammit, Jane, are you *hurt?*"

Anthony felt his hands clench into fists. Ryde was not the only one barely keeping his anger under control. "My lord, you may rest easy. Your sister is unharmed." *Though not for want of my wishing it otherwise.*

Lord Ryde flashed him a blistering look, and then looked past Anthony to his sister. "Well, Jane, does the scoundrel speak the truth?"

There was no answer. Anthony glanced back at her, worried by her silence. He did not like the expression in her eyes as she gazed from him to her brother. She looked quite stricken. *Oh, my dear, I am sorry I did not protect you from this.*

Impatiently, the marquess repeated his question.

She began to tremble. "Stop browbeating her!" Anthony cried. "Can you not see she is at her limit?" He bent down and picked her up and murmured to her under his breath, "Please, my lady, do not fret. Things are not as black as they appear."

"Get your hands off of her!" Ryde grabbed Anthony's shoulder in a fierce grip and began to drag him backwards.

Anthony's own anger snapped. "Sir," he said tightly, "do not cause me to drop her, or I swear I will kill you."

His words seemed to startle the marquess back into some kind of reason. Anthony's shoulder was released, and he was able to turn and set Lady Jane down in the chair. He carefully lifted her legs and set them on the Ottoman. Then he took a deep breath to calm himself and turned to face her brother. "My lord, I believe our time would be better spent if you sent one of your men to fetch a carriage so that Lady Jane can be gotten home as quickly and comfortably as possible."

Lord Ryde's eyes glittered. "Sir, if you presume to give me advice even one more time, I shall —"

"Andrew!"

Anthony and his lordship spun around to regard her. Anthony felt his knees go weak with relief at the sight of her face, which was full of color, and her beautiful blue eyes, which suddenly sparkled with life.

"Dear brother, perhaps you will allow *me* to give you some advice," she snapped.

Lord Ryde had the good sense to look wary. Anthony regarded this fierce new Lady Jane with awe. "Before you say another word to Mr. Winston, I would like you to cross to that door, open it, and look out at that field covered in snow. If it were not for the very fine gentleman who stands before you, you would not need to worry about someone carrying me or whether I had 'come to harm' for you would be discovering me in that field, stiff as a board, frozen dead in the snow."

Anthony felt sudden sympathy for the marquess, whose face had gone deathly pale at her words and who was now staring rather blindly in the direction of Bagshot's front door. Anthony had been in war. He had seen the randomness of death. He knew, firsthand, that sometimes the difference between living and dying was a matter of inches. He looked at Lady Jane, and for a moment he had trouble catching his breath, imagining what his life would be now, today, if yesterday he had decided to turn left instead of right.

It was not a maid who arrived in the carriage from Farthingsgate a half-hour later to look after Lady Jane, but Lady Ryde herself. Anthony was mortified to still be wearing his cursed blanket, but he had been unwilling to leave Lady Jane's side even long enough to change back into his still-damp clothes. He knew that once she departed for her brother's home, it was unlikely he'd be allowed to see her again, despite her repeated attempts to explain events to her stiff-necked brother.

Lady Ryde entered the small cottage with her arms full of clothing, including a bundle she handed to Anthony. Her eyes widened at the sight of him, causing Anthony's cheeks to heat, but still he only grudgingly accompanied Lord Ryde upstairs to Bagshot's bedroom so the ladies could have their privacy.

When they first arrived upstairs, he and the marquess simply glared at each other. Then Lord Ryde exclaimed, "Oh, devil take you, sir! Take off that damn blanket and put on some clothes." He turned his back so Anthony could dress with some shred of dignity in the dry clothes Lady Ryde had brought him. Anthony, grateful to the other man for even this small sign of respect, said in a low voice, "My lord, I know you will not credit it, but I do sincerely regret the worry that you and Lady Ryde must have felt at Lady Jane's absence last night. Believe me, if there had been any way for me to return her home to you, I would have."

Lord Ryde said nothing, but his frosty demeanor seemed to thaw a bit.

Anthony, observing the loose droop of the sleeves and the overlong length of the breeches of the outfit he had just donned, began to suspect that Lady Ryde had snatched the clothes from her tall husband's own wardrobe, but he forbore to comment on the fact. Somehow he did not think Lord Ryde would appreciate the irony.

They waited for some time for Lady Ryde to summon them, and Anthony began to wonder if Lady Ryde could manage the necessary maneuvering to get Lady Jane safely dressed. Foolishly, he mentioned his concern to the marquess. Ryde flashed him a warning look. "Sir, do not try my patience too far. I would sooner have my sister travel home in that ridiculous shirt and blanket than have you serve as her abigail!"

Anthony was brought up short by Lord Ryde's words and made no further protest. He was startled to realize just how distorted his view had become in the space of a single night as to what his rights and privileges were when it came to Lady Jane and her person and her welfare. He wanted charge of all of them; yet he had rights to none. The demoralizing truth of it hit him like a bombshell. He sank down onto the bed, his head in his hands.

"Are you unwell, sir?" the marquess asked, a glimmer of concern in his voice.

"No, my lord," Anthony replied bleakly. "Only tired."

For a while, Ryde left him to dwell on his dismal reflections in peace. Then the marquess cleared his throat. "Sir, it is possible that I may owe *you* an apology having to do with *your* sister."

Anthony sprang to his feet. "What! Is something amiss with Georgiana?"

"No, no! She is sound. It is only—I fear that yesterday, when I grew alarmed at Jane's absence, I rushed to Rosington—"

Anthony's eyes narrowed. "To what purpose, sir?"

Lord Ryde's haughty expression changed. He looked faintly embarrassed. "I thought that you had—that it was possible that Jane was—"

Anthony said coolly, "You thought I had absconded with your sister."

"In a word, yes! Can you blame me, given your reputation?"

Anthony made him no answer. "And when you arrived at Rosington?"

The marquess avoided his eyes. "I demanded an audience with your sister. I did not know her condition then. In retrospect, I should not have taxed her with my fears ... " His voice trailed off.

Once more, Anthony felt his anger flare. He forced his clenched hands to his sides and said tightly, "So let us be clear, my lord. You reasoned that I had kidnapped your sister to ravish her, then spirited her back to Rosington, the house I am leasing from *you*, where *my sister* abides, so that I could do what? Degrade my sister as well as Lady Jane with my debauchery? And this fine bedtime story is what you told my sister during your so-called audience?"

Lord Ryde said stiffly. "I was concerned for *my* sister."

Anthony opened his mouth to issue a stinging retort, but the marquess held up a staying hand.

"I know that does not excuse my mistake, Winston. I was not thinking clearly at the time, and I let my fears color my reasoning. I regret the scene I put your sister through."

It was a surprisingly robust apology, and it drained away most of Anthony's anger. It also drove his spirits even further into despair. Had he sunk so low? Was this, then, the generally held opinion of his character? And what of Georgiana? Would he return home to find that she, too, now believed his soul quite black?

Suddenly Lady Ryde called to them from the narrow staircase. "You may descend now, gentlemen. Jane is dressed, and we are ready to depart."

Sick at heart, Anthony followed Lord Ryde downstairs. As they entered the room where he had passed such precious time with Lady

Jane, Anthony seized the other man's sleeve and pulled him back toward the stairs. "My lord, please!" he entreated tensely. "May I have a moment to say goodbye to your sister—in private?"

Lord Ryde shook his head. "What would be the point?"

Anthony replied hotly, "I think I am entitled to that much, at least, sir!"

Lord Ryde's expression grew frosty. "We will decide what you are entitled to and what actions need to be taken to solve this coil you have landed my sister in—" He pulled out a pocket watch. "Two hours from now. In my study. Do not be late. Go home, inform your sister that you are alive and whole, and then return to Farthingsgate. I will send a groom with you to make sure you do not lose your way. Depending on what we decide, you may make your goodbyes to my sister then."

Anthony stared open-mouthed at the marquess.

"Well, sir? Don't just stand there gaping. Get going!"

Anthony, who felt as if he had just had a reprieve from the gallows, did not have to be told twice.

Chapter 7

Jane sat sideways on the chaise longue in Farthingsgate's large drawing room. She was wearing a dry gown made of soft satin that rustled slightly as she twitched at it nervously. On her left foot, she wore a matching satin slipper. Her right foot was bruised, swollen and bare. Jane made sure to pull back her skirt a little and pose her foot on the little pillow Catherine had placed beneath it. When her brother came in, she wanted to be sure he saw it and was reminded of what he owed Mr. Winston.

There was a flutter of cold air as Catherine re-entered the room and came to sit in a chair by her. Jane pulled the soft silk shawl draped around her shoulders more tightly about her. Strange that she had felt so warm and cozy in Mr. Bagshot's small cottage, but now that she was home at Farthingsgate she could not seem to banish the January chill.

"Oh, my dear. You are trembling. Shall I summon someone to build up the fire, or would you like a small pan with warm coals brought up?"

"No, thank you, Catherine. Will Andrew be coming soon?"

"Not soon, my dear, but eventually. Mr. Winston has arrived, and your brother awaits him in his study. They will discuss what must be done to resolve this ... situation."

"Why must *anything* be done? All Mr. Winston did was save me from the snow!"

"Jane, please! You know exactly why something must be done. Only one of the three men with Ryde when he found you answers directly to him. One is a groom here, but the other two are local farmers. As much as your brother might wish to curb their wagging tongues, he cannot control them. Already, the rumors have begun to spread."

Jane stared moodily down at her hands. "But it is so unfair! Why should Mr. Winston suffer because he did a good deed?"

"Let us see what the gentlemen decide before we jump to any conclusions," Catherine said, flashing Jane a small smile.

"I do not know how Andrew came to think to look for us in Bagshot's cottage," Jane remarked irritably. "Did he go about to all the cottages in the neighborhood?"

"No, some farmers looking for stranded livestock crossed the field and noticed the smell of wood smoke near Mr. Bagshot's home. That made them suspicious, so they summoned Ryde."

"Why should it make them suspicious? Surely a fire burning in January is hardly remarkable?

"It is when Mr. Bagshot has been gone from his cottage for three weeks now. His daughter, who lives in Cornwall, has just delivered him a fine grandson."

"Oh," Jane muttered pettishly. She knew she had no justification for her fractious mood, but she could not seem to shed it. "I wish Andrew had never found us!"

"*My dear! You do not know what you say!*" Jane was startled by the tone of reproof—almost anger—in her sister-in-law's voice. "Goodness, Jane. Your poor brother was half-crazed with fear for you! You vanished from the house—"

"I went for a walk."

"We know that now. We did not yesterday. You did not tell anyone of your intention. And in any case, it would hardly have been reassuring information, would it? Not with the onset of that storm. As it was, when the snow began in earnest, Ryde grew frantic. He even rushed to Rosington—"

"Rosington! Why would Andrew seek me there?"

Catherine turned and stared at the fire. "I think he hoped that Mr. Winston had secreted you there."

"What!" Jane exclaimed. "You mean Andrew thought Mr. Winston had … had … "

"Carried you off. Yes."

"But why would Andrew *hope* for such a thing to be true?"

Catherine met Jane's gaze, and Jane was startled by the bleakness in her eyes. "It was preferable to believing you dead in the snow, my dear."

Jane was overwhelmed with remorse. "Oh, Catherine! I am sorry! I had not truly comprehended how worried all of you must have been!"

"It does not matter now, my dear. We have a happy ending to our tale."

"Perhaps."

Catherine's eyebrows rose. *"Perhaps?"*

"I know Drew means well, and I do understand now that his bluster and anger this morning were because he was so frightened, but it is difficult to have one's entire life decided and laid out for one without so much as a 'by your leave!'" Jane paused, and then added ruefully, "I know that must sound horribly ungrateful to you, dear sister."

To her surprise, however, Catherine smiled at her. "Actually it sounds surprisingly familiar. I believe I said something almost exactly like it to your brother not that long ago."

"It is just that I do not wish Drew to take advantage of the fact that Mr. Winston is such a chivalrous gentleman."

An amused expression appeared on Catherine's face.

"Truly, he is!" Jane exclaimed. "You must believe me! He is not the heartless fellow society claims him to be."

"Yes, *that* I do believe," her sister-in-law remarked drily. "His heart is quite easily visible and clearly as oversized as his fine, broad shoulders."

Jane frowned. Was Catherine quizzing her? "He *is* big-hearted— and very kind."

"Of course he is, did I not just say so?" The corner of Catherine's mouth twitched. "Now I think you must excuse me for a little while. There is something I must do."

In life, as in battle, Anthony reflected, sometimes the outcome is predetermined. Victory or defeat march toward you, as implacable as the grave. Other times, everything is jumbled. Fortune spins her wheel, and you dart in and out of the smoke trying to find your way. Sometimes danger rises up to strike at you with the swiftness of a snake. Other times opportunity rains down from heaven with the unexpected grace of a summer shower. Anthony stared across the desk at Lord Ryde, offering a silent prayer of thanksgiving for the opportunity that had just been poured into his lap. "Would you prefer a reading of the banns, my lord, or shall I procure a special license?"

Lord Ryde frowned. "Special license, I think. The sooner you are wed, the better. I wish to stop tongues wagging as quickly as possible."

Anthony nodded. He was not as sanguine about the ease with which tongues could be stopped—even by a wedding—once begun on their frenzied chattering, but he, too, was eager for speed. He wanted Lady Jane safely in his keeping before things truly became bad.

"Sir, we have not yet spoken of settlements. My sister has a small jointure from her late husband, and I plan to make her a settlement of twenty thousand pounds." Ryde paused, and then added stiffly, "I am sorry it is not more, but I have only recently managed to get my estates into order. If you consider the amount insufficient, my wife is also willing to make Jane a settlement —"

"That will not be necessary!" Anthony exclaimed. "Thanks to a dear uncle who left me an inheritance, I am a man of means. I would be happy to take Lady Jane if she came to me in nothing but her shift."

"That would be an improvement over the shirt and blanket," the marquess remarked, the corner of his mouth almost bending toward a smile.

Anthony smiled in return, trying not to look sheepish that that very same blanket and shirt were neatly folded up and carefully stored away in the chest where he kept his old regimental uniform.

"Mr. Winston, I believe there is only one other matter that we must discuss."

"Yes, my lord?"

"It is the matter of your character and the sort of husband you will be to my sister."

Anthony sucked in his breath. "I will strive in all things to make your sister happy."

Lord Ryde gave a wary nod. "Yes, you say that now, while the bloom is on the rose. But I want your assurance that this wild past of yours is at an end—that you will never cause my sister one moment of heartache with your behavior. Can you make me that pledge?"

"I swear it, my lord," Anthony said heatedly, "on my honor as a gentleman."

Ryde's lip curled in derision.

Anthony flinched. "Very well," he said tensely. "If you prefer, I will swear upon my mother's grave. I will never do anything to harm your sister or shame her or cause her a moment's distress. I would rather cut off my own arm than do so."

Ryde's face relaxed a fraction. "Sir, the reports I have had of you have been very black, but for some reason I believe you." He held out his hand. "Shall we shake upon it?"

Anthony, feeling a huge wave of relief, began to reach out to take the other man's hand. Before he could do so, however, Lady Ryde swept into the room. Anthony surged to his feet. "My lady," he said with a bow.

She surveyed him with a smile.

"Hello, Mr. Winston. You are looking quite fine. That is good."

Anthony was not sure what to make of this comment. Was the lady relieved to find that he was not standing in her husband's stately and imposing study wearing nothing but a blanket?

Her attention swept past him to fix on her husband. She crossed to stand beside Lord Ryde and placed one long-fingered hand on his shoulder. "Dearest, forgive my untimely interruption, but may I have a word with you—in private?"

Anthony awaited Ryde's answer tensely. He wanted no interruptions now, not when things hung so delicately in the balance. He watched the play of emotion on the other man's face. He suspected Ryde was in no mood for interruptions, either. The marquess seemed about to tell his wife so, when she bent to his ear and whispered something. Suddenly, a look of bemused fondness crossed his face. He looked up at Anthony.

"Mr. Winston, could you please excuse us for a moment?"

Anthony, jaw clenched, turned and marched out the door.

Sometimes, in the fog of battle, it is difficult to tell friend from foe. It was ironic, Anthony thought, as he nervously paced the fine hallway outside Lord Ryde's study, that he had come to this house today expecting his greatest and most implacable enemy to be the master of the house and his greatest ally to be its mistress. But as time stretched, and his heart began beating increasingly frantic rhythms and his throat grew tighter and more dry, he began to fear he had entirely mistaken the matter. He feared the happiness that had seemed within his grasp a few minutes ago was now slipping steadily, inexorably out of reach.

The door to the study opened. The marquess stood there, his arm around his lady. "Mr. Winston, I am sorry. As my wife has reminded me, all that we have been discussing here is a matter that deeply affects my sister. My wife feels, and I must agree with her, that it is only suitable to include Jane in the discussion and to consult with her on her wishes as to how we should proceed. Will you please come with us to the drawing room?"

Anthony, his chest tight with disappointment, bowed his head in assent.

He had been so close to securing the right to keep Lady Jane safe, to protect her from the storm that was approaching due to the morning's events. But what chance had he now? She was too innocent to know how fiercely the gale would blow, and there were too many people to tell her that he was a weak reed in which to place her trust.

There was no help for it. Fortune had spun her wheel. He would have to do his best to persuade Lady Jane to marry him. He turned and followed Lord and Lady Ryde down the stately hallway, hoping he was not on his way to snatch defeat from the very jaws of victory.

Chapter 8

When Mr. Winston finally entered the drawing room, marching in behind Andrew and Catherine, Jane was startled by how happy she was to see him. It had only been a few short hours since she had last set eyes on him, but she had missed him. Oh, she had missed him! And she felt warmer now—as if a great Yule log had been dropped onto the fire.

He was no longer wearing Andrew's borrowed togs, but clothes obviously tailored for him and him alone. His coat was green, a lovely deep shade that reminded her of summer and brought out the sparkling emerald of his eyes. His waistcoat was a snowy white, embroidered all over in the same glowing gold as his hair. The sleeves of his shirt were precisely the right length, and his coat fit his broad shoulders so exactly that she longed to run her fingers from collar to cuff and pretend he wore no coat at all.

Suddenly, she was not just warmer. She was *warm.*

She closed her eyes. When she opened them again, he had crossed to stand before her. He made her a very formal bow. "Lady Jane, it is good to see you again." His expression was unaccountably grave. She inclined her own head to him, suddenly shy of this reserved stranger. But when she looked more closely at his face, she realized he did not look unfriendly, he simply looked...she tried to puzzle it out. *Strained.* So strained she was surprised he did not sink to his knees under the weight of it.

Impulsively, she reached out a hand to him. "Oh, Mr. Winston, it is good to see you, too." He took her hand and squeezed it with a fierceness that would have made her protest if she had not seen the look of relief in his eyes. "Will you sit, sir?" she said, gesturing to the chair Catherine had sat in earlier.

"Thank you, my lady." He folded his long body into the small chair and then looked at her, and then away in the direction of her brother, as if waiting for Andrew to speak.

Suddenly, Jane sorely regretted her injured ankle, for she felt an overwhelming desire to spring up from the chaise and rail at her over-mastering brother who had obviously bullied this fine man into some sort of sacrifice that he was too honorable to refuse.

Anthony was grateful for the support of the confoundedly tiny chair Lady Jane had offered him, for he was suddenly completely un-sure how to go on. He had planned his proposal as he had marched down Lord Ryde's long hallway, and he had been ready to be masterful and insistent and to carry his point with a myriad of strong arguments once Lord Ryde placed the matter before his sister. But then he had entered the room and seen Lady Jane, and all his pretty strategies—all rational thought, really—had flown straight out of his head.

She was seated on the chaise with one knee bent and her other leg extended before her, her injured foot propped up on a ridiculous little pillow. He was glad for that pillow, and for the clear view of her poor foot, otherwise he would never have dared approach her. She seemed so different from his lady of the cottage, so far beyond his touch.

She wore a stylish and expensive-looking gown of peach-colored satin, the shade so perfectly suited to her coloring that her skin glowed and her hair shone and the pink of her lips seemed to beckon him from across the room. There was a pretty shawl about her shoulders, and on her good foot a completely useless and completely lovely satin slipper peeped out from beneath her skirt.

What the hell had he been thinking?

At a loss to know what else to do, he crossed to her and bowed, gazing at her injured foot like a talisman, proof that at least for a little while she had been within his reach. He flinched to see how battered her poor ankle looked. He wanted to kiss each and every bruise. Then she looked up at him, and there was a look of greeting in her eyes. He clung desperately to that look, and to the hand she held out to him, trying to fire up his courage, trying to convince himself he still had a chance to win her. He eased his unsteady legs into the chair she offered him and gazed over at her brother—his unexpected ally—desperately willing the man to speak, to set the battle in motion, to force things forward before Anthony completely lost his nerve.

To his everlasting relief, Lord Ryde obliged.

"Jane, Mr. Winston and I have been discussing the difficult situation we find ourselves in. He and I have reached a conclusion about what we think is best to be done, but Catherine reminds me that you, too, deserve a say in the matter."

Jane gazed at her highhanded brother. She had a pretty fair notion of what he was pressuring Mr. Winston to do. "I am still unconvinced *anything* needs to be done about our 'difficult situation.' What do I care about a little gossip? I am not a green girl. I am a widow. If my reputation suffers a little, it can hardly impact my life to a significant degree."

"I beg to differ with you, Lady Jane." The quiet response came not from her brother, but from Mr. Winston. "This particular bit of gossip will hurt very much indeed."

She turned in surprise. "Why should you suppose that to be so, Mr. Winston?"

"Because, my lady, my name—my very blackened name—is attached to it. Gossip is a sort of currency. It has greatest worth when it tells an entertaining tale, when it allows others to feel superior, when it reinforces previously held beliefs. This piece of gossip does all three. The titillating story of an infamous rake who seduces the sister of a marquess on the lord's own property is bound to be a rumor tidbit of the first water."

"But you did not seduce me. It did not happen."

"What is that to the point?" he snapped. "Scandal does not need to be true—only plausible. You were unlucky enough to spend your evening in Bagshot's cottage with *me* and not some nameless mister, so your ruin will be considered not only plausible but assured." She stared at him. The bleak bitterness in his eyes and voice tore at her heart. "Indeed, it is likely that your seduction will be held up as the high water mark of my whole debauched career." His face had gone quite white and his breathing was coming in quick, tense bursts.

In alarm, Jane turned to her brother. "Drew, surely he overstates things! Surely things cannot be so black!"

But one look at her brother's grim expression and the tight grip he kept on Catherine's hand convinced Jane that he, at least, believed every word Mr. Winston spoke.

"Catherine?" Jane pleaded, looking for reassurance.

But Catherine shook her head. "I am sorry, my dear. I think we must trust Mr. Winston's judgment in this. He has suffered the slings and arrows of society's censure. He knows what lies ahead."

Jane turned back to him. "Sir, please! I cannot bear to have you sacrifice yourself to combat what in the end is just a...just a... tarradiddle!"

For a moment, something softened in his green eyes. "My lady, I assure you," he said in a low voice, "it would be no sacrifice."

"What if I were to take the risk and brave the onslaught?"

His jaw clenched. He said harshly, "Then you will be held up as an object lesson to giggling debutantes on the dangers of unchastity. Adulterous matrons will turn their backs on you in disdain. Lascivious widows will laugh up their sleeves at you for getting caught. Your brother will become a laughingstock for guarding you so poorly. And your sisters will become social outcasts, because it will be assumed they share your wild nature."

And our father's, Jane thought, feeling faintly sick.

Suddenly Mr. Winston rose to his feet. He turned to her brother. "My lord, Lady Ryde, would you please allow me a few minutes alone with Lady Jane?"

"Of course, Mr. Winston." To Jane's surprise, her brother rose quickly to his feet, made a deep, respectful bow in Mr. Winston's direction, and offered Catherine his arm. "We will be in my study when you need us."

As the door closed behind them, Jane felt a sort of panic. "Please, sir. *No.*"

But Mr. Winston looked grimly determined. He dropped to one knee and took her hand in his. "My dear Lady Jane," he began. His voice wavered. He began again. "My dearest lady, will you please do me the very great honor of becoming my wife?"

Jane stared down at his bent head, and her breath caught at the sudden thought of what it would mean to marry this man—this sweet, noble, incredibly kind man. Her heart began to pound. What would it be like to wake every morning, as she had this morning, in the circle of his arms? What would it be like to have such a man to protect her and hold her and love her? Her thoughts suddenly stumbled.

He was not marrying her for love, she reminded herself, he was marrying her for duty. The panic began to fill her chest.

And what if she grew to love *him?*

She thought of the great distress she had suffered when Bevin died. She was suddenly quite certain that suffering would be as nothing to what she would feel if she were to love *this* man and then lose him. Her body began to tremble. The panic was now up in her throat.

To love *this* man and lose him? Dear God, she did not think she could survive such pain. He looked up, and she realized she had taken too long to give him an answer. She opened her mouth and closed it. She opened it again and tried to speak, but no words would come. She stared, stricken, into his beautiful green eyes. Right now they looked so full of feeling, she felt as if she would drown.

"Sir, I—" But she could get no further. Suddenly overwhelmed by a choice she felt she could not make, she threw her arms around his neck and began to sob.

Anthony waited for Lady Jane to give him his answer. As he knelt by her side, not daring to look at her, not daring to breathe, he felt like a kite in a March wind. One moment, his spirits would sail upwards, certain she would say yes; the next moment, he would plunge down into despair, equally certain she would say no. He soared and plunged so many times, his stomach felt queasy and his head giddy, but still she did not answer.

At last, he could bear the suspense no longer. He looked up into her face. What he saw there made his breath catch in his throat. He was facing the unexpected terror of the bayonet again, only this time, plunged directly into his heart.

Her blue eyes were filled with panic—and despair. She had the look of a trapped animal, unsure where to turn, desperate for escape. A sudden chill filled him. He had done this to her. He—in his desperation not to lose her and his frenzy to make her understand the danger that lay ahead—had driven her into a box she felt she could not escape. Suddenly she threw her arms around him and began to weep. Feeling as if each painful sob was a punishing lash across his back, Anthony picked her up, set her on his lap, and began rocking her, soothing her, whispering to her that all would be well.

"My dear lady, please! Do not despair. You need not marry me! We will find another way to keep you safe. I promise you!"

But his words did not seem to help, so he just held her and rocked her and desperately racked his brain for a third way, a way that would protect her from the world's scorn, but not require her to marry the most despised rake in all England.

Finally—as the storm of her weeping began to calm, and she settled wearily in his arms, her face buried in the collar of his coat—the answer came. "My dear lady, I have it," he murmured into her ear, stroking her hair and patting her trembling shoulders. "I have the answer. We can simply engage upon a betrothal—do not start, little one, only a pretend betrothal, not a binding one! But it will do. A betrothal will take enough sting out of the tale that it will run its course quickly. And after a time, when the stories have died down and the tongues have ceased to wag, we can quietly announce that we do not suit and go our separate ways."

She lifted her head and gazed at him, her tear-filled eyes wide and staring, "You would do that for me?"

His heart did a painful lurch. "My lady, I would do anything for you."

Chapter 9

Anthony called at Farthingsgate the next day bearing a hyacinth flower in a small blue vase for his betrothed. He was feeling almost cheerful. If the flower he carried could be coaxed to bloom in the middle of winter, then anything was possible. Perhaps with time and patience and careful wooing, Lady Jane might be coaxed into someday declaring their betrothal real. It was an enticing daydream, anyway.

He was shown into the drawing room. He was greeted by Lady Ryde, but Lady Jane was not there. The only other person in the room was Lady Jane's sister, Lady Maria, who kept staring at him surreptitiously. "Mr. Winston, welcome!" Lady Ryde took his arm and led him to a chair. "The doctor is with Jane now, but when they are done, I will have her brought down to you at once."

"Doctor!" he exclaimed, suddenly afraid.

"There is no cause for worry, sir. Mr. Elton is just checking her ankle—to see how she progresses and make sure that she is mending."

"Oh, of course," he said, embarrassed. What had happened to his control, to the impassive mask he was used to displaying before the world? He feared that his ability to hide his feelings, like so much else in the last three tempestuous days, had fallen by the wayside.

"Mr. Winston, may I introduce my sister-in-law, Lady Maria Wentworth?"

Anthony rose to his feet and bowed. "Lady Maria, it is a pleasure."

Lady Jane's sister inclined her head but did not smile. The surreptitious looks were gone. Now she regarded him with the steady, unblinking gaze of a mother about to deliver a scold. Anthony braced himself to hear what she thought of the man who had sunk her sister into so much trouble. But the scold did not come. Instead she said, "Sir, may I offer you a piece of advice?"

Anthony was not sure he wanted to hear it, but he resumed his seat and nodded courteously. "Of course, my lady."

"Take Jane to London when the Season begins. Take her there and hold your head high and face down the tittle-tattle as bravely as you did the French at Busaco. Jane has the courage for it, if you will but ask her."

He stared at her. "How in the world—"

She grimaced. "My husband's brother is in the War Office. I asked him for details about you when I heard you had leased Rosington, for I had heard the gossip and feared the worst. He tells me you are a genuine hero."

He felt his cheeks heat. "No, my lady!"

Her mouth tightened and her eyebrows rose. "You told me, Catherine, but I did not believe you." Lady Ryde gave a small shrug. Lady Maria rose to her feet, so Anthony did as well. She crossed to him, and he sucked in his breath warily, but he let the breath go as she held out her hand. "I wish to thank you, sir."

"Thank me?" Anthony repeated in surprise.

"For rescuing my sister from the storm and saving her life." Her tone was faintly impatient. "Jane is—" The lady paused and cleared her throat. "She is very precious to us." Then she turned and left the room.

Anthony was still feeling a little dazed from his encounter with Lady Maria when a man strode into the room. He was short and sandy-haired. Lady Ryde rose from her seat and crossed to greet him. "Matthew! It is good to see you! It has been far too long!"

She offered him her hands, and the fellow took them. For a moment, he gazed into her eyes with a look of intense longing. Then, as quickly as the look had come, it was gone. He remarked politely, "It is good to see you, too, Catherine."

"So, how fares our patient?"

Patient? Good Lord, was it possible that this besotted fellow was the local doctor? Clearly Lady Ryde had no notion of the fellow's true feelings.

"She is well," the doctor answered. "Your diagnosis was correct. There are no bones broken. It is a bad sprain, nothing more."

"Credit for the diagnosis goes to Mr. Winston here. Mr. Winston, allow me to introduce our doctor and very good friend, Matthew Elton."

Anthony bowed. The other man surveyed him with exasperating thoroughness, then bowed as well. "I am pleased to make your acquaintance, Mr. Winston."

"How long will it take Lady Jane's sprain to heal?"

The doctor considered the question in a deliberate way that made Anthony itch with impatience. "Fortunately, the swelling is not as bad as I would have expected —"

"It is quite bad enough!" Anthony snapped.

"The swelling is not as severe as I would have expected given the amount of bruising," Mr. Elton declared with careful emphasis. "Probably all that time in the snow kept it down. In any case, I think Jane will mend quickly. I would expect—"

"Sir, how do you come to refer to the lady in such a familiar fashion?"

"Hold, Mr. Winston! Hold!" Lady Ryde exclaimed. "As I said, Matthew is an old family friend. He has known Jane since childhood."

"I…see." Anthony took a step back and unclenched his fists. *What the devil was wrong with him? Was he going to go off half-cocked at every alarm, every imagined slight to his beloved?* "Forgive me, sir."

Elton considered him. "It is forgotten already. As I was about to say, I think Lady Jane should be back on her feet again within the fortnight, three weeks at the most."

Lady Ryde started for the door. She called back over her shoulder, "I must go up to Jane now, Matthew, but I hope you will stay? I am sorry I was not here to greet you when you arrived, but perhaps you can join us for luncheon and catch me up on all your news?"

Elton said quietly, "I fear I cannot. Perhaps another time." She flashed him a look of disappointment and then glided out the door. For a moment there was a look on the other man's face—a look of wistfulness and regret and sadness—that was as familiar to Anthony as looking in a mirror.

Poor fellow. Pining away for a lady so completely out of reach.

Feeling suddenly grim, Anthony realized he did not know whether he was pitying the doctor—or himself.

"Mr. Winston?" Belatedly, Anthony realized Elton was trying to get his attention.

"Yes, sir?"

"I feel I ought to warn you. Stories about yesterday's events have already swept the neighborhood and the village and will soon reach most of the county."

Tight-lipped, Anthony nodded. "Yes, I have no doubt. What of it?"

"There is an ugly mood developing hereabouts. You are seen as an outsider, and Lady Jane, having grown up in the area, is considered a sort of—"

"Local princess?" Anthony suggested flatly.

"Exactly! There was already resentment that a man with—forgive me—your reputation had settled into Lady Ryde's old home. Now it is thought that—"

"I have seduced their princess right under her lordly brother's nose?"

"You *do* comprehend. Thank goodness! I do not like the feeling that is developing. I fear something darker and more dangerous may erupt. I urge you, sir, take care!"

Anthony blinked. This stranger was concerned about his safety? He said gravely, "I thank you for your warning, Mr. Elton. I promise you, I will keep it in mind."

The other man flashed him a hesitant smile and then departed.

When Catherine informed Jane that Mr. Winston was waiting downstairs to see her, Jane felt a sudden flaring impatience that she could not simply jump up onto her own two feet and run down to him at once. Instead, a footman had to be summoned to carry her, and before that summons, Catherine insisted Jane change into a fresh gown, and Jane's maid insisted on fiddling with her hair, and then still more time was wasted searching for a slipper to match the gown.

"Really, Catherine, what does it matter?" Jane exclaimed in exasperation. "I only have use for the one, anyway! I can wear any old slipper."

"Dearest, don't you wish to look pretty and composed for your betrothed?"

This caught Jane up short. Mr. Winston was her *betrothed*.

For several minutes, her thoughts simply circled around that one happy thought, and she could not stop her mouth from slipping into a smile. She even joined in the hunt for the slipper by calling out suggestions as to where her maid should hunt for it next. But just as the silly thing was finally found, and Jane slipped it on her foot, it occurred to her that a handsome rake like Mr. Winston had probably seen more than his fair share of satin slippers of every shade—both on and off their owners' feet. The bubbling happiness in her chest subsided, and by the time the footman arrived to carry her downstairs, Jane's spirits were sadly flat.

They revived a little when the footman carried her into the drawing room and she spotted Mr. Winston waiting for her, a pretty pink flower in his hands. Her spirits revived still more when her betrothed—oh, she knew it was not real, but she still found pleasure in applying that word to him—surged to his feet at her entrance and actually scowled at the footman who carried her. For a delicious moment, she wondered if he might actually be jealous, but it turned out he was simply being his usual protective self.

"Careful there, man! Lady Jane is not a sack of potatoes!"

Startled by his fierce tone, the footman actually dropped her a few inches onto the chaise and with a quick bow darted from the room.

"You know," she remarked irritably, not finding the comparison to potatoes at all romantic, "if you scare him like that, he may refuse to carry me at all. Next time he may simply slide me down the banister!"

To her surprise, he did not look at all contrite. Instead, there was a wicked glimmer in his eyes. "As long as I was there at the bottom to catch you," he said, his voice oddly husky, "I would not mind. The view would be spectacular."

She stared at him, wondering where her chivalrous protector had gone. This fellow, with his dancing emerald eyes and his oh-too-knowing mouth, seemed dangerously convincing playing the rake. His golden hair glinted, and he suddenly reminded her of a lion, a lion who was stalking her. Suddenly every square inch of her skin felt hot, and she wondered if she'd taken a fever. He stalked closer, then closer still. She drew a deep, shuddering breath, and his gaze followed the air down, sliding down her throat to focus on the rise and fall of her chest. His broad shoulders seemed even broader as he leaned over her, and her eyes fluttered closed, waiting for his kiss.

But it never came.

She opened her eyes again. His face was only inches from her own, and he was staring at her mouth, his breath coming in small, jagged gulps. Yet he moved no closer.

It was as if her rake and her protector were locked in a battle neither could win. Suddenly, she felt infinite tenderness for both.

She reached up and cupped his cheek. His eyes closed, and his face pressed against her hand, and then his head turned and he pressed kisses into her palm. At first they were soft kisses, light and feathery and sweet. Then his lips became more insistent, and his mouth began to rove, his kisses sliding up her arm, over her shoulder and then slaloming down to the neckline of her gown, his tongue flicking little darting caresses along the tops of her breasts. She felt as if she were falling, as if the soft cushions of the chaise were slipping away beneath her. She clung to him, desperate not to let go. She whispered his name.

And suddenly he went absolutely still.

The stillness lasted a long time, punctuated only by the sound of their breathing. Then he murmured apologetically into her ear, "Lady Jane, I fear we must stop." Slowly he pulled free, retreating to his chair half the room away.

For a long time they just gazed at each other.

Then suddenly Catherine called from outside the door. "Dearest, I am coming in now." And she did. Mr. Winston rose to his feet. "Sir, forgive me," she said, "but as I informed Jane earlier, my husband prefers that the two of you not be left unchaperoned for too lengthy a time."

"He does not trust me alone with his sister."

"Let us just say he thinks it best if we observe the proprieties as much as possible," Catherine countered gently.

He made a bow to her. "Your husband, my lady, is a very wise man."

Anthony watched Lady Ryde settle herself at the far end of the room. Not about to have the infant chair he had been forced to use yesterday foisted on him yet again today, Anthony picked up a larger chair and carried it over to Lady Jane, setting it down as close to her as possible. Now that Lady Ryde's chaperonage would provide a check on his confounded impulses, he ached to be as close to his lady as he could.

He could not quite believe how easily he had forgotten himself and how close he had come to disgracing himself right there in Lord Ryde's drawing room. True, he had been sorely provoked by the sight of Lady Jane in another man's arms, even if the arms belonged to a footman wearing her brother's livery. And true, some mischievous spark had been ignited in his mind by the fantasy image of her sliding down the banister into his embrace. But in the end, what had proved his undoing had been the simple gesture of her reaching up to hold his cheek when he had been struggling so hard not to kiss her. He did not know why, but for one short, delirious moment he had been convinced that she loved him.

It had been a singularly foolish notion.

Frowning, he crossed to pick up the small blue vase containing the pink hyacinth. He carried it over to her and presented it to her with a bow. "Here, Lady Jane, is a gift from my sister."

"It is lovely, Mr. Winston!" she exclaimed, sounding genuinely pleased. "How did she manage to get it to bloom at this time of year?"

"I fear you will have to ask her yourself. It is a dark art, as far as I am concerned."

She chuckled. "I would like to ask her that and many other things. Will she call on me soon? I would very much like to meet her."

"I am sorry, Lady Jane. I do not think so."

Her mouth crumpled. "She does not approve of our counterfeit betrothal?"

"Oh, no," he hurried to assure her. "It is not that. It is just…difficult for her to travel. She usually does not leave the house."

Now her face filled with concern. *Lord, was there ever such an expressive countenance as this?* "Oh, Mr. Winston, is she ill?"

He hesitated. He did not make it a habit to discuss his sister's condition, but Lord Ryde already knew, and Anthony did not think Georgiana would mind if Lady Jane did as well. "Not ill, injured. I fear she suffered an accident last spring—a fall from her horse. At first, the doctors thought the injury was minimal, but she did not recover as expected, and she has not regained the use of her legs since that time."

Lady Jane's blue eyes were now liquid with unshed tears. "Oh, the poor dear! Mr. Winston, I am so very sorry!"

Anthony was surprised how much comfort her sympathy gave him. Usually, he found people's pity mortifying and irritating, but her empathetic anguish made him feel as if she had thrown her two warm arms about him and squeezed him tight.

"Mr. Winston?"

"Yes, my lady."

"If your sister cannot come to me, then I must go to her. May I pay her a call tomorrow?"

"My dear Lady Jane! You are as confined as my sister at the moment."

"Not if you —" She regarded him shyly. "Not if you would be willing to carry me."

"Of course I would be willing! But it would be such a commotion for you. Would it not tire you beyond all bearing?"

"Oh, no! I have been yearning to get out of the house! It is amazingly dispiriting to sit like a lump all day and not be able to do a single thing for myself."

He stared at her, much struck. He had never thought of it quite that way before. Did Georgiana chafe at her inactivity in the same way? She was not such a vibrant, energetic creature as Lady Jane, but still . . .

"Then is it settled?" She asked, gazing at him eagerly. "Shall I ask Ryde if we can borrow his carriage?"

"I have a perfectly good carriage to carry you in!" he exclaimed, stung.

"Oh, I cannot wait to see it! Then is it arranged?"

He sighed. Denying Lady Jane anything was not one of his strengths. "Very well, my de—my lady. I shall come fetch you in the morning. I must warn you though. Georgiana may not be . . . entirely welcoming. She has become quite chary of company."

"I will not take offense. No doubt she is melancholy. Heaven knows I was in no mood for company before—" She stopped suddenly, an arrested look on her face. "Goodness, Mr. Winston. Has it truly been only three days since the ball?"

He watched her, his spirits suddenly buoyant. "Unbelievable, is it not?"

She shook her head, as if in wonder. "So much has happened." She paused and raised her hands to her cheeks. "I feel quite . . . a different person."

He took her hand, squeezed it, and said softly, "Do you, Lady Jane?"

Mutely—looking a little anxious—she nodded.

Chapter 10

Jane was dressed and waiting at an excessively early hour the next morning.

She was certain her first view of Mr. Winston's fine carriage must have been impressive, but she was too distracted by being carried out to it in Mr. Winston's strong arms to have any memory of the experience. He lifted her up onto the seat and climbed in after her, closing the door and sitting down on the bench opposite. He signaled the driver to start. Jane tried to slide gracefully over to make room for him next to her. Without her good foot to push off with, however, the motion was more like the scoot of an infant across the floor, and she flinched in mortification as her bottom rocked its way sideways. A finer gentleman would have ignored her graceless movement, but Mr. Winston's gaze was fixed, eagle-eyed, where it should not be. Feeling a flare of irritation, she gestured to the seat next to her. "Sir, would you care to move, so you do not have your back to the horses?"

"It would probably be wiser if I remained where I was," he said with a chuckle, "but as you have gone to so much *effort* on my behalf…" With his usual fluid grace, he moved to sit next to her. She did not like to be laughed at, but her pleasure at his nearness undermined her efforts to remain angry. He took her hand and lifted it to his lips. "Am I forgiven?"

She tried to resist the smile tugging at her lips, but could not. "Yes."

"I am glad."

For a long time, she could think of nothing else to say. She peeked at his profile, then tore her gaze away and looked about the inside of the carriage, but her gaze slipped back, as obedient to his pull as a compass needle, until she was gaping at him again. And he was no help. He made no effort to offer a subject for conversation, or to begin a discourse himself, or to even look decently away when he caught her staring at him.

To distract her thoughts, she fixed her attention on the scar that slanted like a long, thin accent mark by his mouth. She wondered how he had come by it. Had it been during the same terrible battle where he had received the wound across his chest? Or had it been some other battle? Her heart began to pound a little, thinking of all the battles he had fought in, all the times he had faced death. How glad she was that he had come through whole. But what if he had not escaped? What if she had never had the chance to know him? Never had the chance to kiss him? Her chest suddenly felt much too tight. Unable to look away from that scar, which suddenly seemed so portentous and full of warning, she fumbled blindly for his hand. When she found it, she gripped it tightly.

"Lady Jane, what is wrong?"

"I am sorry, Mr. Winston, I—" She could not go on.

"What is the matter? You look as if you've seen a ghost!"

She trembled at his unfortunate choice of words and buried her face against his coat. His arms came up and held her tight.

"My dear lady, you are starting to frighten me. Please tell me what is wrong."

She shook her head and kept her face pressed against his chest. What could she say? *My husband died, and I fear that you may die, too.* It would sound ridiculous, or—if he took her seriously—would reveal too much. He would guess how she felt…would know how deep…dear God, how had she come to value him so dearly in so little time?

"Lady Jane?" His voice was insistent.

She lifted her head, avoiding his eyes. "It has passed. I am sorry I worried you."

"But what in heaven's name—"

"For a moment, I was overwhelmed by grief." It was as close to the truth as she could bear to speak. She pulled away to a more decorous distance.

"Not over that wretch of a husband of yours, I hope?" She did not answer. "For he was an idiot, pure and simple."

Her lips twitched, and she gave his hand a grateful squeeze. "Sir, were you never taught not to speak ill of the dead?"

"In his case, I choose to make an exception."

Oh, Mr. Winston, you are balm for my soul. "Actually, sir, now that the topic of my late husband has arisen —"

She felt the arm around her shoulders tighten. "Has it?"

"I have a very great favor to ask you. A very great favor indeed."

He peered down into her face. "What is it?"

"As soon as my ankle has healed, I would like you to escort me to London so that I may pay a call on my late husband's mistress."

He suddenly let loose a string of curses that reminded her fondly of the time he had been unable to remove her boot from her swollen foot. When he had run out of steam, he flashed her a sheepish look. "Forgive my language, my lady, but why in —" His lips tightened as he swallowed yet another curse. "Why in heaven's name," he amended, "would you want to do such a thing?"

"The woman has written me twice begging me to come. Apparently, she is in very desperate straits."

Mr. Winston looked as if he were about to suffocate with the effort not to swear again. "That is no business of yours! She has made her bed, now she must lie in it!"

"Actually, Mr. Winston, I believe it was my husband who made — or rather, left unmade — this particular bed." Two bright spots of color appeared in Mr. Winston's cheeks. "Bevin always was most untidy."

He made a strange choking sound.

"In any case," Jane continued, "after promising his mistress that he would care for her, Bevin made no arrangements for the woman either with his man of business or in his will. When he died so suddenly, she was left adrift with no means to sustain herself."

"She could have found herself a new protector!"

Jane frowned. "Apparently, there was some difficulty in that area, though she was rather vague about the details."

His whole face was red now. "You amaze me, my lady! When the trollop has been so abominably forthcoming in every other particular!"

"Sir, you are too harsh!"

"I am not!" he thundered.

Jane noted in surprise that his jaw was practically vibrating and his breath was coming in fast, tight gulps. She wondered why he was so very angry. He continued in a voice that was almost a shout: "She should never have contacted you in the first place! She should never have dumped your husband's dirty linen in your lap! Her difficulties are your idiot of a husband's fault! They are no responsibility of yours!"

She looked up at him, wondering how she could make him understand. "But that is precisely the difficulty, Mr. Winston. She *is* my responsibility now."

He stared at her, his broad chest heaving. She reached up and placed her hand over his heart, willing him to calm. "At first, after Bevin died, Mrs. Chester—that is her name—was able to sell some jewelry he had given her to make ends meet. But there is nothing left now. She is destitute—and ill. Indeed, she says that she is dying." Her voice wavered.

His heart was beating more slowly now. "How do you know that *any* of this is true?" he demanded, but his voice was mild.

"I wrote to Bevin's man of business. He confirmed Bevin's arrangement with Mrs. Chester and reluctantly provided me with copies of the accounts of her maintenance."

"And no doubt you read through them all, tearing your heart out over every jot."

"It *was* painful reading," Jane admitted. "Though now it seems to have lost much of its sting."

"Why can't she address her pleas to your husband's family, to his heir? Surely that would be more suitable?"

"She has tried. They will have nothing to do with her, especially Bevin's brother, the new baronet. He has threatened her with a suit in law if she tries to contact him again."

"Well then, why doesn't she beg help from her own family?"

"She is an orphan. There is no one."

He flashed her a scowling look. "And if I do not assist you in this folly, what will you do?"

"I had originally planned to ask my brother to escort me, but I would greatly prefer your company to his on such an errand."

He scowled at her. "I can well believe that! You have not told him any of this, have you?" His tone was accusing.

Jane was beginning to feel ill-used.

"I had planned to! I had steeled myself to do precisely that the day after the ball."

Suddenly his expression softened. "So that's why you went for your walk in the snow."

"It wasn't snowing when I left! The sun was shining."

"But it is why you wandered so far," he persisted. "You dreaded going home and telling your brother this tale."

Reluctantly, Jane nodded.

He regarded her for some time in silence. Then he said, "Very well, my lady. I will take you. Your brother will probably have my head. But I will take you."

"Oh, thank you, Mr. Winston! You are too good!"

He looked out the carriage's small window. "I would not count on it, my lady." With a sudden swift movement he pulled her into his arms and kissed her.

The kiss was lovely, and intoxicating, and seemed to go on and on, but suddenly he pushed her away. It took her dazed mind a few moments to comprehend why. She had not noticed that the carriage had come to a stop. The door opened, and Mr. Winston picked her up and carried her down the steps before the waiting footman could move an inch. Mr. Winston flashed her a totally unrepentant smile and murmured softly into her ear, "Welcome to Rosington, my dear."

Chapter 11

Jane was startled to see how much Georgiana Winston resembled her brother and how much she differed from him. She had the same golden hair, emerald eyes, and ivory skin. Her features, too, were very like, only softer and in miniature. If Mr. Winston was handsome, she was delicately beautiful. But where he was tall and broad and magnificently masculine, she was tiny, softly-curved, and as feminine as a china doll. Jane, used to being the smallest in a tall family, felt a hulking Amazon beside her.

When Mr. Winston carried Jane into Rosington's small green and gold drawing room, he set her down on a small sofa and wheeled his sister's chair next to it. Jane thanked her for the lovely hyacinth. Two spots of color appeared in his sister's pale cheeks. "I am glad you liked it, Lady Jane." She paused and looked to her brother, as if searching for guidance as to what to say next. Jane wondered if she were shy.

"Georgiana," he said gently, "Lady Jane has asked me how you managed to coax the hyacinth into blooming at this time of year."

"Oh, it is quite a fascinating process—" Miss Winston began. Then she stopped abruptly. She looked down at her hands.

"Please, Miss Winston," Jane urged. "Do continue. I am very interested."

She stared at Jane then shook her head. "You are just being polite. Cordelia—that is our sister-in-law—says I prose on about things no one is interested in. I fear she is right. She predicted it would doom my debut, but then I fell, and my debut never happened. But I would hate to bore *you* . . ." Her voice trailed off.

Jane looked about her, trying to think how to encourage the girl to speak. She had not paid any attention to the room when she had first entered. Rosington had been Catherine's old home, and Jane was quite familiar with the drawing room. But now she saw it was awash in little glass vases of various colors, all filled with blooming hyacinths. Here, in the middle of winter, the room was like a garden. "Oh, Miss Winston!" she breathed. "It is lovely!"

Jane turned and realized the girl had been avidly watching her survey of the room. Now her eyes glowed at Jane's praise. "It is my fairy wonderland," she said softly.

"It is a wonder indeed! Will you please tell me how you do it?"

Slowly, the girl nodded. She began haltingly at first, but grew more fluent as she went. She used her brother to fetch and carry and showed Jane the dormant bulbs and the ones at the base of her blooming flowers. She described how the bulbs grew in water instead of soil and showed Jane how the shape of the vases kept the water from evaporating. She explained how the hyacinths needed weeks in the dark and cold of the cellars so that when they were brought into the light and warmth of the house they were fooled into believing spring had come and bloomed. Jane had a fleeting notion there was a lesson there, but pushed the thought aside. The soft voice finished, and Jane reached out to seize the girl's hands. "Miss Winston, you are a marvel!"

The girl's lovely green eyes grew round as saucers. Then suddenly, to Jane's utter surprise, the girl burst into tears. "There, there, my dear," Jane murmured, trying to soothe her, but it was difficult at a distance.

To Jane's surprise, Mr. Winston—her hyper-competent, unflappable Mr. Winston—seemed totally flummoxed. "But Georgiana never cries," he muttered in disbelief, as if unable to comprehend the catastrophe that had befallen him.

Jane raised her voice to catch the attention of the dazed gentleman. "Sir, can you please lift your sister up and put her on the sofa here next to me?" He did as he was bidden. "And can you go ask the cook to prepare a pot of hot tea with perhaps a few slices of cake? That will give your sister and I a little time to speak privately."

"Of course. Of course. I will be most pleased to!" Mr. Winston hurried from the room as if the hounds of hell were behind him.

Jane watched him go and smiled, then turned her attention to the girl by her side. Miss Winston was crying so hard now that she was unable to catch her breath and was sobbing in great rasping heaves. Jane put her arm around the girl's vibrating shoulders and hugged her close, murmuring in her ear, "Listen to my counting, my dear. Breathe in. One, two, three, four. Breathe out. One, two, three, four." She repeated the words over and over again until the girl's breathing began to slow, and the sobs began to lessen, and finally the tears decreased to a manageable trickle.

A maid came in with the tea. Jane poured Miss Winston a cup, added a considerable amount of sugar, and handed it to her, commanding her to drink it up. Obediently, the girl did. Jane took the cup and set it aside. She took out a handkerchief from her reticule.

"Here, have a good blow. It will make you feel better."

Miss Winston gave a faint, watery giggle at Jane's words, but utilized the handkerchief to great effect.

"Do you wish some cake?" Jane asked.

"I am not hungry."

"No, of course not. I see why you are as slender as a sylph. Very well. You may wait a little while, but then you must eat. You have used up a great deal of energy with your weeping." Jane gave her a few gentle pats on the back. "You know, you remind me of my sister Alex. When she was younger, Alex would never cry. My sisters and I would whine and weep over every little frustration, but Alex—Alex never let any of it out. She would save up all her heartache and all her sorrow like a teapot sitting on barely burning embers. But eventually the teapot would come to a boil, and all that heartache, all that sorrow, would come rushing out in one great burst."

"Is that how you learned about the counting?"

"Yes." Jane said with a smile. "How clever of you to realize that."

The girl winced at the word 'clever.' Suddenly, Jane had a notion as to what might have set off her weeping. "Miss Winston," she said slowly, "this sister-in-law of yours—"

"Cordelia?"

"Yes. Exactly what sort of things did she discourage you from speaking about for fear of boring people?"

"Oh, you know, all the things true ladies are not supposed to be interested in."

"Like how to make flowers bloom in winter?"

Miss Winston nodded, head bowed. "And what butterflies look like when they emerge from cocoons. And what the phases of the moon are. And how far birds travel when they migrate. And why gravity pulls things down but not up. That sort of thing."

"Why, Miss Winston, you are a bluestocking!" The girl started and tried to pull away. "Oh, no, my dear! Please! Do not look like that. I meant it as a compliment. I knew you must be clever, for your brother is exceedingly quick-witted, but it is a pleasure to meet a lady who is interested in interesting things. I have frequently been teased by my sisters for being the bookish one, but all my sisters are clever, and I am glad. And now I am glad to know you. I look forward to the many wonderful conversations we shall have!"

To Jane's alarm, Miss Winston's eyes again began to fill. This time, however, the girl did not burst into tears. Instead, she threw her arms around Jane and exclaimed in the voice of someone delivered from the wilderness, "Oh, I am so happy you are to be my sister!"

Jane eventually managed to coax her into eating some cake. Afterwards, she asked the girl how she was enjoying Catherine's library.

"Oh, it is most prodigious and wonderful!" Miss Winston declared fervently. "Though there are a few omissions—books that I would be happy to recommend to Lady Ryde if you think she would be interested."

Jane smiled. "I'm sure Catherine would be glad of your recommendations, though it is possible that some of the 'omissions' are actually at Farthingsgate. My brother had to make space in the family library for Catherine's additions when they wed."

"Yes, I can quite understand that," the girl agreed gravely. "There are some books I could not bear to be parted from, no matter what the circumstance."

Jane suppressed a chuckle. "And is your brother aware that in addition to providing you a proper dowry he must also ensure that you have adequate library space?"

"Oh, Jane," Miss Winston said, sounding stricken. "I shall never marry. No man would ever want a lady who cannot walk."

Jane gazed at her. "I am not so sure, my dear. I suspect that there are a few gentlemen out there who would be willing to trade ambulation for your extreme beauty."

"Beauty?" Miss Winston said, sounding bewildered.

"Goodness, my dear! Have you never looked in a mirror? Do you not realize you are a veritable Pocket Venus?" The girl stared at her. "What of your brother? Surely *he* has remarked how pretty you are."

"Anthony says all sorts of nice things to me. He is a very kind brother. But that does not make them true."

Jane sighed in exasperation. "Do you think me a liar, Miss Winston?"

"Of course not, Jane!"

"Then trust me when I say that you are a beauty, an incomparable, a diamond of the first water. If you had actually had your comeout, the gentlemen would have been swarming around you like bees!"

Miss Winston blushed. "But Cordelia always said—"

"If I ever meet your Cordelia in person, I fear I shall be sorely tempted to stomp on her with my foot!"

Miss Winston's eyes widened and her mouth began to twitch.

"With my good foot, of course!"

That did it. Miss Winston began to giggle, and Jane began to chuckle, and then both of them began to laugh at once, so that eventually the two of them were bent over double laughing so hard the tears began to squeeze from their eyes.

Mr. Winston rushed in, full of alarm. "What in the world —"

"N-n-nothing to w-w-worry about!" Jane gasped. "W-w-we were just m-m-making p-p-plans!"

"F-f-for Cordelia's f-f-foot!" Miss Winston added.

"And m-m-mine."

Mr. Winston stared at them. "It is almost time for luncheon," he said, regarding them both warily. "I shall wait over here while you two collect yourselves, and then I shall carry you into the dining room."

He moved to the corner and stood watching them.

Jane chuckled and gestured at him with her chin. She felt almost giddy from their laughter. "You see? Your brother, Lord Hercules, makes my point. *I* cannot walk now, but he is willing to cart me about, though I am not nearly as light as you and must be a sore burden to him. Look, he is approaching. Do not repeat what I have said."

Miss Winston grinned. "I will not. I promise."

Luncheon was a pleasant meal. Miss Winston was relaxed and animated, and Mr. Winston seemed in an unusually cheerful mood. Jane watched him with his sister and was surprised to realize that he reminded her quite a bit of Andrew.

Jane was fortunate. For all his highhandedness and bluster, Andrew was a good and kind brother to her. It pleased Jane very much that Mr. Winston seemed an equally good and kind brother to his sister.

The only awkward moment came during dessert when Miss Winston asked her, "Why are you so formal with each other? You are engaged. Why do you not address each other by your given names?"

For a moment, Jane was startled. But she did not think it her place to inform his sister that their engagement was not real, so she said, "Our betrothal is so new, Miss Winston, I do not think either of us have adjusted to it yet. However, you are right. I should call your brother by his given name, and I will, if he gives me permission to do so." Mr. Winston was forced to make the offer, and Jane, quite enjoying herself, made a point of calling him Anthony as frequently as possible just to see him color up upon hearing his name upon her lips.

After he had carried them both back out to the drawing room, he excused himself to go write a letter. After he had gone, Jane said, "I suppose if I am calling your brother by his given name, I should be doing the same with you, Miss Winston. May I?"

"Certainly, Jane! I have been aching for you to do so ever since you threatened to stomp on Cordelia's foot. In return, may I ask you something important?"

Feeling sudden trepidation, Jane nodded.

"You truly care for my brother, don't you?"

Now it was Jane's turn to color up. "Yes, my dear, I do. But you will not be saying so to him, I hope?"

Georgiana shook her head. "No, but I am so very glad, because Anthony made no mention of meeting you at the ball, and he told me about all the other ladies, and then he went for that very long walk, and your brother came and said such worrying things, and then Anthony said you were betrothed, but it all seemed so very sudden, and you were being so formal with each other—" She came to an abrupt stop, one hand flying up to her mouth. "Oh, Jane, forgive me!

So often my thoughts tumble along, and my tongue follows, and, before I even realize it, I am being terribly impolite."

"Don't worry, Georgiana. I am not offended."

"I have just been so very afraid, you see, that there was going to be another duel."

Jane suddenly felt light-headed. "*Another* duel? Goodness, when was the first?"

"Oh, I have done it again!"

"It is all right," Jane said, trying to hide the great tension she felt.

"No, you are upset. I do not blame you. Duels are terrible things!"

Yes, they are, Jane thought bleakly. "When did this one occur?"

"It was a year ago last April. After Anthony kidnapped Regina Hepworth—"

"*Lady* Regina Hepworth, the Earl of Marsbrey's daughter? The one who married—"

"Wild Bill Cross, the Marquess of Darrow. Yes." Georgiana nodded her head vigorously. "That's who Anthony dueled with."

Jane was glad she was seated firmly on the sofa, for the room was now spinning. Wild Bill Cross had been—before his untimely death in a drunken brawl—considered one of the most dangerous and unbalanced peers in all England.

"Jane, are you unwell? You look quite white."

"Forgive me," Jane said, bending sideways to hold on firmly to the sofa. "I feel a little faint. That is all."

"Oh, dear! Shall I summon Anthony or would you prefer to be private?"

"Private. Thank you."

She sensed the girl watching her and was grateful Georgiana seemed to understand her need to be left in peace. After a few minutes, the room began to stop spinning. Jane took several wary breaths and slowly lifted her head. "I am all right now. Thank you for your patience."

"Shall we speak of other things, Jane?"

"No, I wish to know a little more. In this duel, was your brother badly injured?"

The girl's green eyes once again filled with tears. "His poor face was cut all over. Lord Darrow was drunk but also very, very angry. I feared Anthony would be terribly disfigured, but the cuts—though many— were very fine and most healed without a scar."

Jane felt her mouth sag open. Weakly, she closed it. "The scars by his mouth and his eyebrow—those are from this duel?"

Georgiana flicked an anxious glance at her and then nodded. "There are other marks if one knows where to look, but most of the time they simply look like the crinkles one gets when one smiles." She paused and cocked her head slightly. "Unless Anthony forgets to shave, that is. Then he looks as if a tiny pixie has been hacking away at his beard." Jane sensed that Georgiana was trying to cheer her, but Jane could not muster the strength to simulate good humor.

She and the girl regarded each other silently for a time. Then Georgiana said, "Dearest Jane, you are so very sweet, but so very odd." Strangely, this unintended insult achieved what her gentler attempt at humor had not.

Jane felt her mood lighten. "How so, my dear?"

"You have me go on and on about the duel, which so obviously distresses you, yet you ask nothing about the kidnapping, which I would have thought you would find much more...of interest." Georgiana leaned forward. "Does it weaken your affection for Anthony that he could...that he did...that he would kidnap a lady and try to take her away from...from the man she loved?"

It was a very good question. Jane stared at her for a moment, trying to think the thing through, trying to understand what she felt, what she believed. Finally, she said, "My dear Georgiana, I fear it does not."

She saw a look of great relief wash over the girl's face. "Oh, Jane, I am so glad!" She paused. "Could you please, perhaps, explain your thinking to me?"

"Has it weakened *your* affection for him, Georgiana?"

"Not exactly weakened, but perhaps altered it. A bit." The girl looked at Jane imploringly. "It is just—I am quite aware that what a gentleman is to his sister is quite different from what he may be to a lady he...desires." Her ivory cheeks were now crimson.

"You are right, Georgiana. It is a very distinct difference." Jane paused, and then said, "Tell me. Would you like to hear what my judgment of your brother's character is?"

"Oh, very much, Jane! Very much!"

"I think he is a kind and honorable man whom I would trust with my life."

Georgiana stared at her, wide-eyed. "Truly?"

"Truly."

"But then how do you explain the kidnapping?"

"Do you know Wild Bill Cross's reputation?" Jane demanded. "What could be more noble than trying to rescue a woman from *that?*"

Georgiana smiled. "Jane, be serious."

"Very well, my dear. If your brother did this … terrible thing he is accused of, then I can only imagine that his reasons must have been very compelling. Very compelling, indeed. In fact, I—" Jane's voice wavered, and she fought to get it under control. "I would imagine he must have been horribly in love with the lady—so in love, he could not imagine living without her."

"Oh, Jane!" It came out an agonized, sympathetic whisper. Then suddenly the girl's attention shifted from Jane's face to a point behind her head. "Anthony!" she exclaimed, her voice awkwardly high and cheery. "You have finished with your letter?"

Jane whirled around. He had entered the room and was standing not two feet behind her. Jane turned back to Georgiana and flashed her a desperate, wordless question.

The girl gave her head the slightest of shakes.

Jane's eyes closed in profound relief. He had not heard.

Chapter 12

The afternoon had turned quite cold. Anthony placed a blanket over Lady Jane's lap, settled back on the seat next to her, and signaled his coachman to start the horses, trying to ignore how subdued and quiet she was next to him.

The day had been going so well. Lady Jane had somehow managed to coax his sister—the real Georgiana he remembered and treasured—out of her shell. He had spent most of luncheon holding his breath, fearful the real Georgiana would vanish again, but she had remained. And she had laughed. And she had chattered—goodness how she had chattered! And he had looked across at Lady Jane and felt a wistful ache imagining them as a family. Then Georgiana had teased Lady Jane into calling him by his given name, and he had had the exquisite pleasure of hearing his lady call him Anthony as if she really were his, as if they really were going to wed, as if she and Georgiana and he really *were* going to be a family.

And he had thought his heart might burst.

But somehow something had gone terribly wrong. Stupidly, instead of savoring the magic, he had gone off to write a letter. A confounded, unnecessary letter.

When he had returned, his two ladies had been huddled together, speaking of something intently, something that caused Georgiana to look up in guilt, as if they had been interrupted doing something they ought not. Speaking of something they should not.

As Lady Jane had swung around to view him, her face had looked so troubled—so terribly white and distressed—that all his pretty daydreams had crashed around his feet like so much broken crockery. Now she sat next to him, head bowed, hands demurely folded in her lap, and he feared she might never smile at him again.

"Are you warm enough, my lady?"

"Yes, thank you, Mr. Winston. I am quite comfortable."

No more Anthony, he thought wistfully. "Lady Jane?"

"Yes, Mr. Winston?"

"I wish to thank you for paying my sister a call. It has been a long time—too long—since I saw Georgiana as she was today. I have missed her."

She turned to look at him. "I am glad if I was of some help. I do not think she meant to be so distant with you. I think...I think she has simply had a great deal to confuse her."

Her words made him strangely uneasy. "What has confused her?"

But Lady Jane's attention was no longer on their conversation. Instead, she was staring at him. At his face. At his eye. *At his scar?* "Lady Jane?"

She was deaf to him. She lifted a gloved finger and ran it slowly across the raised white slash above his eyebrow. For a moment, he shook at her touch. Then his growing sense of unease blossomed into fear. She looked so grave, so considering. She lowered her finger, turned her head, and stared unseeing at the front of the carriage. He was beginning to go mad with her silence, when she finally murmured, "Your poor cut up face. Oh, I am glad I did not see it."

His stomach turned to ice. "Lady Jane, what were you and my sister discussing when I returned to the drawing room?"

She did not answer him.

"Lady Jane!"

Slowly, as if the words hurt her to say, she replied, "We were speaking of Lady Regina Hepworth and Wild Bill Cross."

"I...see," he said heavily. "And I suppose you would like an explanation of my shameful behavior?"

She shook her head. "No."

Even if I desperately want to give it to you?

"What I would like is for you to make me a promise."

"What sort of promise?" he asked warily.

Please do not say you wish me to go away and never see you again, for I do not think I could pledge such a thing.

"Promise me that you will never, ever do anything so foolish and dangerous again!" Her sweet voice was fervent. "When I think of how Wild Bill Cross could have cut you to ribbons ... " She shook her head and once more buried her head against his coat.

In gratified relief, he reached up to hold her and lowered his head to rest on hers. "My dearest lady," he murmured against her hair, "when I first purchased this carriage, I had no idea what a fine investment it would prove. It is better than a leprechaun's pot of gold. Whenever I get you inside of it, I end up with you in my arms."

She pushed against his chest and snapped her head up to look at him. "How dare you make light of the matter, sir! You might have been *killed!*" Her voice rose on the last word, cracking with emotion.

He sobered. "Forgive me, my fierce little—Lady Jane. I am most humbly touched by your care for my well-being."

Seemingly mollified, she settled back onto his chest. For a long while he just held her like that, content to focus on the rise and fall of her breathing. But then some mischievous inclination caused him to whisper into her ear, "You know, my sweet lady, 'twas *I* that pinked Wild Bill in the ribs. His seconds had to carry him off the field, for he was bleeding like a stuck pig, and if his blood had not been thinned by too much whiskey, he would, no doubt, have turned up his toes then and there."

To Anthony's utter surprise, his lady's response to this provocation was a sharp—and surprisingly effective—punch to his stomach with her small, white fist.

Mr. Winston's departure from Farthingsgate sent Jane's spirits plummeting. The entire family had gathered in the drawing room awaiting her return, and at first she tried to entertain them with stories of her visit to Rosington. She told them about Georgiana and the hyacinths and about the annoying and thankfully absent Cordelia.

Andrew had a good laugh when Jane mentioned Georgiana's concerns about Catherine's depleted library, and Letty sighed.

"Do not tell me we are to have another bookish sister! I shall be made to feel like the family feather brain, no doubt."

Jane turned to her sister in surprise. "Letty, you do know that my engagement to Mr. Winston is of a temporary nature, do you not?"

Letty looked flustered and was uncharacteristically silent. Maria and Alex exchanged a look. Catherine studiously examined the fireplace mantel, and both Jane's brothers-in-law stared down at their boots. Suddenly Andrew swooped down on Jane and picked her up. "Well, my dear sister, since your bogus fiancé is not present, I suppose I shall have to serve as your cart-horse into dinner."

"Andrew!" Catherine exclaimed in reproof.

"Fear not, dear wife," he quipped as he strode past her and out the door with Jane in his arms. "I will not expect you to go about the house with carrots in your pockets for me."

Jane's spirits sank further during dinner. Her big, warm family felt oddly removed from her. When dinner was over, she asked to be excused, and Andrew carried her quietly up to her bedchamber. When he turned to go, she asked him to send Letty up to see her. Her sister entered Jane's room a scant five minutes later.

"You wished to see me, my dear?"

"I want you to tell me everything you know about Lady Regina Hepworth."

Letty frowned. "Oh, Jane, must I? Somehow gossip is not nearly so enjoyable when one's sister is in love with the man who figures so prominently in all the *on-dits* about a scandal."

"Letty!" Jane exclaimed in consternation. "Is it so very obvious how I feel about him?"

"Of course it is—I mean, not at all, dear Jane."

"And I suppose the rest of the family knows?"

"Well, of course. Even *Edward* can see—"

"Oh, never mind! Tell me about Regina Hepworth and Wild Bill Cross."

"Must I?"

"Yes! And you must tell me everything. Do not leave out a single detail. Tell it like one of your stories, if that makes it easier for you."

"I suppose that would help—a little." Letty drew herself up, and her voice took on a dramatic cadence. "It was Lady Regina's first season," she intoned, gazing about Jane's boudoir as if expecting to find an audience there. "She was acknowledged the premier beauty of the year's debutantes, and the gentlemen were circling round her like wasps at a picnic. It was even rumored Wild Bill Cross was interested. Then a relative nobody with a sketchy reputation as a rake began wooing her." Letty paused and peered enquiringly at Jane.

"It's all right, Letty. Please continue."

Her sister grimaced. "This mere mister was something of a war hero with an eye for the ladies. He was neither titled nor particularly wealthy, so his rakish exploits made little impression on the *ton,* but he was reputed to have tried to elope with one lady and to kidnap another—the fiancée of his best friend and military comrade."

Jane could not help herself. She made a small wincing sound.

Letty reached out and seized her hand. "Please. Can I not stop?"

Jane shook her head.

Letty flashed her a wary look. "The rakish mister proved an extremely determined suitor. He pursued Lady Regina relentlessly, especially at any events Wild Bill Cross attended. Soon it became clear that the two men were the only real horses in the race for fair Regina's hand. Some speculated that despite his lack of title or fortune, the nobody might win, for the earl's daughter seemed quite smitten with his charm and leonine good looks." Jane's sister came to an abrupt stop.

"Letty, continue!"

"Oh, Jane, I don't want to! You were already quite white, and now you look as if you're going to cry. I don't want to make you cry."

"It doesn't matter if I cry! I need to know."

Letty shook her head, but continued in a softer voice. "But the fair Regina was sensible enough to prefer a marquess to a mister. Unfortunately, just as she succeeded in bringing the notoriously skittish Lord Darrow up to scratch, she was kidnapped by a masked marauder. Wild Bill, incensed that his lady had been seized right under his nose, set off in hot pursuit."

Jane could no longer hold off the tears. They began slipping down her face. She tried to be silent, but a single sniffle alerted her sister.

Letty said accusingly, "You are crying!"

Jane angrily shook her head.

Letty frowned, pressed her lips together, and then continued, cantering along at a faster pace. "The furious marquess caught up with the absconding villain, who turned out to be Lady Regina's rakish former suitor. Determined to avenge himself, Wild Bill challenged the man to a duel. Mr. Winston—I mean, the other suitor—chose swords, and the men fought the next morning. Despite Wild Bill's daunting reputation, it was the nobody who pinked the lord and won on the field of honor, but Lord Darrow triumphed in the end, as he and the fair Regina were wed. The discarded suitor disappeared into the sunset, or, at least, from the knowledge of the *ton*."

Jane was weeping openly now.

Letty threw her arms around her. "Oh, my dear Jane. It was all so long ago."

"It was only a year and a half!"

"Nearer to two!" Letty insisted.

"And if he was so besotted with Lady Regina that he would risk a fight with Wild Bill, do you not think it likely he loves her still?"

"It is *possible* he does not," Letty said with false cheeriness.

"You are very poor at comforting, my dear!"

"Oh, Jane! I didn't want to tell you about it. You made me!"

"I know. And I thank you for it. Really. Better to know, than not."

"Are you sure? I would think not knowing was better actually."

"And she is a widow now?"

"I fear so."

"Do you think she still cares for him?"

"Well … they do say she was quite wild for him at the time."

"Again, Letty, not the right answer!"

"You asked me."

"I know. You have seen Lady Regina. Is she *very* beautiful?"

"Oh, my goodness, yes—I mean, no, not at all. Quite a crone really."

"Oh, Letty!" Jane exclaimed, caught between a laugh and a sob.

"My dear, please tell me how I may help!"

Jane quieted. "I fear there is no help, nor easy answers. I shall just have to be brave, I think."

Letty frowned and rose to her feet. "In my experience, bravery is not usually a remedy for heartache." She bent down and kissed Jane on the cheek. "Still, I hope you sleep well, dear sister."

"Thank you, Letty, I shall try."

Chapter 13

As it turned out, Jane was not destined to sleep well or even to sleep the night through. She woke in the middle of the night to find Catherine standing over her bed, a candle in her hand.

"My dear, I am sorry to disturb you." Something in her sister-in-law's tone frightened Jane into full wakefulness.

"Goodness, Catherine! Whatever is the matter?"

"My dear, I—" Catherine started, then stopped. "Your brother is outside. He wishes to speak with you. May he enter?"

Jane's heart began to pound, and her mouth went dry. Unable to speak, she nodded. Andrew, white-faced and grim, came to stand by her bed. For a moment, he just stared down at her, not saying a word. "Dear God, Drew," she whispered. "What has happened?"

"Janey, Mr. Winston has been attacked."

A cold numbness spread through her.

"Is he dead?" she finally managed to utter.

Drew shook his head. "No, thank God. He is badly injured, but he lives. Matthew is tending him now."

Jane sank back against her pillow and took the breath she had not realized she had been holding. The numbness slipped away and all she could think of was how desperate she was to move, to go, to see him. "Drew, please!" she exclaimed shakily. "Take me to him!"

"Of course, my dear. We will go at once."

Ryde carried Jane into Mr. Winston's bedchamber, darting wary glances at his sister's white face. If he had not been in such a grim mood, he might have laughed at the irony of carrying his sister into the bedchamber of the man he had suspected of seducing her less than three days ago. But seeing the grievous injuries that had been inflicted on the man, Ryde was not inclined to laugh. Instead, he felt an anger rising in him that frightened him with its violence. He wanted to get his hands on the bastards who had done this and beat each one unconscious with his bare, slamming fists.

He felt Jane stiffen in his arms. He had debated with her about the wisdom of seeing Mr. Winston in his injured state, but she had insisted, and Ryde was in no mood to deny her anything. He was too conscious of having failed her by failing to protect Winston. He called to Matthew to set a chair for her near the bed, then gently set her down, disentangling her from the greatcoat he had wrapped about her to protect her from the cold January night.

For a moment, he could not drag his gaze away from the expression of devastation on her face at the sight of Winston's injuries. Then giving himself a slight shake, he asked Matthew to follow him to a distant corner of the room to speak.

"So?" he asked his old friend tensely. "He will survive, will he not?"

"I believe so. His injuries are many and might well have felled a lesser man, but he is surprisingly strong. You would not believe the scar on his chest—"

"Bayonet attack at Busaco."

"My God!"

"Apparently, he has also survived a sword fight with Wild Bill Cross," Ryde remarked, with a slight lightening of his spirits.

Matthew's eyebrows rose. "He must have the devil's own luck. He would not have survived tonight if he had not had a pistol with him. He managed to fight his way back to the carriage and seize it to drive his attackers away."

"That was not luck," Ryde said grimly. "That was you."

Matthew shook his head, looking uncomfortable.

"No, my friend," Ryde insisted. "You do not know how many prayers of thanksgiving I have offered up to the Almighty that Winston took your warnings seriously, when I did not. I did not believe that men from my land could be so stupidly and viciously violent. I was a fool. Has the coachman come to?"

"Yes. He says there were three of them. They blocked the road, and when the coachman jumped down to move the obstacle, the men seized him. He cried out, and Mr. Winston alighted from the carriage to help and was set upon, too. They must have knocked the coachman unconscious at that point, for he remembers no more. I have a suspicion he may have recognized one of the attackers, but he has not admitted it."

"By God, he will admit it to *me!*"

"Ryde, go easy!"

"Easy? Look what they have done to him! To my sister! I'll see them hanging from the nearest gibbet before the week is through!"

"Might not that—forgive me, Ryde—but might not that just feed the ill feeling that led to this attack in the first place?"

"I will protect me and mine," Ryde growled, "and woe betide the man who thinks otherwise. I tell you, Matthew. Right now I would gladly eat their livers in the marketplace!"

"I understand. Cleaning up the man's wounds, I felt pretty bloody-minded myself. But please, when your temper has cooled a little, consider whether a little mercy might not be wise."

A discourteous rejoinder rose to Ryde's lips, but instead of giving voice to it, he took a deep, steadying breath. "Matthew, I have learned the folly of ignoring your advice. I promise you, when my temper has cooled, I will consider what you say."

"That is all I ask."

"Now, to a more pressing topic. Can Winston be moved to Farthingsgate without causing him further injury?"

Matthew flashed him a quizzical look. "I suppose so, if he were transported flat on his back in a wagon. You feel he would be safer there?"

Ryde grimaced. "I want him under my roof, protected by my men. And I want him there for Jane's sake. If I do not bring him home with us, she will insist on spending all her time here. Can you have him ready to travel by nine tomorrow?"

"I believe so. Yes."

"Then I will make the necessary arrangements for his transfer. In the meantime, is the staff here able to accommodate you and provide you what you need for Winston's care, or shall I send some of my people from Farthingsgate?"

"I think the household can manage well enough for now, but can you make arrangements for Miss Winston? There is only the one footman here if she needs shifting, and I believe she was used to having her brother carry her most of the time. I will be happy to help her myself while I am here, but once you have moved her brother to Farthingsgate, I fear she may feel adrift."

"Of course, she must come when he does."

"Thank you. I've been quite worried about her. She is downstairs now and seems quite lost."

"I am glad you had the notion, Matthew. As it happens, I need to make amends to the lady."

"She is quite a vulnerable little thing," Matthew added.

Ryde regarded his old friend in surprise. "Indeed. And now, I think I must bid you good night. Take good care of him for me, Matthew."

Matthew glanced toward Winston's unconscious form. "Do you think Jane is ready to leave? You have only just arrived."

Ryde shook his head. "I do not think I will be able to pry my sister away from the poor fellow's bedside before morning. However, I must return to Farthingsgate as soon as possible to make things ready. With you present to keep an eye on things, I think I can safely leave Jane here. Before I leave, however, I will check on Miss Winston for you."

To Ryde's amused surprise, Matthew's shoulders seemed to sag in relief. For a moment, Ryde's mind was distracted from the problem of Mr. Winston by his friend's surprising focus on Winston's diminutive sister. Was Matthew concerned about the girl because of her medical condition, or did he have a more personal interest?

It occurred to Ryde that—if one liked tiny women—Miss Winston might be considered a rather attractive young lady. And Matthew was not exactly a giant himself, so perhaps it made sense that petite little things appealed to him. "Do you wish me to pass on any particular message to the young lady?" Ryde asked.

A sudden wave of red passed over Matthew's freckled countenance as he hastily declined Ryde's offer.

For the first time that wretched evening, Ryde's face relaxed into a smile.

Chapter 14

Jane stared down at Mr. Winston's battered face in despair. An hour had passed, but it was no easier to gaze at him, for she kept noticing new cuts, new bruises, new spots of blood. Everywhere she looked there was hurt. She remembered Georgiana—had it been just that afternoon?—talking about his poor cut face after the duel. As horrible as that must have been, this was worse, far worse. She hated the men who had done this to him. She wanted to kick them and hit them and yell curses at them for hurting him so.

And it was all her fault.

She knew, without anyone needing to tell her, that it was because of her that they had done this to him. Because of what they thought he had done to her in the cottage. She regarded Matthew, who was inspecting some hidden damage beneath the sheet.

"Is there nothing I can do?"

Matthew straightened and looked at her, then down at his hands. "He could do with a good washing."

Jane felt a rush of eagerness. "Yes, Matthew. Please! How should I go about it?"

"I'll have some hot water and strips of linen sent up. You will need to be exceedingly gentle, for he is one mass of abraded flesh, but if you can get the blood off of him and especially the dirt before it can work its way deeper into his wounds that would be a help."

She waited impatiently for the hot water to come. When the foot-man finally arrived with a huge cooking pot full of boiling water, Matthew directed him to set it right up against the grate so it would remain warm. Then he poured out some of the boiling water into a basin and added some water from the ewer to cool it. He brought her the basin and some linen strips and showed her how to gently dab at the skin rather than scrub at it.

"Start with his face," Matthew told her. "If you finish with that, I'll start you on his neck and shoulders." He tucked the sheet in around Anthony's still form as if he were tucking in a child at bedtime.

It was a long, slow process, but Jane did not care. The longer and slower, the better. It gave her something to focus on so she would not go mad. She was grateful when Matthew excused himself and slipped from the room. She wanted to be alone with her Anthony.

She started on the left side of his face. She cleaned away the dirt and blood near several cuts on his cheek and dropped a light kiss on an undamaged area near his ear. His poor eye was swollen shut, but she soaked the linen with a little extra water and tried dabbing the dried blood away from his lids and lashes. At some point, she began to cry, but she ignored the tears, and kept dabbing, cleaning off the scrapes on his forehead and chin. She washed away the dried dirt and blood above his ear.

Oh, my poor love, what have they done to you?

She started in on the cuts on his nose, and for a moment she was lost in remembering his checking her own nose for frostbite. Tenderly she cleaned and dabbed at his face, and whenever she found a bit of skin not scraped or cut or bruised, she kissed it.

Matthew Elton watched Jane just long enough to make sure she understood how carefully she must work cleaning the wounded man. He knew Ryde would be furious with him for suggesting such a task for her, but Jane needed a way to be of use. Matthew had known both her and Ryde since they were all children together, and knew Jane was not the sort of lady to sit idly by when there was trouble, especially when she cared about the person in trouble. That she cared about the battered man in the bed was patently obvious.

There was not much more he could do for his patient now but wait and pray, so Matthew left Jane to her washing and headed downstairs to check on Miss Winston.

He paused on the threshold of the drawing room, noting that conditions there were much improved. Leave it to Ryde, his blessedly practical friend, to make sure the candles were fresh and the fire burned brightly and that the small, beautiful girl in the rolling chair by the fire had a shawl over her shoulders and a book on her lap.

She seemed a shy little thing, but there was something about her eyes that fascinated him. They were pretty, of course—beautiful really—but what intrigued Matthew was that they were so *aware*. It was as if they were trying to take in everything in the world all at once. He shook his head. He was being fanciful. Then suddenly those big green eyes turned and gazed directly at him, and he had the unnerving sense they were trying to take in all of *him* at once. He felt quite overwhelmed by that gaze, yet he could not look away.

The book on her lap began to slip down her leg. Startled, she reached out to grab it, but it was already past the reach of her hand. Her left leg bounced up a little trying to stop the book's momentum, but it was too little too late, and the book clattered to the floor.

Matthew, feeling a sudden racing excitement in his chest, hurried forward to retrieve it for her. He picked up the thin volume and handed it to her with a flourish. "Allow me to restore this to you, Miss Winston," he said, unable to keep himself from grinning.

"Thank you, Doctor Elton," she said, regarding him quizzically. She seemed unsure what to make of his beaming good humor, or the fact that he kept staring at her leg. He knew he should not, but he was so eager to see if the motion could be repeated.

He searched his mind for some way to stimulate the proper response. But he was tired, and it was late, and he decided he did not want to wait to come up with something better.

He reached out and set his hand down at the very top of Miss Winston's thigh.

Her leg twitched and her foot came flying up right into his shin.

Despite the acute pain, Matthew smiled.

Instinct was a wonderful thing.

Matthew and Miss Winston stared at each other in the flickering light of the drawing room candles. He realized that he was surprised as well as disappointed by her response to his very improper action. He was surprised, because her bright eyes held an almost avid look of curiosity. He was disappointed, because while her lovely face look startled, there was none of the outraged disapproval he belatedly realized he had hoped to find there at his overly intimate touch.

He was tired of being overlooked. He was tired of being ignored. He was doctor to half the county, yet he might as well be the lowliest servant when it came to his neighbors treating him with the courtesy they accorded every other gentleman of their acquaintance. He was a devoted friend to Ryde, yet he might as well be the village idiot, when it came to his high-born friend heeding his advice. He adored Ryde's wife, yet he might as well be a genderless eunuch when it came to her seeing him as a flesh-and-blood man worthy of notice.

Suddenly, Miss Winston spoke. "Doctor Elton, I must ask you. Why did you do that? It was extremely pleasant, but highly improper. Could you please explain it to me?"

Matthew cleared his throat. "I wanted to see if I could make your leg move a second time." It was not a proper explanation, but his thoughts were too occupied by the news that she had enjoyed his touch.

Astonishingly, it did not seem to matter. She understood anyway. Her eyes sparkled and her mouth curved into an appreciative smile. "Oh, that was very clever of you! You knew that if you touched me in that way I would kick out as a sort of reflex. But why are you so interested in seeing my leg move?"

How could he clarify it for her? "Miss Winston, I was told that you could not walk because you had suffered an injury to your spinal column."

"Yes. I fell from my horse." She was watching him intently, as if determined to know his meaning not just from his words, but from his very countance. "You have reason to doubt that assessment?" she said sharply.

Startled by her quick comprehension, he gave a wary nod. "You must understand, I am not an expert in injuries to the spine —"

"Yes, sir," she interrupted impatiently. "I accept your caveat. Please, continue!"

"I—it is my understanding that if your spinal cord were truly damaged in such a way, you would not be able to make your leg move the way that you just did—twice."

There was sudden hope in her face. Matthew felt a wave of guilt. "Please, Miss Winston, you must not get your expectations too high. Most likely it is some other sort of injury that prevents you from walking."

She nodded, but he was not sure she had really heard his warning. "Doctor Elton, how can we test your hypothesis?"

"My hypothesis, Miss Winston?"

"That my spine is uninjured. Do you feel competent to examine me? Would you be willing to do so, if you are?"

Where had all this force come from? She was such a little thing, so delicate and fragile-looking, yet in the face of her sudden determination, Matthew felt as if he'd stepped into a gale. "I would be happy to examine you, Miss Winston. Indeed, I am eager to do so."

"Now?"

"Not *right* now, Miss Winston. It would hardly be suitable— here, alone, in the middle of the night! Perhaps in a few days, at Farthingsgate. There will be an abundant supply of ladies there to provide you proper chaperonage."

"Forgive me, Doctor Elton. Cordelia assures me I am totally lacking in ladylike sensibility." She paused, then added with surprising heat, "Though, I must say in this particular instance I could wish Cordelia to the devil!"

He started.

"I have done it again!" Her lovely eyes fixed him with an imploring look. "*Can* you forgive me, Doctor Elton? I am not trying to outrage you. I am just so eager. It is good to have a strand of hope, however fragile, to cling to. It has been so very long, you see."

Again, Matthew felt a stir of uneasiness. He had been a fool to raise her hopes. Then he remembered the battered man upstairs. She was that poor man's sister. Surely she deserved a little hope to hold on to on such a dark night as this? He flashed her his brightest smile.

"My dear Miss Winston, you could never outrage anyone. Forgive *me*, for being so awkward in my address as to give you the impression that you could."

"Oh, Doctor Elton! What a masterfully courteous thing to say!"

Gratified by her praise, he made her a small bow. "It is only because you bring out the gallant in me, Miss Winston."

Suddenly she looked quite shy. "Do I?"

Matthew regarded her. The gale had suddenly transformed into a coaxing summer breeze. "Yes, Miss Winston," he said gently, "you most certainly do."

Her expression turned wistful. "Then may I ask you a very awkward and perhaps inappropriate question?"

Wary, but curious, Matthew nodded. "Of course."

"Today, when Lady Jane visited, she said something I find difficult to credit, and I was just wondering . . ."

"Yes, Miss Winston?"

"I was wondering if you could tell me if it was true or not."

"In my experience, Lady Jane's pronouncements are usually quite reliable, but I will be happy to give you my opinion, if that is what you wish."

"That is precisely what I wish."

"Then go ahead, Miss Winston. Ask me your question."

Suddenly her lovely porcelain skin blushed pink. She did not speak.

"Miss Winston?"

She gnawed at her lip. He resisted a strong impulse to reach up and caress that lip with his finger. "Do you think," she finally said, "it is true that I am . . . that I might be considered to be . . . that there might be gentlemen who could find me—pretty?"

He opened his mouth and then closed it again.

Miss Winston's bottom lip began to quiver. "I should have known Lady Jane was simply being kind. Forgive me, Doctor Elton! I did not mean to embarrass you by asking such a ridiculous—"

"You are not just pretty," he blurted out.

Her eyes widened. "No?" It was barely a whisper.

"I think you are the most beautiful creature I have ever seen."

Her rosebud mouth formed into a perfect 'O.'

He waited, his stomach in knots, wondering what amazing, confounding, astonishing response she would give to his ridiculously forthright declaration.

But, for once, not a single syllable passed her lips.

Jane looked down at the basin in her hand and frowned. The water was cold and filthy, full of bloody linen and washed-off dirt. Where in the world was Matthew? She had expected him to return by now. She needed clean, hot water and fresh linen strips so she could continue to bathe Anthony. With her hobbled foot, she could hardly get them herself.

Angry with her absent friend, she rose to stand on her one good foot. Perhaps she could *hop* across to the grate? The empty ash bucket was there. Perhaps she could dump the soiled water into that and scoop up some fresh water directly from the pot?

It turned out, however, that hopping was not an ideal mode of transportation with a basin full of dirty water in one's hands. After only a few hobbled jumps, the sloshing of the dirty water grew so great, it spilled on the floor and all down her skirt. Muttering a curse she was glad no one was there to hear—except, of course, her dear Anthony, and she would have given anything to have him awake enough to hear it— Jane grimly hopped back to the bed, and set the now empty basin on the floor. What was she to do now?

She had no idea when Matthew intended to return. She looked down at Anthony, at his poor battered face, at his blood-matted hair. And at the sheet Matthew had pulled up almost to his chin, no doubt to hide Anthony's more serious injuries from her sight.

Confound it! If she could not distract her thoughts by continuing to bathe him clean, then she had to know. She had to ascertain how badly he was hurt under that sheet. Slowly, terrified by what she might find, Jane lifted it.

To her shock, he had not a stitch of clothing on.

For a long moment, she could only stare. He was so impressive, so handsome. Her warrior prince without the blanket. Then she had a sudden thought that filled her with dread. She peered wildly about the room searching for his clothes, desperate to assure herself that his assailants had not left him stripped and naked in the road. She saw his boots first, and her heart began to slow. Then she saw his ragged, bloody clothes in a pile in the corner, a pair of seamstress scissors tossed on top.

Now the tears came in earnest.

Someone, probably Matthew, had had to cut Anthony's clothes off his beaten body.

She reached out and ran a finger along the long scar on his chest. *Please, my darling, be strong one more time. You've chased off death before. Do it again—for me.*

She was relieved to see that his torso was not as battered as his face, though there were three ominous bandages, all soaked through with blood. Jane gently peeled one back and swore. It was a cut, deep and jagged. One of his attackers had had a knife.

She began to cry again. Then, angry with herself, she swiped at her eyes with an impatient hand. Crying would do him no good. She could not bathe him. Fine. She would inventory his injuries, committing each one to memory so she would never forget what he had suffered for her sake.

It took a long time.

She started with his head. Holding it gently in her hands, she lightly ran her fingers through his blood-matted hair to assure herself that his skull was still whole. Then she moved down. His face had taken the greatest beating. She sighed over his swollen eyes and his bloodied cheeks and nose and chin. His poor lips were split and broken. She pressed a soft kiss at the edge of his mouth.

Next she inspected his throat. There was a single set of bruises, the imprint of a choking hand. Furious at the marks and wishing she could erase them from his skin, Jane gently trailed kisses away from the bruises, as if trying to lead Anthony's sleeping mind away from the memory of those cruel fingers.

His beautiful broad shoulders were relatively unscathed, as were his sides. Perhaps his thick coat has served as a shield. But Anthony's arms were bruised, and his knuckles were bloodied. Jane dabbed a wet piece of linen against them and realized with relief that it was from the other men's blood. Jane lifted his hand and pressed it against her cheek. *Oh, my brave darling! I am glad you punished them—at least a little. I wish I could do the same.*

The cuts on his torso worried her. As did the bruises forming across his ribs and near his stomach. She glanced further down, dreading what injuries she might see there. But apparently Anthony was well-endowed with the masculine instinct for self-preservation, for the area looked unharmed.

Feeling her cheeks heat, she forced her gaze lower—to his legs. His thighs were badly bruised, and there was a scrape on one leg and another blood-soaked bandage on the other. His shins were slightly less battered; maybe his boots had protected them. Finally, she gazed at his feet. His feet were completely and gloriously unmarked.

Jane was so grateful for this small miracle that she let the sheet fall and hopped down to the end of the bed. Lifting the bottom of the sheet, she stared happily at his unmarked feet for several minutes, then leaned forward and kissed the tops of them, tears of relief slipping down her cheeks. She was startled by how soft his skin was there, almost as downy as a babe's, which, of course, only made her cry harder.

Suddenly he made a groaning sound and shifted in pain.

Jane straightened abruptly and peered at him. Damn the dwindling candles! She could not make out his face clearly. She hopped frantically up towards the other side of the bed, listening for more sounds, searching for more movement. When she had gone far enough to gaze into his face, she scrutinized his one good eye. To her delight, it was part-way open.

"Oh, my dearest Anthony!" she cried. "Please tell me that you are awake!"

His only response was another loud groan. Then his eye fluttered shut.

But it was enough.

Chapter 15

Anthony woke to incredible pain.

For a moment, he thought he was in Portugal, a bayonet wound in his chest, but then he opened his eyes. He was not in some filthy field hospital, but in a large, soft bed in a luxuriously furnished bedchamber he did not recognize. Where the hell was he? He closed his eyes again, trying to remember. What had he been dreaming?

Men had been attacking him, and he had shot one with a pistol. A beautiful girl had been crying over his feet—no, not just crying, *kissing* his feet. A giant had been arguing with the girl about a wagon. A stream of people had paraded past his bedside, whispering.

But the girl never left.

This was doing no good. The dreams were nonsense. They did nothing to help him understand where he was. Why he was here. Why he hurt so damn much.

He snapped his eyes open.

Then he saw the girl. She was real and sitting in a chair next to him. She was bent over, her folded arms resting on the bed, her head resting on her folded arms. She was asleep. He didn't understand why she was asleep. There was bright sunshine slanting in through the windows.

He wanted to understand.

Then she opened her eyes and raised her head and turned to look at him, and she smiled—a huge, beautiful smile brighter than the sun. Somehow, *she* was what he needed to understand. She was *all* he needed to understand.

The pain became too much. He closed his eyes, not wanting her to see his pain, not wanting her to see his tears.

Someone poured something down his throat.

The pain eased.

He slept.

Jane woke to the feel of someone lifting her from a chair. Drowsily, she struggled to open her eyes. "Did I fall asleep?"

"Of course you fell asleep!" a voice thundered in her ear. "You have had no true rest for three days!"

"But Drew, where are you taking me?"

"To your bed! So you can get a decent slumber. In a horizontal position. I am tired of finding you collapsed in every chair in this accursed room!"

"But Drew, I cannot leave! What if he wakes?"

"Someone shall fetch you."

"But—"

"But me no buts! Any more argument from you on the subject, and I shall send him shooting back in the wagon to Rosington!"

"*Drew!* You would not!"

"Try me!" he snapped.

Jane, overcome by another yawn, allowed her head to sag against her brother's chest. "You are too hard," she mumbled into his waistcoat, her eyelids sagging closed.

"As a diamond—where you are concerned, sister mine," he said in a softer tone as he laid her gently on her bed.

She slept.

Georgiana looked up. "Hello, Doctor Elton."

"Hello, Miss Winston. I gather it is your turn to stand vigil with your brother?"

"Yes. Lord Ryde has carried poor Jane off to bed." She turned to look at Anthony. "Does he look better today?"

"He has been looking better every day, I think. I am very pleased with his progress." He crossed to examine the bottle on the small table near Anthony's bed. "Do you know how much laudanum your brother has had today?"

"I do not know precisely, but I have been marking the bottle each time he is dosed, for Jane is so fatigued, I feared she might give him two doses without realizing it."

He looked at her with that considering look that made her feel he actually knew she had a brain in her head. "A wise precaution, Miss Winston. Yes, I see the marks."

"Will you be—do you think it might be possible to reduce the amount he takes?" She watched him closely, hoping he would not take offense. He was a wonderful doctor, and she did not want him to think she questioned his ability.

He flashed her that slightly crooked smile that always left her breathless. "Do you think it would be advisable to do so—in your considered opinion?"

She nibbled nervously at her lip. "I have heard that the habit for laudanum, once begun, is difficult to break."

"That is quite true. Which is why I plan to halve your brother's dose today and halve it again tomorrow."

"Oh, I am glad!"

"Glad because your brother will be having less laudanum or glad because I am taking your very fine advice?"

"Have I offended you?"

"Of course not. As I said, it is very good advice." He gave a chuckle. "Perhaps you should consider becoming an apothecary, Miss Winston."

"Oh, Doctor Elton! I would like nothing so much! It would be so wonderfully interesting to learn about medicines and how they work and why they work and what the dangers are and how one should prepare them. Tell me, how does one go about it?"

He was staring at her with that wide-eyed, astounded look people got when she said something truly outrageous. She never liked getting that look, but usually she could tolerate it. Receiving it today from Doctor Elton, however, and about her interest in medicines, which had fascinated her since she was a little girl, made her want to cry.

"Miss Winston! Whatever is the matter?" He rushed toward her. She was not sure how to answer him.

He knelt down by her chair like some knight in a story. "Please tell me."

She hesitated. But the obvious concern in his face brought the words tumbling out—and the tears. "I truly *would* like to be an apothecary, and it makes me s-s-sad that you think it is such a s-silly notion."

"Here, my dear."

He handed her a very large and very fancy handkerchief embroidered with his initials. Had some sweetheart given it to him? She blotted at her eyes, fretting about how red they must look now.

"I do not think it is a silly notion, Miss Winston. I was just surprised. Would you like it if I brought you a book about medicines to read?"

She felt as if he had just handed her a bouquet of large red roses. "Oh, Doctor Elton. I should absolutely adore it!"

When Jane finally woke, her room was quite dark. She felt an overwhelming melancholy at having slept the day away. Her maid came bustling in and urged her into a hot bath. That made her feel better, as did putting on fresh clothes and having her hair brushed, stroke after soothing stroke. When she finally summoned a footman to carry her to Anthony's room, she felt quite restored.

Maria was there, sitting next to his bed with baby Ada on her lap.

"Thank you," Jane said. "It was kind of you to watch over him for me."

Her sister shook her head. "It was a pleasure."

The footman set Jane down in her chair, and she leaned over and gave Ada a kiss on her sweet, bald head. "I will watch him now, Maria."

Her sister rose to her feet. "Have you eaten any dinner yet?"

Jane shook her head. "I will have something sent up on a tray."

Maria frowned. "Take Ada for a few minutes." Jane gathered her niece in her arms, and Maria left the room. Jane bounced the tot up and down on her knee, and Ada started to coo and giggle. Jane felt a fierce pang of yearning and gave the child a tight hug.

"Jane." His voice was so weak she couldn't be sure he had spoken at all.

"*Anthony?* Oh, curse it! I cannot hop to you, for I have Ada on my lap. Are you in pain?"

"*Yes.*" The single syllable was barely a whisper, but so thick and drawn out that Jane flinched.

Fortunately, at that moment, her sister returned carrying a tray. "Oh, Maria, please take Ada! He is awake!"

Jane was grateful for her sister's quick understanding and tactful action. In what seemed like one continuous motion, Maria set down the tray, scooped up her daughter with one hand, pulled Jane to her feet with the other, and glided to the door. "I expect you wish to be left alone with him?"

Jane nodded.

Maria exited quietly, pulling the door shut behind her.

Jane hopped to Anthony's side. "Hang on, my love. I will get your medicine." She moved a little farther, to the small table where the laudanum bottle sat. To her surprise, there was a neatly written note on the table from Georgiana indicating that Matthew wished to reduce Anthony's dosage. Detailed, careful instructions followed. For a moment, Jane was furious with them both. Did they not know how Anthony suffered? Did they not care?

Then she realized Matthew would not have made such a decision unless he thought it was in Anthony's best interest. Still, it rankled. She squeezed the reduced number of drops into a glass of water and carefully crossed back to Anthony, foregoing her usual hopping and setting her weight firmly upon her sore ankle so that she would not spill a drop.

She gently lifted Anthony's head. "Here, my sweet. Drink."

He did so, watching her above the glass. His one good eye glittered at her in the candlelight, full of unshed tears. His other eye was still swollen shut. A tear squeezed between the swollen lids and rolled down his cheek.

"Oh, my dearest. I am sorry the pain is so great."

He continued to watch her silently. Before, at the higher dose, the laudanum would take effect almost immediately, providing him relief. Now, however, it took much longer. His mouth was set in a tight white line, and he weakly reached out for her with one questing hand. She put her hand in his. He squeezed it with surprising force.

She had to distract him from his discomfort. But how?

Then she had an idea.

Jane began reciting to him all that had happened, as if she were telling him one of Letty's stories, as if they were children gathered round the fire ready for a grand tale. She told him of his attackers. How he had fought them so bravely; how she had washed his knuckles clean from their blood; how the man he had shot with his pistol had been found two days later—dead.

She told him of how they had brought him to Farthingsgate to heal. How she had ridden with him in the wagon all the way, despite her brother's objections, because she wanted everyone to see how proud she was of her injured hero. How everyone in the house, every dear member of her family, as well as his sister and Matthew, had come to see him and watch over him and pray for him to heal. She told him how determined her brother was to find the two men still alive who had done this to him and bring them to justice.

And then, just as he finally drifted off into merciful sleep, she told him how very much she did—and always would—love him.

Chapter 16

Ryde looked down at the two men cowering on the filthy straw. He took savage pleasure in their bruised faces and torn clothing. Some of the bruises looked old. *Mr. Winston's doing,* he thought with satisfaction. Ryde was glad Winston was such a formidable man to cross. He had been outnumbered three-to-one, yet he had managed to shoot one of his attackers dead and mark both the others.

Ryde turned his back on the prisoners. He was due to meet with Sir Henry about the convening of the assize court. "Your lordship, please!" one of the bastards begged him from behind. "You must speak for us! We were only trying to avenge Lady Jane's honor."

Ryde whipped around to face the man, cold fury in his throat. *"How dare you!* My sister's honor is my affair! It is no business of yours! The man you nearly killed is likely to become my sister's husband. Do you think I mean to offer mercy to the men who tried to murder my future brother-in-law?"

The man stared up at Ryde in horror, the certainty of death in his eyes.

Ryde saw that look and took a shuddering breath. For a moment, he felt his fury flicker. Then he thought of Jane. Grimly, he turned his back on the men a second time and strode away.

"Well, Jane? Do you approve of my decision now?"

Georgiana watched Doctor Elton as he conversed with Jane about Anthony's progress. Her brother was doing better—so much better that Georgiana had half-feared Doctor Elton would not come today. She hated to think how disappointed she would have been not to see him.

"Yes, Matthew," Jane replied. "I will own it. You were right and I was wrong. Anthony's awakenings have grown more regular, and when he does come to the surface he is no longer so overwhelmed by pain. He notices his surroundings more, and he no longer mutters deliriously about giants."

Doctor Elton nodded, and Georgiana realized she was gaping at the man in a decidedly unladylike fashion. She quickly looked away.

"But Matthew," Jane said in a worried voice, "Anthony *is* safe now, isn't he? Please tell me there is no longer any risk that he will succumb to his wounds."

"I believe he is quite safe, Jane. His healing requires time, not prayer." He turned and looked right at Georgiana and smiled.

Georgiana's heart began to pound.

"Miss Winston, now that my exam of your brother is over, I have a gift for you." He crossed to a table by the door and picked something up, then crossed to her and handed her an immense book, so heavy she needed both hands to receive it from him.

"*Oh, Doctor Elton!*" she exclaimed in an awestruck whisper. She ran her fingers over the heavy red leather cover, then reverently opened it and gazed down at the title page. "Dr. Buchan's Domestic Medicine," she murmured aloud. Her gaze traveled to the bottom of the page. "Why it was only published last April! It must be brand new!"

He nodded. "I purchased it while I was in Edinburgh."

"But I cannot take this from you!"

"I wish you to have it. I can send for another copy."

She gazed up at him raptly. *Oh, was there ever such a man?* "It is the most precious thing anyone has ever given me."

His crooked grin grew so wide it lit up his entire face. "Miss Winston?"

She realized too late that she had been staring at him. Her gaze dropped and fixed once more on the precious book in her lap, which she cradled like a baby.

"Miss Winston, there is something else."

She gazed at him expectantly.

His dear freckled face began to color up. He cleared his throat. "About your back. If you are ready, then so am I."

Jane looked from him to Georgiana. "Ready?" she repeated, sounding completely at sea.

Georgiana regarded him happily. "I believe Mr. Elton is ready to examine me." Seeing Jane's expression, she added, "Do not worry, Jane. He means nothing improper. He wishes to inspect my back, because he does not believe my spine is injured at all."

"Is this true, Matthew?" Jane demanded in a startled voice.

"Yes. I believe it is possible that her spine is whole," he replied in his most careful doctor tones. Georgiana's lips twitched. She often felt tempted to twit him when he spoke like that, but today all desire to tease him was gone. She was feeling too grateful. He continued to Jane, "I will know more after I have completed my examination."

"When can we begin?" Georgiana demanded.

"Now, if you please. Lady Ryde awaits us in your chamber. If you do not mind my carrying you, I will take you there at once."

Too excited to speak, Georgiana nodded her assent. He picked her up in his arms, and she was surprised to realize how very strong he was. He was not nearly as tall as her brother, but his muscled arms held her in a grip every bit as powerful as Anthony's own. Extraordinarily content to be in the arms of her pocket Hercules, Georgiana lifted her hand in a happy salute to Jane as he carried her out the door.

Jane glared at her brother. He had summoned her from Anthony's bedside to tell her that the men who had attacked Anthony had been captured, but now he refused to grant her very reasonable request. "Why will you not take me to see them?"

"Jane, be sensible! The prison is no place for you. And why would you wish to look upon those two miscreants in any case?"

"I wish to tell them exactly what I think of them."

"To what end?"

"They no doubt have some distorted notion that they acted on my behalf. I wish to set them straight on that point and a few others."

"That is ridiculous," he said, but something flickered across his face, something that convinced her that he knew it was not ridiculous, but the absolute truth.

"They said as much to you, didn't they? They said they did it for me!"

He was not fool enough to deny it again. "Can you not let it be, my dear? They will be punished, I promise you."

"Drew, I must see them. I cannot explain it to you, but I—I need it. Will you please take me to the prison tomorrow?"

Her brother stared at her for a long time in silence. Then with a heavy sigh, he said, "Very well, my dear. I will take you."

Matthew stared at the shawl draped over Miss Winston's naked back and willed his racing heart to slow. Where were his objectivity and disinterest? He had to start soon, or she would wonder what the matter was. Catherine stood on the other side of Miss Winston's bed, facing her. She was holding a blanket over Miss Winston's front to provide her some modesty.

Clenching and unclenching his jaw, Matthew willed his fingers to be steady and gently pulled the shawl aside. Her back was beautiful. Her skin was the palest ivory. Her gold hair fell in soft waves onto her shoulders. He started doing sums in his head, trying to steady his thoughts. He was checking her spine, not her suitability for bed.

But Lord it was hard.

Gently, he placed his thumb and forefinger on her neck. Her skin was like down, so soft and warm he wanted to bend down and rub his cheek against it. Forcing the thought away, he tried to focus on her perfect-looking vertebrae.

"Miss Winston," he asked softy, "can you bend your head forward for me?"

She did as he asked. He slid his thumb and forefinger on either side of her highest cervical vertebra and began palpating it carefully. He slowly worked his way down her neck, and by the time he reached her thoracic vertebrae, his focus had been restored. He worked his way down all twelve and was elated. Each seemed perfectly, blessedly normal.

"Miss Winston, can you lean all the way forward? Yes, that is perfect."

As he began to examine her lumbar vertebrae, he became even more careful and slow. If the problem was anywhere, it was likely to be here, but by the time he reached her sacrum, he still had found nothing. He began to feel almost light-headed with relief. Was it really possible that her spine was whole?

Then why could she not walk?

He turned away and asked Catherine to help Miss Winston back into her shift. When she was covered, he came round to face her, where she was sitting on the bed.

"Miss Winston, may I examine your legs?"

She was, as usual, too quick. She demanded excitedly, "Does that mean you found nothing wrong with my back?"

"It could be that I am not experienced enough—" he began, but she was having none of his caution.

She threw her arms around him and hugged him. "Oh, Doctor Elton, thank you!"

The fine linen of her shift was so thin she might as well have been wearing nothing at all, and he was acutely, hotly aware of every single curve of her delectable body. Catherine came up beside her and whispered something in her ear.

Immediately, her grip on him fell away and she scooted backwards away from him, avoiding his eyes. He was torn between wanting to groan from the loss of her warmth and wanting to exclaim with excitement over her movement on the bed. "Miss Winston, could you do that again? Scoot backwards from me, I mean. I want to watch your muscles work."

Her face came up then, and she no longer looked embarrassed. Instead, she tilted her head at him, a mischievous look sparkling in her bright green eyes. "La, sir! Do you say such sweet things to all your patients?"

Chapter 17

Anthony woke and everything seemed familiar. He was in a big, soft bed. Bright sunshine slanted in through the windows. A girl with brown hair sat beside his bed. She was bent over, her arms resting on the bed, her head resting on her arms. She was asleep.

Jane.

He struggled to sort out the jumble in his head. Had he dreamed of her like this or had it happened before?

Fragments of memory popped to the surface of his awareness like hole-riddled pieces of cork. He closed his eyes and let them float to him. They were so light, if he grabbed at them, they bobbed out of reach. Slowly they came. Carefully he gathered them up, anchoring them in his mind with the one solid line that did not yield.

Jane.

He *had* woken to find her here before. Repeatedly. He would wake to pain, and she would give him something to drink, and she would hold his hand and talk to him until the pain eased, and then he would go back to sleep.

She was always there. His one fixed star.

How long? How long had he been in this bed? How long had she been keeping watch? No wonder she was so tired, poor thing. Why had no one come to make her sleep? Where the hell was her overbearing brother? After all, this was his house.

Startled, Anthony turned to gaze about him. The abrupt movement made him wince. Of course. That was where he was. Farthingsgate. She had told him so herself when she had told him ... Curse it! It kept skittering away. And it was important. Somehow he knew it was damnably important.

He took a painful breath. He had to think. He had to remember.

She had been holding his hand, and he had been clinging to it fiercely, fighting through a wave of pain so overwhelming he had feared it would wash him away from her forever. She had begun to speak. It had been hard to focus on her words, but he had fought to do so. She had told him a story, and her words were like a net she wove around him to keep him safe. Slowly, dazedly, he had realized the story was his own, but she told it like a fairy tale. And at the end . . .

At the end she had said . . .

No, it could not be.

He gazed down at her bent head. He was no prince, entitled to his fair reward. He was a rake, entitled to ... nothing. Painfully, he lifted his hand to touch her, but let it drop back to the covers. She needed her sleep. What was her brother about letting her run herself so ragged? For that matter, what was Ryde about letting her take up virtual residence in the bedchamber of a man with Anthony's reputation?

No doubt he knows you are as incapable of action as a eunuch in the sultan's harem. A painful chuckle tried to tremble to life in his battered gut, but all he could do was splutter and groan.

Jane roused at the sound. Her head turned and she looked at him, starting at the sight of him awake. "Anthony! Are you in pain?"

He realized it had become their traditional call and refrain. Even before he answered, she rose to her feet, a cane that had been resting against the bed in her hand. She began limping past him toward a small table.

"No," he croaked. Egad. He sounded like a toad.

She had already begun measuring out the draught. She looked up, surprised.

"No," he repeated, trying to sound firm. At least, he no longer sounded amphibian. He gathered himself up to push out more words. "Want. To. Talk."

"Oh, my darling! Of course." She crossed back to the bed and sat down by him again and gazed at him with a sweet, expectant smile.

"Jane," he said, perspiring with the effort to pronounce her name as he wanted to, like a caress. Instead, the appellation fell to the ground like a dead fish. He clenched his hands in frustration. "How. Long."

"A week, my dear. It has been a week." She reached out and placed a hand on his arm. "But Matthew says you are mending splendidly."

"You. Must. Sleep."

Her eyes widened, and her chin came up. "I *have* been sleeping. When I am awake, I prefer to be here with you."

Infuriating woman. How was he to argue with her, when his tongue felt like it belonged to an ox? "Tired," he ground out angrily. "You look ... tired."

She looked affronted, and she rose to her feet. Good. He wanted her to be angry with him. Maybe then she would leave and get some rest. But she did not make for the door. Instead, she moved closer. Leaning over him, she carefully put her arms around his neck. "And you, my dearest Anthony, look so wonderfully fine, I think I could cry."

The next time Anthony awoke, Jane was gone. He told himself he was glad, but his disappointment at her absence felt like a new bruised place he had only just discovered.

He had not been left alone, however. At first, he thought the lady sitting in the corner was his sister, Georgiana, for she had Georgiana's golden hair. Her attention was fixed on something in her lap, however, and after a bit he realized it was an embroidery hoop. This could not be Georgiana. The lady looked up and regarded him gravely, and he realized the sister was not his, but Jane's.

"Lady ... Alex," he grunted.

"Hello, Mr. Winston. It is good to see you awake.

"Is Jane ... sleeping?"

She did not answer him. Instead, she said, "Are you uncomfortable, sir? Jane instructed me how to administer your medicine." She rose to her feet and came to sit in the chair pulled close to his bedside. *Jane's chair.*

He frowned. "Tired of ... sleeping."

"That is understandable. Rest is important when the body needs to heal, but you have had a great deal of healing to do. I do not blame you for being heartily sick of that bed." He was surprised by the sympathy in her voice, and he felt a rush of gratitude to her.

"It is good … of you … Lady Alex … to keep watch . . .with me."

She flashed him a wide smile so like her sister's that Anthony's breath caught. "No, indeed, Mr. Winston. It is a prize I elbowed my way past both my sisters to obtain." He stared at her, and she laughed. "Do not look so astounded, Mr. Winston. You are our resident hero. Watching over you is quite a sought-after honor."

"Lord Ryde … does not mind … Jane … in my room?"

Her expression turned grave. "My brother regrets failing to protect you, sir. He is not inclined to object to anything Jane asks of him."

"Jane's idea … bring me here … to mend?"

She shook her head. "No, that was Andrew."

"Why?" Anthony was grateful to be back down to one syllable. The pain was crowding in on him in earnest now, and he was starting to perspire with the effort of squeezing out each word.

"My brother has always been a protective fellow. His instinct is to guard his own fiercely. He wanted you close—and your sister, too."

"But we … are not … *his* … responsibility." Anthony gasped with the effort to get the words out.

She frowned. "Sir, you and Miss Winston are family, or as close to it as makes no difference. How could my brother *not* feel you to be his responsibility?"

Anthony's mouth fell open. He clamped it shut and tried to understand. *Family?* His betrothal to Jane was a sham. The marriage would not happen. He would not *really* become part of this large, affectionate family. The knowledge was painful, but it was no surprise. So why did Ryde consider them his responsibility? It made no sense!

"Mr. Winston, you look—pained." Lady Alex's voice was anxious. "Shall I get you your medicine now?"

"Would … like … to wait." He did not want to sleep. He wanted to think.

"Of course. Perhaps you would like me to fetch your sister to you then? She is downstairs discussing healing herbs with Mr. Elton."

Anthony felt his bruised mouth curve into an uncomfortable smile. "She must … adore … that."

Lady Alex flashed him a grin full of good humor. "It is quite clear that she does. Beyond all reason." Her eyes twinkled, but his poor befuddled brain could no more tease out the meaning behind her words than it could solve the puzzle of Ryde's unexpected hospitality. It was too tired. *He* was too tired. And he hurt.

"No," he told her thickly. "Leave her ... be."

"Then since I suspect our conversation has sorely taxed you, may I read to you?"

Anthony, who had not been read to since he was a boy being dandled on his mother's knee, was not quite sure what to make of this offer, but managed to croak politely, "Thank you ... Lady ... Alex," before closing his eyes and sinking down into the bedclothes as the pain pressed in on him. To his surprise, her gentle voice did manage to distract him from the worst of his discomfort, but after a while even her soothing tones were not enough to see him through. Feeling a defeated man, he asked her for his dose of laudanum. She brought it to him, handing him the glass as if she were presenting him a medal instead of tossing him a crutch. He could not meet her eyes.

"Jane is right about you, Mr. Winston," she said gravely. "You are, indeed, a *very* brave man."

"Jane ... thinks ... *that?*"

To his very great satisfaction, Lady Alex nodded.

Catherine had been searching for Jane everywhere. She had looked in Mr. Winston's room and Jane's bedchamber and the drawing room and the dining room and the library and even the kitchen—for, of late, Jane had been eating very irregularly—but she could not find her anywhere. Finally, it occurred to Catherine to check the chapel. To her great relief, she found Jane immediately. She was sitting huddled on one of the back pews, a look of misery on her white face.

"Oh, my dearest!" Catherine exclaimed. She came and sat down next to her and wrapped an arm around her. "Andrew has told me how bad it was. I am so very sorry!"

Jane laid her head on Catherine's shoulder. Catherine reached up and stroked Jane's hair and patted her, as she would a small child. She waited patiently for her to speak, but her usually voluble sister-in-law was completely silent. They remained like that for some time. Catherine was beginning to grow alarmed at the continued silence, when Jane finally said in a very small voice, "I am so ashamed."

"Whatever in the world have you to feel ashamed about, my dear?"

"As we were leaving, Ryde and Sir Henry went ahead. One of the men—" Jane came to an abrupt stop.

"One of the men what?" Catherine demanded sharply.

"He seized my skirt and pulled at it and...and . . ." Jane's voice broke.

Catherine's heart thundered in her chest. Her imagination assailed her with all sorts of lurid possibilities. "Please, dearest! Tell me!"

"He begged me for *mercy!* He said he has a small daughter. He told me her name." Jane began to cry.

Catherine's eyes closed briefly with relief. Then she rocked Jane as she wept. When the tears had finally stopped, Jane turned her wet face to her.

"Catherine, what am I to do? I cannot bear to think of that little child without a father. I want to be implacable and strong...but I cannot! I fear I must go to Andrew and tell him—beg him—to speak to Sir Henry and ask for mercy for those men."

Catherine hugged her tightly. "Do not fear! Your brother will not be angry with you for asking such a thing. To show Christian compassion is not a thing to be ashamed of."

Jane shook her head. "It is not Drew's reaction I fear. It is Anthony's. He suffered so frightfully at the hands of those men. I feel if I ask for mercy for them, I am betraying him. And I fear he will think I do not care about what he suffered, when everything he suffered was because of *me!*"

Catherine was not sure what to say. Jane had the right of it. It was a very real possibility that Mr. Winston *would* take serious offense at Jane's plea for mercy.

"I think," she finally said, "that you must go to your brother and do what is in your heart, what you feel is right about those two men." Jane regarded her mutely. "After that, I think we must trust Ryde. He has a good head on his shoulders. He will know what is to be done about Mr. Winston's reaction to the news."

Jane nodded, but said nothing. Catherine sighed. She suspected her attempt to comfort her sister-in-law had been a signal failure.

Anthony was back in Portugal.

The battle was raging, but he had stopped before this small, terrible house. Why he had stopped, he could not remember. He could hear the battle in the distance, but here it was quiet. Then a baby cried.

Of course! *That* was why he had stopped. He had to get the baby and take it with him. He had to keep it safe. He entered the house and searched for the child, but the two lower rooms were empty. He climbed the tiny stairs.

The woman was lying on her stomach: skirts up, arms splayed at her sides. She did not move, did not breathe. Cold dread slid up his throat. Slowly, Anthony knelt down beside her. Reaching out a hand that shook, he touched the soft brown hair. Then he turned her over.

And he screamed.

Jane watched Anthony sleep, wondering if he would ever forgive her for what she had done tonight.

Her brother had been surprisingly kind and understanding. He had promised to ride and see Sir Henry in the morning. He had cautioned her that there was no guarantee her plea for mercy would sway the judge. It was quite possible the men would still hang. Jane had told Drew she understood. Then she had fled the room and come here.

At first, she had been alarmed that Anthony was still sleeping. She had expected him to be awake. Then she remembered Alex telling her, when she and Ryde had arrived from the prison, that Anthony had delayed his afternoon dose of laudanum by nearly two hours. Alex had been admiring, but Jane had been too troubled to pay her sister much heed. Now she peered anxiously at Anthony's sleeping form and watched his chest. The strong rise and fall of his breathing reassured her.

To her relief, he was wearing a fresh linen shirt. She lifted it up and inspected the new dressings Matthew had placed on his stitched and healing knife wounds. This morning one of the wounds had started to bleed, seeping through the bandage and his shirt. The sight of the blood had unnerved her, but then Anthony had woken, and she had disregarded it in her joy that he was lucid and speaking to her.

Yet here he was, still covered in the marks of violence. Violence she had signaled she did not want avenged. How could he not hate her for that? She turned away and slowly limped over to a chair in the corner where he would not have to look at her when he awoke. She buried her face in her hands.

Suddenly Anthony gave a fearful cry.

She jerked upright, knocking over her cane. Heart pounding, she began to hobble toward him. "Anthony! What is the matter?"

His eyes opened and his gaze swept the room in wide-eyed panic.

"Anthony, please! Tell me what is wrong!"

His attention swiveled toward her voice. His eyes fixed on her with an intensity that stopped the breath in her throat. She leapt the last few feet to his bedside, and he grabbed her and pulled her to his chest.

"Jane!" His heart was beating so hard it felt like thunder. *"Thank God!"* She tried to take his hands, hoping to offer reassurance, but his grip on her did not loosen, but instead grew tighter.

"Do not leave ... I need you near ... I was so ... terrified!"

"Of course, dearest. I will not leave. But what frightened you so?"

He did not answer, but she saw that his eyes were full of tears—frightened, terrified tears. Her stomach clenched. *What on God's green earth?* Then she realized. Realized the one thing that could have panicked her brave, dear Anthony. It was—it had to be—the memory of the terrible attack he had just endured. Her guilt twisted deeper. She tried to pull away, but he would not let her go. So maneuvering around his hold, she levered herself up onto the bed until she was lying next to him. "Be still, my love. There is nothing to fear. You are safe."

He shook his head, adamant. *"You ...* are safe."

She had no idea what he meant by that, but he seemed to grow calmer, so she stroked his hair and kissed his hands and let him hold her as tightly as he wished. After a while, she tried to pull free so she could bring him his laudanum, but he refused to release her. She could feel the tense grip the pain had on him. "Please my darling, let me fetch your medicine, so you do not hurt so badly."

But he shook his head and tightened his hold. "Want to. . . show you ... I am brave."

The words were so unexpected and so heartrending she gave up trying to coax him. Instead, she turned carefully in the circle of his arms and nestled against his side, determined to remain there as long as he needed her to.

Even until the end of time.

Chapter 18

Anthony woke to find Jane asleep in his arms. He sighed with relief. *She is safe.*

He recalled his terror from the night before, when he had relived his old nightmare only to find the dead woman on the floor was Jane. His stomach clenched at the memory, and for a moment he thought he was going to be sick. He turned his head away and took a few heaving breaths. Slowly the nausea subsided.

It had only been a dream. A damned, horrific dream. He focused on the truth of that until he grew calm. He turned back to look at her. There was a painful sort of pleasure in holding Jane like this. Waking with her like this. Gazing down at her sleeping face like this. It was so easy to imagine that she was really, truly his. Would always be really, truly his.

And why should she not be? called a small enticing voice in his head.

Anthony tried to ignore the voice. He knew only too well the folly of listening to it. He had listened to it once before, and the result had been … catastrophe.

He looked away from Jane's sleeping face and tried to fix his attention elsewhere. His gaze searched about the room, but the room was still dark, and there was nothing to see. A faint wisp of light was slipping in under the curtains, but it was still earliest morning. No doubt even the servants were still safely in their beds.

I should simply lie here with her until the whole house stirs about us,

Anthony thought ruefully. *Then Ryde will come storming in here with his horsewhip and force me to marry her and make me the happiest man on the face of the Earth.* He gave a low chuckle.

Jane stirred.

Sorry, my love. I did not mean to wake you.

She made a soft sound and raised her head a little. Then she burrowed against his bandaged chest. He gave a gasp, for it hurt like hell, but he was too entranced at having her so close to push her away. Instead, he closed his eyes and focused on the rest of her body, tracing each warm point of contact into a constellation of delight that kept the pain at bay.

His one fixed star.

He slept.

Jane woke to find her face pressing against Anthony's chest. She realized, with a sort of panic, that she was lying right on top of one of his wounds; she could feel the raised softness of the bandage through the thin linen of his shirt. Slowly, carefully—so as not to wake him— she lifted her head away, terrified she would find she had set the thing to bleeding again. But she could see no blood. Her eyes closed in relief.

Fearful of what other inadvertent damage she might be doing to his poor, healing body, she tried to ease out of his arms, but his grip was steely, and when she tried to slip downwards to escape, she felt his hands slide down to prevent it.

"Just where ... do you think. . . you are going?" he asked sternly.

"I was afraid—I thought I might be hurting you."

"I hope I am ... a little tougher than that."

She gazed up into his face, relieved to see the terror of last night was gone, vanished as if it had never been. His expression was calm.

"Will you not ... come back up here?" he asked as lightly as if he were asking her out for a drive. She slid back up into the tight circle of his arms, trying to keep a pillow of air between herself and all his many hurts. But he had other ideas. He pulled her fast against his body. "I will not ... break," he murmured into her hair.

"But you have not had your laudanum since yesterday afternoon. Are you in pain?"

He chuckled. "I fear I will be old and gray...and every time...I encounter you on the street...you will say to me...'Are you in pain?'"

She felt the sudden prick of tears in her eyes. Were they to be mere strangers then, passing each other on the street someday?

"My lady...forgive me...I only meant to tease."

And now he was back to calling her 'my lady'?

"I did not take offense," she assured him. "I was simply . . ." Her voice trailed away, as she realized she had absolutely no idea what to say. Fortunately, he did not press her about it. Instead, he bent his head and began softly kissing her ear. "My love!" she protested. "You must not! Your poor lips, they are still healing!"

"My lips...are my own affair!" he growled softly, but he desisted. His gaze, however, when he lifted his head, was oddly intent, and Jane was uneasily reminded of a hawk who has just spotted a mouse in a field. "But that brings up a topic...I have been meaning...to discuss with you."

"Yes?"

He eyed her speculatively. Then to her surprise he said, "I suppose...I worried you last night?"

She did not wish to embarrass him by dwelling on his fear. "Not terribly, my dearest," she lied. "Only a little."

Suddenly, he grinned at her. "There you go...doing it again."

"Doing what again?"

"Dropping endearments...from your lips...as if...they were the merest trifles. Just in these five minutes...I have been graced...with a 'my dearest' and a 'my love.'"

She stared at him—once more at a loss for anything to say.

"So which is it?"

"Which is what?" she said, beginning to feel sorely tried.

"Am I your dearest...or am I your love?" His green eyes were twinkling wickedly at her now.

She was sorely tempted to poke him in the ribs, but—as she had no real desire to do him harm and as his ribs were, according to Matthew, quite bruised—she settled for turning her back to him and murmuring in exasperation, "At the moment, you are neither!"

But turning had been a strategic mistake. He turned, too, and spooned her back, wrapping his arms around her breasts.

"Does that mean that...at one time...I was both?" His voice was low and his bruised lips now caressed her neck.

"Anthony, please," she whispered, completely overset by his touches, "I do not think—"

He ignored her. "I have a memory... of you telling me a very fine tale... It concerned the exploits of a handsome and brave rake. At the end . . ."

He had heard her! Dear God, he had heard her! Through the pain and the drug he had heard her—and *remembered.* What was she to do now?

"Was it... true... what you told me... at the end?" His voice was now so deep that it sent little rippling waves through her—like a stone skipping along the surface of a pond. "I find I need... very much... to know."

How was she to answer him? This very morning her brother was headed to Sir Henry to bear her pleas for mercy. She was a Judas, waiting to betray him with a kiss. How could she tell him she loved him and then do such a thing to him? She tensed in his arms.

His hold on her loosened. "I think... I have my answer."

No! She could not have him think that either. She turned abruptly in his arms and—as gently as she could—took his face in her hands. "My darling Anthony," she murmured, her heart breaking with tenderness. As softly as she could, she began kissing his face.

She barely brushed the places that looked most sore with her lips, virtually blowing kisses as her mouth swept by. On the places that were healing, however, her mouth lingered, her lips nuzzling and caressing, trying to give comfort. And where he was whole... where he was whole, she saluted him with a concentrated passion she could only give rein to. The areas were small, but she kissed and licked and stroked each beloved inch as if it contained the entire universe of her being.

She was trembling by the time she reached his mouth. She darted her tongue between his bruised lips. Gently she prised them apart and plunged inside. She felt herself spinning into the hot wetness of his mouth. She was a child twirling in her joy. She was a bird unfurling into flight. She heard a sound, but could not tell if it was her groan—or his.

Suddenly, she was torn away. His strong hands were pushing her from him. "Off... the bed!"

She did not understand.

"My lady... *off the bed!*"

Then she heard the footsteps in the hall. She scrambled sideways, slipping off the edge of the bed and crashing to the floor—onto her bottom.

"*Jane!*"

"I am fine," she assured him, rising shakily to her feet and sinking into the chair. *All but my dignity.*

The door opened and a small chambermaid entered, her arms full of equipment to light the fire. The girl's eyes widened when she spotted Jane sitting in the chair next to the bed, her face no doubt as red as the curtains keeping out the importunate morning light.

"Oh, my lady! Beggin' your pardon." The little maid's glance flicked from her to Anthony. "Shall I come back, ma'am?"

Mouth clamped tight to avoid breaking into hysterical giggles, Jane shook her head.

As the self-conscious maid toiled on and on lighting the cursed fire, Anthony furtively watched Jane and brooded. The pain was beginning to sweep in on him now, like a foolishly forgotten tide, but he was too distracted to care.

Blast it! Did she or did she not?

Her manner said she did. Her care of him, her heedless endearments, her unwillingness to cause him pain—they all declared the answer *yea*.

Her family's behavior said she did. Their hospitality to him and their calm assumption that he and Jane would wed—both declared the answer *yea* as well.

Her body said she did. His blood was still on fire from the frenzy of her kisses. Indeed, if the maid still crouched before the fire had not approached when she had, he probably would have used this fine, big bed to finish what he had started in that small, silly chair in Bagshot's cottage, consequences be damned. He closed his eyes for a moment, savoring the thought of it. However, with eyes closed, the pain began to wash against him more insistently. He opened his eyes again and fixed his gaze once more on Jane.

Her body most definitely declared the answer *yea*.

And so? demanded the determined and coaxing voice inside his head. *Surely that is enough?*

No, it is not *enough,* his reason retorted.

There were only two entries on the negative side of the ledger as to the state of his beloved's heart, but they loomed vast and ominous.

First, she would not acknowledge her love, though he had virtually begged her to do so. It was hard to imagine a reason for that, except that she did not, in fact, love him.

Second...second was his own experience. She was a lady and he was a rake, and he knew that no matter how deeply he loved her, no matter how desperately he wanted to make her his, the odds that she could bring herself to soil her heart by granting it to the likes of him were...nil and none.

He shut his eyes and turned away. The pain closed in, and he welcomed it. He was tired of fighting against it. He heard a clatter as the chambermaid collected her things, then the door to the room opened and closed.

"Anthony?"

She was leaning over him. He could feel her closeness, but somehow could not bring himself to open his eyes.

"Anthony?" she persisted. He felt the backs of her fingers skim softly along his jaw. "Can I not get you some medicine?" Her tone was pleading.

Mutely, he nodded.

He heard her go to fetch it. When she returned, she said gently, "You must sit up to drink it. I cannot tip it into you while you are bent away like that."

Feeling like a scolded child, he snapped his eyes open and straightened up in the bed. He held his hand out for the glass angrily, and when she handed it to him, he tossed the draught off as if it were a tankard of ale. He only regretted that he did not have a counter to smash the glass down on afterwards. He would have liked to see it shatter into a thousand pieces.

"Anthony, could you look at me?"

Rigidly, he turned his head to meet her eyes.

She ran her tongue nervously across her lips. For a moment, he recalled all too vividly the wonders she had performed inside his mouth with that tongue. Then he forced himself to focus.

"Yes, my lady...what do you want?"

She flinched.

He had not meant his voice to sound so furious, but he found he did not have the will to apologize either. He was not in a gentle mood.

"I want . . ." Her voice trailed off. What the devil was she about? Suddenly, she looked as guilty as if she were about to commit some mortal sin. "I want . . ." she began again. Her beautiful blue eyes fixed on him, silently pleading for something he did not understand. It was as if she wanted his *forgiveness*. But for what?

"Devil take it . . . Jane . . . what is the matter?"

"You asked me a question a little while ago. Now I want to give you my answer."

So *this* was the source of her guilt. He tensed, wishing he had never asked. It was bad enough to fear. He feared what it would be like to know.

She reached out her hand to him. Not sure what else to do, he took it.

"I want to tell you, Anthony—my dearest Anthony—that everything you heard me say that night was true. It is what I felt then. It is what I feel now. I love you."

Anthony stared at her, uncomprehending. Obviously the laudanum had taken effect more quickly than he realized, and he was hallucinating.

"Must you look so disbelieving?"

"What?"

"Your face is so full of doubt," she cried. "It is as if you do not trust my assurances—as if you do not trust *me.*" She pulled her hand free.

"Jane!"

"Well?"

"But you cannot love me," he protested.

"Why not?" She sounded angry now.

He could not explain it. It would hurt too much to explain it. He clutched at straws. "If you loved me . . . then . . . you would not be so deathly afraid . . . to marry me."

"I am not the least bit afraid to marry you!" she snapped.

"You aren't?"

"Of course not."

"Then will you?"

"Will I what?"

"Marry me."

She did not look angry anymore. "Is that what you want, Anthony? Is that what would truly make you happy?"

It was the stupidest question to ever pass the lips of his normally intelligent lady. However, she was his beloved, so he refrained from saying so. Instead, he said simply, "Yes."

"Then I will."

His heart began to race. "And this is . . . a true betrothal?" he demanded. "With a reading of the banns . . . and a trip to London to purchase wedding clothes . . . and a honeymoon to plan?"

She laughed. "Goodness, my dear! You sound like an eager mama planning the wedding of your firstborn."

"Why are you still down there?" he demanded, too giddy to take affront at this aspersion. "Get up here, madam," he commanded. She climbed back up onto the bed next to him. He pulled her close and kissed her soundly without a single protest from her about his bruised lips. When he was done, his giddiness had transmuted into a glowing, happy contentment. He nestled his head on her breast and murmured sleepily, "So . . . my dearest Jane . . . what then *is* the groom's proper role . . . beyond planning the deflowering of his beloved?"

For some reason, she turned as beautifully pink as a sunset. "Dearest, I am a widow."

"Ah. Then perhaps we may begin the honeymoon early?" he said coaxingly. "I am so very eager to . . . eager to . . ."

But the cursed laudanum took effect and he could not remember what he had meant to say.

Chapter 19

Anthony woke and looked eagerly about the room, but Jane was not there. Instead, Matthew Elton stood by a window. The light was bright, though winter thin. Anthony guessed it was early afternoon. Elton crossed to him and grinned. "You are becoming as regular as clockwork, sir. Seven hours of sleep per dose. And I am glad to hear from Jane that you are trying to wean yourself from the laudanum. If you can hold off and not take another dose until evening, I will be well pleased."

Anthony grimaced. "I would be well pleased... if I never had to take another dose... ever. I am heartily sick of the cursed stuff... and of sleep... and of being confined to this damned bed... I want to be up and about."

And I want my Jane.

He wished she were here. He had a superstitious need to see her and touch her and assure himself that his fairy tale was real.

As if sensing his thoughts, the other man said, "By the way, Jane wished me to tell you that she will be back soon."

"Where is she now?"

"I believe she is down with Ryde. He has just returned —" Elton's voice came to an abrupt stop. "May I examine your dressings now?"

Irritably, Anthony signaled the man to go ahead. He was tired of being poked and prodded like a Christmas turkey, but he knew the true reason for his upset was his fear that Jane's vow to marry him was nothing more than a laudanum-induced hallucination.

Elton seemed satisfied with his inspection. "Sir, let me congratulate you. You have the constitution of an ox—an extremely strong, extremely fast-healing ox. Those knife wounds had me worried, but they are healing just as efficiently as the rest of you. I can only hope your sister takes after you when it comes to the strength of her constitution."

Anthony had no idea why the strength of Georgiana's constitution should be of interest to Mr. Elton. However, he had just had a notion which he was too impatient to get started on it to give the matter further thought. "Elton, can you find me ... some breeches? I would like to get up and go sit ... in that chair over there ... and feel like an actual man again ... and not some cursed bed cushion." Anthony pulled back the bedcovers and swung his legs over the edge of the bed. He was eager to accomplish the task before Jane returned.

"*Wait, sir!*"

Anthony pushed his feet down on the floor and struggled against the soreness and stiffness he felt everywhere. Slowly he rose ... and promptly collapsed.

To his surprise, the diminutive doctor caught him in an iron grip before his head hit the floor. "Dammit, man!" gasped Elton, "I told you to *wait.*" The doctor heaved him back up onto the bed. Anthony could only lie there, waiting for the room to stop spinning and for his churning stomach to stop rocking. He pressed his face into the bedclothes to hide his humiliation.

"Sir, you may have the constitution of an ox, but you are still human," Elton commented drily near his ear. "You have been gravely injured, have been taking laudanum by the bucketful, and have been off your feet for nearly nine days now. You cannot expect to rise like a phoenix from the ashes of your sickbed! Let us take it slowly, bit by bit. Once your head has ceased swimming, I will help you to rise to sit on the edge of the bed. You can dangle your legs and allow your poor body to adjust to the notion that it must vie once more with gravity to get blood to your brain."

"I do not wish ... Jane ... to see me like this," Anthony muttered into the sheets.

"I think Jane will be a while yet," Elton assured him. "In the interim, may I wish you happy?"

"She spoke of it...to you?" Anthony exclaimed, his relief so strong, it set his head to spinning again. His miracle was real.

"I believe she announced it to her entire family—as well as to your sister. It was Georgiana who told me."

"Georgiana?" Anthony repeated, confused. "Why should she tell you such a thing...and since when are you and my sister...on a first-name basis?"

The doctor's freckled face turned quite red. "Actually, I have wanted to discuss that with you for a few days now, but I wished to wait until you were stronger."

Anthony suddenly felt the need to be upright. He lifted his head and then his shoulders. "Well?" he demanded, feeling as if he were on a seesaw rising and then plummeting to the ground. If only the damned bed would stop rocking.

Fortunately, Elton came straight to the point. "I would like your permission to pay my addresses to your sister."

Anthony wondered if he had taken a new dose of laudanum and forgotten it. "I beg your pardon?"

Elton was now frowning at him. "I would like to pay my addresses to your sister. Do you object?"

"Of course I object." The other man's expression was now a fierce scowl, or so it appeared to Anthony as he watched the other man's face rise and fall. Fearing he would be sick, Anthony closed his eyes. "You do realize...but that is stupid...you are a doctor...you must realize...she has an injured spine...she cannot walk...sadly, she will never walk—"

For some reason, the other man made a harrumphing sound.

Anthony soldiered on, determined to finish before he cast up his accounts. "If you pay court to her," he said panting, "she will think you mean to marry her...and...and...I will not have her...hurt in such a way!"

"But I *do* mean to marry her," Elton said, his voice quite close. Suddenly, the man was pushing Anthony's head down and hauling his torso up so that Anthony was left crouched like a dog with his head between his paws and his tail in the air. He would have protested the ignominy of the position, if it didn't immediately make his head feel much better. Anthony took a few relieved breaths.

"What did you say?" he said weakly, still not ready to open his eyes.

"I said I do intend to marry your sister. Indeed, I am determined on it. And as for her spine—I do not believe there is actually anything the matter with it."

Anthony's eyes snapped open. "And on what basis … do you make that amazing … pronouncement?"

"I examined her myself, and—"

"You did *what?*"

"And I found that—"

Anthony was furious. "Sir! On whose authority … did you take it upon yourself … to do such a thing?"

Elton shook his head and gazed up at the ceiling. "Lord, save me from stiff-necked giants! I swear, you and Ryde are two peas in a pod!"

Anthony was taken aback by this comparison. He moderated his tone. "Sir, I believe I am entirely within my rights … to enquire by whose authority … you examined my sister!"

"By that of the lady herself!" Elton snapped. "I considered that sufficient. Now do you mean to keep blustering on like a fool, or do you actually wish to hear what I discovered?"

"Tell me," Anthony said stiffly.

So Elton did. When he was done, Anthony—now seated on the edge of the bed—regarded him with a mixture of hope and anxiety. "And you truly believe there is a chance … that with this treatment of yours … she might be able to learn to stand upright again?"

Elton smiled. "Oh, I am quite sure of *that*. It is the walking I am less sure of, but the only way to know is to try."

Anthony's hopes rose in the face of the other man's confidence. He knew firsthand that Elton was a cautious and competent doctor. He did not think him the sort of man to promise a thing he could not deliver. But still he worried. "If you cannot fix her legs … if you cannot make her walk … then what happens when you also … withdraw your offer of marriage? That would be a devastating blow."

Elton's expression, which a moment earlier had been all friendliness, was now colder than the January wind rattling the windowpanes. "And why would I do such a thing?"

"Was not your interest in my sister … predicated on the notion that … you might be able to … well—fix her?"

"My interest in your sister is predicated on my deep esteem for her, my affection for her, my—oh, curse it, if you must know, my love for her! That has nothing to do with whether she can walk, skip, or dance. I do not need to fix her, for she is not broken, and if she would have me, I would be happy to marry her tomorrow to prove as much to you!"

Anthony was about to ask the overwrought doctor if he carried a special license about in his pocket, but he was not really inclined to vex the man. He was too hopeful that Georgiana's opportunities for happiness were not as circumscribed as he had once feared.

And if Elton truly was able to help his sister walk again . . .

Well, then this was a day for miracles indeed.

Jane tiptoed into Anthony's bedchamber expecting to find him asleep. Instead, he was sitting in a large wing-backed chair, his feet propped up on a real Ottoman, his golden head bent forward as he read a small green volume. He looked up at her. "It is about time you arrived . . . Is this the sort of neglect . . . I can expect from you once we are wed? I have been expecting you this half-hour . . . at least."

She opened her mouth to answer him, then closed it again as she belatedly noticed the twinkle in his eyes. He was teasing her. She had been so distracted and worried about her brother's news that she had missed that Anthony was teasing her. She looked closely at him now, trying to commit to memory the look of warm contentment on his face, the mischievous sparkle in his green eyes, the eager set of his poor, bruised mouth. He looked happy. She wanted—so desperately—for him to keep looking happy.

She smiled down at him. "I do not know what you have to complain of, sir," she said, surveying his fresh shirt, overlong breeches, and fine Turkish slippers. "It is obvious that *someone* has been taking great pains with you. You look so amazingly kempt."

"How sharper than a serpent's tooth . . . is the tongue of my betrothed."

She laughed. "I suppose Andrew donated those clothes to you?"

"Strictly speaking, Lady Ryde gave them to Elton . . . who gave them to me . . . but yes, he was the original donor . . . though I cannot imagine . . . how you can tell."

She smiled and perched herself on the portion of the Ottoman not occupied by his feet. "At least, his footwear seems to fit you properly."

She resisted the impulse to run a finger along the top of his bare, slipper-clad foot.

He was watching her, and when she looked up at him, an odd expression appeared on his face. "The girl weeping over my feet!"

"What?"

"Seeing you there ... perched over my slippers ... reminds me of an odd dream I had during those first, confused days ... I dreamt there was a girl ... with pretty brown hair ... who wept over my feet." His head tilted, as he considered her. "But what was more ... extraordinary ... was that afterwards ... she kissed them." Jane turned away, avoiding his eyes. "Only now I begin to wonder ... if it really *was* a dream."

"It sounds silly enough to be a dream," she remarked loftily.

His hand reached up and gently turned her head so she had to meet his eyes. "It did not feel silly at all. It felt ... magical. As if a fairy princess were ... bestowing some sort of ... healing blessing on me."

She looked down at his slippers. "That night was terrible," she said, suddenly caught up in the memory of it. "And your feet—they were so wonderfully unmarked. It seemed as if every last inch of you was covered in hurts, but *they* were not."

"Every ... last ... inch ... of me? Jane! Just how much of me ... did you see that night?"

She was silent for a moment. Then she said, "Matthew had you covered with a sheet. But he—he wasn't there, and I simply had to know how bad it was."

"But I had ... my clothes on?"

"Matthew had cut them from you."

"But I still had ... my smallclothes—"

She shook her head. "Dearest," she said in a small voice. "You had wounds everywhere!"

He instinctively looked down.

"Oh, no, my dear, not there! You protected yourself well enough to avoid that!"

Two bright spots of color appeared in his cheeks. "Really, madam! I begin to wonder ... who is the true reprobate ... in this relationship!"

She made a face at him. "This from a gentleman who took advantage of my need to change from my wet things to steal a peek at me!"

He had the grace to look sheepish. "You knew?"

She nodded, and then her mouth slipped into a smile. "Of course,

I would have been highly insulted if you had not."

"Come here, future wife," he said, pulling her from her perch on the Ottoman onto his lap. He wrapped his arms around her. "When we are married ... you may kiss my feet to your heart's content ... as long as I have the opportunity ... to steal a peek now and again."

"You are very fortunate, sir, that you are so riddled with sore spots that I cannot decently poke you for saying such a thing."

His wicked green eyes twinkled at her, "Madam, you do know that in a marriage ... it is the husband . . .who is supposed to do the poking?"

"*Anthony!*"

"Forgive me, my dear," he said, sounding genuinely contrite. "My high spirits are having an unfortunate effect on my tongue. I will do better, I promise."

Suddenly, there was a peremptory knock at the door. Jane slipped from Anthony's lap and rose to her feet just as the door opened and her brother strode into the room. Drew paid no heed to her closeness to Anthony. His attention was focused solely on her, on asking her an unspoken question. *The* unspoken question.

Ashamed of her cowardice, Jane gave her head a faint shake. Perhaps if she had had more time, she would have been able to steel herself to tell Anthony. But she knew it was not true. She could not tell him, because she could not bear to snatch his happiness away. Her brother was right. He would have the courage to do it. Sadly, she did not.

Anthony looked up at Lord Ryde standing in the doorway and felt a cold, dizzying wave of apprehension that made the hairs on the back of his neck stand on end. It was the old feeling, the feeling that had come over him before all the truly terrible things that had happened in his life—before Busaco, before the elopement with Regina, before the recent attack—but why was he having it now?

Anthony shrugged it away. No doubt his mind was just nervous at the similarity. This was too much like Bagshot's cottage, when Jane's brother had burst in to spoil the magic of their time together. But there was nothing that could be spoiled now. Jane's heart was his, and soon she would be his wife, and there was nothing for Ryde to rail at, for Jane had sprung to her feet as lightly as a deer and moved away, perhaps not very far away—she was still using a cane after all, but far enough that her large brother could have no serious cause for complaint. They were a betrothed couple after all.

A *truly* betrothed couple.

Anthony clung to the thought like a shield as Lord Ryde strode into the room. He did not rail at Anthony. He did not look at Anthony. He did not even glance at the curious proximity between Anthony and Jane. Ryde simply fixed his gaze upon his sister.

The feeling at the back of Anthony's neck returned.

It suddenly occurred to him how very quick Jane had been to pop up, almost as if she was not surprised by the knock, almost as if…she had been expecting it.

The beat of his heart quickened. He watched as Lord Ryde flashed Jane some meaningful but—to Anthony—totally incomprehensible look. Then he watched Jane look down as if she were…ashamed. Anthony's jaw clenched. Damn her stiff-necked brother! What had he communicated with that look to make her feel such a thing?

Jane suddenly gave her head a faint shake, as if offering her brother some answer in the negative. But devil take it! *What had been the question?*

The marquess crossed to Jane, patted her shoulder, and ordered her from the room so he could speak to Anthony in private. Anthony was not sure whether to be relieved at the lofty peer's gentle tone with his sister or absolutely terrified by it.

What the devil was happening?

Anthony regarded Jane, desperately parsing her reaction to her brother's order for some hint as to what sort of catastrophe was rolling toward them, but she did not react at all. She uttered no protest; she registered no complaint; she offered no explanation. She simply crossed to Anthony with her head still bowed, dropped a kiss on his hair, and murmured four words that filled his heart with dread:

"Forgive me, my love."

Chapter 20

Anthony regarded Lord Ryde with battle-ready wariness.

"May I sit, sir?" Lord Ryde made the request in a mild, almost friendly tone.

Anthony gave a stiff nod and gestured toward a nearby chair. "As you will, my lord. It is your chamber after all ... and your furniture."

Ryde seated himself in the chair Anthony had indicated, folding his long body into the small chair with evident discomfort.

First rule of battle: *always discommode the enemy in any way you can.*

"You are looking well. Much better than when I checked on you last."

Anthony resisted the urge to inquire when that was. He had been unaware of any visits by his titled host. Perhaps the marquess had visited him while he slept.

"I am still weak," he replied, "but Elton seems satisfied ... I am grateful to be alive."

Second rule of battle: *always encourage the enemy to underestimate you.*

A look of discomfort passed over Ryde's face. "Sir, I wish to offer you my deepest apology."

"Apology, my lord? For what?"

The marquess replied tightly, "For failing to see you properly protected from this horrific attack on your person."

Anthony blinked. "You could not know it would occur."

"Matthew warned me."

"He warned me as well, my lord. It was I who failed to mount ... adequate defenses. Not you."

"You did well enough. I expect Jane has told you that the attacker you shot is dead?"

Anthony thought back to Jane's tale of the brave rake. This had not been a part of the tale he had wished to dwell upon. "Yes, I suppose she did, my lord."

"Enough my lords, man! I can bear no more. Jane has told me your news. You are to be my brother soon. Call me Ryde!"

At first, Anthony found this simple declaration so disarming and such a relief he was ready to call truce then and there. Then he noted the expression on the other man's face. Ryde still look guarded and circumspect and almost as uneasy about what lay ahead as Anthony himself. Grimly, Anthony realized the true battle was yet to come.

Third rule: *never let the enemy lull you into a false sense of complacency.*

"My lord—Ryde. I do not wish to be rude. . .but I grow weary and may soon ... need to ask for my laudanum. Was there a particular topic ... you wished to discuss?"

The other man nodded. "The topic of mercy."

"Did you say *'mercy,'* sir?"

"Yes. I wondered what your thoughts on that particular virtue were."

For a moment Anthony could only stare at the other man, hopelessly as sea. "I fear I am unused to being called upon ... to extemporize on any virtue, sir ... It is usually only vice ... I am considered expert enough ... to have a valid opinion about."

Ryde frowned. "I am serious, sir. Do you hold with the biblical injunction: 'an eye for an eye and a tooth for tooth?' If you had your attackers before you now, would you wish to see them hanging from the nearest gibbet—as I did, the night I first beheld the violence they had wrought upon you—or would you show them mercy and see them live?"

Anthony regarded the other man. Had Ryde truly felt such anger on his behalf? He tried not to let the thought please him, but it did. He considered the question gravely. The other man seemed quite intent on his response. Anthony had the uneasy feeling that this might be a test—one that he must pass, or risk—what? He replied slowly, "It has been my experience ... that death only begets death ... I have seen men — " He paused and swallowed against memory. "I have seen men go mad ... with the thirst for vengeance."

"Then you would come down on the side of mercy?"

Anthony nodded. "I will live. I see no reason ... for anyone else to die. If my attackers ... are sufficiently punished ... I have no appetite to see them swing." Ryde's face filled with relief. Had he passed the test? It seemed he had. "Of course, first they must be caught."

"Oh, they have been, sir!" Ryde assured him with a smile. "Indeed, I have already been to the prison to see them, as has my sister. You should have heard the abuse she heaped upon their heads. I was quite shocked to learn the breadth of my sister's vocabulary."

Anthony felt a sudden roaring in his ears. "Are you telling me that you took Jane ... *my Jane* ... to such a place? To encounter such men!" His voice was roaring now. "For what reason, sir? Tell me ... you had lost your mind ... for that is the only justification I can forgive!"

Ryde stared back at him, all blood drained from his face. Even his lips had gone white. "Sir, how *dare* you speak to me—in my own house—in such a fashion?"

"I dare, sir, because while I was forced to ... to *moulder* in that confounded bed over there, you took ... you took my beloved Jane to a damned *prison* ... and forced her to ... to view all the pain and misery of the accursed place ... and exposed her to the ... the foulness of those men ... and I was not even there to ... to ... protect her!" Anthony's voice trailed away as he realized his anger was gone, like an outgoing tide, leaving only his deepest feelings behind—bare and exposed. He turned his head away from the other man's gaze. "You are her brother, sir.... Why would you do such a thing?"

"Because she asked me!" Ryde snapped, his breathing as hard and rasping as Anthony's own. "Because she needed to see those men and confront them! I owed her that much, at least. And *I* was there to protect her, for God's sake! I did not send her there alone! As for pain and misery, what the hell do you think she has been looking squarely in the face these past nine days and more? Do you think anything she heard or saw in that damned prison could affect her as much as casting one single glance down at you in all your battered gore?"

Anthony felt battered indeed by the other man's words. He had not considered how terrible it must have been for Jane to see him in his injured state. He had been glad of her concern, he had been grateful for her care, he had chafed at her worry—especially when all he had wanted to do was touch her, but he had never imagined how deep her distress had been. He thought of her weeping over his feet because they were unmarked. What a damned fool he had been! "Why didn't she tell me?" he murmured.

Ryde heard and mistook his question. "She feared you would be angry with her," he said, sounding calmer. "She wanted to be Nemesis, your avenging goddess, and at first she was quite fierce enough to frighten even me. However, once her anger was spent, she could not ignore the sense of doom in the air. One of the scoundrels begged her for mercy. She wanted to be unyielding and simulate a heart of stone—"

"But Jane being Jane," Anthony said simply, "she could not." For a moment, he and the stiff-rumped marquess exchanged a look of complete understanding.

"You do not hold it against her?" Ryde asked.

Anthony shook his head. How could he? Jane's tender heart was part of what he treasured most about her. Curse it, the woman could not even turn her back on her dead husband's mistress. "What did she do?" he asked wryly. "Throw herself at the feet of the magistrate ... to beg leniency for them?"

Ryde grimaced. "No, she had *me* do that."

Anthony resisted the urge to laugh. "And was the fellow moved?"

Ryde shrugged. "It is difficult to say. The assizes are in two weeks. He has promised to consider transportation to Australia as a possible alternate sentence. But we shall have to see." He paused, and then said, "Will you mind it if that is how he decides?"

"As I said ... I escaped with my skin. As much pain as the bastards caused me ... it will not give me any particular joy to see them hang. Though if they live, I would take relief in knowing ... that they are far away ... and can never hurt me or mine again."

"As would I." Ryde gave a gusty sigh. "I am glad those are your sentiments. Jane will be much relieved. She feared you would interpret her urge for mercy as a betrayal."

"That is ridiculous," Anthony said flatly.

"Yet there are some men who would not be as understanding as you."

"Then they are fools."

Ryde smiled. "We are agreed."

Anthony wondered if Jane's dead husband had been such a fool. Is that why she had feared Anthony might prove such a dolt as well? Anthony sighed, pushing his jealous demons back in their box. "I still do not understand why she was so cursed keen ... to visit those men in the first place. *I* certainly have no desire ... to see their ugly faces again."

"Uglier still thanks to the marks you gave them," Ryde murmured with a grin.

"Thank you," Anthony said. "I have to confess to a certain satisfaction ... hearing that. But the point remains ... What did she hope to achieve?"

Ryde seemed to consider his words. "My sister is not a stupid woman."

Anthony stared at him. "You have no need ... to inform me of that, I assure you."

"She realized that those men acted on what they thought was her behalf."

Suddenly the hairs were back up on Anthony's neck.

"She blamed herself for the attack—no, control your choler! I am not saying that it is so. I am merely describing her belief. I think she felt responsible for every bruise, for every wound."

There was a rock of ice forming in Anthony's gut.

"She thought the harm that had come to you had come through her, and I think that made her feel she owed you a debt," Ryde continued on, compounding Anthony's sudden doubts into an avalanche of cold.

A debt, he thought bleakly. *That* was what he was to her. No longer merely a despised rake, but a millstone hung round her neck. A huge debit in her accounting book that had to be set right. Ryde kept droning on, and Anthony could think of no way to make him stop.

"So that is why she went to the prison. I think she felt she owed it to you to face those men and punish them with her anger."

Poor naive fool, Anthony thought bitterly. Did Ryde really think Jane, his fine honorable Jane, would consider visiting a couple of villains in prison sufficient payment for such a debt as this? Especially after she had spoiled the payment by asking for mercy for the men?

Anthony closed his eyes.

No. Jane would not consider that nearly enough sacrifice to square up their account. But there was one sacrifice she might think sufficient.

"Mr. Winston, do you feel unwell? Shall I summon Matthew?" Ryde's anxious voice broke in on Anthony's reverie.

Slowly, Anthony nodded. If Ryde went in search of Elton, then Anthony would have a few minutes of solitude in which to fight the ruin of his dreams. He heard Ryde's heavy footsteps move away, and the door open and then close. Now that he was alone, Anthony brought out his cache of precious memories. He fought to assure himself that all his fears were baseless; that Jane's declaration of love had been real; that all his dreams of happiness were not based on a noble lie.

But the trouble began almost at once.

He remembered lying there, his arms around her soft breasts, his lips on her sweet neck, begging her to tell him that her words of love were true. But she had not. Instead, she had stiffened tensely in his arms.

Why? Was it because her words of love had only been a sop to a suffering man waiting for the pain to cease?

He had given voice to his disappointment, and she had responded—not with a vow of affection, but with frenzied kisses. He had thought, then, that she had just been passionate with affection.

But how much more likely that she had been desperately trying to make up for the fact that she did not love him and could not bear to tell him so.

And then she had filled his heart with joy by proclaiming that she did indeed love him, would always love him. He could swear *that* had felt real, except... Jane had reacted oddly, or rather overreacted, to his rather understandable disbelief.

It is as if you do not trust my assurances—as if you do not trust me.

Had she been so touchy because she was hurt by his skepticism—or because she was in reality telling him a lie? A noble, well-intentioned but completely unforgivable lie?

He wanted to shake her. He wanted to shake himself. Why had he let himself believe in a fairy tale?

Yet, Anthony was not yet ready to call retreat. After all, he had asked Jane to marry him, and she had said yes, and she had seemed happy and content at the prospect, almost as happy and content as he.

But even this, he suddenly realized, was no proof, for now he remembered her manner of acceptance: *Is that what you want, Anthony? Is that what would make you truly happy?*

He had thought she meant to set the seal upon his happiness. Instead, she had been calculating the accuracy of her reckoning.

One hand in marriage for one beating near to death.

Acknowledging himself a defeated man, Anthony buried his face in his hands.

Fourth rule of battle: *be wise enough to know when the battle is lost, else you may be trapped where you stand—and cut to pieces.*

Chapter 21

"Good morning," Jane forced herself to say brightly, as she opened the door to Anthony's bedchamber. "I have brought some neighbors who wish to make your acquaintance." She pointed to the tall, white-haired lady on her right. "This is Mrs. Howard, and this—" Jane gestured toward the short, round lady on her left, "is Lady Dent. Ladies, this is Mr. Winston."

Anthony was by the window, sitting in his usual chair. Sunshine glinted on his golden hair, and Jane noted with surprise how recovered he looked. Somehow it had crept up on her without her even noticing. His bruised face was almost healed. A few new scars were scattered over his countenance, but they only made him look more roguishly handsome than before. His broad shoulders were no longer hunched in pain. Reflexively she glanced over at the small table, but the laudanum bottle was gone and had been for several days. His long legs looked strong enough to actually hold him upright, and his bearing—even relaxed in the large chair—consisted of that crisp, military posture she knew of old.

He surged to his feet as the sight of them. "Good morning, ladies. It is a great pleasure to make your acquaintance."

Lady Dent erupted in a loud harrumph. "Stuff and nonsense, young man! What use have you for the likes of us? Rakes only take pleasure in the company of rose-cheeked chits and loose widows."

Jane winced. Two bright spots of color appeared in Anthony's pale cheeks.

"*Ada!*" Mrs. Howard exclaimed.

"What's wrong with what I said? It's the truth!"

"Really, Ada! *Think!* He is Jane's young gentleman!"

Was he? Jane wondered, sneaking a look at Anthony from behind her lashes. He had spent the past week studiously ignoring her. She would come and sit with him and try to talk, but he would treat her as if she were of less interest than some chair or the Ottoman on which he propped his feet.

Lady Dent's protuberant eyes regarded Mrs. Howard belligerently. "So?"

"Jane is a widow!" Mrs. Howard said with an impatient snap.

Jane tensed as understanding began to dawn on Lady Dent's face. She opened her mouth to speak, but Jane, fearing further embarrassment, said hurriedly, "Ladies, will you not be seated? What is new in the village?"

Mrs. Howard gave her a hesitant look. "I fear that all anyone talks about is the attack on Mr. Winston and the arrest of the two laborers from Atkins farm."

Anthony's face was now shuttered. For once, Lady Dent kept tactfully silent.

"Oh," said Jane, realizing how stupid her choice of topic had been. But now her mind was a blank. She could not think how to turn the subject at all.

Fortunately, Mrs. Howard had no such problem. "Well, for my part, I am much more interested in this happy news about Mrs. Barrett."

"Happy news, ma'am?"

"Has Catherine not told you? Mrs. Barrett is expecting a child!"

Jane tried to fix a smile upon her face, but it was difficult. "We are surrounded by happy tidings of late." Suddenly, she realized Anthony's attention had snapped back to her. She dared not meet his eye, for fear she would burst into tears.

"Yes, I have seen your sister's babe," Mrs. Howard continued. "Quite an adorable little thing. You must quite dote on her. There is nothing like a baby to cheer one's days."

"Yes, ma'am," Jane replied, feeling the dangerous march of tears up her throat. She darted a quick look at Anthony. He was watching her intently, and it was clear he comprehended her distress with devastating clarity.

Mrs. Howard was still going on about Emily. "I gather Mrs. Barrett's interesting condition is the reason she and Mr. Barrett did not come to visit at Christmas. She is due to take to her bed sometime in late March, I believe."

The tears were in Jane's eyes now, threatening to spill. *Last March, I was awaiting Maria's child,* she thought dismally. *This March I will be awaiting Emily's.*

Lady Dent made a disparaging noise. "Obviously, *Mr.* Barrett wasted no time. They were only married in July!"

Mrs. Howard pointedly ignored her. "Now I understand why Catherine is so keen to go to Town for the Season," she said with a smile. "I think she does not trust Emily to safely deliver a baby without her being by her side to see that it is done right!" She broke off and peered at her. "Jane, whatever is the matter?"

"Ma'am," Anthony said suddenly, pointedly re-entering the conversation and drawing Mrs. Howard's attention to himself, "do you ladies plan to travel to Town for the Season as well?

"We usually venture there to shop," Lady Dent said gruffly. "For a few weeks, at least. I have a house in Curzon Street."

"Why do you ask, sir?" said Mrs. Howard.

"I think Lady Jane and I might travel to the great metropolis as well."

This was news to Jane. She turned to stare at him, her tears forgotten. He flashed her an undecipherable look, but then he smiled at her, and Jane's whole body relaxed. If Anthony were at her side, she could welcome Emily's baby with equanimity. Indeed, if he were at her side, she could welcome a hundred babies that were not hers and still not falter.

"And will your sister travel with you, Mr. Winston?" Mrs. Howard asked.

"I do not know, ma'am. Travel is difficult for her."

Mrs. Howard nodded. "Yes, that is why Ada and I are eager to meet her while we are here today. My nephew has told us all about her and sings her praises very highly."

"Forgive me, ma'am. Your nephew?"

"She means Matthew," Jane interjected. "Mrs. Howard is his aunt."

"Ah, I see. Well, ma'am, I am surprised you have not already made Georgiana's acquaintance. Is she not to be found downstairs?"

"She is out taking a ride with Matthew at the moment," Jane told him quietly.

"Georgiana is out for a ride? But Georgiana hates to go for rides."

"Well, she seemed quite eager to take this one."

"Poor chit!" Lady Dent murmured lugubriously. "Young Matt means to pop the question today, and no doubt she is fool enough to have him." She added in a slightly less mournful tone, "Though as husbands go, he will probably be better than most."

Jane looked at Anthony. His face was once again completely shuttered.

"Ada!" Mrs. Howard expostulated. *"That was supposed to be confidential!"*

Lady Dent thrust her chin in Anthony's direction. "Fellow's her brother. Doesn't he have a right to know?" Mrs. Howard's thin lips clamped tightly shut, and she scowled at her friend fiercely. Lady Dent scowled back.

Anthony was now staring off into space, seemingly not listening to any of them. Jane wondered how he felt about his sister being courted by Matthew Elton. Did he disapprove? He had had little enough opportunity to see how happy Matthew made her, or how Georgiana's face lit up every time he walked into a room.

"Well, I think he will make her an excellent husband," Jane said, trying to reassure him.

"Speaking of husbands," Lady Dent said, fixing Jane with a beady stare, "when are the two of you to be leg-shackled? I listened carefully in church Sunday, but I did not hear the preacher mention you. Did I miss it—the first banns, I mean?"

Jane had an urge to succumb to the vapors. "Ma'am, we have not yet set a date—"

"Goodness, Ada!" Mrs. Howard snapped. "Poor Mr. Winston is still recovering from his wounds! And in any case, since when are you so eager to see any lady hurried to the altar? You are usually the one urging her to cry off!"

Suddenly, Jane sensed Anthony's attention snap back to them with a vengeance. "Is that why you have come today, ma'am?" Anthony said, addressing Lady Dent. "To urge Jane to cry off our engagement?" His voice was cool and smooth and exceedingly polite, but there was an edge to it so sharp, Jane flinched. "If so, you have the right of it," he continued. "I do not think she realizes how poor a bargain she has struck."

Both ladies were leaning a little back in their chairs now, eyeing him warily.

"Anthony," Jane murmured in a low, imploring tone.

But he would not look at her. She watched the sharp rise and fall of his chest and ached with the desire to do something, anything to fix what was wrong between them. But how could she fix something she did not even understand?

"Ladies, I am sorry. I think our visit has wearied Mr. Winston beyond bearing. Let us go see if Georgiana is back from her ride."

She herded the silent ladies out of the room and cast one yearning look back at her beloved, but he was staring fixedly out the window.

Georgiana watched as Doctor Elton spread a fourth blanket on the ground. The January sun was shining through a thin layer of clouds and the temperature was quite mild. The snow from the big storm had melted and the ground was brown and bare and dry, but still he fretted she would catch cold. Finally, he came and lifted her out of the dog cart and carried her over to her woolen throne. When he sat down next to her, she smiled.

"This was a very fine idea, Doctor Elton. It is such a beautiful day and I am so very happy to be outside—with you."

"And I with you, my dear Miss Winston," he said, his voice oddly deep.

Something about his voice made Georgiana's stomach feel quite odd. She looked at his face, trying to rid herself of this sudden nervous feeling, but though his dear freckled face looked quite the same, the intent expression in his dark eyes made the nervous feeling grow rather than diminish. She wanted to look away, but could not. "Doctor Elton?"

"Yes, Miss Winston."

"I am feeling a little strange."

"Are you?" he said softly. "How so?"

"I feel all ... fluttery inside. And my skin feels hot, though I can feel that the breeze is cool when it blows against my skin."

"And how do you feel when I do this?" He lifted her hand and kissed the inside of her wrist between the edge of her glove and the cuff of her pelisse, where her skin was bare. She trembled. Slowly he folded her glove back, his lips brushing caressing strokes against each bit of skin as he exposed it, until her whole hand was bare and had been kissed. Then his tongue began flicking soft little circles in her palm.

Her eyes closed. Slowly, the warm, wet, mesmerizing circles began to slow, until his mouth was absolutely still in the center of her palm. He pressed one last kiss there. Then his mouth was gone. She opened her eyes, startled by the sudden withdrawal of his lips.

"Doctor Elton?

"Matthew, Miss Winston. Please call me Matthew."

"Matthew, that was ... very nice. Might we do it again?"

He laughed. "Of course! But first I have a question to ask you."

"You do?"

"Yes, I do. If I had planned this better, I would have had you up on a higher perch, but you will just have to imagine looking down on my bowed head as I kneel at your feet."

"Goodness, Matthew, why should I ever do such a thing?"

"Because my darling Georgiana, I am about to ask you to marry me."

"Truly?" she whispered, feeling quite overwhelmed.

"Truly, my dear. Will you have me?"

She nodded, unable to speak.

His warm arms came round her, and he lifted her onto his lap. "Now what is the matter? I am unused to this sort of silence from you."

"I am j-just so h-h-happy," she said before bursting into tears.

He was quite patient with her blubbering. He held her close and rocked her and offered her his huge handkerchief, which had been nicely laundered since last she used it.

"Matthew, may I ask you a question?"

He grinned at her. "Ah, now I know you are back to normal. What would you like to ask me?"

She peered at his face, scrutinizing it carefully. "You are not proposing to me because you feel you must, are you?"

He frowned.

"I understand that when you teach me to walk again you will need to handle my limbs quite a bit, more than is really respectable I suppose, but I do not mind. I would not expect you to marry me because of it —"

"My darling little skeptic." His husky tone set her stomach to fluttering again. "I am sorely tempted to handle your limbs this very moment, for they are such beautiful limbs." He took a long, shuddering breath. "But in answer to your question, no, I am not asking you to marry me for propriety's sake. I am asking you, because —"

"Yes, Matthew?"

"Because I adore you, you exasperating poppet! Now may I please kiss you properly, before I explode?"

"Of course, dearest Matthew!"

His strong arms drew her closer. Her eyes closed, then snapped open again, as she had an anxious thought. "You were indulging in hyperbole, dearest, were you not? A gentleman deprived of a kiss is not truly in danger of—"

Her words were cut off.

A considerable time later she rubbed her cheek against the soft silk of his waistcoat and murmured contentedly, "Goodness! I never knew kissing could be like that. I feel like a bottle of champagne that has had its cork plucked out and has fizzed all over the place."

For some reason, he groaned. "Darling, I fear that is not a metaphor I find particularly helpful at the moment."

"Is something wrong? Is there anything I can help you with?"

He made an odd, choking noise. Then he pressed a sweet kiss upon her hair. "Do not fret my love. It is nothing that a long dip in a cold pond will not solve."

"You are jesting, my love, are you not? I would not wish you to catch cold!"

He began to laugh. "Oh, Georgiana. Life with you will never be dull."

For a moment, she was affronted, for she hated to think that he was laughing at her, but she felt so cozy nestled against his chest and so happy with his strong arms holding her tight, that she decided to be forgiving. "Matthew?"

"Yes, my love."

"How long will it take for me to be able to stand—even just a little?"

"I do not know, sweetheart. I would guess several months."

"That long?"

"I know it is difficult to be patient, but—"

"It is just that I would dearly like to be able to stand at our wedding."

"Oh, my love! If that is your wish, then of course we must wait!"

"Yes, I suppose we must," she said sadly.

He pushed her a little away from his chest and looked into her face. "I am very gratified by your eagerness to wed. I am eager, too.

However, my greatest wish is for you to be happy. If waiting means you can stand at our wedding, I am well content to wait."

"Thank you, dear Matthew. You are right; we should wait. I was being foolish. I suppose I was too swayed by your kissing."

"My kissing?"

"Yes, you see, I thought that if your kissing could make me feel so exceedingly fine, then—well, it occurred to me that what we would be doing during our honeymoon —"

"Georgiana," he said sternly, "do not even consider following that train of thought to its conclusion, or I will have to hie me to the nearest pond this very instant, I swear!"

"Devil take it, Matthew! What is this sudden obsession with ponds?"

"Never you mind, my dear. I see I must distract you. What other wishes do you have about your wedding?"

Georgiana suddenly felt wistful. "It is not practicable."

"What?"

"It cannot happen."

"Tell me!"

"I would so like to dance with you."

"My dearest! Shall we dance now?"

"Please, Matthew, do not tease—not about this."

"My heart. I would never do that." He lifted her up in his arms and began humming, then singing to her.

"Matthew, I never knew you had such a beautiful voice!"

He began spinning her around as if they were waltzing. She wrapped her arms around his neck and laid her head on his shoulder. "Oh, promise me that we shall dance like this at our wedding!"

"I promise, my dearest. Truly, I promise."

Chapter 22

Anthony reached the end of the garden walk and turned, ready to march back the way he had come. Elton had set Anthony the task of an hour's walk each day to increase his stamina. If he did this for a week, *perhaps* he would be permitted astride a horse. Anthony was desperate to ride, so here he was, like an obedient child, performing his first day of required pacing. It rankled to have to seek permission to do something he had been doing since he was a lad out of short pants, but it was Ryde's stable and Ryde had given strict orders that no horse was to be saddled for him unless Elton gave the order.

Grinding his teeth, Anthony marched.

He tried to keep his thoughts fixed on his need to exercise, but all too soon his thoughts flicked back to Jane. He had spent a week trying to distance himself from her, trying to push her to see the folly of an engagement based on a lie. But despite his forced indifference, despite his increasingly uncertain temper, despite the fact that he fought with every ounce of his strength to keep her at arms' length, his effort was in vain. Loving Jane was like sinking into a bog. The more he struggled to free himself, the more quickly and deeply he fell.

Anthony marched more quickly, wishing he had a sword with which to take a few slashing whacks at the shrubbery or a pistol to knock down a few branches from a passing tree. He was still haunted by her face yesterday—when Elton's aunt had spoken of another woman's baby. Anthony had seen the pain in her face and had wanted to kneel at her feet and wrap his arms around her and beg her to be happy.

Suddenly a golden-haired lady wearing a warm-looking pelisse and a blue bonnet, which she held onto firmly in the strong January wind, stepped into his path. "Hello, Mr. Winston."

"Hello, Lady Alex. What are you doing out here in the cold?"

"I was searching for you. Our holiday is at an end. Godfrey and I and the twins are returning home. I came to bid you goodbye."

He was touched. "That was exceedingly kind of you, Lady Alex. I will be sorry to see you go, and I wish you and your family a safe journey."

She smiled at him, but her eyes looked troubled. "Sir, I wish you did not speak of kindness as if it were a thing quite foreign to your experience. It is not that out of the way for a sister to wish a brother goodbye before leaving."

"But we are not—" Then he stopped and made her a small bow. "I still value the gesture, whether it is in the common way or not."

"Then I am glad I made it." She reached out and touched his arm. "Mr. Winston, my husband and I make our home in London. If you should ever need our assistance, I hope you will not hesitate to contact us. My brother can supply you our direction. I do wish the best for you and Jane, and I look forward—very eagerly—to the news that you are wed." She was watching him closely now, as if searching for an answer to some puzzle.

He avoided her eyes. "Thank you, ma'am, for your very kind offer. Jane is very fortunate indeed in her sisters."

"As we are in her." Frowning slightly, the lady turned to go. "You know, Mr. Winston," she called back over her shoulder as she went. "It is possible to be *too* noble. I hope you will not fall into that trap."

Two days later, Anthony was once again taking his constitutional in the garden when he turned to find a figure waiting for him on the path. This time the lady had dark hair and was wearing a bright scarlet redingote at the very height of fashion. Anthony wondered if his host should consider naming his gravel path "The Sister Walk" for it seemed Anthony did nothing but discover Jane's sisters there.

"Good morning, Lady Charlotte."

"Good morning, Mr. Winston." Her voice was wary. "I have come to bid you goodbye."

Anthony felt a pang. Farthingsgate was a sore trial to him at the moment, but the one thing that comforted him about the place was how full it was of the St. John family. The affection and vitality of the boisterous clan gave the large and intimidating house a sense of friendliness and warmth. But now one by one they were leaving. "I am sorry to hear that, Lady Charlotte," he said with genuine feeling.

She cocked her head slightly to one side. "You are?"

"Of course, but I wish you and your husband a safe journey."

"Thank you, sir, and I wish you ..." Her voice trailed off. She took a step forward and seized his hand. "You know, Mr. Winston, your sister *is* very clever, but I would not mind having her as a sister. She is a pretty little thing, and it would be a pleasure to take her to Town and dress her and take her about in my lovely little phaeton. It would have been excellent fun to find her a husband as well, but Matthew has stolen a march on us on that front, so I will have to give up my matchmaking ambitions." She gazed up into his face and flashed him a faintly anxious smile. "But planning a wedding is almost as pleasant—two weddings, I mean! Oh, Mr. Winston!" she exclaimed, a sudden catch in her voice. "There are to be *two* weddings, aren't there?"

For some reason, she was impossible to lie to. "I begin to think that it might be best if there is only one, Lady Charlotte."

"Oh, no sir, you are wrong!" Unbelievably, her green eyes filled with tears. "You are quite, quite wrong."

"That is kind of you to say, Lady Charlotte."

"It is not kind. It is right! You and Jane belong together. That is the proper ending to the story."

"Story, Lady Charlotte? What story?"

She looked chagrined. "That night Jane first visited your sister—the night you were attacked—Jane asked me to tell her about you and Lady Regina. About how you ..." Her voice trailed away.

"Kidnapped the lady?" he offered tightly.

Her mouth crumpled. "I did not know you then, sir. I told her the whole tale. It made Jane ... cry. I am sorry I made her cry. But then you were attacked, and Jane refused to leave your side, and the betrothal turned real, and it seemed the story was to have a fine, romantic ending. Only now Jane wanders around looking lost, and you march around looking angry, and I would like to fix things, only I haven't the faintest idea how!"

He gazed down at her. "It is kind of you to want to help, Lady Charlotte but some things cannot be fixed."

"Oh," she said dismally. She released his hand and turned away. "So it is true. You *do* still love her."

His chest felt tight. "Yes, if you must know, I do—"

But Lady Charlotte had already wandered despondently away, her voice floating back to him. "And now she is a widow—and free."

Anthony stared after the lady, perplexed. *Free?* It was a true description of Jane—at least, how he should think of her, but it was odd for Lady Charlotte to describe her so. He suddenly had an uncomfortable notion that there had been a misunderstanding.

He started after her, but Elton had been canny about his limitations. Anthony could not get his legs to move half as quickly as he wished them to, while the lady walked at an extremely fast clip. She was still talking to herself. Anthony strained to hear what she was saying.

"Jane *said* he must love her quite desperately to do such a thing!"

Anthony's chest was starting to ache rather alarmingly, but he tried to speed up. Instead, he began to slow.

"It is not as if Lady Regina is *that* much prettier than Jane!"

What the hell? Anthony tried to speed up a second time, but now his knees began to buckle beneath him. Devil take the woman! Was she Atalanta come back to life? Her voice was now so faint, he could barely make out her words: "I suppose *that* is the reason he is so determined to venture to Town for the Season."

Anthony tried to soldier on, but his lungs were on fire. He paused to catch his breath. He could no longer hear any of Lady Charlotte's mutterings. After his breathing had steadied and his heart had slowed enough that he did not fear it would jump from his chest, he continued along the path until he reached the point where the house was again visible. He scanned from left to right, searching for the red-clad figure, but she was nowhere to be seen. There was only a carriage preparing to start off down the drive.

Sensing it was important to clear up the misunderstanding as quickly as possible, Anthony started toward the carriage, but he was too late. He raised his arm to signal it to halt, but Lady Charlotte and her husband merely waved goodbye as the carriage rolled by.

꙳

Lady Maria came to make her farewell in the library. Anthony had set down his book and was pacing the room. Outside, it was snowing, and Anthony was surprised how much his body missed its daily exercise along The Sister Walk. As he stalked about the room, he came across a curio case full of miniature paintings of the family. He gazed down at the one of Jane, trying not to smile at the sweet expression on her face. Then his gaze passed to the next portrait in the case and all desire to smile vanished.

The painting was of an excessively handsome young man with chestnut hair and haughty brown eyes. Anthony had the uncomfortable feeling the fellow was looking down his nose at him. He could not know who the man was, yet he felt an uncomfortable certainty nevertheless, especially when he noted the small black ribbon tied in a knot through the ring at the top of the frame.

Lady Maria came up behind him. "Yes, that is Jane's Bevin."

"He looks quite full of himself."

Lady Maria chuckled. "Between you, me, and the bedpost—he was. But Jane loved him, so we put up with him and tried not to mind his arrogant ways."

Anthony was surprised how much it hurt to hear that Jane had loved her asinine husband. He knew it to be true, yet somehow he had managed to push the knowledge into a far corner of his mind. "Was he good to her?" he asked. He had already made up his own mind on the matter, but he was curious to hear Lady Maria's opinion.

She seemed to weigh her words. "I believe Jane thought he was."

"What do you mean?"

"He was fond of her, in his way. He did the usual things that courting gentlemen do, and Jane felt admired. But as a husband, he never truly put her first—in anything. He would be kind enough to her, but only as an afterthought, like patting a dog on the head as one heads out the door."

"Jane did not mind such treatment?"

"She did not know any better. Bevin was the only serious suitor she had before she married. She never had anyone to compare him to."

"You cannot be serious!" he exclaimed in disbelief.

Lady Maria gave him a warm smile. "I am glad *you* appreciate how wrong it was. Bevin never did. He always believed that Jane had been most fortunate that he had taken an interest in her when no other gentleman would. Sadly, Jane believed it, too."

Anthony swore. "Forgive my language, Lady Maria."

"You are forgiven, Mr. Winston. To be honest, there were times I felt like swearing myself over the matter. Unfortunately, Jane was the first of us to enter the marriage mart, and since my father was still alive then, she bore the brunt of society's disapprobation."

"I do not understand, ma'am."

"My father's reputation made things very hard for her."

"Your father's reputation?"

"Mr. Winston, have you never made the connection? Our father was *Wild Ryde.*"

He stared at her for a long time in silence, wondering who Jane's asinine gentleman was now. *Good God. She had been saddled with this sort of misery* twice. "I suppose I should have realized, Lady Maria, from your brother's title, only your brother is so very—"

One fair eyebrow rose. "Proper?"

"Indeed. That is just the word. It makes it difficult to imagine him associated with anything—or anyone—exceptionable. I gather he is very different from your father?"

"Poor Drew has always held himself to a ridiculously high standard because he is much more like our late father in temperament than he ever wished to admit. Fortunately, Catherine has made him very happy, and she has taken a great deal of the starch out of him." Lady Maria turned to face him. "And now, sir, I would like to see my sister happy." She paused, flashing him a kind but faintly reproving look. "Can you not tell me what is the matter between you two?"

Anthony gazed at her consideringly. "I might speak, ma'am, if I knew our discussion would be confidential. But you are Jane's sister. As fine as your principles may be, it will be difficult to keep secret what she will no doubt try to pry from you."

She scowled. "Why must gentlemen be so coy!" she exclaimed in irritation. "Very well, sir, you have my word. I swear. I will not repeat anything you say—to anyone."

"Thank you, ma'am. You are an honorable lady. I know I can trust your oath."

She flashed him a look full of impatience. "Speak, man! Speak. What has caused this ruction between you and Jane?"

"She lied to me, ma'am," he said simply.

"How dare you, sir! Jane is no prevaricator!"

"She feels she owes me a debt. She blames herself for the attack on my person."

"That is nonsense!"

"I agree, ma'am. But Jane believes it to be true. She thinks to discharge this debt by marrying me. I suspect you are aware of my feelings for your sister, so I will not enter into them here. Let us simply say that no matter what I feel, I do not find the notion of such a payment... pleasing."

"Sir, you are mistaken. Jane reciprocates your affection."

He shook his head. "No, ma'am," he said crisply. *"That* is the lie."

For a moment, Lady Maria—calm, reserved, proper Lady Maria—looked as if she wished to box his ears. "Oh, sir, I regret ever agreeing to that devil's oath of yours! You mean to do something completely stupid, do you not?"

"I mean to follow your advice, ma'am."

"My advice?" she spluttered.

"I mean to take Jane to Town and face down the gossips, ma'am."

"And?" she snapped angrily.

"And, in the process, I mean to convince Jane just what a poor bargain she has struck. But I will need your help ma'am."

"What makes you think I mean to help you in this mischief?"

"I want to make sure that when I give Jane cause to break our engagement, all blame accrues to me—and to me only—and she is held blameless by the *ton*. That will be your job."

Lady Maria's mouth had dropped open. She snapped it shut. "You expect me to blacken your already blackened name—"

"For your sister's sake, ma'am."

"Oh, Mr. Winston, I could shake you!"

"All I ask is that you help me."

Her eyes narrowed. "And if I do not?"

"Then I may have to resort to more... drastic means to achieve my end."

"Sir, you make my blood run cold."

"But will you do it?"

Her mouth twisted into a frown of deep disapproval. "You have me between the devil and the deep blue sea, sir. What choice do I have?

Chapter 23

As Anthony approached his accustomed turn in The Sister Walk, he saw a shadow flicker past his vision. Someone was coming up behind the high yew hedge that lined the path here. Anthony wondered who it could be. There were no more St. John sisters to bid him farewell. Lady Maria had been gone three days now. The only St. John sister remaining in the place was Jane, and she had, of late, taken to avoiding his company with more determination and skill than he had ever managed when trying to avoid hers. But the figure that now appeared was not a lady at all. It was Ryde. Anthony was startled and alarmed by the grim look on his face. "Sir, what is it? Tell me nothing has happened to your sister!"

"She is well." Ryde paused. "I have had news of the two men who attacked you."

Anthony looked at the anguished planes of the other man's face and the haunted look in his eyes. "The magistrate did not come down on the side of mercy," he said quietly.

Ryde shook his head, looking faintly dazed. "They were hanged this morning."

"I am sorry, sir."

Ryde regarded him in surprise. "You truly are, aren't you?"

"Yes."

Ryde sighed, and his gaze grew unfocused. "I fear I am to blame.

My anger burned so fiercely during that first interview with Sir Henry. I was so extravagant in my calls for vengeance. Matthew warned me to consider and be cool—but I have ever been so ... *uncontrolled.* " His eyes closed.

"Sir, those men fixed their own fate. You are not culpable in the least."

"I keep imagining: if only I had been more careful in my watch over Jane, if only I had heeded Matthew's warnings, if only—"

"Enough!" Anthony snapped crisply, clasping the other man's shoulders and giving him a slight shake. "If only, if only, if only! Those are the two words most quickly guaranteed to drive any thinking man to madness. Ryde, you must trust me in this. What is done is done! You cannot change it by wishing. You cannot fix it by grieving. If you truly feel a sense of responsibility, then put your energy into assisting their widows and orphans. It does no good for you to torture yourself by looking back. There is only one path. You must go forward."

Ryde was staring at him now, but he no longer looked dazed, and some of the color was back in his cheeks.

"Does Jane know the news yet?" Anthony asked.

"No," Ryde said grimly. "I must tell her, though how I will manage it, I do not know. I had hoped to have Catherine at my side, but she is feeling indisposed."

Again? It occurred fleetingly to Anthony that Lady Ryde had been suffering indispositions quite frequently these last two weeks. Then his thoughts snapped back to Jane. The words were out of his mouth, before he could consider their folly: "Sir, *I* will tell your sister the news."

Ryde's relief was plain. "Thank you, Winston. I am most grateful."

Anthony had searched most of the house for Jane. Instead, he found his sister tucked away before the fire in the library. "Georgiana, do you have any notion where—what the devil is that?"

She looked up with a pleased expression. "It is a contraption Matthew fashioned to help me strengthen my legs. I pretend I am skating and push the little blocks of wood forward and back with my feet. Is it not clever?"

He considered the device. "Yes, but I hope it does not tire you too much."

"I like the feeling of growing tired. I had not realized how much I dislike being still. It was slowly driving me mad." She paused and regarded him closely. "But you did not come here to discuss Matthew's contraption or my state of fatigue. Did you wish something?"

"Yes, do you have any notion where Jane can be?"

"You are looking for her?" Her tone of amazement made his temper flare.

"Yes! What is so surprising in that?"

"Nothing, except you have been at such pains to avoid her this past fortnight."

"Georgiana! Must your eye be so keen and your tongue so blunt?"

"I am sorry, Anthony, though I am hardly the only one to have noticed. As for my tongue—you are right, I must learn to control it. Matthew sorely teases me about it." She did not seem vexed, however, for her mouth slipped back into its familiar besotted grin.

"Georgie, I asked you if you knew where Jane could be," he reminded her.

"Have you tried the nursery?"

"The nursery! But the boys are gone and so is baby Ada."

His sister nodded. "But I think you should look there all the same."

As it proved, his sister was right. Anthony walked into the small, cheerful room full of battered toys and faded wallpaper to find Jane perched on a small chair. She was staring out at the austere February landscape, baby Ada's forgotten doll hugged tightly to her chest.

Anthony's own chest tightened.

He had last seen the doll a week ago, when he had come upon Jane and the small tot playing a sort of game. The baby would fling the doll to the ground with a cooing giggle, and Jane would scoop it back up and thrust it back into the baby's chubby fingers, telling the child what a fine, strong arm she had. He had watched them unobserved for nearly five minutes before Jane had looked up and caught him at it. He had quickly excused himself and fled, but the memory had stuck to him like a burr. "You miss the little imp, don't you?"

She spun around abruptly, almost toppling from the chair. There was a look of acute embarrassment on her face. "Anthony!"

"I am sorry if I startled you. I came to see if you would be willing to keep me company while I finish my required perambulation along The Sister Wa—in the garden."

"You wish my company?" she exclaimed, sounding as surprised as Georgiana had.

He pressed his lips together to force his temper down. "Yes," he finally said. "Will you join me?"

"Yes, of course." She rose to her feet. "Let me fetch a bonnet and pelisse."

"Make sure they are warm ones. The snow has melted, but the wind blows cold."

"Do not fear. Andrew has given me a new pelisse that is entirely lined in fur. It is so warm, I am sure I could wade through drifts a yard high and not notice."

Her words conjured up a flurry of memories. To his chagrin, she seemed quite aware of the direction of his thoughts, for she came forward and touched his arm. "Forgive me, Anthony. I did not mean to remind you of something you perhaps wish to forget." Before he could tell her that he had no wish to forget anything, she hurried off toward the door. "I will meet you downstairs as quickly as I can."

She was as good as her word. As they walked outside, he offered her his arm, and she took it, and he felt dangerously happy as he placed his other hand atop hers, locking her to him as they strolled along.

"I am glad to have this opportunity to speak with you," she said, when they had gone some way and were about to enter The Sister Walk. "I wished to tell you that I have spoken to Ryde, and he has agreed to take me to London in three days' time."

"I thought I was to take you!" he exclaimed, feeling aggrieved.

"Anthony, you are not yet fit to travel, and I have had another letter from poor Mrs. Chester. Her situation grows more dire, and I feel I cannot postpone any longer."

"Of course, I am fit to travel! All that is required of me is to sit in a cursed carriage for hours on end. It will not be any different from how I spend all my days of late, eternally on my——"

"*Anthony!*"

He grinned at her. He had forgotten how wonderful it was to tease her. "And have you actually explained your purpose in going to London to your brother?"

"Not yet. But——"

"You do realize that you will give the poor man an apoplexy?"

She scowled at him, which made him feel even happier. "It will not be as bad as that."

"No? Let us imagine the conversation. Dearest brother, I wish to visit the great metropolis so I may supply money to my dead husband's mistress, because my fool of a husband did not properly provide for her maintenance before he went to his great reward."

Jane actually stopped and stomped her foot. The sound of her half-boot impacting the gravel rang out like a pistol shot. "Sir! Why are you being so abominable?"

"Because it is one of the great joys of my life to provoke you." He felt oddly giddy.

"Then you must be as delirious with happiness as a drunkard in Bacchus's garden!"

"Now that you mention it, I do feel a bit intoxicated," he said, feeling a sudden impulse so strong it made his heart pound.

"Why do you have that strange look on your face?" Her voice was wary.

"Probably because I have such an excellent imagination."

"What does that have to do with anything?"

"I can imagine quite precisely how good it will feel to do this." He turned her to face him and bent his head to kiss her. He had caught her off guard. Her lips were still parted in surprise. He brushed his mouth against their warmth and slipped his tongue between them, caressing them into parting still further. He wanted her to open to him completely.

He had intended to be gentle. But it was wonderful to be kissing her with unbruised lips, and he had missed her mouth, and he became obsessed with questing for the taste of her against the warm, wet pressure of her tongue. His lips became more insistent. Again he became obsessed with pressure, but this time it was the rhythmic kneading of her lips, the push and the pull, the arc and twist, the parry and thrust of her flesh yielding to his. He wanted her surrender. He needed it. Now.

She made a soft sound.

For a moment, he could not comprehend the shimmering boundary between self and other. He and Jane were spiraled together so tightly he could not make a motion or take a breath that was separate. Yet somehow the sound started a wave, and the wave began an unraveling, and the unraveling sent him hurtling upwards, surfacing and gasping for air.

Her chest was heaving just as hard as his was.

For a moment, he took savage pleasure in the fact. Then the thought that had been circling round and round his oblivious mind became comprehensible.

She does not love you.

He was a fool.

For a moment, he could not bear to completely separate from her. He leaned his forehead against hers—waiting for his heart to slow, his breath to steady, his blood to stop simmering with the need to touch her. "I suppose I should apologize for that."

"Do not," she said sharply. "Please. Do not!" He was startled by her vehemence.

"I should not have let myself get distracted. I brought you out here to tell you something—something I wish you did not have to hear. If I promise to behave myself, will you walk with me a little farther?"

Jane pushed back against his chest, and looked into his face. "You mean to break our engagement," she declared flatly.

He stated at her, totally nonplussed. Here was his chance. After two long weeks, she had handed it to him without a fight. With a kiss. A kiss that still trembled through him. A kiss that made him weak. A kiss that made him desperate not to give her up.

I am a fool.

He would pay for this moment of frailty. He knew he would pay. But he could not do it. Not now. He told himself it was because of the terrible news he still had to give her. But he knew that was a lie. A desperate, prevaricating, face-saving lie. The truth was: he was not ready. He was like a wounded man going before the surgeon to have his leg off. He knew it was going to happen, knew it was as fated as the sun setting into night, but still he had to beg for one more day.

He took her hands in his. "No, my dearest, it is not that. Please, walk with me."

Her blue eyes, strangely dark and shining from the cold—surely it was the cold and not tears?—closed. Once again, their foreheads touched, and he wished he could stand like this forever. Then she drew away, slipped her hand in his, and turned.

"Yes, Anthony. I am ready."

So they walked. He led her to the very end of The Sister Walk, to a small stone bench he had wistfully contemplated each day during his pacing. Just as he always did in his daydreams, he led her to the bench and sat her down and took his place next to her. But he did not slide his arms around her, and he did not kiss her, and he did not lay his coat on the ground and lift her onto it and cover her in his warmth and make her once and truly his. He simply sat there next to her on the cold stone bench holding her hand.

He told her the news of the two men who had died that morning and would never see another night. To his surprise, she did not flinch or exclaim or even move. He wondered at her equanimity, until he looked down into her white face. His heart lurched in his chest. He knew that sightless look, knew that frozen demeanor. He had seen it times uncounted on the faces of men in shock, contemplating the carnage of the battlefield. But he had never had to endure it on the face of someone he loved.

"Jane—my Jane! *Look at me!*"

It took her a long time to obey—a frighteningly long time. He jerked her onto his lap, chafed her hands, wrapped his arms around her, and turned his back as a break to the wind so she would not have to deal with the cold when the trembling began.

The storm, when it broke, was intense but mercifully brief. He rocked her and squeezed her so tightly he feared he would bruise her, but he knew bruises would be easier to bear than the soul-numbing, trembling cold. After a while, she relaxed in his arms, and he could feel the warmth begin to flow into her again. He wished he had his strength back and could carry her to the house in his arms, but he knew he would falter. So he simply held her on the bench waiting for her own strength to return, and cursed his idiocy in delivering such news to her out in a cold garden instead of before a warm fire. Eventually, she took a long shuddering breath and raised her head.

"Anthony?"

"Yes. You are restored?"

She gave a faint nod. "Can you forgive me?"

For a long, fogged moment he thought she was asking forgiveness for her lie—for pretending that she loved him. He panicked. He was no longer angry with her for the falsehood. That safety had fled. Now, he simply clung to the lie—a drowning man hugging his pitiful, waterlogged plank of wood. He was not ready to have her take it away.

"Anthony, did you hear me? I want to know if you can forgive me for grieving over those two men after—after the terrible things they did to you." She reached up and touched a new scar he sported on his cheek.

He sank back against the firm support of the bench and gazed up in satisfaction at the blueness of the sky. The sun had emerged from behind a cloud. Somewhere, a bird actually began to trill. "Do not fret, my dearest Jane. Do not fret. At this moment, I could grieve for them myself. They are not here to enjoy the beauty of this day."

He squeezed her hand. "And I am."

Chapter 24

As Jane gazed out the window of the rented post-chaise she and Anthony were traveling in, she heard a loud horn sound on the road behind them. *Good!* she thought wearily. Perhaps having the mail coach upon his tail would prod their laggard of a coachman into increasing his speed. She had been expecting their arrival at The White Boar, the hostelry where they were to spend the night, for hours. Anthony was looking grey and worn, and she did not feel particularly well herself. The springs of the post-chaise were old and stiff, and though they moved at a snail's pace along the rutted road, the rise and fall of the seat was reminiscent of a ship tossed by a stormy sea.

Still, the discomforts of the journey might have been easier for Jane to endure if she had been able to pass a few of the long hours in discourse with Anthony. However, beyond a few desultory remarks when they had first settled in their seats, he had spent most of the journey in taciturn silence. She had attempted to start any number of conversations on a variety of topics, but his monosyllabic responses had ground each one to a halt. She felt sorely aggrieved by this, for conversation with him was one of her keenest pleasures, the quicksilver give and take of their repartee almost as stimulating as his kisses.

She had never experienced that sort of exhilaration conversing with Bevin. Her late husband's address in public had always been adroit and polished. He had been hailed as quite a wit by his circle of friends, but he had never made *her* laugh. She had assumed that was because her sense of humor was odd. So often a thing had struck her as funny but had left him entirely unmoved. They had also never bantered. Bevin had hated to be teased—he had had far too much dignity for that—and it had certainly never occurred to him to tease her.

Yet what had truly proven a revelation to her in her discourse with Anthony was how he could skim along her thoughts with darting speed, following every twist and turn of her mind with effortless grace. When she and Bevin had spoken in private she had often fretted at the lags and digressions in their conversation, and she had frequently felt ashamed that her husband seemed to find her thoughts as strange and wild and impossible to navigate as a labyrinth.

The horn of the mail coach sounded once more behind them. It was closer now, but their own speed had not increased one jot. Jane sighed and cast a covert glance at Anthony.

He looked tense and uncomfortable, which was not surprising considering his position. Despite the chaise's narrow width, he had folded his long body so tightly onto his side of the bench, that he and Jane only made contact in three places: at the tip of his broad shoulders, the swell of her hips, and along the shared boundary of their thighs. Jane could well imagine the effort it had taken for him to maintain himself so rigidly against the jostling of the carriage hour after hour, but her sympathy was limited. If he thought by such heroics to spare her the temptation of wishing for his touch, he had failed abysmally.

Those three points of contact were more than sufficient to make her acutely, achingly conscious of his nearness every moment of the trip. If he would only talk to her, he would accomplish far more to maintain the propriety of her thoughts. But with nothing but the relentless motion of the carriage to distract her from her warm awareness of his body, those three points of contact were like so many flints sparking increasingly heated and licentious imaginings in her agitated mind.

Finally, she could take the silence no more. "I begin to think I erred in not making this journey with my brother," she grumbled. "He might have railed at me about Mrs. Chester, but he would not have left me in this oppressive silence."

To her disappointment, Anthony did not rise to this provocation, but instead said in a flat voice, "I apologize for having proven such a poor companion, my lady."

"Oh, do not 'my lady' me! That is just your polite way of wishing me to the devil!"

"I would never wish any such thing!" he snapped back angrily.

"Well, you obviously wish me somewhere far away. You must find my company tedious indeed if you cannot even look at me." Her voice was now as strident as her temper, but she could not seem to get either under control.

"That is ridiculous!"

"Is it?"

"Yes! I have simply been immersed in my own black thoughts!"

"Well, that is lowering information, for as black as they are, they seem to amuse you more than I do!"

"They amuse me not at all! They are an affliction!" His voice was now a roar.

"Still, not as great an affliction as my company appears to be!"

"Tell me, did you ever quiz that imbecile of a husband of yours as sorely as this when he neglected you to go off to his doxy?"

Jane's breath caught in her throat. It was as if he had suddenly slapped her. Where had her gallant Anthony gone—her knight errant who protected her from harm? The silence stretched between them as taut as a drum. Then his voice burst into the silence, "Jane, please! Forgive me! I should never have said such a thing." His voice was low and filled with remorse, but she could not look at him for fear she would burst into tears.

"You call him an imbecile, but it was I who played the fool. It is cruel of you, however, to fling my stupidity in my face."

"Jane, I wish you could see. *He did not deserve you!*"

"To the contrary, since you seem to hold us both in such contempt, I can only conclude we were a well-matched pair."

She heard him suck in his breath at that. She turned to stare out the window so he would not see the tears now filling her eyes, but despite her blurry vision she realized a surprising fact. At long last, their dilatory carriage had turned into the courtyard of The White Boar.

There was a loud knock on the door of Jane's chamber. She assumed it was someone with the dinner she had ordered. But it was not dinner. It was Anthony.

He stood on the threshold of her chamber looking much restored—too restored. He was wearing his beautiful green coat, the one whose shade perfectly matched his eyes, the one he had worn that night he had come to Farthingsgate to propose. His golden hair was well-brushed and sparkled in the candlelight. His face was grave and exceedingly repentant.

"I have come to apologize and to ask—no, to beg—that you will let me make amends by escorting you to dinner downstairs. I have bespoken a private parlor, and I promise that I will be so garrulous you will be tempted to plead a headache just to escape my inane chatter. Please, will you join me?"

What was she to do? It was impossible to remain angry with him—not with him standing there, looking like a naughty schoolboy desperate for forgiveness. Reluctantly, she agreed. However, all notion of childishness vanished the minute she took his arm. Despite his air of pliancy and affability, his body seemed to vibrate with a tension that made his proffered arm feel like an invitation to much more than a walk.

As they were forced closer together on the narrow stair, Jane realized just how overpowering his manly aura was tonight. She was tempted to swoon just to press herself against him. Fortunately for her dignity, they reached the lower floor quickly, and he once more drew away. But whatever magnetism was churning through him did not only affect her. As they passed through the crowded public rooms of the inn to reach their private parlor, Jane noticed every feminine eye swivel their way, and glancing back she saw more than one lady fan herself vigorously as she gazed after Anthony's retreating back, despite its being a crisp February evening.

When they reached their private parlor, Anthony was all solicitousness. He helped her to be seated, summoned the boy to bring their food, served up her plate himself, and poured her a small glass of wine. When he had done, and the boy was gone, and the door was closed, and she had taken her first few hungry bites of food, Jane looked up to find him watching her, his own food untouched.

"Sir, are you not hungry?"

He shook his head. Instead, he took a long drink of his wine. "I am sorry the trip has been such a miserable trial for you so far."

"Most of the unpleasantness has been no fault of yours."

Two bright spots of color appeared in his cheeks. "Only the worst of it, eh?'

She gave a tiny shrug. "Eat, sir! It will improve your disposition. It has already worked wonders on mine." She returned to her food.

He continued to watch her, taking sips of his wine without his gaze ever leaving her face. He did not say a word.

"I thought I was promised witty conversation."

He seemed to gather himself up. "Of course, my lady. What topic would you like?"

"Perhaps we can begin with you promising never to call me 'my lady' again for as long as we both shall live."

"I cannot," he said, pouring himself a second glass of wine.

"And why not?"

"Because you will always be 'my lady' in my heart."

Now *she* was the one unable to shift her gaze from the face across the table. That had been unfair of him, but oh so very sweet. "Anthony, please. Eat something!"

He did not even bother to refuse. He just ignored her. "And what topic now, my lady?"

He was so abysmally, achingly handsome. She stared at him in his fine green coat and had a sudden memory of him that very first night, when he had played Jack Flash all decked out in his military red. He had looked quite startlingly fine in his borrowed togs. How much more dazzling must he have looked in his real cavalry uniform? She was sorry she had never had a chance to see him in it.

"I am curious to know why you resigned your commission."

The sudden transformation of his face reminded her of that same night, when they had been dancing and she had glimpsed all the tumultuous feeling he was capable of in his eyes, only to have them go quite opaque, hiding... everything. Suddenly, not only his eyes but his entire face was as cleared of feeling and impossible to read as a painting on the wall.

He poured himself a third glass of wine. "You have seen the scar upon my chest," he remarked lightly. "Do you blame me for losing my nerve? A dear uncle left me an inheritance, and I no longer had to risk my life to maintain my life, so I resigned."

She laughed. She could not help it. It had not been a particularly droll answer, but it was such a ridiculous one, that she could not stop the humor bubbling in her chest. "No, sir, do not tease me. What was the true reason? I genuinely wish to know."

To her surprise, there was not a flicker of humor in his face. He stared at her. "That is the tale. Ask anyone who knows me. They will tell you."

She began to feel angry. "Anyone who knows you knows that cannot be the tale! Why are you so unwilling to tell me the truth?"

He blinked at her. Twice.

She had a sudden notion. Trying to hide her distress, she said lightly, "Do not tell me they forced you out over the matter of Lady Regina?"

His face relaxed, and he shook his head. "Do you think the War Office cares tuppence about society's tattle? As long as a man can sit his horse, keep his nerve, and kill a sufficient quantity of the enemy, any flaws in his character are of little matter to them." He took a deep drink of his wine, and added grimly, "Even if his soul ends up black beyond redemption."

Suddenly afraid, she reached across the table and seized his hand. "Anthony, why in the world should you fear for your soul?"

He blinked again but did not answer.

Her food forgotten, she rose and came around the table. She knelt beside him and put her arms around him. "Please, tell me."

He shook his head. "I could not bear to have you despise me."

"What foolishness that is! I could never despise you, no matter what passed between us or whatever you did." Impulsively, overcome with feeling, she laid her head in his lap. "You are my one true knight."

Slowly his arms crept round her, and his fingers twined in her hair. Little by little, his hold on her tightened, until she was lost in the warmth and safety of his embrace. But suddenly his strong fingers pushed her from him. "You must move away. Now!"

She lifted her head, startled. "Anthony! Whatever is the mat—" She stopped abruptly. His face—his whole beautiful face—was bright scarlet. She glanced down. It took her a moment to comprehend what she saw. Whenever she had seen Bevin in such a state, he had already been in her bed, unclothed, about his business. She looked away, certain her own face must now be as scarlet as his.

"Return to your chair!" he said through teeth that barely unclenched enough to get the sound out. She hurried to obey. She was sorry for his mortification, but a part of her wished she dared sneak a tiny look. She had never realized a man could experience such a thing when he was not actually in the act of—

Her hands flew up to her heated cheeks. "Anthony?"

"You are not the only one to wish this misbegotten journey had never begun! Finish your dinner, and I will take you back to your room."

"I am finished," she said, realizing she could not eat another bite. Her stomach was in a nervous whirl, and her head felt light and giddy.

So he offered her his arm and marched her back up to her room. This time his arm conveyed no thrilling vibration. It was as cold and unbending as a rod of iron. He bid her a curt goodbye at her door, and she watched him walk away. To her surprise, he headed back toward the stair that led down to the public rooms. He glanced back, and she quickly shut her door, but she remained standing by it for a long time, wondering. She had heard stories about public inns—about serving girls who sometimes served other needs as well. Had Anthony gone in search of such a woman to ease his need? The thought made her feel sick inside.

Slowly she began making her preparations for bed. She had left her maid behind at Farthingsgate, so she undressed herself and searched through her portmanteau for her nightdress. Before she slipped it over her head, she glanced at her reflection in the clouded mirror that stood to one side of the room. Had Anthony found her form pleasing when he had snuck his look in Bagshot's cottage, or were her charms the same as any naked woman would have for any gentleman? Would any woman do? Was Anthony off to put the matter to the test this very minute?

She tugged her nightgown on with trembling fingers and went to lie in bed, but she was too restless to stay there for long and began to pace the small room, thinking of Bevin, trying not to think of Anthony, wishing she had had the courage to invite him to her bed so he would not now be in search of pleasure elsewhere.

She began to cry.

How strange it was that the whole time she had been married to Bevin he had had a mistress, yet she now felt more pain and jealousy at the thought of Anthony spending one night in the arms of another woman then she had over Bevin's entire history of betrayal. What sort of woman was she? Anthony was not even her husband yet!

A sudden painful thought occurred to her. *What if he never was?*

What if the recent cooling of his affection meant he no longer wished to marry her? Three days ago she had been sure he meant to break things off. What if he had meant to, but had taken pity on her because of the terrible news about his two attackers. What if he were only waiting for a better time to cry off?

She would never know what it was like to lie with him—and she so wanted to know. Of late, it seemed to be almost all she could think of. When she had married Bevin, she had known nothing. When they had been newlyweds, she had hoped he would teach her things, but he had never seen the need, and after a while, she had been too embarrassed to ask. He had been patient with her—up to a point, but then he had gone on with what he was about, and she had managed as best she could. He had been dutiful at first, visiting her almost every night, but his visits had been brief and to the point and he had departed to his own chamber when he was done. She had never felt any great desire for him to linger and, as time went on, it had been more a relief than not when he had failed to visit her. She had assumed that was how relations were between man and wife. Of interest and a pleasure to the gentleman, an obligation to the lady, but a way for the lady to show her gentleman she loved him and was a good wife. Then Anthony had burst into her life, and she felt as if she were constantly on fire. What would it be like to wait in her bed for Anthony to come to her, for Anthony to touch her? The thought of it made her dizzy.

Suddenly, she heard a noise at her door. She crossed to it and listened warily. The sound was repeated. It was not quite a knock; it was more like tapping. "Jane? Oh, Jane! Are you there?" The words were spoken in a slurred whisper.

She slid back the lock and swung the door wide. *"Anthony?"*

He was listing almost sideways. "Sorry. Bit foxed. May I come in?"

Jane yanked him inside and closed the door. Even at the height of the laudanum, she had not seen him like this. He leaned heavily on her, and she had to use all her strength to keep the two of them upright. "What in heaven's name are you about?" she demanded.

"Had to ask you a question."

"How much have you had to drink?"

"A fair bit. Needed it. Had to drown my sorrows." He peered at her owlishly. "That ain't the question."

Jane didn't care about his question. If she didn't maneuver him into a seated position soon, they were both going to topple over onto the floor like two felled trees. He was so ridiculously large, she feared what damage he would do to his newly healed body if he fell so far. "Anthony, please! Let me get you into the chair!"

"Don't want to go anywhere 'til I've asked you," he said stubbornly.

"Very well, ask me!" she panted, managing to tip him slightly, but in the direction of the bed, not the chair.

"Dearest Jane," he enunciated carefully.

"Yes?" she gasped, managing to move him a few more feet by turning him, as if they were doing a very heavy, very awkward waltz.

"You don't truly think... I hold you... in contempt, do you?"

She turned him again. She had no breath left to speak. They were almost to the bed.

"Feel such deep... respect... for you, fair kills me to think you could. Think that, I mean." To emphasize the point, he threw his arms around her in an enthusiastic bear hug and lifted her up into the air. They both toppled backwards. Anthony landed on the mattress, and Jane landed on top of him, face down on his chest.

"*Whoops!*" he exclaimed cheerfully.

Once again, she had no breath to say anything, this time because it had been knocked out of her. She rolled to one side. After a few panicked gasps, she could breathe again.

"Where did you go?" he demanded. "Oh, *there* you are!" He pulled her back on top of him. "Oh, Jane, my Jane. Forgive me for what I said in the carriage. I was jealous, that's all. It is so unfair."

"Jealous?" she said, bewildered. "Jealous of whom? And what is unfair?"

"Your loving that bastard, but not loving me."

"But Anthony, I do love —"

"Too bad he's dead," he interrupted. "Would love to call him out. Pink him like I pinked Wild Bill." He grinned at her. Suddenly, his eyes narrowed. "You're not wearing any clothes."

"I am wearing a nightgown."

His hands slid down along her sides. "Thin thing. Feels like you don't have anything on underneath."

She did not answer, just closed her eyes and nestled against him with a sigh.

"Don't like it. Want to see you." With a sudden burst of energy he reached down and yanked her nightgown up, managing to pull it clean over her head and throw it on the floor in one fluid motion. He surveyed her, obviously pleased with himself. "That's better!"

"Anthony?" she asked in a small voice. "Shall I get beneath the covers now?"

"Why the devil should you do that?"

"So you can—I thought you wanted to . . ." her voice trailed away in mortification.

He peered at her. "Like lookin' at you, my beautiful Jane. Do you mind?"

"No, Anthony. I suppose not, though I do feel a little embarrassed."

"Silly to be 'barrassed. You're beautiful. In fact, think I'm going to kiss you now."

"Now?" she exclaimed, totally confused. "But you do not need to kiss me now. You already have my clothes off. That is why I asked—"

"Don't *need* to kiss you. *Want* to kiss you."

At first, Jane was so excruciatingly self-conscious, she could not enjoy it, though it was a lovely kiss, sweet and tender. Then she stopped thinking about how wanton she was to be lying on a fully dressed gentleman without a stitch of clothing on and thought about how the gentleman was Anthony and how she loved him and how wonderful his warm, strong arms felt holding her and how his mouth tasted of wine. Then his kiss made her so happy she wanted to cry.

After a bit, he began caressing her and murmuring all sorts of sweet things to her and she stopped worrying that she might make him impatient. She did not know when he would order her under the covers so he could have his release, but she would not mind at all. In fact, his touches were so tantalizing and lovely that she began to yearn for the moment herself. Yet just as she thought that, she noticed that his caresses were growing gentler and gentler and more and more languid until he went completely still. She tensed. Had she disappointed him? Then she looked up at his dear face and realized the wine had finally caught up with him. He had fallen asleep.

His arms were wrapped tightly around her. She tried to shimmy out of his grip, but just as she thought she would be able to slip free, he turned on his side and carried her with him. Now she was well and truly trapped. His grip on her was tighter than before, and now his weight was holding her down, not just his arms. She twisted and turned and twisted again, until she felt like a corkscrew, but still she could not wiggle free. Finally, she accepted the embarrassing fact that she was not going to be able to get free and would have to remain as she was throughout the night.

Worn out, yet strangely content despite the mortification she knew awaited her in the morning, Jane fell asleep.

Chapter 25

Anthony woke feeling as if his head were about to break in two. At first, the pain distracted him from all else. Then he realized he could not remember where he was, or why he was lying fully dressed on the bed, or who the woman was whose perfect, round breast was cupped so pleasantly in his hand. But suddenly he was filled with a sense of impending doom so strong he jerked backwards from the woman's sleeping form and lifted his head as if to rise. That proved a grave mistake.

His head began to play a resonant duet with his pounding heart, throbbing so hard he wondered how his neck managed to keep the thing attached. He drew deep heaving breaths and fought hard to keep from emptying his stomach all over himself, the woman, and the bed. Slowly, he forced himself to calm. His head's throbbing reduced to a dull ache, his heart's pounding to a steady march, his heaving belly to a constant nausea, acrid but under-control. Careful not to move suddenly again, Anthony surveyed the room, trying to determine the source of his panic, trying to remember where he was and how he had come to be here in such a state.

He had been drinking heavily, there was no need for memory to know that much, but why had he been on such a bender? It had been a year—no two—since he had been so bosky he had awoken to such discomfort, and then he had the excuse of wanting to blot out the memory of his ridiculous folly over Lady Regina Hepworth.

What folly had he been trying to forget last night? A single name suddenly rang through his thoughts with the force of a trumpet announcing the end of the world.

Jane.

Slowly, feeling like a condemned man, he turned his head to look at the naked woman lying next to him in the bed. She was turned away from him, curled up like a kitten before the fire, but the hair was right, and the alluring curves were right, and—ignoring his throbbing head, he leaned over her to see her face—the beloved features were right.

What the hell have I done?

He desperately grabbed at remembrance, but his thoughts were a jumble and his mind a fog. His gaze flicked about the room, searching for something to jog his memory. His attention fixed on a white heap of linen on the floor. Her nightdress. That—was familiar. His jaw clenched. He remembered now. Devil take him! He had yanked it right off of her and thrown it on the floor!

His heart began to pound again. *Did I force her?* Dear God in heaven, surely even in his drunken state, he would not force her! *If I have,* he thought grimly, *I will find a pistol and put a bullet in my head.*

"Jane!" he called into her ear, desperate to know. "Jane, you must wake—and tell me! Are you hurt?" His voice broke. "Did I hurt you?"

She turned to face him. For a moment, his breath caught at the sight of her. She was so damn beautiful. Then her eyes opened sleepily and fixed on his face. "Anthony? What are you doing here?" Suddenly she seemed to remember—something. Her face turned pink. She looked down at herself, then up at him. "Would you mind," she said in a whisper, "closing your eyes for a moment?" Feeling like the lowest scum on the earth, he did so. He felt her scramble off the bed and heard the sound of rustling fabric. "Thank you. You can open your eyes now."

She had pulled the damn nightdress back on. She might as well have heaped burning coals upon his head. He rose to his feet and crossed to stand before her. "You must tell me!" he exclaimed, his voice sounding wild even to his own ears. "Last night—did I hurt you?"

Her eyes opened wide, and to his utter astonishment, the corner of her mouth twitched as if she were trying to suppress a smile. "Is that 'hurt' in the traditional sense of the word or in my brother's sense?"

"In any damn sense you please!" he cried. "Just tell me! I shall go mad if you do not—this very instant!"

"Forgive me, Anthony," she said, her tone grave. "Last night, you did not hurt me—in either sense of the word." Then, to his utter mortification, she chuckled. "You fell asleep before you could do so."

"Oh, Jane," he said mournfully. "I did not try to force you, did I?"

She shook her head. "You were as gentle as a lamb."

His eyes closed in relief, and then it suddenly occurred to him to be affronted by the portrait she had painted of him. His eyes snapped open. "Forgive me, ma'am, for inflicting my drunken, comical, impotent attentions on you!"

"Oh, hardly impotent, my dear!" she exclaimed softly, an impish twinkle in her blue eyes. "Surely you recall our misadventure at dinner!"

"Jane!" He had not meant it to come out a bellow.

"Shhh! Not so loud, my love. Forgive me for teasing you. It is simply such an unfamiliar pleasure. I could never tease Bevin, you know."

Partially mollified by this intelligence, he moved closer to her. "And you forgive me for last night? I did not traumatize you with my drunken advances?"

She shook her head, but her gaze dropped and she would not meet his eyes.

"Jane?"

"No, truly. You were actually quite—" she stopped, and he waited, a fine dew developing on his forehead as he waited for her to finish, "—sweet." She looked up at him and smiled.

Again, he did not quite like this characterization of his ardor, but at least she had not found his embraces distasteful. He took another step forward.

Sunlight was beginning to pour through the windows. Her nightdress was as thin as a spider's web, and as the sunlight illuminated it from behind, her tempting body was outlined in a glorious halo of light. He took another step forward. And another. "Jane, my dearest—" he whispered.

"Anthony, please stop."

He came to an abrupt halt. "Forgive me," he said, chagrined.

"There is nothing to forgive. But if you come any closer, I will be tempted to try to finish what you began last night, and since I have no notion how to go about such a thing, I fear I will mortify us both."

For a moment, he was struck quite dumb. Then he wanted to shout from the rooftops that he would gladly teach her anything she wanted to know. But she was not done speaking. He closed his mouth on his joy and listened.

"In any case, my dearest, we dare not tarry—even for that. The maids are probably already up and about. You must return to your room before anyone knows you spent the night here. You do not mind, do you? I just could not bear to cause Drew any more scandal."

"I shall slip away like a thief in the night—or rather, the early morn—but may I claim a kiss first?"

"Very well. One. But quickly!"

He had seized her waist and tipped her back before she had finished the last word. He kissed her deeply, plundering her mouth with all the satisfaction of a pirate king contemplating his newly-won gold. When he restored her to an upright position, her blue eyes were huge and full of wonder. "I like that expression on your face, my dear Jane. I must make a habit of coaxing it from you at least once a day, I think." With an exultant grin he marched from the room.

He returned safely to his own chamber without encountering a soul. He changed his clothes and mussed his bed and readied his luggage for the day's journey without the grin ever once leaving his face. It was only much later, as he and Jane sat companionably in a much more comfortable post-chaise on the road to London, that it occurred to him to wonder at Jane's rather extraordinary avowal that she did not know what she was about when it came to seducing him—she who could turn his knees to water with a single touch. Devil take her late husband! She had been married to the man for three-and-a-half years. Surely he had taught her *something* in all that time? It was not as if she were naturally cold. Indeed, he could not think about how very warm she was without … he slipped his arm around her waist. She made a contented sound and settled her head upon his shoulder.

Well, *he* was going to be her husband soon. Sheepishly, he acknowledged to himself that all his fulminations about her sacrifice and lack of love for him had turned out to be sound and fury signifying nothing. He was going to marry her and that was that. His drunken intrusion into her bedchamber had guaranteed the thing. But if he had achieved his heart's desire by unfair means, he was determined to make Jane happy with her lot. She might not love him, but now he knew he could offer her blandishments to compensate for the lack. And maybe over time she would learn to love him. A man could dream.

He leaned over and kissed her sweet-smelling hair. A man could daydream as well. Today he knew precisely what his daydream was going to be. When he and Jane were wed, he was going to give her an education—a very *complete* education.

It was his duty.

He grinned.

&

They arrived at the home of Lady Alex and Lord Godfrey early that evening. Anthony was surprised by how happy he was to see them both. Dinner was pleasant and afterwards he lingered with Lord Godfrey over his port, sensing the man had something to say to him. He soon realized why Lady Alex's husband was regarded so highly in government circles. While managing to speak with the utmost tact and diplomacy, Lord Godfrey quickly sketched a very precise and very daunting picture of what the current situation was in Town regarding the gossip about Anthony and Jane and the night they had spent in Bagshot's cottage.

Apparently things had been subdued until Regina had arrived back in Town to set up court at Darrow House. As Wild Bill's widow, her status was higher now than it had been while the crazy peer was alive, and she was using her exalted rank as the dowager marchioness to full advantage, establishing her own social circle to rule before the Season got into full swing. She also seemed eager to resuscitate the old stories about her kidnapping and rescue, for both gave her a cachet she could not achieve otherwise.

"Now that there is an even blacker mark against my name and a juicier story for the *ton* to consume, I suppose Regina is worried she will not get her proper share of attention?" Anthony asked.

"You comprehend exactly," Lord Godfrey replied. "Lady Darrow's story is nearly two years old. If Jane is considered—forgive me, Winston—an innocent victim of your attentions, then she will become a more interesting and sympathetic character for Society to focus on."

"So Regina feels she must blacken Jane's name or risk eclipse as wronged maiden of the hour?" Anthony had trouble swallowing his fury. Had she not already extracted her pound of flesh from him?

"That is the situation in a nutshell, and I fear Lady Darrow has been hard at work already. Jane's father's history has been dredged up, as has the old gossip about her brother.

Anthony almost choked on his drink. "Ryde? What possible aspersion could anyone cast against that paragon?"

The other man's expression grew frosty. "Some have accused him of scheming to marry Catherine for her money," he said stiffly. "He was her trustee before their marriage."

"Forgive me. I meant no offense. Anyone who thinks your brother-in-law married his wife out of anything but the deepest affection is a fool."

The other man nodded. "Unfortunately, as we both know, fools are often the first to give free rein to their tongues." There was a slight bitterness in the other man's tone that alarmed Anthony.

"Sir, have you and Lady Alex suffered harm from this as well?"

"Winston, I related Lady Darrow's scheming not as a complaint but as a warning from one brother to another." He held out his hand, and Anthony took it.

"I deeply regret having brought such trouble down upon your family."

"*Our* family, Winston. And do you think any of us would prefer the alternative—Jane frozen to death in a field? Now, let us speak of more pleasant things. Alex informs me that you and Jane mean to accomplish several wedding-related errands tomorrow. I will be happy to put my carriage at your disposal—"

"That is very good of you," Anthony interrupted hurriedly, "but I do not wish to put you to any inconvenience. I will hire a carriage to take Jane and me about tomorrow."

Lord Godfrey eyed him sharply. Anthony knew the other man was intelligent enough to suspect that he planned to take Jane somewhere he did not want her family to know about. Anthony prepared for resistance, but Lord Godfrey simply gave him a stiff nod. "Very well, sir. Just remember that this family is under siege. Take care."

Anthony could not help but find Lord Godfrey's warning prophetic the next day, as he gazed down the dim hallway of the dirty, broken-down building they had come to in search of Mrs. Chester. Anthony's every instinct was to carry Jane bodily from the place, but he knew she would refuse any order to retreat, so instead he braced himself, determined to protect her no matter what dangers lurked in the fetid shadows.

Jane's attention was fixed on a grimy door. She lifted a gloved hand and knocked. Anthony could make out no reply, but Jane must have heard one, for she turned the knob of the door and entered. Anthony followed, wishing she had heeded his admonition to allow him to go first. The stench of the room was horrendous, and there seemed to be no one there. Then Anthony looked more closely at the mussed bundle of bedclothes on the filthy bed in the center of the room. His stomach clenched. A tiny, emaciated woman lay there, and as he watched her, he became aware of the painfully labored sound of her breathing.

Jane rushed forward to the bed. "Oh, Mrs. Chester!" she cried. "Forgive me for taking so long to come. What can I do to make you more comfortable?" The woman murmured something in reply, but she spoke in such a low whisper Anthony could make none of it out. Even Jane, right at the woman's bedside, seemed to have difficulty. She leaned closer over the woman, and the woman spoke again. For a moment, Jane stiffened. Anthony was about to join her at the woman's bedside, when Jane came to him instead.

"What did she say to you?"

Jane did not answer. Instead, she peeled off her gloves, took off her bonnet and shawl and coat, and handed them all to Anthony to hold

"What the devil?" he exclaimed, but she paid him no heed. Instead, she returned to that awful bed. Gently, she moved the tiny woman to one side and began gathering up the soiled bedclothes from beneath her.

"*Jane!*"

"Somebody needs to do it, and unless you are offering, it shall be me. It would help, however, if you could lift her for me."

Jaw clenched, Anthony searched for an unsoiled surface to place Jane's things. He could find none, so he laid his coat on the floor and put her things atop it. Then he crossed to the bed and picked up the woman. The poor creature felt pitifully light, and he felt an odd tightness in his throat. Jane tied the soiled linens in a bundle and set them off in a far corner. Then she found some fresh sheets in a cupboard and made up the bed. He had purposely fixed his attention on Jane to occupy his mind as he held Mrs. Chester, but he let his attention wander and his glance dropped down onto the face of the woman in his arms.

To his chagrin, her faded blue eyes were full of tears and her face with mortification. "Forgive me, sir," she said in a tiny whisper, "for this inconvenience. It is most kind of you to assist me in such a fashion."

"No, ma'am," he replied gruffly. "It is no inconvenience. I am honored to be able to help." She gave him a tremulous smile, and he realized with a shock that she must have been quite lovely once.

Jane had finished with the bed. Anthony was about to lay Mrs. Chester back down, when Jane exclaimed, a note of anguish in her voice. "We cannot lay her back down in her wet things!" But there were no other clothes to be found in the whole wretched hovel.

Somehow Anthony was not surprised when his beloved commanded him to shut his eyes.

He wasn't sure what she intended, for even she could not mean to literally give the woman the shift off her own back, but he had underestimated his Jane. Eyes closed, he felt her peel the woman's clothes off and begin slipping some other item on over the woman's bare skin. He shivered a little at how thin and fragile the woman's skin felt. When he was allowed to open his eyes, he found Mrs. Chester practically disappeared inside the folds of Jane's new fur-lined pelisse. Strangely resigned to his darling's starts, he gently laid Mrs. Chester down on the bed and merely murmured under his breath, "You will freeze on the ride home." As he expected, Jane paid him no heed, but instead went to fetch her shawl to make the woman a pillow. Turning away, so Mrs. Chester would not see him, he rubbed his hands clean on his breeches and then pulled out his pocket watch.

"Jane, I fear we must leave in a few minutes. The carriage will be returning."

Jane hurried to his side. Her voice was slightly wild. "Anthony, can you please give me some money? I did not bring any. Stupidly, I only brought a cursed ruby brooch Bevin once gave me, but she is in no fit state to sell the blasted thing."

Seeing the look on her face and startled a little to hear her language, he did not scold her for her impracticality. He fished some guinea coins out of his pocket and dropped them into her hand. "Thank you!" she cried, pulling his head down and giving him a quick kiss.

She crossed back to Mrs. Chester and set the coins on a small, dirty table by the bed. Then, to Anthony's surprise—though he should have seen it coming—Jane reached down and pinned the ruby brooch onto the bunched folds of the pelisse. Mrs. Chester was staring at Jane now, tears slipping down her gaunt cheeks. She murmured something, and Jane exclaimed, her voice cracking, "Shhh! There is nothing to forgive. I promise you, I shall return tomorrow and see that you are moved to a better place, a place where you will be cared for properly." The pitch of Jane's voice was growing higher and higher.

"Jane, I fear we must be leaving." Anthony turned his back to her to gather up her bonnet and gloves and lift his coat from the floor. "Jane, did you hear me?"

But Jane was bent over the woman once more, listening intently to what Mrs. Chester was saying. Suddenly, a stricken look crossed her face.

"Jane?" he exclaimed. *Damnation!* What had the woman said to her, to cause her to go so white? "We must leave. Now!"

He made the woman in the bed a quick bow, and tugged at Jane's arm, practically dragging her to the door. She raised a silent hand in farewell to the woman and let him guide her out of the building with so much ease his fear increased. He wrapped his coat around her before they stepped outside. He scanned the street for footpads. All was quiet, and to his great relief, the carriage was waiting. He trundled Jane quickly inside, signaled for the driver to start, and popped her bonnet on her head and her gloves on her hands.

"Jane," he demanded, when he was done, "what in the world did that woman say to you to put you in such a state?"

"She told me— " Jane said in a dazed voice. "She told me that she bore Bevin . . . a son."

Chapter 26

Jane and Anthony argued about the child all the way home. Jane was frustrated that Anthony could not seem to grasp the situation. Bevin had a child, a two-year-old son, who would soon—when his mother died—be without anyone to watch over or protect him. Of course Jane had to do something about it.

When they arrived at Godfrey's townhouse, Anthony paid the driver and tipped him three guineas to make up for the stench they had left in the poor man's cab. They tried to enter the house without notice, but the smell was so bad, the butler actually swayed when he opened the door to them. Then Alex leaned over the banister to determine the source of that "ungodly odor," and all attempt at stealth was lost.

"Change and bathe, at once," Alex adjured Jane, as they climbed the stairs to their rooms, "and then I will speak with you in the drawing room." She turned to Anthony, "Godfrey would also like a word with you, Mr. Winston, if you please. He will await you in his study when you are less ... malodorous."

It felt good to bathe and to dress in clean clothes, but Jane's thoughts were circling round and round so very quickly that she was relieved when Alex's maid finally released her, and she could run downstairs. She hoped to see Anthony before he spoke with Godfrey, but when she arrived downstairs, he had already disappeared into Godfrey's study. Jane had a nervous feeling that events were repeating themselves. Just so, she had waited when her brother had called Anthony before him to answer for the events at Bagshot's cottage. Now he was being scolded again for her sake. Was the poor man never to be left in peace?

Alex catechized her about Mrs. Chester while they waited. Jane answered her sister's questions distractedly, anxious for the men to appear. Yet when they did, Godfrey and Anthony behaved more like allies than antagonists. Anthony crossed the room and came to sit beside her. "Jane, my dear." He took her hands in his. "Lord Godfrey and I agree that you cannot return to Mrs. Chester's tomorrow."

Jane had forgotten her history. This was how it had been before, too. The men had gone off to decide her fate without her having any say. Well, she had had her fill. "I do not believe either of you is in a position to decide such a thing," she snapped, pulling her hands free.

"Godfrey, forgive me, but you are my brother-in-law, not my keeper. As for you, sir, you are not my husband yet!" Both men stared at her. "I *will* return to Mrs. Chester's tomorrow, and I *will* see that she is moved to a better place. Then I *will* take charge of her son— Bevin's son—and bring him back here with me, so that I may ensure he is properly raised and cared for." She glared, in turn, at each of the three people in the room and dared them to contradict her. Alex and Godfrey looked away, but Anthony jerked to his feet.

Towering above her, he said fiercely, "Have you no sense, woman! Just how much scandal do you think your poor family can bear?"

She had never experienced his wrath like this before. "What do you mean?"

He began pacing before her. "Let us set aside the issue of Mrs. Chester. I am quite willing to go tomorrow and see to her removal to any place of your choosing. But what in *hell* do you think you are doing waving your dead husband's bastard under the nose of the *ton*, when they are already baying for your blood and that of all your kin!"

Jane's heart began to hammer. "Why should they care about Bevin's son? Bevin is dead. The gossips cannot hurt him."

"They will not think the child his. They will think him *yours!*"

Jane stared up at him in bewilderment. "But Bevin and I had no child, and I was with Bevin's family for the first few months after his death. They know I was not increasing."

"*Precisely.*" Anthony's sharp, impatient syllables made her feel like she was having her knuckles rapped. But suddenly she understood. People would believe the child her bastard, not any sort of child of

Bevin's. It would be the obvious explanation, especially for a widow already steeped in scandal. She glanced over at Alex and Godfrey. They were busily looking everywhere but at her.

She said in a small voice, "How stupid of me."

His voice gentled. "Not stupid, my dear, just … innocent."

"Sir, I am a widow, not some green girl!"

Anthony shook his head, his expression softening. "In your heart, my dear, you are as green as the buds in spring."

"Well, if I am green, sir, you are as hard as flint. I cannot believe you expect me to turn my back on my … my responsibilities to my husband's memory."

"Do you have any care for your family in what you do," he demanded tensely, "or is your obsession with your beloved Bevin too all-encompassing?"

"Sir, whatever you may think—whatever the gossips may think—I cannot stand by and abandon Bevin's child!"

Anthony was back in motion, marching up and down. "Yes," he railed, his voice rising almost to a shout, "heaven forbid you abandon *anything* that execrable husband of yours decided to discard! His sick mistress, his bastard child. Perhaps we can find an old, lame dog he cast off for you to adopt as a pet."

"How can you compare a child—a baby—to a *dog!* Can you not comprehend how much it *hurts* that she could give him a son when I could not?" Her voice caught. "Can you not see how dearly I wish that child had been mine?" She buried her face in her hands.

There was a long, painful silence. Jane looked up. Anthony was staring down at her, his face quite white. "Trust me. I see all too well."

She felt sick to her stomach. She wanted to go to him, wanted to tell him she was sorry and beg his forgiveness, but Alex and Godfrey were there, frozen like two statues, and she could not find the words or make herself rise from her seat.

"Very well, madam," Anthony continued, "you desire a solution; I will offer you one. *I* will take the child. People can think he is *my* bastard." Behind him, Alex gasped and Godfrey paled, but Anthony paid them no heed. Jane's chest grew so tight she could not breathe, but blithely he continued, "No one will remark on such a thing or find it in any way remarkable. I am the sort of man people expect to fairly litter the countryside with his bastards. No one will turn a hair."

The next day Anthony and Godfrey set off with two footmen to retrieve Mrs. Chester and the baby and bring them to the house. Jane awaited their return in the drawing room, starting up at every sound in the street or every time she heard a door open or close. After a while, Alex joined her in her vigil. They did not speak much. Alex was no doubt still mortified by the scene from the day before, and Jane—Jane felt as if she were drowning in sensibility, one emotion after another surging through her in waves. She feared if she gave tongue to any of what she was feeling, it would carry her off in a flood.

Alex kept busy with her embroidery hoop. Jane envied her focus and her calm, nimble fingers. Jane tried passing the time with reading, but she could not make her eyes focus on the page and would fling the book down, pace up and down, and then grab it back up again when the thoughts in her head pressed in on her too much.

"Jane, my dear! Such arrangements as the men are making are bound to take a while. Please! Calm yourself. I fear you will make yourself sick maintaining such a fevered pitch."

"Oh, Alex. I cannot stop. I cannot sit. I have used him very badly, have I not? Letting him take the child on as his own?"

For a long time, Alex considered her words. "I think Mr. Winston's offer was an act of great gentility and affection. He must love you very much."

Jane tried to speak, but it came out a sob. She began pacing again. When she could finally get the words out, she said, "I should not have accepted his offer, should I?"

"I do not know. Perhaps there was no other choice."

"But I hurt him by accepting. I hurt him quite terribly."

"Yes, my dear. I fear that you did."

"Oh, Alex! Do you think I will lose him because of it? I do not think I could bear to lose him! Not now!"

Alex came to her and put her arms around her and hugged her tightly. "Jane," she said softly, "I think if you tell him what is in your heart, all will be well."

Suddenly, outside in the street, there was a clatter and the sound of voices. Jane ran to the window and looked out. "They have arrived!" Before Alex could stop her, Jane had run out into the hall and past the astonished butler to throw open the front door herself.

Anthony stood on the steps, a toddler in his arms. The child's head was on his shoulder. Its small arms were tight about his neck. Anthony was gazing down at the child's sleeping face. For a moment, Jane dared to hope that all was well, and she was forgiven. Then Anthony looked up and saw her standing in the doorway, and all hope died. His face was white and strained, and when he saw her, his mouth tightened into a sharp, pained line.

She could not bear it. She could not bear to have him look at her like that, as if he had not a drop of love left in his heart for her. She turned and ran. "Jane!" she heard him call after her.

She ran back to the drawing room. Alex was gone. The room was empty. She found a chair in the farthest corner. She turned the chair so its back was to the door, then she climbed up in it, drawing her legs up as if she were a child, curling herself up into a ball, pushing the world out so it could not tell her what a fool she had been. Her arms were tight around her legs, and she pressed her face against her knees.

"Jane." She turned. He was in the doorway, the child still asleep on his shoulder. "Enough of that," he said. "Come. Sit on the sofa."

She did as he asked. He laid the sleeping tot in her lap. "Jane, this is John." Her arms came up to hold the child. He was warm and—surprisingly—clean. She noted his damp hair. "You washed him before bringing him home."

Anthony gave a small shrug. "Godfrey insisted."

Jane examined the boy's face. "He does not look much like Bevin— except for the hair."

"He may resemble his father more when he grows." Each word was a hard pebble tossed in her lap.

She looked up. "Anthony, I did not mean—I am relieved it is so."

He nodded curtly, his disbelief plain.

"No, truly, Anthony. I prefer that that is the case."

He turned away.

The sick feeling was back. Desperate for him not to leave, she said, "And what of Mrs. Chester? I did not see the lady in the carriage. Is she coming separately?"

He turned back and came to sit next to her. His voice was gentle. "I fear I have some bad news on that score. The poor woman did not make it through the night."

Jane stared down at the little child in her lap. *"She is dead?"*

"Yes, Jane. I am sorry."

Dead. Too many people were dead. Poor Mrs. Chester. The men who had been hanged. Bevin. And Anthony—almost. It had been so very close. She swallowed hard, thinking how close it had been. If he had not had his pistol. The sick feeling in her stomach grew and grew until she could not breathe. Her head tingled. Her vision darkened.

"Anthony, take John. Quickly. Please."

"What in the world—"

But she had no time left for words. She thrust the child at him and as soon as he had a grip, dropped her head between her knees.

"Jane!"

The world swirled round in polka-dotted shadows. She focused on her breath. One. Two. Three. Four. *He is not dead.*

"Jane! Are you ill? Shall I summon your sister?"

She shook her head. One. Two. Three. Four. *He is whole.*

"I think perhaps I ought to." His voice was anxious.

"No." One. Two. Three. Four. *He is here.*

"But what do you need?"

"You." One. Two. Three. Four. *He will not leave.*

"What did you say?"

"You. I need you. Please. Will you stay?"

There was a long silence.

One. Two. Three. Four. *Please let him not leave!*

"Yes, Jane. I will stay."

One. Two. Three. Four.

The darkness went away.

She was playing a game with John—rolling a wooden ball back and forth and pretending John had knocked her over when he managed to roll it into her—when Alex came to say that Anthony wished to go for a ride with her in the park to cheer her spirits.

Jane had no real desire to go riding, but she was eager to please Anthony, and she wondered if perhaps he had suggested the thing because he needed to be outside and on a horse himself. After all, most gentlemen were horse mad, and Anthony had been in the cavalry.

She turned little John over to Alex, and went upstairs to change into one of her sister's riding habits. Not for the first time she regretted that she was the shortest of her sisters. Alex's scarlet habit looked lovely on Alex, but on Jane it was too tight in some places and drooped in others. She waited in the drawing room for Anthony to return with their hacks, and when Alex came to tell her that John was safely installed up in the nursery with the twins, Jane declared woefully, "Anthony will be sorely ashamed to appear in public with me looking like this! It is a beautiful habit, Alex, but if fits me so ill!"

Her sister smiled at her. "It fits you ill in some places, dear sister, but regrettably fine in others. Heavens, I envy you your curves."

Jane regarded her in surprise, "Are you teasing me?"

"No, my dear. I fear I am not."

"But you look so elegant in your gowns. I always feel as if I am bulging out of mine."

"Somehow, I do not think Mr. Winston minds the bulges."

"*Alex!*"

"Simply an observation, my dear. By the way, I have a rather dashing hat that sets off that scarlet to perfection. Would you like me to fetch it for you?"

"Oh, yes. Please!"

So Alex fetched the hat, and Jane stood as tall as she could and waited for Anthony to return. When he did finally enter the room, she was gratified by the look of admiration that flashed across his face. It was quickly gone, replaced by a look of fixed blandness, but Jane was satisfied. At least, she knew he would not be ashamed to be seen with her.

She was pleased when he helped her to mount, instead of leaving it to a groom. Then he swung up into the saddle himself, and his face relaxed into a huge grin of contentment. He had needed to be astride a horse indeed. As they trotted sedately toward the park, she slanted covert glances at him. She had never seen him on a horse before, but he looked as if he had been born on one, he sat it so perfectly. His natural grace, which had always captivated her, was magnified. He seemed more centaur than man. She imagined him in his cavalry uniform storming across a battlefield. That must have been an awesome sight.

She gave herself a little shake. They were in the middle of London, not some war-torn patch on the Peninsula. They were out for a leisurely ride, not some pitched battle. Yet she remembered how he had looked in Bagshot's cottage—a blanket slung low on his hips, a knife gripped tightly in his hand. The jacket he wore fit him well and looked quite fine, but she could not help imagining him wearing no jacket at all, perhaps not even a shirt . . .

"You seem deep in thought."

She started. "I was just reflecting—"

"Yes?"

"I like how you look on a horse."

His eyebrows rose. "Why thank you, my lady."

To think she had once been irked with him for addressing her so. Now it was like he had forgiven her and was ready to cry friend. "I am so glad you suggested this," she said happily.

He flashed her a quizzical look. "Riding?"

"Yes! It is wonderful to be outside and to be with you and . . ."

"And?"

"That is all, really. I am just happy to be with you."

He regarded her warily. "You are?"

"Yes! Is that so difficult to believe?"

He did not answer, but the set of his shoulders seemed to relax. They rode in companionable silence. It was early in the year, and London was still relatively empty. They met few people, and no one that they knew. Then they reached the park. Jane did not notice the two gentleman riding toward them. What she noticed was Anthony. Suddenly he sat very tall and erect, as if he were riding into battle. There was no emotion visible on his face, but his jaw was clenched so tightly she wanted to reach up and rub it to make it relax, and his eyes were shuttered and as watchful as a hawk's. She was about to ask him what was wrong, when the two men rode by, each pointedly turning his face away from him, giving him the cut direct. Her stomach churned, and she had to fight the urge to ride after them and slap each one upon his nasty, disdainful cheek. When they had safely passed out of hearing, she demanded in a whisper, "Who were those horrible men?"

Anthony's cheeks looked hollow. "Former comrades of mine—from my regiment."

"And they treat you so?" she exclaimed in outrage. "You, who almost died on the battlefield!"

He gave a small shrug. "You must not mind it."

"How can I not mind it? I wish I could kick them both—in a very sensitive place!"

"Jane!" he exclaimed, sounding quite shocked, but his face relaxed.

Yet the nastiness was repeated. Once the source was a couple, unknown to Jane, riding in a laundalet. Another time it was two ladies and a gentleman riding horses. From a distance, the three looked familiar. When they drew closer, Jane recognized Bevin's brother, Cedric, the new baronet, and his wife and sister. She was about to make introductions, when the threesome rode by—pointedly ignoring her and turning their faces away from Anthony.

"How dare you, sir!" Jane cried after Cedric in a choked voice. "I am your sister!"

Anthony put a hand on her arm, perhaps trying to calm her, perhaps trying to direct her away. Cedric checked and turned his horse, returning to stare down at her as if she were something foul lying on the ground. "Did you address me, madam?"

"I did, sir! What sort of manners are these? Have you no regard for what is due your brother's memory?"

"I think that a question more pertinent to ask of you!" he replied with a sneer.

"Sir, be careful what you say to the lady," warned Anthony, his tone as flat and threatening as a cobra ready to strike.

Cedric's wife blanched, and she brought her horse near and whispered in her husband's ear. He licked his lips nervously, but addressed Anthony in an odious tone, "Sir, I do not make it a habit to converse with men who kidnap innocent ladies."

"That is well, sir, for I do not make it a habit to converse with sniveling bastards who leave their nephews to starve in the street. Jane, let us move on."

She nodded stiffly, and the two of them rode away, leaving Cedric and the two ladies to goggle after them.

They rode quite a distance in silence before he finally said, "I am sorry you had to go experience such treatment."

"No, it is I who am sorry! Oh, Anthony! How can I ever apologize to you for that horrendous scene? That Bevin's kin should treat you so, when you have done what no man should ever have to do for Bevin's child! Can you forgive me for placing you under such an obligation? It was wrong of me—so terribly wrong! I am ashamed to have done it!"

For a moment, he gazed at her in the old way: as if he were happy to look at her, as if he believed she meant him well, as if there was room for her in his heart again. Then suddenly his expression changed. Some emotion—some *passion*—filled his face to bursting, as if the sheer quantity of feeling was too great to be contained.

Wildly, Jane turned, searching for the focus of his attention, the source of all that white-hot fire. Then she saw. A lady was driving a high-perch phaeton with matched white horses toward them. Even from a distance, Jane could see that she was beautiful. Her hair was jet black, her skin was palest ivory, she was tall and graceful as a nymph, and she wore an exquisite rose-silk gown with a matching hat set atop her glossy ringlets. As she drew closer, Jane saw how perfect and delicate her features were. Her eyes, Jane noted with despair, were the same sparkling green as Anthony's own. Suddenly the lady looked at him more closely and gave a start of recognition. Jane wondered if she would cut him as the rest had, but instead she brought her horses to a halt and stared at him boldly, calling out in a trilling voice as beautiful as her face, "Why, Mr. Winston, is this your new whore?"

Jane's stomach clenched. For a moment, Anthony seemed too stunned to react. Then he exclaimed fiercely, "Dammit, Regina! If you were a man—"

"But, you are so intimately aware that I am not. Tell me, do you still yearn for me with all the passion of Paris for his Helen?"

"Do not push me too far—"

"Or what? Shall you kidnap me a *second* time?" She laughed. It was the light, airy laugh of a faerie queen. Jane began to tremble. "I fear I must be off, Anthony. *Au revoir.* Perhaps we shall meet again." She flashed him a dazzling smile. "That could prove quite—stimulating." She slanted a flirtatious look at him from beneath her dark lashes. Then setting her horses to the trot, she drove away. Jane waited in silence. All she wanted to do now was return to her sister's house.

"My dear, I cannot find the words to tell you how very sorry—"

Jane shook her head, desperate for him to stop. She could not bear for him to offer her an apology—as if for some ordinary insult—when her whole world had just crumbled beneath her feet. "Home," she whispered. "I wish to go home."

"But, my dear, please! We must talk. I wish to explain—"

Again she shook her head, more frantically this time. *"No!"*

There was a long silence. Then Anthony said in a weary voice, "Very well, Jane. Let us go."

Chapter 27

When Anthony and Jane returned from London, it was clear he had recovered enough that it was time to move back to Rosington. Georgiana did not mind the change of venue. After all, Mr. Elton could visit her as easily at Rosington as he could at Farthingsgate, but Anthony found the shift back to their rented home wrenching. He missed Jane sorely. Awkward as their interactions had been during the journey home, at least they had been together. He had been able to see her and—on occasion—touch her. Now he was in one house and Jane was in another, and they might as well have been at different ends of the Earth as on neighboring estates for all the opportunity he had to see her.

Anthony was actually glad to have responsibility for little John that first week. The child was sweet-natured and jolly and active enough to keep Anthony's mind off the worst of his lovesick woes. He found further distraction in the process of finding the boy a foster family among the tenant farmers on the estate. He settled on a newly married couple: Ellen and Tom Rowick. Ellen was a kind woman whose mothering instincts were already in full bloom. Tom was a strong, clever man who could read and write—important qualifications as Anthony someday hoped to send little John to school. Both seemed well-disposed toward the rosy-cheeked boy, and they had convinced Anthony they could be as close-mouthed as he needed them to be about the boy's origins.

Once John was settled, Anthony visited him in the mornings. In the afternoons he took long rides past Farthingsgate's imposing drive, but he never called on Jane. He feared the estrangement that had developed between them after Regina's insult would somehow harden into something more permanent if he did. It was a superstitious notion, but he felt it so strongly he dared not ignore it. He still writhed to remember the incident—his emotions seesawing between fury and the deepest mortification. To think he had once been so deeply in love with Regina that he had been willing to risk everything to be with her. He called Jane green, but he had outdone his lady by far in his foolish belief that Regina had a heart, let alone one that could be touched by him. Now he wished he could blot all remembrance of his folly from his memory—and from Jane's.

After a week, Ryde came to visit. Anthony was startled by how happy he was to see the man. It was as if he were having a visit from some long lost comrade-in-arms.

"So, Winston, how go things here with you and your sister?"

"Fair enough, sir, though I weary of always walking into a room only to find my sister's betrothed with his hands roaming free—rehabilitating her with gusto!"

Ryde chuckled. "Ah, I feel your discomfort, though I have not had to deal with that particular issue for a while now. Then it was *your* rehabilitation that was the issue."

Anthony felt his face heat as he poured the marquess a brandy. "You have your revenge, sir. I suppose it is a sort of cosmic retribution."

"No, only God's humorous way of providing us with brotherly understanding for one another." Ryde's expression grew grave. "Speaking of which, what has passed between you and Jane that causes her to mope about as if she has no hope of happiness in the world? You two have not broken off your betrothal, have you?"

"I stand as fixed in my desire to marry her as ever. Whether she will still have me is a less certain question, but she has given me no indication that she means to cry off."

Ryde blew out his cheeks. "As the two of you are as mercurial as the blasted weather, I find neither of those statements particularly reassuring."

"My feelings for your sister have not changed one iota since that night when you and I faced each other across the desk in your study. I loved her then. I love her now. I am quite certain I shall love her always."

"I appreciate the avowal, Winston, and it does ease my mind a bit. But I would feel a good deal better if Jane did not burst into tears for no reason whatsoever, and if my other three sisters were not all sending me anxious letters about the state of your romance."

"All three?"

Ryde nodded gloomily. "Maria writes me lengthy missives full of dark hints that you plan to break the engagement. Letty writes me equally lengthy letters full of florid prose detailing your undying passion for that detestable Darrow creature. And Alex writes short, cryptic notes hinting that Jane has so misused you over this wretched business of Brawley's by-blow that you mean to wash your hands of her altogether. Having four sisters is a thoroughly exhausting business."

"You have my sympathies, sir. One is quite enough for me."

"Speaking of this Brawley matter, I must express my gratitude —"

"There is no need, sir!"

"Of course there is need! Godfrey has written to tell me how bull-headed Jane was being and of how deadly the gossip would have proven had she had her way!"

"You are a very epistolary family, aren't you, sir?"

"You're not going to distract me that easily. We are all in your debt."

"I did the thing for Jane and for Jane only."

"Understood. The family is grateful all the same. And speaking of the boy, my sister has asked if she may visit him. I fear that tongues will wag, but I told her I would seek your opinion on the matter."

Anthony looked up. "My opinion?"

"Yes, why do you sound so surprised? I know I can trust you when it comes to issues of Jane's welfare. And the child is under your protection. It is up to you to decide how matters should be conducted."

"Thank you, sir," Anthony said, gratified. He paused and then said, "I think it would be safe for Jane to visit little John on Tuesdays, for on Tuesdays the Rowick's man of all-work labors at another farm."

Ryde took a sip of his brandy. "You trust the family to keep silent about her visits?"

"I do. They are very fond of the boy, and I have made it clear that I will recompense them for their reticence, but will withdraw him if there is any breach of privacy."

"Very well. I will tell Jane she may begin her visits tomorrow. Good. That leaves only the matter of the Season and our visit to London to discuss. You and your sister will, of course, join us at my house there."

"I am not sure that would be wise."

"Winston, the family must stick together and present a united front."

"I understand that, sir. Truly I do. But I have grave doubts about the wisdom of taking Jane back to London this Season."

"I will not have my sister—I will not have anyone in my family—cower in the shadows. We will meet this thing head on."

"But I fear Marchioness Darrow intends—"

"Godfrey has already written me about what that woman intends, as has Maria, Maria's husband, and even Letty! The battle must be waged."

"But Jane has already suffered grievous insult from the woman, and I could do *nothing* to protect her. One cannot call out a woman!"

"No. More's the pity!"

Anthony stared at him.

"You need not raise your eyebrows to your very hair, sir," Ryde remarked dryly. "I do not intend to call Lady Darrow out however much it might tempt me." He raised his glass and regarded it. "Someday, Winston, when you and I are very, very drunk, I will tell you the tale of another heinous female—one I would gladly have called out if not for her gender." He suddenly flashed Anthony a determined look. "I was the ultimate victor in *that* battle of wills, as I expect you will be in this one." Ryde tossed back the rest of his drink.

The next day Anthony sat on his horse amidst a stand of trees and waited for Jane's arrival at the Rowick farm. It was all very well for Ryde to breezily assume Anthony could best Regina and reclaim the St. John family honor, but Anthony could not for the life of him think how he was to do it. Regina had an almost insurmountable advantage. She knew how to manipulate the *ton's* opinion to achieve her own ends, while Anthony fought vainly to defeat the rumors and falsehoods that sprang up hydra-like at his feet.

Suddenly, he was distracted from his grim thoughts by Jane's arrival. She dismounted and crossed to kneel down before the small boy in the yard. Anthony wished he had the courage to approach her. He longed to be back at the inn, kissing her as if he owned the world. She was his lady. He had to protect her. But how?

He thought about Regina's veiled invitation in the park. No doubt the woman thought to ensnare him again so he could serve as a puppet in some new scheme. But what if he turned the tables and ensnared *her* instead? Could the idiot fish become the fisherman? He considered the matter for the next two hours as he watched Jane play with little John. It would be a chancy scheme, but some chance was better than no chance at all.

He kept vacillating back and forth the following week. One moment he would think he could do it. The next he would be sure he could not. He began to feel like a weather vane, spinning in the wind. His only true north was Jane.

Sadly, he watched her second visit to little John from as great a distance as the first. He had sent several notes to Farthingsgate in the hopes she would invite him to visit, but though she answered his letters politely, she made no mention of a visit or of missing him or of thinking there was anything strange about an engaged couple who never saw each other.

He was beginning to ache with the need to touch her.

By the third week he could wait no more. Whether she was over her upset about Regina or not, he had to see her. He decided that Tuesday, when she visited little John, he would be there to greet her.

He was up with the sun and pacing about the house, too eager to stand still or sit or do anything of use. He went for an early morning ride and ventured up Farthingsgate's drive until he could see the house. He gazed at the window of Jane's bedchamber like a mooncalf.

He could not help himself.

He was too agitated to eat luncheon and was almost out the door nearly an hour early in his haste to head to Rowick farm, when a boy arrived bearing a note from Tom Rowick saying Jane had sent a message indicating she was not coming. Lady Ryde was ill again.

Anthony felt such a wave of disappointment he nearly kicked the legs out from under the little Sheraton table the note from Tom had been left on. If Lady Ryde was ill, Anthony could not call at Farthingsgate today, and tomorrow Ryde's household would begin the long journey to London. He and Georgiana were set to follow on Thursday. He would not have a chance to see Jane for at least *four* more days. How was he to wait? He had already reached his limit of waiting—and exceeded it.

Suddenly Elton entered the room in far too jolly a mood.

"Why the devil is Lady Ryde sick all the time?" Anthony snapped. "It is a cursed nuisance!"

Elton stared at him. "What are you talking about?"

"Lady Ryde. She is ill again and now Jane must stay with her instead of coming to see little John. What the devil is the matter with the woman? These indispositions never seem serious, but they come and go with the annoying frequency of the tides!"

"No one has said a word about them to me! How long has this been going on?"

Seeing the concern in the other man's face, Anthony began to feel uneasy. "A month perhaps, five weeks at the most. Surely if something were seriously wrong, Ryde would have summoned you?"

"I would hope so, though I have been so distracted of late; perhaps he did not trust me to pay proper attention . . ." Elton's voice trailed away. "I think I shall ride over there now and see for myself—just to be sure. You will give Georgiana my apologies?"

Anthony nodded, wishing he had an equal excuse to make the trip.

He was not sure how he was going to manage four more days without Jane.

Chapter 28

Jane closed her book with a sigh and set it down on the table in Catherine's bedchamber. She had been planning to visit little John today. She had also gathered up her courage to stop at Rosington afterwards and see Anthony. But Catherine had taken ill, and now Jane was going nowhere. It was enough to make her cry in frustration.

She had spent the past three weeks trying to convince herself that the scene in the park had never happened, that Anthony did not truly feel the passion she had seen on his face, that her own place in his heart had not been completely eclipsed by the reappearance of Lady Darrow in his life. Three weeks had passed, and she still had not succeeded in the self-delusion. It was not simply the fact that the Faerie Queen, with all her terrible beauty, possessed an older and far stronger claim on Anthony's affections than any Jane could claim. It was also that Bevin had shown her the folly of believing herself safely and exclusively loved. Yet she had come to realize the question was not about Anthony's sentiments but her own. Was she strong enough to accept that she might never possess more than half of his heart? It was a painful thing to contemplate, but after more than three weeks without him, Jane was beginning to think that she could.

Suddenly there was a loud knocking on the door. Catherine, who had been dozing fitfully, lifted her head from the pillow. "Jane," she said in a strained whisper, "who is that?"

"I do not know, my dear. I will see. Is your head still ailing you?"

"No, it is my stomach—*oh, Jane, please pass me the basin!*"

Jane did as her sister-in-law asked and flinched a little at the sounds of Catherine's distress. There was more knocking, but Jane waited for poor Catherine to finish before she opened the door. To her surprise, Matthew stood there, his freckled face quite pale. He pushed past her. "Where the devil is your brother?"

"Out visiting Mr. Bagshot. Why?"

He did not answer, but instead crossed to the bed. "I could hear you out in the hall! How long have you been ailing like this? Why did you not call for me?" To Jane's surprise, Matthew sounded angry.

Catherine's face was whiter than the sheets, but she pulled herself up to a sitting position. "Jane, now that Matthew is here, you can go say goodbye to your little John."

"Are you certain?"

Catherine gave a faint nod. "It will give Matthew and me a chance to talk." She paused, eyeing the basin as if she might have need of it again. "We have not talked … in quite … some time. Please, Jane!"

It seemed an odd time for a tête-à-tête, but Jane had no wish to cause her sister-in-law further distress by arguing the point, so with a nod to Matthew, she slipped from the room. Perhaps *he* could figure out these troublesome episodes of illness Catherine kept experiencing.

Her worries about Catherine faded as she passed Rosington's drive on her way to Rowick farm. Oh, she missed Anthony! She missed him terribly. Her whole body ached with missing him. She was so caught up in imagining how good it would be to see him again that when she arrived at the farm, she did not, at first, notice that anything was wrong.

She was surprised that Mr. Rowick did not come out to help her dismount, but she was still distracted with thoughts of Anthony, so she slid awkwardly from her horse and began to look around for little John. But she did not see the boy anywhere. Aside from the low, negligent clucking of the chickens, the yard was eerily quiet.

Jane's dreamy state vanished. Suddenly she was focused entirely on the missing boy. Where in heaven's name could he be? And where were Mr. and Mrs. Rowick for that matter? How could they leave such a little boy alone? The house was empty. She began circling the yard, but could find no sign of him. Jane was beginning to grow frantic, when she heard John's peeling laughter ring through the still air.

She started towards the sound. It had come from a nearby field.

Then the laughter stopped abruptly. Jane, already worried, felt a stab of panic. She began to run, desperate for a glimpse of him. At first, she saw nothing but the stand of trees that blocked the field from view. Then the field opened up before her and she saw the tot. He was not alone after all. Anthony's golden hair glinted in the sun. He had little John up on his shoulders, and he was holding the boy's chubby legs as he twirled him round and round and round.

John's little arms were outstretched in glee. Anthony's face was lit up with a grin so broad he looked like a little boy himself. Jane's breath caught in her throat, and she felt an ache in her chest that grew and grew.

Anthony stopped abruptly when he saw her, and his face grew grave. Then he lifted John off his shoulders and whispered something in the boy's ear. The boy nodded, and Anthony set him on the ground. Then both of them, boy and man, rushed toward her and seized her in their arms. John wrapped his small arms around her legs. Anthony wrapped his long arms about her waist. He pressed his forehead to hers. "I have missed you."

"And I, you," she said, her voice trembling.

"Me too, me too, me too!" John crowed into her skirts.

The hour that followed was one of the happiest of Jane's life. When the time came for them to bid the little boy farewell, Jane had to hold back tears as the little fellow wrapped his arms about her neck and solemnly kissed her cheek goodbye. He saluted Anthony in the same way, though his aim missed and the kiss ended up on Anthony's nose. Then Mrs. Rowick, who had returned from visiting a neighbor, lifted John into her arms so he could wave to them as they rode away.

They were halfway home, when Anthony said to her, "Would you mind if we paused here before I return you to your brother's house? There is something important I wish to tell you—and ask you."

Jane was suddenly unsure she was ready to hear what he had to say, but gave her assent. They stopped in a small meadow and tied their horses to two trees. Anthony laid down his coat for her to sit on and sat behind her. He wrapped his arms around her and put his head on her shoulder. She decided that if she had to hear something painful this was at least a very fine way to hear it and relaxed against him with a sigh.

"Jane, my dearest Jane, I have an apology to make to you."

"Anthony, if this is about the park, I would very much prefer—"

"No, this is not about the park. I am quite aware you do not wish to talk about that, and I am willing to honor your feelings in the matter—up to a point. Someday, though, we will have to speak about it." She gave an involuntary shiver. "But not today," he assured her, pressing a kiss on her cheek. "Not today." He ran a hand through her hair. "The apology I wish to offer you is about John—about the harsh words I used and the anger I directed at you, simply because you would not abandon the child as your wretched brother-in-law was quite willing to do."

"Oh, Anthony! You have nothing to apologize for. You have been so good to John—and to me!"

He pressed a second kiss on her cheek. "I was jealous, as you so rightly accused me of."

"I should never have said such a thing."

"But it was true. I still am."

"You have no reason to be! I wish I could convince you of the fact!"

There was a long silence, and then he said, "If you tell me it is so, Jane, I believe you." His arms tightened around her. "Now, may I ask you a question?"

"Of course, my dear. Ask it!"

"Would you mind, if—after we are wed—I were to adopt John, and we were to raise him as our own child?" She could feel his body tense as he waited for her answer.

Her chest ached. "Why in the world would you wish to do such a thing?"

"I have grown rather ridiculously fond of the fellow."

"Yes, my dear. So have I. But I know how you feel about Bevin, and he is Bevin's child! Will that not grate on you unbearably after a while?"

There was another long silence. "Jane, do you remember that night at the inn—"

"Of course, I remember! Do you think I could forget it?"

He pressed a kiss against her hair. "You asked me why I resigned my commission, and you did not accept the reason I gave you."

Startled by this sudden twist in the conversation, Jane nodded—waiting.

"You were right, of course. You also asked me why I was worried for my soul. It was as if you knew the two were bound together, though I cannot fathom how you knew." His head pressed back down on her shoulder. "You always know the truth of me, Jane, when no one else does. How do you do it?"

She did not answer. Something was coming, something that made her feel she dare not even breathe, lest she stop it in its tracks.

"I resigned my commission, Jane, because I did fear for my soul. I feared what I might become if I did not." His voice trembled slightly. "My dear, I wish to tell you something now. Something quite terrible. I have never spoken of it to another living soul. Do you wish me to stop, or do you think you can stand to listen to it?"

Fear dipped and fluttered in her stomach, but she reached up and cupped his cheek in her hand. "Tell me."

"I must set the scene a little." He paused, as if collecting his words. "The big battle was approaching, and we were tussling with the French over a village. We had taken it from them, they had seized it back, and we were on the brink of scooping it up a second time. The village was being taken house by house. I and my group of men were charged with maintaining an area that had already been wrenched from French control. There was still sporadic fighting, and in the distance we could hear the much bigger battle that was beginning on a nearby ridge. I chafed at what was essentially sentry duty. I wanted to be away to the real battle. Finally, orders came that released us to join the fray. But as we were leaving, I heard … a noise. I sent my men ahead and stopped to investigate a small house on the very edge of the town."

He stopped and was silent, and Jane tried to twist in his arms to see his face. "No, my dear, please do not," he said. "It is easier for me, if you do not look at me." Chastened, she resumed her original position.

Anthony continued. "I went inside the house. It was small and dark and dank. It made me strangely afraid. I searched, but could not find the source of the noise. I climbed the stairs to check above." His voice was growing more and more ragged. Jane desperately wanted to touch him, but knew she must not. She forced herself to keep still.

"When I got to the top, I saw her. She was lying face down on the floor."

Do not speak, Jane reminded herself sternly, as the swooping in her stomach became a spinning in her head. *Do not say a word.*

He continued hoarsely, "It was obvious that she had been … violated. I knew she must hear me, for with each step I took toward her, my boots seemed to thunder on the floor, but she did not move. Her back—there was no motion, no rise and fall. I knelt down on the floor beside her and called to her, but she did not answer." He took a deep, tense breath. "I turned her over." Jane felt him swallow convulsively and reach out blindly for her. She seized his hand in both of hers. "She was staring up at me, eyes wide open. He had cut her throat."

Jane could be strong no longer. She twisted round in the circle of his arms and pulled him tight against her, his head on her breast. He gave a small shudder and then burrowed there, his arms tightening around her so fiercely she thought her ribs might break. They remained like that for some time, but just as she began to relax into the silence, his voice continued. Implacable. Inescapable. Apparently the horror was not over.

"There was something clenched tightly in her right hand. Her fingers were closed over it, but I pried them loose. It was a button—a damn silver button—with the torn thread still hanging from it." His voice seemed to be coming from very far away. "I recognized the button."

She clamped her mouth shut, but too late to stop the gasp from emerging.

"It belonged to a comrade of mine, a man as close to me as a brother." He took a deep breath. "I determined to confront him, to call him out for committing such a horror, but I never had the chance. During the battle I met the bayonet. At it turned out, he met worse and was killed outright in the fighting. When they told me—" To her shock, a stifled sob rattled in his throat. "When they told me, I was *glad*. He went to his maker—unshriven—with that horrible stain on his soul, and I was ... *glad*."

Jane lifted his face and tried to kiss it. He shook her off. "No! You do not know the worst."

Dear God, surely there cannot be worse?

"You do not know *my* crime."

Jane's heart skipped a beat. And then another.

"The noise I heard, the reason I stopped in the first place was that I had heard a baby crying. Her baby. When I found her body, it was sitting there crying piteously at her side. It had a little cup. I filled it with milk. And ... and ... I left it there."

He suddenly lifted his head and stared into her eyes. "Do you understand, Jane? That poor baby—*I left it there!* I had to report to the battlefield directly, and I did not think I could carry it with me. How could I charge into battle with a baby in my arms? I meant to return afterwards and take it, but then I was wounded, and I was completely off my feet for weeks. When I was finally able to return, I found the house burned to the ground. I never knew, could never find out, if the baby was still inside when it burned." His eyes closed. His head leaned forward to press against hers, and he began to weep. Finally, after a long time, the sounds of his distress dwindled into silence.

Jane let it settle over them like a blanket. Slowly her arms slipped up to encircle his neck. She kissed him: lightly on the cheek and then tenderly on the lips. She wanted to comfort him, to chase away the shadows, but she did not have the words. She did not know what to do. She just held him.

Slowly, infinitesimally, he relaxed in her arms.

"Jane?"

"Yes, my dear."

"Do you despise me now?"

"That is a very stupid question, my dear. You know I do not." She gave his neck a gentle nuzzle.

He relaxed still more.

"And you forgive me for telling you such a horrific tale?"

"My dear, I do not know how you have borne it all this time pressing on your heart, but I am glad that you trusted me enough to finally unburden yourself. I am honored."

"You see why John is so important to me?"

"I think I do."

"God has given me a second chance. Thanks to you I did not leave *this* child behind to some unknown fate." He gripped her hand and squeezed it. "So, my dear Jane, what is your answer? Do you think you could bring yourself to raise Mrs. Chester's child as your own, with all the pain that that may entail?"

She gave a small chuckle. "If you can bear to raise Bevin's son as your own, then I can certainly bear to raise his mistress's as mine. Indeed, I think I have the far easier side of the bargain."

His eyes opened wide. "You do?"

She grinned at him. "Yes, my jealous darling, I am quite certain of it."

Chapter 29

Despite the sudden addition of Matthew to their party, the trip to London in Drew's coach was considerably more comfortable than riding in a rented post-chaise. Yet Jane must have looked almost as white-faced as Catherine by the time they reached Town, for both Matthew and Ryde treated her as gently as if she were made of porcelain. Jane was embarrassed by their solicitude, for while Catherine's fatigue was due to her continued indisposition, Jane's exhaustion was simply due to lack of sleep. During their overnight stay at The White Boar, Jane had been besieged by memories of Anthony's visit to her chamber during her last visit to the inn.

Jane had been a little shocked at how vividly she could recall each detail of his visit. She was even more shocked at the effect those details had upon her—both body and mind. Each one was like a potent little mouthful of brandy, warming and intoxicating her. Like a drunkard who could not get enough spirits, she kept poring over each recollection, closing her eyes and reliving the entire sequence over and over again. Each time, her body would grow hotter, her thoughts more wild, until there was nothing to do but pace her room at a feverish pitch, all hope of sleep vanished.

Both Jane and Catherine sought their beds with alacrity when they reached St. John House in London. Jane woke the next morning feeling much refreshed. Letty, who had called early to welcome them to Town, greeted Jane as she descended for breakfast with the news that Emily Lowery had delivered her baby—a little girl named Emma— two days earlier. When Catherine appeared, Jane was relieved that she seemed to be feeling so much better. Unfortunately, Catherine was also so excited by Letty's news that she decided the three of them should pay a call on the new mother that very morning.

Jane felt great trepidation about seeing Emily's new baby, but she was not about to admit the fact, so she agreed to the plan and went off to change. As it turned out, Jane had been right to worry. The baby was beautiful—with ten perfect fingers and two intent blue eyes that already searched out her mother's face. When Emily invited Jane to hold the newborn, Jane lifted the baby up in arms that trembled. For a moment, her longing for her own little baby seemed to swallow her up, and she closed her eyes. Then she thought of little John, and of Anthony whirling him around while the child crowed with glee, and she was able to open them again and smile down at little Emma.

"She is quite—" Jane came to an abrupt stop, not bothering to finish the compliment, for Emily was not paying her the least bit of attention. Instead, all Emily's focus was on Catherine, who was leaning close to her bed and whispering something in Emily's ear. Jane passed baby Emma to Letty, who seized the baby with glee and hurried away. Meanwhile, Emily gave an exclamation and beamed up at Catherine with a congratulatory smile. Catherine leaned down to receive Emily's hug. Jane's eyes narrowed. So that was how the wind blew.

"Oh, Jane!" Letty exclaimed in a low voice. "I want one of these. I want one so very badly!" Jane, surprised by her sister's tone, crossed to where Letty stood by the window and put an arm around her shoulders.

"I know, my dear. Little Emma is a bad influence. She is so very beautiful."

"Actually, Jane," Letty dropped her voice to a whisper, "she is not beautiful at all. She is red and wrinkly and her hair is quite thin. But I want one just the same. Why do I long for it so very much?"

Jane was caught between a cough and a snort. When she could catch her breath, she squeezed her sister's shoulders in affection. "Oh, my dear, I do not know the answer, but I think most women feel the same. Maybe it is the way we are made."

"Do *you* feel the same?"

Jane looked into her sister's eyes. "Exactly the same."

Letty sighed. "That makes me feel better." She carried baby Emma back to Emily and returned to Jane. She murmured in a conspiratorial tone that had just the slightest bit of naughtiness in it, "Perhaps Mr. Winston can be persuaded to give you one soon."

"Oh, he already has."

Letty's mouth fell open. "*Jane!*" she exclaimed in a strangled whisper.

"Forgive me, dearest. I meant little John. Anthony wishes to adopt him once we are wed."

Letty's mouth snapped shut. "You almost gave me an apoplexy!" She flashed Jane a cross look. "Do you think the idea wise? People are bound to talk. It seems an odd notion."

"We are agreed upon it, Letty."

"Oh, very well. At least, if Mr. Winston is making such plans, he cannot mean to break the engagement and run off with Lady Darrow!"

For a moment, Jane lost her balance and felt herself sway. She caught herself and settled her feet heavily against the floor. "Why would you suppose such a thing, Letty?"

"Oh. No reason. Just a silly notion I had."

"And what gave you the notion?"

"Nothing! Just something Mr. Winston said."

"What did he say?"

Letty looked decidedly uncomfortable. "It is not important, Jane. I am sure he did not mean it."

"Letty, what did he say?"

There was a long pause. In a small voice, she said, "Just that he still loved her."

Jane groped behind her for a chair and sank down into it. "Oh. Just ... *that.*"

Catherine crossed to them. "Emily needs to feed the baby so we must be going." She looked more closely at Jane. "Is something wrong, my dear? You look positively ill."

Jane shook her head. *I will cling to my half of Anthony's heart, and I will not despair.* "I am fine, Catherine." She rose to her feet and pretended she was Anthony marching into battle as she went to offer Emily the compliment she had meant to offer her ten minutes earlier.

ॐ

When they returned to the house, Jane pled a headache and retreated to her bedchamber, but Catherine followed her there. "My dear, I know it is not a headache that ails you. I am sorry that I have been neglecting you of late, but will you please tell me what Letty said to you that caused you such distress?"

"It is nothing that I did not already know," Jane said wearily.

"Can you not tell me? You did not used to be so secretive with me."

Jane felt a sudden rush of anger. "Do not speak of secrets to me! Not when you have been keeping a very large one from me and others for over a month now."

Catherine would not meet her eye. *"You know?"*

"I finally guessed when I saw you whisper your news to Emily and I saw her reaction. It is interesting that you confide your secret to her the moment you see her, but you have not seen fit to tell me in all this time!" Jane was awash in her sense of grievance. "Have you told my brother?"

"Not yet. I was afraid he would not let me come to London. You know what he is like, Jane! Once I tell him, he will wrap me in cotton wool."

Jane eyed her. "Perhaps he should. Both my sisters had sickness at the beginning—Alex, especially—but neither was as ill as you have been. What does Matthew think?"

"He is a little worried, but he says that some women do have stronger sickness at the outset. It is not usually a problem in the long run."

"But sometimes it is?"

"It can be," Catherine admitted. "However, Matthew thinks it is a good sign that the truly bad bouts only last a day or two."

"I think you should tell Drew."

"I promise I will tell your brother as soon as we return to Farthingsgate, but right now he is so worried and distracted about you and Mr. Winston that I do not wish to give him anything else to worry about. You will not say anything, will you?"

Jane frowned. "To be honest, I am surprised he has not discovered the truth already. He usually chases after any issue regarding your welfare like a terrier after a rat."

Catherine's mouth twitched. "A very pretty metaphor, my dear. I think perhaps the rat your brother is fixated on at the moment has a prior and justifiably superior claim on his attention." A loud, tinkling laugh suddenly burst from her throat.

Jane felt a flare of anger. She was in no mood to be laughed at. Then she realized her sense of humor was in sad need of repair. "Very well, Catherine," she said with a reluctant smile. "I suppose we rats must needs stick together." She held out her arms.

Her sister-in-law's laughing eyes suddenly filled with tears. She rushed into Jane's arms, and Jane hugged her tight. "Forgive me, my dear," Catherine said in a voice that was half chuckle, half sob. "My emotions, of late, seem to overwhelm me quite easily. You know, I would have told you my news sooner—truly, I would have—only I feared it would grieve you. You do not mind very much, do you? I fear it makes me rather disgustingly happy."

Jane, wondering at herself, not only managed to smile, but to chuckle. "No, I do not mind. As to your happiness, we shall see just how happy you are eight—"

Catherine shook her head. "Matthew thinks seven."

"—seven months from now, when you take to your bed to give birth to the son or daughter... of a giant."

Catherine's eyes widened to the size of saucers.

As Anthony carried Georgiana up the front steps of Ryde's impressive mansion, he was relieved to see the front door swing open and spill golden light on them. They had been expected hours ago, and Anthony had feared there would be no one left awake to greet them. But it seemed his fear had been misplaced.

His sister was worn but rigid in his arms. As each mile brought them closer to London, she had grown more tense and quiet. She had a strong aversion to crowds and strangers, and here was a place filled to bursting with both. She was also missing Elton.

Anthony demurred when Ryde's butler, whose fine, bald head reminded Anthony a little too forcefully of an egg, offered the services of a footman to carry Georgiana. Instead, he carried her himself and followed the prim and proper butler up the grand marble staircase, past a large drawing room, gallery, and ballroom to the 'blue' drawing room reserved for the family. Feeling quite small in the face of all this magnificence, Anthony swallowed hard and squared his shoulders. As the butler opened the doors before him, Anthony could see that the elegant room was filled with the St. John clan.

He relaxed a little. He and Georgiana moved forward into the room, and Ryde rose to greet them. So did Matthew Elton, who rushed across the room and arrived at his sister's side, full of solicitous concern, before Anthony could lower her into a waiting chair. "My dearest Georgiana, you must be quite fatigued from your journey. Have you had any opportunity to stretch your poor muscles—"

"Elton!" Anthony snapped. "Give us five minutes in the room before you begin obsessing about my sister's limbs, if you please!"

To Anthony's great satisfaction, the man colored to the very roots of his sandy hair and fell back a step. Then Anthony saw the happiness on his sister's face, and he could not remain angry with the fellow. Georgiana's sudden smile seemed to far eclipse all the light put out by the rather astonishing number of candles burning in the many chandeliers and candelabra about the room. And here Anthony had always taken Ryde to be a frugal man.

No, he reflected, it was good to see his sister so cheerful and content. But Elton had best beware. If he ever did anything to rob her of that shining happiness, Anthony would not be answerable for his actions. Suddenly, he realized Ryde was watching him, a wry smile twitching at his lips. Anthony had the uncomfortable notion that the man could read his thoughts with the same unnerving clarity his imp of a sister was in the habit of displaying.

Anthony spun around. Speaking of which, where *was* his beloved? Every other member of the St. John family was present and accounted for, but he could not see his Jane anywhere. Dammit, where was she? Was she not as eager to see him, as he was to see her? He had woken before the roosters this morning in his chamber at the inn, afire with the memory of that other morning, when he had woken with her naked in his arms. He had been on a low, restless boil all the weary day and evening, just waiting until he could see her again and touch her—and now she was not even here. It was too much!

Ryde seemed to sense his distress. "Jane will be down in a little while, Anthony. She has been suffering a mild headache today and has spent most of the time in her room, but I know she is eager to see you and wish you welcome."

Full of gratitude to the man, Anthony extended his hand. "Thank you for your welcome, sir. I am sorry we are so late in arriving." He gestured to the assembled family. "I hope we have not discommoded anyone."

"No, we have been having a council of war. Come. Join us." Ryde gestured for him to sit in an empty chair between Lady Ryde and Lady Maria. Anthony did so, and instantly became the focus of all four St. John women.

"Ladies," he said, feeling a bit uneasy. "I trust that you all are well?"

They murmured polite responses and then fell silent. Anthony addressed himself to the gentlemen. "Lord Godfrey, Mr. Crawford, Sir Edward—I thank you all for being here to welcome us to Town. It was very kind of you."

Lady Maria's husband, Sir Edward, who was of such a shy disposition that Anthony had only heard him speak twice during his entire stay at Farthingsgate, suddenly released his grip on his wife's hand, rose to his feet, and came to stand before Anthony's chair. "Just wish you to know, sir, that we are all behind you one hundred percent. These rascals with their tittle-tattle should be ashamed." Taking a deep breath after having delivered this heartfelt speech, the gentleman made Anthony a quick bow and returned to his seat.

"Thank you, sir," Anthony replied, quite touched. "Your support is appreciated."

Crawford was next to express an opinion. He did not rise from his seat, but his usually benign face was creased in a fearsome scowl. "It would give me great pleasure, sir, to call out the first jackass who dares offer you insult." Lady Charlotte's face turned quite white.

"That is a deucedly tempting offer, sir," Anthony replied hurriedly, "and I am greatly in your debt for it, but I think—perhaps—we must exert iron control over our honorable impulses. After all, we do not wish to cause any disquiet to our ladies, do we?"

Crawford cast a fond glance at his wife and shook his head regretfully. "Yes, I suppose you are right." Lady Charlotte's shoulders sagged in relief.

Lord Godfrey now spoke, "Winston, the truth is that we are—all of us—completely at your disposal if there is any way we can be of assistance to you in this matter."

"That means a great deal to me, sir."

"Enough with all this sentiment," Ryde remarked crisply, "let us get down to strategy. We can have no notion how to proceed until we get the lie of the land. To that end, Maria has obtained invitations for all of us to attend Lady Attlington's ball a week from today."

"It is expected to be a sad crush," interjected Lady Charlotte, finally showing some animation, "and everyone who is anyone is expected to be there."

"Lady Maria, I am most impressed," Anthony said lightly. "I hope you did not have to work too hard to arrange the invitation." *Or grovel at the feet of some harridan not worthy to kiss your shoe to get her to invite such a blackguard as me.*

Lady Maria regarded him with a beady eye. "Lady Attlington is a patriotic woman, sir. I did not have to twist her arm to get her to include a hero from the Peninsula at her affair. It is you who do her honor with your attendance—not the other way around."

Anthony stared at her, his heart swelling in gratitude.

Ryde nodded. "Exactly. Now we shall attend in a group. We shall all meet here first, and then travel together to the ball. I will coordinate the carriages. Since the event will be crowded, we should have an excellent opportunity to observe without enduring too much scrutiny ourselves."

Anthony sighed to himself at Ryde's naïveté. They—none of them—knew what they were in for, even this wonderfully managing patriarch of this wonderful, beloved family. With a start, he realized they were his family now. He had to protect them as much as he had to protect Jane. He would have to do battle with Regina in the only way he knew how. He shuddered a little at the thought. Stepping back into the arena with that woman was like venturing down to Hades to try to bargain with the devil.

At least he was not setting forth alone. "Sir," he said, standing up and addressing Ryde, "you have called this a council of war. I fear that achieving our desired outcome in this war may prove as difficult as one of the Iron Duke's victories, but I want you to know—each and every one of you—that I have never entered a battle in my life as glad of the army at my back as I do this one."

Chapter 30

Anthony marched up the stairs toward Lord and Lady Attlington's ballroom. Jane glided beside him, looking as regal as a queen. She wore a new gown—a pretty, rose-colored thing—that shimmered as she moved and revealed more of her curvaceous figure than it ought, with the result that he was doubly on guard with each gentleman they encountered. He kept watch lest any man show his Jane too little courtesy—or too much.

Lady Charlotte had been correct. The affair was a sad crush. So much so that Anthony wondered if anything would be accomplished beyond them toiling their way up this grand staircase and then back down again. His army was arrayed behind him. Even Georgiana had come. She was being carried up in Matthew Elton's arms, and Anthony worried the man's strength would give out before they ever reached the ballroom and Georgiana's rolling chair.

The ladies in his army were looking pretty and defiant, and the gentlemen dapper and a little fierce. He was determined to do his best by them, but did his stratagem have any chance of working? He had already determined that Regina would attend tonight. Earlier he had been buoyed by the news, but now he felt much less sure, especially with Jane so close. How was he to feign enough passion to entrap Regina when the woman he truly burned for was literally within his grasp?

He grimaced. Not that he wouldn't give a great deal to grasp a little more of her. Since they had been in London he had hardly had a moment alone with Jane and few opportunities to do more than brush his lips across her gloved hand. He was beginning to feel quite desperate to touch her bare skin and taste her warm mouth again, and he had begun to fantasize about the morning at the inn with a fervor he did not deem entirely healthy.

Suddenly the lady on the step above them swayed and tipped backwards. Anthony caught her, steadied her, and lifted her back onto her step. Her escort looked back at him with a look of irritation; apparently the gentleman preferred that his lady fall then have another man handle her. The man's face looked familiar, but Anthony could not place him. The other fellow's recollection proved more facile. There was a flash of recognition, and the man's slight frown turned into a look of icy disdain and anger. He pointedly showed Anthony his back and whispered something heated to his lady. She turned and stared at Anthony, then shifted her attention to Jane, sneering down at her as if Jane were some Cyprian sneaking into the ball to have a romp.

That look enraged Anthony. He was sorely tempted to slap her, woman or no, to make her stop. But Jane did not flinch or look away. Instead, she gazed back at the woman—her expression proud, even haughty. Then she deliberately flashed Anthony a warm look and a wide, glorious smile. The woman's cheeks turned crimson, and she turned away in a huff. Whispers cascaded up the staircase, and soon a multitude of faces stared down at them. Jane gazed coolly back up at them, her smile never wavering. Daunted by her calm dignity, one by one the faces turned away. Anthony's grip on her arm tightened. He leaned close to her ear and whispered, "Do you have any notion how very much I love you at this moment?"

Suddenly, the calm dignity was gone. Her blue eyes widened; her cheeks grew pink; her lower lip began to quiver. Anthony began to fear she was going to burst into tears right there on that accursed step. "What did you say?" she demanded in a hoarse whisper. The crowd moved up a step, but she did not budge. He slid his arm around her waist and urged her up, slanting a sideways look at her. What ailed her? She acted as if he had spoken some great revelation, something he had never said before, something—

He froze, dumbfounded.

Now the crowd was pushing at *his* back. Mechanically, he helped Jane up another step. He *had* told her so before surely? Explicitly?

Openly? How could he not? He felt as if the words and the thought behind them were grooved into his heart. But as he racked his brain for when he had done so, they moved up nearly a dozen steps, and still he could not come up with a single instance. Worse, Jane was still waiting for him to confirm what he had said. "My dearest Jane—" he began in an undertone, as they took another step.

But they had reached the summit. The ballroom was finally visible, and so was a familiar head of raven-black hair. Regina loomed ahead near the threshold of the ballroom like an omen of doom—a call to arms as insistent as the beat of the drum and the smell of powder. How was he to set forth on his campaign to woo her without Jane secured to him with the certainty of his heart?

"Jane," he began again—this time more hurriedly, more insistently. "Look at me, Jane." She turned, her face still filled with hope, but her eyes with uncertainty. He wished he could banish that doubt with a kiss, but that was the problem. He had assumed she could read his body's single-minded devotion as easily as she seemed to read his thoughts.

"Jane, no matter what happens tonight, no matter what I do or say—promise me that you will remember that I love you."

The doubt sparkled and was gone. "I promise," she whispered, her blue eyes alight with a look of happiness. Now he truly wished he could kiss her, but the crowd relentlessly pushed then forward toward the ballroom, and all he could do was squeeze her hand and smile. His chest grew tight with that familiar mix of icy fear and tense anticipation he had not felt in nearly two years.

The battle was about to begin.

They were an island. An island besieged in a sea of hostility.

Jane gazed around them, her mood bleak. Anthony had known it would be like this, but they had not listened. They had not believed. He had experienced it. He had lived it. He knew. And still he had been willing to come. She marveled at it.

She had not had an inkling of what lay ahead of them when they had first entered the ballroom. She had been floating on a cloud, an irrational but oh-so-wonderful cloud of happiness and joy. Despite his feelings for Lady Darrow, Anthony loved her and had told her so. As soon as everyone had reached the ballroom and assembled in a tight group, he had led her out to dance. It had been a minuet, and it had reminded her of their first night together, when they had passed below the mistletoe and kissed for the first time.

So she remained on her cloud. Her sisters began to dance, each with her own husband, and Andrew danced with Catherine. Georgiana did not dance, of course, but Matthew stood beside her chair, and they talked. Things did not seem so bad.

Jane danced with her brothers-in-law and with Andrew, and the other gentlemen took turns dancing with the other ladies of their party, but no outside gentlemen came near, and Jane began to notice the hostile looks, the sneering disdain thrown their way like dirty water, as people began to become aware of who they were, who Anthony was. Anthony danced one more dance with her. Then he was clearly done with dancing. "My love," he murmured, holding her hands in his, "perhaps things will ease a bit if I move away. I will see you in a while."

And he slipped away.

She watched his golden head move through the crowd with a tight throat. Then she turned back and surveyed her poor family. She could not believe the damage one short hour had wrought. Edward—dear quiet Edward—was gazing about the room with hot, glittering eyes, as if ready to call out the next man who did not give Maria her proper due. George was even more in a frenzy. Letty was literally sagging on his arm, desperate to keep him from some impulsive act that would lead to disaster. Godfrey kept gazing about in a daze, as if unable to comprehend the magnitude of what was taking place. And Andrew—Andrew was staring off at nothing, Catherine's hand gripped so tightly in his own that Jane feared he would bruise it. *Oh, my poor proud brother, what catastrophe have I brought down on your head?*

Jane realized something had to be done—and quickly. Her brother was wrong. This was one instance when solidarity was not a rock, but an anchor that would sink them all. She had to save her family from drowning. She crossed to George. "Do not let them see your distress," she commanded him in an undertone. "Take Letty to that corner of the floor over there—" She pointed. "And keep her dancing with her head held high until your feet grow sore. Do not return to us. Keep her there. Understood?" George's frenzied expression calmed. He was a man with a task. He nodded, determined, and led his wife away.

Jane gave similar injunctions to Edward and Godfrey, pointing them to different corners of the floor. They moved off, and she turned to her brother. "Drew, you must take Catherine away, over there, away from me. *Please!*"

"We will not abandon you," he insisted, and Catherine nodded her agreement.

Jane looked into their stubborn faces, and knew they would not act to save themselves. Then she looked over at Georgiana's strained face, and Matthew standing sentry over her, and she knew what the answer must be. "Very well. Then I must abandon you." Without a backward glance she plunged into the crowd and hurried away.

For a while, she simply moved. She noted the whispering that followed her, like some stalking animal, as she sought to lead it away from the ones she loved. She had been hurt when Anthony had left them, but now she understood. He, too, had been trying to lure away the tiger.

She threaded her way around lines of dancers and out toward the punch bowls, but after many minutes of constant movement, she was not sure where else to go. Then suddenly she saw a familiar head—its glossy black ringlets threaded with lavender ribbons—and without really knowing why she did it, she began to follow the beautiful woman through the crowd. Perhaps she could plead with her to have mercy? Perhaps she could beg Lady Darrow to forgive? It was a forlorn hope, but Jane was desperate, and any hope—any action she could take—seemed worth pursuing.

Though Lady Darrow was a tall woman made taller with her black hair piled high, Jane still had difficulty tracking her through the throng of people that filled the Attlingtons' ballroom to bursting. Jane kept losing sight of her, and she would have to stop and launch herself up onto her tiptoes to try to see her again. One time when she did this, Jane realized the other woman was doing exactly the same thing. As she watched, Lady Darrow popped up, suddenly taller than she had been a moment before, her head swiveling from left to right, obviously looking for someone. If Jane was following Lady Darrow, then whom was Lady Darrow following?

Jane realized the lady was headed toward the doors at the end of the ballroom. Then Jane saw Anthony's golden head. He was by those very same doors, and, to Jane's complete shock, he turned and went out. Was he leaving—without a word to her? *Without even saying goodbye?*

Suddenly, with a premonition of doom, Jane saw Lady Darrow follow him out. Jane rushed to catch up, skirting past and around people without even an attempt at apology. When Jane skittered to a stop outside the doors, she looked down the long staircase but saw neither of them. She looked back and realized Anthony had turned to the right and was circling around the outside of the ballroom. Twenty feet behind him trailed Lady Darrow.

There was no one else about. Where was he going?

There was a second staircase at the far end of the ballroom and to the left, but the ballroom doors were closed on this side, so no one was using it. Anthony turned left and started down the stair, then stopped. He turned and glanced back up behind him. Jane shrank back into the shadows against the wall, but Lady Darrow gazed down at him and smiled. He had seen her—he *must* have seen her—and that smile so full of challenge and invitation. He did not react, however, but simply turned round again and continued down the stairs, as if nothing untoward had happened.

Slowly, gracefully, like a cat who has just stretched and is ready to do a bit of hunting, Lady Darrow followed him.

Jane's stomach began to churn.

She waited until Lady Darrow descended and turned left into a hallway at the bottom of the stair before dashing down herself. In her haste, she missed a step and almost took a bad tumble, but she clutched the banister just in time. When she finally reached the bottom, her heart was pounding, not because of her near escape, but because far down the hallway she could see Anthony's arm reach out from an open doorway to take Lady Darrow's dainty gloved hand in his.

He pulled her inside.

The door closed.

Jane found a small, curtained alcove, almost a sort of closet, at the very end of the hall. She stepped into it, pulled the curtain nearly shut and peered out, determined to keep watch. It hurt to stand there so still and silent. It hurt dreadfully. Jane wanted to scream and stamp her feet and sob Anthony's name. More tempting still, she wanted to throw open the door and grab Lady Darrow by her hair and drag her out into the hall and shake her until she fled in terror. Then Jane's anger flickered out and all she wanted to do was curl up into a ball on the ground and cry. But she was too afraid Anthony would find her there weeping. So she stood and waited.

She was sorely aware of time ticking by. Her mind painted very vivid pictures of what was probably going on in that closed little room. She could imagine each touch, each kiss, each embrace. They had been in there long enough to do so much. They had already been in there longer than most of Bevin's visits to Jane's bed. The tears began slipping down her cheeks. Longer, even, than she had spent enjoying Anthony's drunken caresses the night at the inn. Panic began rising up her throat. Was that woman going to claim him totally—steal him from Jane completely—in that cursed little room?

Oh, Anthony, how could you do this to me? You said that you loved me.

Then she remembered her promise to him. She was to believe in his love, no matter what happened. No matter what he did. How could she possibly do it? Still, she had promised.

He loves me, she asserted with no real conviction.

She tried again. *He loves me.* Suddenly Jane pictured Anthony holding Mrs. Chester while she cleared away the messed sheets. *He loves me.* She saw him and little John rushing toward her to capture her in a hug. *He loves me.* She heard the menace in his voice when Bevin's brother insulted her in the park. *He loves me.* She saw the look of wild despair on his face when he feared he had hurt her when he was drunk. *He loves me.* She felt him comforting her on his lap as she mourned the two men who had nearly beaten him to death. *He loves me.* She tasted his tears as he confided his terrible secret to her. *He loves me.*

Suddenly the door to the room opened. Lady Darrow peered out, looking first one way and then the other. Apparently deciding that the coast was clear, she hurried from the room and toward the stair.

Anthony followed more slowly. Jane dreaded seeing his face. She feared she would see the same self-satisfied look Lady Darrow had worn, or worse—the sated look Bevin always had...after. But as he glanced about before heading down the hall, Jane realized she could make out no emotion on his face at all. The only indication that he was not a statue were the two bright spots of color on his cheeks that usually signaled embarrassment. Was he embarrassed now? Was he ashamed?

Jane was so desperate for some sign, some strand of hope to cling to, that she was willing to take those two spots of color as proof that she still had some lodging in his heart. He left the room and loped away toward the staircase. Once he was safely gone, she slowly wiped her tears away on the curtain and emerged.

She reentered the ballroom with a group of new arrivals to avoid notice. She could not see Anthony or Lady Darrow anywhere, but Letty and George were in one corner still dancing and Maria and Edward were in another, standing together sipping punch. Jane could not spot Alex and Godfrey, but Andrew and Catherine were dancing a waltz in the center of the room, holding each other tenderly.

Jane felt more tears prick at the back of her eyes.

"Lady Jane!"

She almost leapt into the air. He had come up behind her without her even noticing, and when he had spoken his mouth had been only inches from her ear.

"Lord Farleigh," she acknowledged stiffly.

"How do you do this fine evening?" Even delivering this innocuous pleasantry, his voice held that barely-leashed intensity she remembered of old.

"Well enough," she lied, finally turning to regard his dark face. "And you?"

His sharp blue eyes did not miss the evidence of her tears. "No better than you, I fear." He shifted his gaze from her face to where Catherine and Andrew were dancing. "This is the first time I have set eyes on her since that day we both remember so well." His attention flicked back to Jane's face. "Though at the time I did not know what a pivotal role you played in the interruption of my wedding."

Jane's heart began to pound. Nine months earlier she had recalled her brother from London just in time to prevent Catherine from marrying the wrong man. Now the wrong man stood before her, and she was afraid. "I was not trying to hurt you, sir, only to assist my brother and Catherine. You tricked her cruelly."

"Lady Jane, have you ever loved without hope?" There was such bitterness and pain in his voice, Jane flinched. He saw her start, and suddenly his expression gentled. "Forgive me, ma'am. I did not mean to frighten you. Your reproving look is justified. I am to blame for my own fate. Sadly, that does not make it any easier to accept." His gaze latched onto Catherine again. "She is … happy?"

Jane actually began to feel pity for him. "Yes."

"I am glad. Your brother treats her well?"

"Of course. He loves her just as deeply as you do."

One eyebrow rose and he made her a small bow. "Thank you for that acknowledgment, ma'am. Yes. I do love her deeply. I also wish her well. Will you tell her that for me? Will you tell her that I wish her happiness and all good things?"

"Sir, I cannot!"

"Lady Jane, do you not owe me that much at least?"

"But my brother—"

"Please. I am begging you." His proud eyes implored her. Somehow, tonight of all nights, she could not deny their appeal.

"Oh, very well, sir. I am a fool, but I will do it."

He seized her hand and raised it to his lips. "Thank you, Lady Jane!"

"Sir, release me, please!"

He let her hand go and grinned at her. Seeing the radiance of that grin, she swayed a bit. She had always wondered what his appeal for Catherine had been. Now she knew. She began to turn away.

"One last thing, Lady Jane—before you go. When is the happy event to be?"

Jane rounded on him in shock. "Sir, how in the world do you come to know of that? My brother does not even know yet! You and Catherine—you have not been in communication, have you?"

The grin vanished. "Would I need you to bear my message to her if I had any hope of communicating with her more directly? I have composed enough letters to her to fill a small library, but I have never sent a one, and she has certainly never attempted to contact me."

"Forgive me, Lord Farleigh. But then I do not understand. How do you know the true state of things?"

"Lady Jane, I am a father myself. My late wife died giving me a daughter. And I have five sisters to boot. I recognize the signs when a woman is in that . . . interesting condition—especially a woman I care as much about as Catherine. Your brother truly does not realize?"

"You need not look so pleased about the fact, sir!"

The grin was back, this time less happy and more mischievous. "Allow me my small pleasures, ma'am. It is nice to know there is *something* I do better than he!"

"Lord Farleigh!"

He seized her hand again. "Forgive me, Lady Jane. I did not mean to vex you. You will give Catherine my message, won't you?"

"I have already said so!"

"Simply making sure." He kissed her hand with extravagant gallantry and made her a deep bow. Then glancing over her shoulder, he said, "There is a very angry-looking gentleman bearing down on us quickly. I would rather not take any questions that might get back to your brother, so I will bid you a quick *adieu*." He disappeared into the crowd.

Jane turned. She saw the angry-looking man charging toward her like a bull in a field. It was Anthony. "There you are!" he snapped, his green eyes furious. "I have been searching for you everywhere!"

"Have you?"

"Yes! Where the hell have you been?"

"Sir," she said coolly, "please watch your language."

"I—very well, forgive me. But devil take it, Jane! I could not find you anywhere. Then I see you hidden away in this damn corner—"

"Sir, again. Can you not speak two sentences to me without uttering a curse?"

He clamped his mouth shut and blew out his cheeks. "Very well, ma'am. I will strive to watch my language if you will, in turn, tell me who that blasted fellow was who kept snatching up your hand and kissing it!"

"An old acquaintance."

"An old *acquaintance?* He seemed to be acting in a damn sight more forward manner than a mere—"

"Sir, I refuse to be catechized in this manner, especially with such language."

He stared at her, as if he had no idea what to make of her behavior. "Jane, please," he said in a softer tone.

But she was in no mood for softness. She needed to remain icy if her anger was not to burst into a conflagration the entire ballroom would witness. "Take me back to my brother," she said coldly. "It is time we were leaving. This evening has been a complete debacle from start to finish."

He regarded her searchingly. Then, his mouth set in a tight, white line, he made her a small bow and led the way back to her family.

Chapter 31

Two days after the Attlington ball, Anthony sought a private interview with Ryde. Lady Charlotte had obtained several new invitations for them—to a musicale at Pinnock House, a rout held by Lord and Lady Palmer, and the Duchess of Hereford's ball—but Anthony was determined to persuade Jane's brother that it was time to disband the St. John army. He had already communicated with Regina, and she had confirmed that she would attend all three gatherings. The campaign could proceed, but Anthony was damned if he was going to see Jane laid bare witnessing the ostracism of her family again. Ryde fumed and fussed, but in the end he was too sensible not to acknowledge Anthony's point. He understood that having her family around her had made Jane more vulnerable, not less. He agreed to let Anthony escort Jane to the other three events alone.

The matter settled, Anthony went in search of his beloved. He was to accompany her on a shopping trip she had intended to take with Lady Ryde, who was once again indisposed. He had never been clothes shopping with a lady before, but it made for a surprisingly pleasant afternoon. He could sit and stare at Jane's figure to his heart's content while the dressmaker held up dresses and bolts of material in front of her, and Jane turned this way and that, and he was free to imagine her in her fine new dresses—or out of them.

It was also wonderful to be with her without the taint of Regina hovering in the air between them. Not that Jane knew anything of his campaign or what he was forced to do to pursue it. Still, Anthony knew, and he hated how it had made him feel. If he had not already begun to sense progress, he would have been tempted to discard the entire scheme. However, to his surprise, he already sensed Regina softening to him.

"Oh, by Jove! That peach stuff," he exclaimed, as the dressmaker draped a few folds of some satiny material over Jane's shoulder. "That's the thing!"

"*Monsieur* has impeccable taste," the dressmaker said with a small nod. "The color sets off Madame's skin to perfection."

Indeed, it does, Anthony thought. He pondered rather feverishly how lovely Jane would look standing there with just a few wisps of the peach material draped over her and nothing else. Then he could slide his hands beneath the cool satin and caress that fine looking skin and slowly tug the wisps away …

"Anthony!"

"Yes, Jane?"

"We are finished. It is time to go."

"Of course, my dear." He rose to his feet and offered her his arm.

But he could not shake his imaginings, and when they were safely back in the carriage and the door was closed and the horses had started up, he could control himself no longer. "My beautiful Jane," he said as he slid an arm around her waist and tipped her back in her seat. He kissed her, and—feeling a little desperate—his hands and mouth began seeking every bit of exposed skin he could find, but it was not much. She was wrapped up like an Egyptian mummy. His fingers fumbled with the buttons of her pelisse, and after lengthy exertions he managed to tug it open. His reward was to touch the lovely, soft expanse of skin rising up above her gown from the swell of her breasts. But touching it was not enough. Not today. Not in the state he was in. He had to kiss that lovely skin. His tongue kept dipping lower and lower until it was sneaking down beneath the neck of her gown. She gave a gasp of pleasure, inciting him to even greater fervor. He began tugging and pulling at her gown and her stays until he managed to slip one hand in to cup her breast. "Oh, my love," he murmured.

Suddenly, his warm, yielding darling was gone. She tensed and stiffened. "Remove your hand, sir."

It was easier said than done. He inadvertently ripped her stays and then the neck of her gown in the process of extracting it. "Jane, I am sorry. I have just missed touching you so very much."

"That is all love is to you," she snapped, her voice furious. "Kissing, touching, satisfying your body's need. That is why you say you love me. You wish to lie with me. No doubt once that has been accomplished, you will move on to the next lady—any lady—and that will be your new love."

"Jane, you cannot believe that!" To his utter mortification, his voice broke as he added, "You, who have always believed the best of me."

"I no longer know what to believe!" She buried her face in her hands and began to cry. He wanted to comfort her, but he did not dare touch her, and he could not think of a single thing to say to her.

They rode the rest of the way home in miserable silence.

Damned but the deception was growing more difficult.

He had had to lie to Jane so he could slip away to meet Regina is this little hole of a room, which had taken a good stiff bribe to a footman to discover in the first place. It was only the second lie he had ever told her—the first being the one about all women being the same with their clothes off—and he hated the thought of it. He also wondered how Providence would punish him for it. Obviously his punishment for the first lie had been that awful scene in the carriage.

It was damnable irony that she thought him so blinded by lust that he could not differentiate one female form from another, when these tortuous sessions with Regina were making it clear that Jane had spoiled him for all other women, even one he had once been so desperate to bed he'd risked crossing swords with Wild Bill. Indeed, Anthony was finding it difficult to even feign lust for Regina now. He was too achingly aware that she was not Jane.

"Anthony, I would like another kiss now." Regina's tone was faintly aggrieved.

He had been too lost in thought. He looked down at her with her head in his lap. He did not want to kiss her. He was not sure he could stand to kiss her. He closed his eyes and pretended it was Jane with her head in his lap, calling him her one true knight.

For a moment, that helped.

But Regina did not taste like Jane, and she did not smell like Jane, and her skin did not set him on fire like Jane's skin did, and her curves were not the right shape—Jane's shape—to do anything but annoy him.

He broke free and desperately searched for an excuse he could give Regina for his unwillingness. She looked quite disappointed and was regarding him with a considering eye. He feared his fumbling embraces were making it clear that he no longer cared for her a whit.

"Regina," he said thickly, "forgive me, I am in too much of a brown study to be of any use to you or myself." That, at least, was true. "I—" He paused, wildly casting about for something she would find credible. "I feel the difficulty of our situation too keenly." Another partial truth. "If only," now it was time for the whopper, "if only," he repeated mournfully, turning his head away so he could try to imagine he was saying this to Jane, "I could kneel at your feet," he said in a deeper tone, "amidst all that glorious music upstairs and declare myself your one true love." His voice trailed away. He *did* wish he were upstairs with Jane now, this very instant, listening to the music, her head resting on his shoulder. But he was forgetting, he was forbidden even that pleasure now. He sighed.

"Oh, Anthony!" Regina exclaimed huskily. "When did you become so devilishly romantic?"

He blinked. Regina had *believed* his twaddle?

Her hand slipped inside his waistcoat and tugged at his shirt. He tensed. At the Attlington ball, Regina's amorous inclinations had proven far more accelerated than he'd anticipated. He had chosen this room because it was small and cramped and boasted nothing upon which to lie but a very small, very narrow sofa. Regina liked her creature comforts, and he hoped the limits of the room would discourage her from getting any serious ideas. It had been a near run thing last time, but he had slipped by. He would never be able to simulate enough passion to bed her, however. It was a physical impossibility.

Fortunately, as her hand finally slipped beneath his shirt, it moved upward and not down. He gave a little a shudder of relief. Regina seemed to interpret this as passion. Her hand stroked his stomach and then moved up to caress his chest. "My dear Anthony, I have been thinking over what you said last time. I have given it *considerable* thought, and I think I have a plan as to how to redeem your good name."

Anthony's pulse quickened. She felt it, and placed her hand over his heart. "Patience, my dear," she said coyly. "Patience! This room is too cramped to give you your proper due tonight, but I promise you will not have to wait long."

"What is your plan, Regina?" He tried not to sound too eager.

"I have come up with an excellent tale of how you abducted me—"

"But, Regina, I did *not* abduct you—"

She flashed him a warning look, and he was silent. "That you abducted me only to prevent Wild Bill from doing so. Everyone will believe it of him for he was so foul."

He suddenly felt a twinge of pity for her. "Did he treat you *very* badly, Regina?"

"Oh, no!" she exclaimed with a tinkling laugh. "I had him wrapped around my little finger, actually. And he was so drunk most of the time, I had to put up with very few inept advances. He provided me with wealth and an excellent title and then got himself killed quickly so I could enjoy what he gave me. He proved a most excellent husband."

Anthony was staring at her. He looked away before she could see what he was feeling. She began to kiss his chest. He could not stand it. He drew away in a sudden abrupt gesture and jerked to his feet, almost spilling Regina to the floor. He did not care.

"Anthony, whatever is the matter!"

He spoke the truth. "I was simply contemplating what my life would have been if you had chosen me instead of Wild Bill." He gave another shudder. *Shackled to this—with no honor. Worse, with no Jane!* He suddenly found it difficult to breathe.

"Why, Anthony, your chest is heaving! I know how deeply you loved me before, but I must say, it is quite *stimulating* to learn how ardent your affections remain still." She twined her arms around him and rubbed her body against his.

He broke free again. "Regina," he said, once more speaking the truth to her, "you have no notion how you torture me." Then, without pausing to see how she interpreted his words, he fled the room.

Anthony and the Faerie Queen had been alone for a much shorter period this time when he burst from the room, but Jane knew better than to take comfort from the fact. She had noticed with Bevin that often the more heated his passion, the more quickly he was done and departing from her bed. Anthony certainly looked in a passion, she noted sadly, his face full of far too much feeling rather than too little.

There had been no handy alcove this time, so she had risked keeping watch from another room. She feared he would see her as he stormed by. The door was open too wide, and he had surprised her by exiting so abruptly. But apparently he was so wrapped up in his own thoughts that he was blind to all else. Jane eased the door closed before Lady Darrow emerged.

Oh, she wished she had never quarreled with him in the carriage. She was losing him, and instead of clinging to him as long as she could, she seemed determined to fling him away, sacrificing everything because she could not have all of him. She leaned against the door, listening for the sound of Lady Darrow's departure. She longed to go upstairs and find Anthony and be with him, and she was impatient for the lady to be away so she could do so. But Lady Darrow seemed determined to thwart her even in this. It took nearly ten minutes for the lady to finally leave. When the sound of the Fairie Queen's footsteps finally receded, Jane emerged and hurried upstairs herself.

The orchestra was playing a mournful air, and a soprano stepped forward to sing a painfully lovely aria in Italian. Jane paused at the doorway to listen, feeling as if the music were speaking directly to her soul. It warned her that all love ends in loss, and she had best enjoy her love while she could.

"Jane! Where the devil have you been?"

She whirled around. His beautiful green eyes were dark with anger, but she did not care. "Oh, Anthony!" she cried, so very happy to see him. "May we leave now—right now? If I listen to this music much longer I shall start weeping."

His expression softened. "Yes, it is cursed beautiful. Let us away." He held out his arm to her, then dropped it back to his side. "Forgive me, Jane. I was forgetting."

"I would very much like to take your arm." He stared at her in surprise, but offered it to her with alacrity. She took it, trying to memorize the precious feel of it. They walked without speaking, and she was content with the silence. At last she said, "Anthony, I am sorry."

She felt his arm—no, his whole body—tense. "For what, Jane?" His tone was sharp.

She bowed her head. "For my aspersion to you in the carriage. For accusing you of feeling only lust and not love. I know I was wrong."

They had reached the porte-cochère. Anthony drew her back into the shadow of a column. "Jane, you do not know—you cannot comprehend—how much it means to me to have you tell me that. I had feared that I had lost your good opinion forever."

He looked an eager question down at her, and she nodded, lifting her face to him. He kissed her with such a tender, gentle kiss that she was back listening to the music again, only infinitely finer and infinitely more poignant. Her stomach trembled and her heart swelled with the ache of it. "Jane, there is something I must tell you—"

She pressed her lips to his mouth to stop him. She could not bear to have him declare the truth of his feelings for Lady Darrow now—at this moment. She kissed him deeply, desperately, as if it might be the very last time. It was Anthony who pulled away.

"*Jane!*" he exclaimed hoarsely. "Have a care! We are on an open porch!"

She smiled up at him. "And you call yourself a rake!"

"What has come over you?"

"I do not wish to waste the precious minutes I have to spend with you."

He seemed not to know what to make of this. His face was wary but his eyes sparkled. Jane's body began to tingle anticipating the carriage ride home. This time, she would deny his hands and mouth nothing.

"But Jane," he persisted, "you were so angry with me. I do not know what has wrought this change in you." His tone was suspicious.

"My dear, I simply realized that your heart is not too fickle, but too fixed." She added softly, "I cannot blame you for that."

She heard his breath catch, and something altered in his face, but she could not make out his expression. One of the nearby torches had burned itself out, and his face was now swathed in shadow. "Jane, what exactly is it that you think you know?"

She was not about to admit that she had spied on him. That would be too humiliating. In any case, she feared to be explicit. Once the truth was spoken aloud, it could not be ignored or escaped from. She skirted around the point. "What does it matter? Can we not simply enjoy this fine evening and the chance to be together?"

He shook his head. "*It matters!*" He practically barked the words at her. He was breathing heavily and obviously waiting for an answer.

Well, he could wait all night. She was not going to give him one. They stared at each other in the darkness, clearly at an impasse. Finally, without a word, he offered her his arm and led her out to the light so they could summon the carriage. With a heavy heart, Jane knew there would be no importunate advances for her to indulge during the long ride home.

Chapter 32

ane turned her horse down one of the more obscure bridle paths. She was grateful her brother had been willing to let her venture out alone after Anthony had canceled their ride together. She was in no mood to be tethered today and wanted no company of any kind, not even the silent presence of a groom.

She was losing Anthony so quickly. He was slipping through her fingers like an outgoing tide, and she could think of no way to secure him. She had been happy thinking of this outing. She had been looking forward to it so very much. Then the letter had come for him, sealed with scarlet wax and smelling of Lady Darrow's scent, and he had abruptly announced he could not go. He had looked abashed about it, he had hemmed and hawed and asked if they could go another time, but he had stuck fast in placing Lady Darrow's summons over his promise to ride with her in the park.

That had hurt. More than Jane had comprehended in the moment. At first, she had simply been angry—thoroughly, gloriously angry. She had stormed from the room determined to enjoy a ride without him. Now, however, her anger had deserted her, and as she rode along the lonely bridle path at this unfashionable morning hour the true pain of it sank in. Lady Darrow had but to snap her fingers and he would rush to her side.

The Faerie Queen had won.

Anthony no longer seemed to even want to touch Jane. Since the night of the musicale, he had been as distant as the moon, his contact limited to his proffered arm and nothing more. All she could think of were his kisses, but he would not so much as brush his lips across her ungloved hand.

Without thinking, she had ridden into a part of Hyde Park usually abandoned to nannies and children. She became aware of shrieks and laughter and far too many perambulators full of other people's babies. She began to turn her horse, then stopped abruptly. In the distance, she could see another rider. Her breath caught at the sight of him—a golden-haired centaur recognizable in an instant. Had he come to join her after all? Her heart began to pound at the thought. Then with a crash of spirits so profound she almost slid from her horse, she realized he had not even seen her. He was riding toward a small closed carriage. There was no crest or insignia on the vehicle, only two painfully familiar matched white horses. Anthony drew alongside it, dismounted, and tossed his reins to the carriage's driver. Then he climbed inside.

Unable to do anything else, Jane began to cry. The tears rolled down her cheeks until the front of her habit grew quite wet.

"Lady Jane?"

She looked behind her. To her utter amazement, there stood Lord Farleigh, a stale loaf of bread in one hand, a dark-haired girl tugging impatiently on the other. "Lizzie, my love, give me a moment, please. Here is some bread. Go feed it to the ducks." The girl went scampering off. "Lady Jane, it seems I never see you but you have tears in your eyes." He handed her up a handkerchief.

"Thank you, sir," she said, wiping her eyes and face gratefully. He looked away. Jane thought he was being tactful, but then she realized he was looking after his daughter.

"I must keep a watchful eye on my Lizzie, especially near the water, for she is a fearless child and sometimes prone to be rash when curious. Would you mind dismounting so that we may talk a little without my taking my eyes off of her for too long?"

Jane was surprised and touched by his fatherly concern. She had a clear remembrance of visiting this portion of the park with her own father. He had not cared so dearly for his consequence as to disdain such an outing with a daughter who had plenty of servants to mind her. Smiling at the memory, Jane said, "I will be happy to, Lord Farleigh, if you will but aid me to dismount." He cast another careful look after his daughter, and then turned back to Jane.

"Of course, ma'am." He reached up and began to lift her down.

Her boot caught in her stirrup and her motion checked abruptly. He swayed, trying to regain his balance. She made the mistake of trying to shake her foot free.

They went down in a pile, her bottom coming down with surprisingly force on his chest, knocking the wind out of him. She quickly rolled aside and peered at him anxiously. "Oh, Lord Farleigh, I *am* sorry!"

He took a couple of heaving breaths and stared at her. Then to her utter shock, he burst out laughing. "Do you think depriving me of a wife not sufficient punishment, Lady Jane? Must you also s-stomp on my c-chest with y-y-your — " Here he broke down completely into helpless guffaws.

At first she was affronted. What sort of gentleman was he to laugh at her when she was so mortified? Then the sound of his laughter began to tug at her, and she imagined how satisfying it would be to stomp on Lady Darrow's chest in just such a fashion. She began to chuckle, too. Soon they were doubled up on each other, laughing as if they would never stop. Finally, the almost painful waves of mirth began to subside, and Jane was able to straighten up into a sitting position. She realized Lord Farleigh's daughter Lizzie was staring at them from a distance, her grave eyes wide with alarm.

"It is all right, Poppet," he assured her. "We are fine. We have just been laughing." He exchanged a look with Jane. "Sometimes when people have been sad, they feel better after a good laugh." The girl seemed to accept this explanation and returned to the ducks. He crossed his legs and rose to his feet. Then he held a hand down to Jane. "At the risk of another catastrophe, may I help you up?"

She smiled, and he helped her to rise without incident. He turned to take his habitual glance after his daughter, and when he turned back, she could sense that the effects of the laughter had left him. He was suddenly full of nervous tension. "Sir," she said, determined to end his suspense. "I gave Catherine your message."

"You did?" He sounded torn between gladness and fear.

"Yes."

"I do not suppose she sent any sort of response?" His voice was wistful.

"On the contrary, she told me to tell you that she thanks you for your message and wishes you all good things in return."

The intensity of the emotion in his face made her sway a little. "She forgives me?"

"Completely. She said that she only hopes you can find your own happiness," Jane paused, not wanting to hurt him, "as she has found hers," she finished carefully.

He suddenly seized her in a bear hug and whirled her around. "Thank you, Lady Jane! Thank you very, very much!"

"You are…welcome, sir," Jane said, panting a bit for lack of air. Sensing her distress, he loosened his hold and set her back on her feet.

"Forgive my exuberance, Lady Jane," he said with a grin.

She did not reply. She was distracted by the sound of an approaching horse. She turned, startled. She could not believe how fast the horse was galloping toward them. Then her gazed shifted from the horse to the rider, and she gave a gasp of shock. It was Anthony, bearing down on them as if they were French invaders setting up camp in Hyde Park. He vaulted from his saddle while the horse was still in motion and landed not two feet from her, his expression so fierce she kept wondering when he would notice that he had forgotten his sword. "What the *hell* is going on?" he roared.

Lord Farleigh wisely remained silent.

"Anthony," she said in an unsteady voice, "allow me to introduce Lord Farleigh. Lord Farleigh, may I introduce Mr. Winston my—"

"*Betrothed.*" The word came out a snarl.

Lord Farleigh's eyebrows rose. "Ah." He turned and called to his daughter. "Lizzie, my dear, can you come here?" The girl arrived with well-behaved promptness. "Lizzie, this is Lady Jane Brawley, an acquaintance of mine, and this is Mr. Winston, who is Lady Jane's fiancé. Can you please go and shake hands with both of them before we leave to go home? It is almost time for your luncheon."

Jane marveled at the man. With a single masterful gesture, he had completely defused what had suddenly felt like a very dangerous situation. Lizzie solemnly shook Anthony's hand and then Jane's, and then returned to her father's side. "Come Poppet, away we go home." Lord Farleigh flashed his daughter a fond smile. Then he gave Anthony a tight nod, made Jane a deep bow, and took his daughter's hand and led her away.

She and Anthony watched their slow progress for some time, before he turned to her. "Well, Jane?" he demanded tightly, his anger seeming to reignite now that the little girl's dampening presence was gone. "Will you explain to me what I have observed here between you and that gentleman? For I fear if you do not do so soon, I may—"

"I will be happy to do so," she interrupted, "once you explain to me who it was you were visiting in that carriage with the memorable set of white horses. I assume that rendezvous is the reason you broke our appointment to take a ride in the park?"

He paled. "Jane, I—"

"No, it is of no moment. I do not require an explanation. I simply wish to return home. Would you mind helping me to mount?"

He did so silently. He noticed Lord Farleigh's handkerchief lying on the ground where she had let it slip during her graceless dismount. He picked up the crumpled piece of linen and smoothed it out on his palm before holding it up to her. "Did you drop this?"

Fearful that he would know she had been crying over him, she snatched it up. "Yes. Now may we go?" He did not answer. He simply mounted his horse with his cavalryman's grace and set off.

Letty had warned Jane that Lord and Lady Palmer's rout was expected to be terribly crowded. Yet as Jane and Anthony worked their way up the main staircase into one of the series of drawing rooms that had been opened up to accommodate the prodigious number of guests, Jane still managed to spot Lady Darrow's glossy black ringlets in the crowd. She wondered how soon it would be before Anthony excused himself to go keep tonight's rendezvous. Jane was no longer angry or even sad about the state of things. She was simply resigned. It would be a relief when he finally told her their betrothal was at an end. At least then she would be done with this constant waxing and waning of hope.

She had felt one of those useless rushes of optimism during their return from the park that morning. Anthony's jealousy had seemed to burn so bright she felt sure he must still love her—at least a little bit. But she had been wrong. When they arrived back at St. John House, all he had seemed to care about was convincing her not to accompany him to the rout. She had foolishly let her jealousy get the best of her and had angrily assured him she would not get in the way of his visit with Lady Darrow, but she was going—with or without his escort. He had backed away from her as if she had slapped him.

So here she was, working her way through a crowd which seemed even more hostile to her than normal, while Anthony marched silently beside her. Her only consolation was that hardly anyone expressed open hostility to *him*. Perhaps the Faerie Queen had thrown some fairy magic his way? Jane hoped it was true. At least then some good would be coming from all this pain.

To her great surprise and very real pleasure, Jane spotted Letty as they finally reached the second drawing room. Anthony went off to find Jane some refreshment, and she worked her way toward her sister. "Letty!"

"Oh, Jane! I hoped I would find you in this crush."

"It is very good to see you, Letty, though I ought to scold you for coming and should probably urge you to leave at once. But I cannot bear to! Please, come stand by me and tell me tales of someone else's scandal for a change!"

Letty gave her a warm hug and looked about her. "Where is Mr. Winston?"

"Procuring me some punch."

"Ah."

Jane sighed inwardly. No one could pack as much innuendo into a single syllable as her sister. "Out with it, Letty. What are people saying now?"

"Well … do you wish the good news or the bad?"

"The good—definitely the good. I do not think I can bear the bad at the moment."

"It seems Mr. Winston's reputation is rising hourly. There is now a story circulating that Mr. Winston only kidnapped Lady Darrow in order to save her from Wild Bill, who was planning to carry her off himself."

"But Letty! That is wonderful!"

"Not entirely."

Jane had a sudden urge to shake her blunt sister. Could she not spare her five minutes of happiness before pouring a pan of cold water over her head? "Why not, Letty?"

"Because I have it on very good authority that the person circulating the story is Lady Darrow herself."

"Well, of course. It would be, would it not?"

Letty stared at her. She said slowly, "Now that Wild Bill is safely planted, they say she means to take up where she left off with Mr. Winston."

Jane said nothing.

Letty gazed at her mournfully. "Oh, Janie, then it is *true*?"

Anthony suddenly appeared with Jane's glass of punch. "Good evening, Lady Charlotte."

Letty flashed him a wrathful look. "It may be to you, sir. It is not at all to me!"

Anthony regarded her with a look of bewilderment, then passed Jane her punch. "My dear," he said, two bright spots of color appearing in his cheeks. "You will excuse me for a little while?"

"Of course, Anthony." She gave him a formal nod as if he had just begged her some boon, and she had granted it. He flinched. Letty watched the interplay between them, looking confused. He made them each a quick bow and departed. Jane watched him go, unable to take her eyes off him as he moved through the crowd.

"Oh, good Lord!" Letty suddenly exclaimed at her side. "The fat is in the fire now!"

For a moment, Jane panicked. Did Letty somehow know where Anthony was going? Then she realized her sister's attention was not fixed on his retreating back, but on a handsome couple standing next to the doorway he was about to pass through.

"Who are they, Letty?" Jane demanded.

Letty gestured with her chin. "That's the *other* girl he is said to have kidnapped!"

"Dear God!" Jane exclaimed, sprinting forward. She had to stop him before he walked right into them. His reputation was just beginning to recover. The last thing he needed was the revival of yet another scandal. But the crowd was too thick, and Anthony's long legs enabled him to move through it far more quickly than Jane could. She was at least fifteen feet away from him when the couple by the door spotted him. Jane braced herself for a scene, but to her surprise, they did not step into his path to confront him nor turn their backs on him. Instead they moved quietly aside and watched him pass from a safe distance. The expression on the man's face filled Jane's heart with wonder.

It was the look of a man consumed by guilt.

Anthony was having a surprisingly hard time getting Regina to accept what he was telling her. "I thought I made it clear this morning when you summoned me so imperiously to your carriage. I am weary of all this skulking about and wish to be done with it. I do not think we should meet again."

Just as she had this morning, Regina paid him no heed. He might have been a fly buzzing about her head, for all the attention she paid his words. She was fixed on trying to kiss him. Thinking that perhaps he could at least get her attention that way, he let her. Her mouth was hungry and wet, but he disengaged his mind and let his thoughts wander.

Of course, they snapped—as they had been doing all day—to what had happened *after* he had left Regina's carriage. He had emerged frustrated and upset. He had sacrificed his chance for a ride with Jane for a guilt-ridden assignation that had accomplished nothing. At first he was in such a brown study, he did not notice the couple in the distance cavorting on the ground. It was their odd position that caught his attention, for they were doubled-up on each other in a very curious way. Then the woman straightened up, and there was something unnervingly familiar about the line of her neck and shoulder, the curve of her breast, the color of her hair. Anthony mounted his horse and rode closer.

He still was not sure it *was* her. No doubt because he could not stand the notion that it could be. Both she and the man had now risen to their feet. They were talking intently. Anthony rode closer still. The woman took the man's hand. The man lifted her into his arms and spun her around. Anthony saw her face.

He did not remember riding up to them. One moment, he was watching Jane at a distance, horror-struck with recognition. The next he was standing right in front of her, so full of anger he could not breathe.

"Anthony! Oh, Anthony!" Regina murmured huskily. "I can never get enough of your kisses."

"Regina," he said wearily. "You must do without them, because we must stop seeing each other." She was sitting on his lap, and he could not seem to shift her. "Did you hear me?" Now she was busy trying to kiss his neck. *"Regina!"*

She finally looked up. "Of course, Anthony. I understand. You are not the sort of man to sneak around in the shadows."

Except that that is precisely what I have been doing.

"Do not fear, Anthony." Her hands slid under his waistcoat again. "Your reformation progresses apace. Soon I will be able to welcome your devotions openly." Her hands began skimming downwards this time. She began trying to unbutton his breeches.

Anthony's mind was suddenly filled with the image of Jane's head inclining regally to him when he had excused himself to come here—to do *this*. How could she accept such a thing with such calm? As if it did not matter to her. As if she did not want to scream with rage as he had wanted to do this morning when he had seen her with another man.

Regina's fingers had wiggled their way inside. Cursing silently, he seized her small hand, and, without any gentleness at all, yanked it away. *"No, ma'am. I have told you. It is over."*

She stared at him, disbelieving. "But Anthony—" She tried to coax him with her mouth. He jerked his face away, suddenly distraught. It occurred to him why Jane might accept his being here, in *this* room, with such equanimity. Was she using the opportunity to meet that bastard in another one? While he was stuck here with Regina, warding off her irksome advances, was Jane in another room accepting his?

In a fury, he surged to his feet, Regina still in his arms.

"Oh, my dear," she sighed. "You are being so masterful tonight. Whatever has come over you?"

Without bothering to answer her, he deposited her unceremoniously down on the sofa and rushed to the door. Without a word to her, he left the cursed room. The campaign was over. He hurried down the hall and up the stairs, but when he got back to the drawing room where he had left Jane, she was nowhere to be seen.

He looked about him wildly, his heart beginning to beat a battle cadence. He searched through all the drawing rooms, but could not find Jane in any of them. Grimly imagining what he was going to do to that dark-faced bastard when he found them, Anthony sprinted back down to the ground floor rooms again. He began flinging open doors. He found her in the third room he checked. She started at the sight of him and fell back several paces, her blue eyes wide, her lovely skin crimson. Feeling as if a dragon were breathing flame in his head, he slammed the door shut behind him. At least she was not lying naked on the overlarge blue sofa that seemed to fill the room. She still had her clothes on. That was something. "Where is he?" he demanded thickly.

"What?" She looked at him blankly.

"Dammit, Jane! *Where is he?*"

"Anthony, what the devil are you talking about?"

"Your dark-faced cicisbeo from the park. Where the hell is he? I've a mind to beat him to a pulp."

"Are you talking about Lord Farleigh?" Her voice was disbelieving.

"Of course I am!" he roared. "Unless you have other lovers scattered about Town I am unaware of." Suddenly, unaccountably, she smiled at him—a huge, happy, exultant smile that made him want to shake her until her teeth rattled. "You will not be smiling when I am done with him," he assured her through clenched teeth.

"Anthony! You really *are* jealous, aren't you? This morning in the park I thought you must be, but then you didn't want to bring me tonight," a cloud passed over her face, "and I knew it was because you were meeting *her*, and I decided to give up hope, but you really are jealous!"

"Ma'am, as you know, I am not a patient man! Tell me where he is or I shall break this room apart to find him!"

"Anthony! Lord Farleigh is not here. I have no notion where he is. Probably he is at home, in his bed, sleeping soundly."

He gaped at her. "Then you and he were not..." His voice trailed off raggedly, and he was unable to keep from staring at the overlarge sofa. "But then why the devil are you in this room and not upstairs?"

"If you must know, I was waiting for you to finish your tryst with Lady Darrow."

He stared at her. *"You were spying on me?"*

"If you must snatch every last shred of dignity from me, yes! I heard you leave a while ago, but she lingered. I thought I heard her depart, but she was so quiet I was not sure she had gone, so I thought I had better wait a little. Then you burst in and began your accusations."

He was suddenly filled with a soaring hope. "And the other nights when I could not find you, you were spying on me then, too?"

She flashed him an angry look. "You truly want your pound of flesh, don't you. Then *yes!* What else could I do? I knew sooner or later she was going to steal you away from me!"

He was so full of hope now he felt as if he were atop a snow covered peak laughing down at the world. "And that argument we had in the carriage— that was because of this, too? You knew I had been with Regina?"

"Does it really please you to lay me bare this way?"

He realized just how much pain he had given her with his blasted campaign to woo Regina. She did not know it was a sham. She had no idea how little pleasure he had taken in the whole misbegotten venture. He thought of her keeping silent watch while she thought he was enjoying the sort of pleasures he had just been desperately afraid she had been indulging in. He would have to explain it all to her, every last bit of it, down to the last detail. But not now. Now there was only one thing he had to do. He sank to his knees before her. "My beloved Jane," he said softly, bowing his head. "Can you ever forgive me?"

"Oh, get up! I cannot bear to see you bent over like that, as if you were—"

"A penitent sinner waiting for absolution?"

"Stop it! Get up!"

"Only when you say you forgive me!" He cast a quick glance up. She was scowling at him. He relaxed a little.

"I'm not sure you deserve to be forgiven." Her tone was grumpy.

He relaxed a little more. "Then I shall be down here a very long time, and if you leave I shall have to follow you about on my knees."

"Perhaps I should have some special shoes fashioned for you."

"Cruel woman. Did I mention that, while I am down here, I would be happy to kiss your feet?"

"Sir," she said in a tone that was supposed to sound stern but burbled slightly with the sound of suppressed laughter, "are you not aware that foot kissing is a thoroughly depraved occupation?" She paused, and then added in a tone that suddenly held no amusement at all. "Though not nearly as depraved as what I am sure you have been doing while locked away in your secret little rooms."

"Jane," he said, unable to resist the temptation any longer to wrap his arms around her legs and press his head against her. "I know you will not credit it a whit, but what passed in those rooms gave me absolutely no pleasure at all. I spent every excruciating minute keenly aware that the only joys—carnal or otherwise—that I will ever find in a woman's arms will be in yours and yours alone."

She pulled free of his grip.

His stomach lurched. She did not believe him.

Then she was kneeling down beside him, peering at him. "But you love *her!* I saw it in your face!"

"I do not know what you saw in my face, my dear, but the only woman I love—and will love until the day I die—is you."

Her arms slowly crept up to encircle his neck. "Anthony," she whispered.

"Jane," he said softly, lifting her up with him as he rose to his feet. "Now, I would like to give you a very long and a very thorough kissing, but I insist on going somewhere else to do it." He glanced down with a shudder. "I think I have developed a phobia of that accursed sofa."

She stared down at the piece of furniture in bewilderment.

He said "I will explain it to you later, my love."

Chapter 33

Anthony was in a mood to celebrate. It was warm, and the sun was shining, and he wanted to be outside in the fresh March breeze with his beloved. He thought of going for their postponed ride together, but the associations of yesterday were still too fresh. Besides he wanted Jane closer than that. He wanted her directly next to him, close enough to feel her thigh against his, close enough to snatch a kiss if ever they found a secluded spot. He had no carriage in town, and Ryde had only the formal coach, which did not suit Anthony's purpose or his mood. It was unlikely Regina had been able to undo in a single night all the improvement in his social standing, so this one morning—before she unleashed the storm to once more sink his name—he wanted to parade around town like a peacock, his beautiful Jane at his side.

Fortunately, George Crawford had precisely the thing he needed, a fine barouche with a lovely set of greys. Anthony set off to call on Lady Charlotte's husband first thing to ask for the loan of the thing. Crawford greeted him warmly and was most obliging. and while his host went to make arrangements for the equipage to be made ready, Anthony penned a quick note to Jane and dispatched it with a footman telling her to make herself ready for a fine drive about Town.

Suddenly, Lady Charlotte entered the room. "Well, sir," she said, a fearsome scowl upon her face, "what have you to say for yourself this terrible morning?"

"Forgive me, Lady Charlotte, but I must disagree with you. The morning is not terrible but wonderful! Indeed, I am tempted to crow like a rooster in my happiness in it."

"Yes, no doubt you are pleased with Lady Darrow's machinations to puff up your good name. But what of my sister, sir? Are you equally pleased with the slanders your fancy lady has planted left and right accusing Jane of seducing you and forcing you into an engagement?"

"What!" he sputtered.

Lady Charlotte's green eyes widened. "You did not know?"

"Of course I did not know! I shall wring Regina's lily white neck for this!"

"No, sir! You must not! I do not think Jane would like it if you were hung for murder!"

Anthony was torn between amusement at the frightened look on Lady Charlotte's face and consternation that he had not seen this coming. Regina would have no use for him unless Jane was out of the picture. "Fear not, Lady Charlotte. I was only using a figure of speech to express my fury at Regina—and myself. I was a fool not to anticipate this."

"Oh." She kept flashing wary glances at him but said no more. He should have tried to make conversation, but he was in no mood. He and Lady Charlotte stood in silence until her husband returned to the room, a jolly smile upon his face. "All's ready for you, Winston. Hope you and Jane enjoy your ride. Had Cook pack you a picnic luncheon. Nothing more romantic than a picnic, I always say."

"Thank you, Crawford," Anthony said, shaking the other man's hand.

All the way back to St. John House, Anthony tried not to let Lady Charlotte's news ruin his mood. He would take Jane back to the country, and they would be married, and they could remain there for the rest of their lives if need be. A pox on the *ton* and their wagging tongues. He had no need of society. He just needed his Jane.

But what did Jane need?

Would she begin to pine for all the things she could no longer enjoy? Would she grow to resent him for what he had cost her? He pushed the worries away. Today he was simply going to be happy. Unfortunately, when the barouche pulled up in front of St. John House, he saw a sight that made him entirely forget his pledge to remain content in the day. Regina's phaeton was parked in front of the door. Her tiger was seated on the curb as if anticipating a long wait.

How dare *she!*

He took the steps three at a time and slammed the knocker so hard the butler's eyebrows were drawn into a single frowning line of disapproval when he opened the door. "Sir?" he intoned icily. No doubt it was as close as he could come to a reprimand to a guest of the house.

"Where have you put Lady Darrow?" Anthony demanded.

"In the red drawing room, sir, but—"

Anthony did not wait to hear more. He charged past the butler and hurtled upstairs. He burst into the red drawing room to find Regina mercifully alone. "How dare you seek me beneath this roof, ma'am!" His fury only seemed to grow at the sight of her.

"I did not come to see you, sir! I am here to pay a call on Lady Jane."

"You can have nothing to say to that lady worthy of her hearing!"

"That is a matter of opinion. I think she will find news of your visits to me highly intriguing, especially the more intimate details."

Anthony suddenly had a hard time remembering his training as a gentleman. He forced his rigidly clenched hands down at his side and exclaimed, "Ma'am, were you born with the manners of a whore, or did you simply acquire them over the years?"

Regina burst to her feet and stormed toward him, her chest heaving. "Do not speak to me of whores, sir! When I am done with that lady of yours, she will have to *aspire* to the social standing of the lowest drab in Covent Garden. You have used me, sir! You pretended to love me just to achieve your ends!"

"You mean as you used me two years ago to bait your hook and catch Wild Bill?"

Her hand came up to slap his face. He caught it, and if he was ungentle in his hold of her wrist, he did not care at all. "Do you know what I suffered because of your lies, Regina? You begged me to run off with you. Then you sent your maid to tell Wild Bill I had abducted you. You told me that you loved me, and then you sent him after me to kill me!"

"Let go of my arm, sir! You are hurting me."

He let her go and took a step back, unwilling to be so close to her. She flounced her shoulders. "Well he did not do so. On the contrary, you nearly killed him!"

"Yes, that must have frightened you!" he said, taking grim relish in the thought. "You must have dreaded that your golden prize was about to slip through your fingers."

Suddenly, to his surprise, she moved nearer again. "Anthony, I know you are bitter. I can understand your ... resentment. But are you truly so angry with me that you will let *your* golden prize slip through your fingers?" Her voice was soft and husky now, and she reached up and ran a finger along his jaw. "You know what a fine passion we share. I know how you burn for me." She tried to slip her hand inside his waistcoat. "Can we not come to some sort of understanding?"

He took another step back. "Ma'am, you have nothing to offer that I desire. My golden prize is the lady upstairs."

Regina made a disparaging sound. "What prize? She has no money, only middling looks, and it is said her dead husband was more fond of his mistress than of her, especially when it came to her efforts in bed."

His hand was half-way raised to strike her, when he realized she was as angry as he was. She was trying to goad him into violence, no doubt to blacken his name still further. He dropped his arm. "Poor Regina. It must be hard to be put so completely in the shade."

"In the shade—*by her?* That is laughable, sir!"

"Is it? She was born above you, ma'am. She is the daughter of a marquess, after all, while you are but the daughter of an earl. But it is her character that has lifted her to such exalted heights above your head. She is a woman of honor. She breathes honor as if it were a holy wind. You trample even the semblance of honor beneath your feet like dung."

"You are a fool, sir!" Regina exclaimed. "What is character in a woman? Nothing! No man ever longed for a woman's touch because of her honor. No man ever bedded a woman for her virtue. Pretty she may be, but she is nothing out of the ordinary! I am beautiful. Men abase themselves at my feet. Given a choice between her and me, you cannot mean that you would pick her!" Her small pink lips tightened into a white line.

He said quietly, "Never, Regina—not if you stared into the sun until you turned quite blind, could you conceive the splendor I see when I look at her. I would sooner spend a lifetime lying like a dog on the floor of her bedchamber hoping to catch a single glimpse of her nakedness than waste a minute partaking of the full measure of your paltry pleasures. Indeed, I gravely doubt I could find enough satisfaction in your arms to fill a thimble—could I tup you morning, noon, and night!"

Suddenly, he saw the furious line of Regina's mouth relax into a smile. At the same moment, reflected in a pane of glass, he noted a figure standing in the doorway behind him. He spun around. It was Jane—her blue eyes huge, her mouth open in shock.

Damnation! How much had she heard? More to the point—how little? Before he could ask her, Jane abruptly turned and fled.

"I do believe she quite appreciated your little quip about tupping me morning, noon, and night, Anthony," Regina remarked coolly.

"Go to hell, woman!" he cried as he ran from the room. He almost collided with the butler, who was hovering in the hall. "Did you see which way Lady Jane went?"

The butler looked quite shocked by the question. He drew himself up, very much on his dignity, and slowly began, "Sir, it is not my place—"

Anthony cut him off. "It *is* your place to show Lady Darrow out. Please do so at once!" And he ran on. Jane was not in any of the other drawing rooms, nor the music room, nor Ryde's study, nor even in any of the hidden alcoves in the library. Anthony ran downstairs to check the front door, but when he looked out, he could see no sign of her on the street, only Regina storming off in her phaeton.

She did not vanish into thin air!

Then he realized the obvious place—her bedchamber. He raced back up the stairs. He was so distraught and so desperate to find her, he did not think to knock, but simply burst into her room. She spun around in surprise, wearing nothing but her stays and shift.

"Anthony!"

"I—Jane, forgive me, but I—" He came to a stammering halt. It was so precisely like the morning at the inn. Sunlight was slanting in through the windows, shining through the thin linen of her shift, outlining her body in a golden glow. For a moment, he could not remember why he had come or what he had meant to say.

"Shut the door!" she hissed.

At least, she had not thrown him out. It was a start. He turned to close the door, using the action as an opportunity to gather his wits. "Jane," he began again.

"It is a good thing my maid is not here!" she scolded him.

"Forgive me, I was not thinking. I was just so determined to speak with you." He took a few steps toward her.

"Why?"

"I fear you may have misconstrued what you heard me say in the drawing room."

"You words were very clear. I believe I understood them perfectly."

He took a few more steps toward her. "You heard only a part, not the whole! Please, Jane, may I tell you the rest?"

"There is no need. I understand fully, I assure you."

"I would not have you think I still have feelings for that woman."

"It is quite clear how you feel about her, and how she feels about you."

"How *she* feels about *me*? But you were not there long enough . . ." He crossed the distance between them in three long strides. "Jane, just how much of my conversation with Lady Darrow did you manage to overhear?"

"A fair bit," she said, avoiding his eye.

"A fair bit?"

"Pretty well most of it. I must say, I did like that bit about her trampling honor underfoot as if it were dung."

"Jane!"

"Sorry, dearest."

"You have become quite adept at spying and listening at keyholes. It quite turns my blood cold."

"As well it should, my dearest. Please remember that next time you try to keep a secret from me." She grinned mischievously up at him.

"You little minx!" He slid his arms around her waist.

"I thought I was your golden prize."

"You look very golden in this outfit," he murmured. "The sun shines through it and outlines every curve in a nice golden glow." He began tugging gently on the laces of her stays. "Jane, I do not understand. If you heard all that I said, why did you go running off? You gave me quite a scare."

"After I heard what you said, I very much wanted to see your face."

That pleased him. He tugged a little more energetically at the laces. "Did you, my love?"

She nodded. "But you had your back to me, and all I could see was the Fairie Queen. I did not want her to see how happy you had made me. So I ran up here and was happy in private."

He chuckled. "The Fairie Queen. That's your name for Regina?"

"Yes, is it not apt?"

"Exceedingly so." The last lace was undone. "I suppose that makes me Tam Lin?"

He slipped her stays off her shoulders and they fell to the floor. Jane's eyes widened. "I suppose it does."

"Then you must be the one true love who saves me from the Faerie Queen's clutches." He ran a finger caressingly along the neckline of her shift. Her eyes closed. He kissed her mouth and then her neck and then his kisses moved lower. "Jane," he whispered, "may I?"

She nodded.

He undid the drawstring of her shift with trembling fingers and then pulled it wide to reveal her breasts. For a moment, he just wanted to gaze at them. Then he cupped first one and then the other. They felt so warm and perfect in his hands. He was just about to kiss them, when there was knocking at Jane's door. Her eyes flew open and she tugged her shift closed. Anthony groaned silently in frustration.

"Jane, dearest," called Lady Ryde. "May I come in?"

"*No!* I mean, I am changing, Catherine. May I meet you downstairs?"

"Of course, my dear. I thought since your maid has the toothache you might need assistance."

He watched, arrested, as every inch of her skin turned pink. "Thank you, no. I think I can manage."

He heard Lady Ryde's footsteps move away. Jane took a long, shuddering breath. "Oh, Anthony, that was so mortifying!"

"Calm yourself, my dear. All is well."

She was fumbling with the drawstring of her shift, but her fingers were trembling too much to actually manage to tie it. "Here, my love, let me," he said gently, feeling guilty that she had been given such a scare. He leaned over and picked up her stays and helped her slip it back on.

"Please, sweetheart, my fingers are so clumsy. Help me to lace it back up."

He struggled with the task. "I am considerably more expert at doing this in the other direction," he muttered.

"Of course you are, my dear, but do you think that the most tactful thing to tell me at such a time?"

"I am sorry. Do you forgive me?"

"Perhaps. Though the notion of your lying on my bedchamber floor desperate for a glimpse of my nakedness is beginning to have great appeal. Perhaps that is how we shall begin our honeymoon."

"Jane! You wouldn't!"

"I thought you said you would find that sufficient for the rest of your days," she said with a low chuckle, as he helped her put on the dress she had set out to wear for their ride.

He remarked with great feeling, "I find the prospect has considerably less appeal than it did ten minutes ago."

For once, Jane was grateful for George's obsession with picnics. She enjoyed sitting on this blanket picnicking with Anthony. The ride in George's barouche had been fine as well, though there had been enough unpleasant encounters with members of the *ton* to make it clear the Faerie Queen had already begun her work blackening Anthony's reputation again.

Jane, however, did not care. Anthony loved her, and they had found this secluded spot to picnic, and he had his head in her lap, and she was happy. She was blissfully happy. She bent down and gave him a kiss. When she had done, he grinned up at her. "Hmmm, my dear, that was very pleasant. What was the occasion?"

She smiled down at him. "Only that I love you."

His green eyes suddenly grew quite wide, and beneath her arm she could feel his heart pounding with surprising force.

"Whatever is the matter?"

"It is just so devilishly fine to hear you say that," he said, his voice strangely deep. "I mean, I knew it—or, at least, I hoped it, but it is so exceedingly reassuring to have you say the words out loud."

"Anthony, I told you so at *Farthingsgate!*"

"Yes, my dear, but I thought you were lying then —"

"*Lying!*"

"Yes, on account of the beating I took. I thought you were taking pity on me. It was so very obvious how besotted I was with you, and I believed that you were simply trying to make me feel better."

She was angry now. "And I suppose all those liberties I let you take with my person, those were all out of pity as well? Heavens, I never knew what a philanthropic character I possessed! Perhaps I should start a society providing kisses and caresses for all the suffering gentlemen here in the grand metropolis!"

"My dear!"

"Perhaps I should begin with Lord Farleigh. He is quite heartbroken over his loss of Catherine. Maybe I should volunteer to cheer him in his hour of need!"

"Jane! Now you are purposely provoking me!" His tone was light, but she noted that his face had gone quite white, and it suddenly occurred to her that it was not surprising he felt unsure of her love, of any woman's love, after how he had been mistreated by Lady Darrow.

"Oh, Anthony, I am sorry! I was just piqued, because I have been pining for you since that first night in Bagshot's cottage, and it was somehow mortifying that you did not realize it." She leaned over and gave him a second kiss, this one a great deal less tender and a great deal more passionate than the first. Somehow, when she was done, they had completely switched positions. His head was no longer in her lap; she was sitting on his lap, completely encircled in his arms. She sighed with contentment.

"Anthony," she said after a bit, "am I to understand from what I overheard this morning that you never kidnapped the Faerie Queen at all? She simply said that you did?"

"Hmmm, what did you say, my love?" He was busy kissing her neck and seemed to be paying her words no heed. She repeated the question.

"I thought we were eloping," Anthony finally responded, pausing for a moment before brushing his lips along the side of Jane's throat. "But Regina decided an abduction would help her snag Wild Bill. My dear, why do all your pelisses have to come up so very high? It makes things devilish difficult for a fellow."

"What about the first girl you are reputed to have kidnapped—I believe her name is now Mrs. Brand—did you really abscond with her?"

His mouth stopped moving, and his fingers stopped trying to unbutton her pelisse. "I am not at liberty to discuss the matter with you," he said stiffly.

"Anthony! Your reputation is in tatters because you are reputed to have kidnapped that girl as well as Lady Darrow, and you are not 'at liberty to discuss the matter'?"

"It is not my story to tell," he persisted stubbornly, his jaw set in an obdurate line she had come to know well.

"Very well. I see I will need to get the story directly from Mrs. Brand."

"Jane, you would not!"

"I think, my dear, you know that I would."

"I forbid you to do any such thing!" She simply gave him a look. He sighed. "You are not going to prove a very biddable wife, are you, my Jane?"

"I simply wish to know the truth! Will you not tell me the tale?"

So he told her. It turned out Mrs. Brand had been the daughter of one of his captains. She had wanted to marry Mr. Brand, one of Anthony's good friends and fellow lieutenants, but her father did not approve. The couple had planned an elopement, but the father was suspicious, and kept Mr. Brand under close watch. So Anthony had volunteered to be the one to carry the future Mrs. Brand off to an inn.

"But I do not understand. After the two eloped, did they not make it clear that you had only been an intermediary?"

His expression grew shuttered. "They did not end up eloping."

"Why not?"

"Her father came to an understanding with Jack—Mr. Brand—the very night Susie and I ran off to the inn. After that, they couldn't admit they had been planning to elope, so we left it that I had tried to force her, and Jack had rescued her before any harm was done."

Jane was furious. "And they left you to take all the blame? That is shameful!"

"Jack wanted to tell her father the truth, but Susie feared her father would call off the wedding."

"Why did they not tell him the truth after the wedding!"

"Almost immediately afterwards we were sent down to the Peninsula, and it did not seem all that important."

Jane was so full of anger, she began to feel as if fireworks were going off in her chest. "All that important! Your honor was stripped away, you were labeled a kidnapper, and it was not important? I am amazed her father did not call you out!"

"He had Jack do it." His tone was matter of fact. When he saw her face, however, he quickly added, "Of course, Jack was careful, and so was I, and there was no real harm done. I only got a small poke, really."

Every single firework was now exploding at once. She leapt up from his lap. *"Your own friend, the man you sacrificed so much for, had the gall to call you out?"*

"Jane, please, calm yourself," he beseeched, jumping to his feet as well. "It is not as bad as that."

She turned her back on him. She was starting to cry now. "It is worse!"

His hands slipped round her waist. "No. Jack didn't mean me any harm, and—in any case—I didn't do it for him."

Remembering Mrs. Brand's pretty face, Jane felt a sudden stab of jealousy. Slowly, she turned back to face him. "You loved her, didn't you? What was the matter? Wouldn't she have you?"

He shrugged again, looking embarrassed. "I was not the charming swashbuckler that Jack was. She could not even see me, let alone care for me."

Jane gave a loud, unladylike snort. "Mrs. Brand is not a very clever woman, is she?"

He hesitated. "She has a very vivacious personality and is very sweet really, though you might not believe it from this tale, but no, I suppose—in retrospect . . ." He stared off at the distance, as if considering the fact for the first time. "But how could you know such a thing, Jane? Have you met her?"

Jane gave another snort. "Any woman who could not see you amongst any company of men would have to be an idiot! Even the Faerie Queen knows your value, even if she sells it cheap!"

He looked startled but pleased. "Jane, you are wonderfully good for my pride. Do you know that?"

"I suspect your pride would not be so humbled, my love, if you were not such a lodestone for scheming females who do not value you as they should! I suppose the lady you eloped with was another of the same ilk? What was her tale? Did she inveigle you into eloping with her and then run off with some other fellow leaving you to take the blame?"

Two bright spots of color appeared in his cheeks.

"Oh, Anthony!" she cried, suddenly filled with tenderness for him. "You are a complete fraud!"

"What do you mean?"

You are no rake, sir! You are some misplaced knight-errant from another time, wandering the countryside, having your heart repeatedly assaulted because you are too gallant to protect it properly. It is a good thing it is finally in my keeping, for I know it for the treasure it is, and I shall always—*always, my dearest*—keep it safe."

To Jane's surprise, Letty was waiting for them at St. John house when they returned from their picnic. When they entered the blue drawing room, they found her pacing back and forth at a frenzied pace. "Letty, whatever is the matter?" Jane exclaimed.

"Oh, Jane! Thank goodness you are home! I trust you had no misadventures on your picnic?" Her eyes fixed on Anthony. "No gentlemen came up to accost you?"

"Letty, what in the world?"

"Mr. Winston, I gather you are no longer in Lady Darrow's good graces?"

Anthony slipped a proprietary arm around Jane's waist. "Most decidedly not, Lady Charlotte," he said with a grin. He flashed Jane a decidedly warm look, and then repeated proudly, "Most decidedly not."

"Letty what is wrong?" Jane said, starting to feel alarm.

Letty threw out her arms. "Nothing but complete catastrophe! Last night Lady Darrow made a new conquest: Lord Charles Burston."

Jane gazed at her sister blankly. "My dearest, this affects us how?"

"Oh, Jane, you are hopeless! Do you not know the *reputation* of Lord Charles?"

"No, Letty, I do not even know the identity of Lord Charles. Who is he?"

"He is the youngest son of the Duke of Braedeen, but that is not to the point. Or rather, I suppose it is, as he has run wild since he was a babe due to his exalted status."

"Letty, the point as it pertains to us?"

"The point, dear sister, is that the man is reputed to have a fierce temper and is prone to calling gentlemen out left and right! There are some that say he is more deadly than Wild Bill ever was. Some whisper he has planted at least five gentlemen that he has fought—and some claim it is six!" Her voice caught in a breathless little catch.

Jane suddenly began to grasp what her sister was getting at.

"Oh, no!" Jane cried. "You do not think—"

"I do not think, Jane, I know!" Letty exclaimed. "The stories are already flying."

Jane began to feel lightheaded. She reached out and gripped Anthony's hand tightly.

He looked down at her hand with a look of concern. "Jane. Lady Charlotte. Please. Can one of you enlighten me as to what we are discussing? I find it a little difficult to follow the breakneck speed of your conversation."

Letty frowned at Jane's beloved as if he were dimwitted. "Mr. Winston, you had an audience with Lady Darrow this morning, did you not?"

Anthony regarded her with a wary look. "Yes."

"You did not, by any chance, seize her arm in a violent grip during your ... discussion, did you?"

"I—she raised her hand to strike me, and I stopped her. That is all."

"Sadly, that is not the tale she is telling. She says you grew violent when she refused your proposal."

"Proposal!" he choked. "The only one receiving a proposal—and, I assure you, ma'am, it was not an honorable one—was me!"

Letty's mouth fell open. *"Mr. Winston!"* There was a note of awe in her voice that would have made Jane giggle if she were not fighting quite so hard just to draw breath.

"Letty," Jane cried. "Lord Charles—he does not intend to call Anthony out?"

"Oh, indeed he does! Sir, you must take to your bed—no, better yet, you must decamp to Rosington this very instant!"

Jane flinched at her sister's disastrous phrasing.

Anthony drew himself up into what Jane had come to think of as his battle pose. He said quietly but fiercely, "Lady Charlotte, I know you meant me no true insult, but please do not ever repeat such a suggestion to me again."

Poor Letty, who had never faced even this mild, well-contained version of Anthony's wrath before, fell back several steps and regarded him with wide eyes.

Jane felt a surge of despair. Her brave Anthony would do nothing to save himself, and she could think of nothing to do to save him. The familiar panic was rising up her throat, but she did not care. She did not bother trying to fight it. The darkness filled her head, and she let it.

Chapter 34

Jane had frightened the whole household with her swoon, and when she woke she found Matthew hovering over her bed telling her not to consider rising from it for at least a day. Apparently, it was not her faint that worried him, but the extremely hard rap on the head she had received when she hit the floor.

"Why you could not have aimed for the edge of the carpet, Jane, I cannot fathom," he teased her. Matthew was not the only one in her crowded bedchamber. Andrew came over and squeezed her shoulder and kissed her forehead. Catherine gripped her hand. And Letty, white-faced and teary, drew near and begged forgiveness.

"Oh, dear sister, I feared I had quite literally scared you to death!"

Jane chuckled, which was a mistake. It made her head ache painfully.

Matthew shooed them all out, telling them that she needed her rest. She thought she was alone, when Anthony appeared from the corner. "Oh! I did not ... see you there ... at all." She spoke softly so as not to aggravate her pounding head.

He did not say a thing, just bent down and kissed her cheek. He would not meet her eyes. Then she noticed the blood.

"Dear God ... what has happened? There is blood ... all over your waistcoat! Do not tell me Lord Charles —"

"Not my blood," he said hoarsely.

She suddenly realized that her hair felt quite matted and sticky. She reached up towards the back of her head. She wore a veritable turban of linen strips, and when she pressed the center of the turban—

"*Oww!*"

She looked back at him and caught his gaze before he could look away. His eyes were full of tears

"Anthony?"

"You frightened me, love. You truly frightened me. Do not ever frighten me like that again."

In the hours that followed, he resolutely refused to leave her bedside. Jane quickly realized that as long as he was watching over her he was safe from Lord Charles. So—much to Matthew's consternation and eventually his concern—her convalescence dragged on and on. Anthony also grew more and more worried, which made Jane feel guilty, but she preferred a worried Anthony to a dead one.

Finally, after a week had come and gone, Letty arrived with some hopeful news. The Duke of Braedeen had taken seriously ill, and Lord Charles, along with his two older brothers, had been summoned to the duke's bedside at the family seat in Scotland. Lord Charles was expected to be safely out of town for at least a fortnight.

Jane made a miraculous recovery. When she announced that she wished to rise from her bed, Anthony was so relieved he gave her a full and lengthy open-mouthed kiss right there in front of her brother. Jane was so mortified that she wished to sink below the floorboards, but Anthony was unrepentant, and Andrew simply turned his back on them and stalked out of the room, calling over his shoulder for Anthony to come see him in his study when he was done with Jane's "rehabilitation."

"What in the world did he mean by that?" she demanded when Anthony was finally done kissing her.

"It is a private joke, my love," he said with a grin. "Never mind."

Jane was not sure why she summoned her sisters and Georgiana to meet with her the following morning, except that she needed to talk, and she knew the gentlemen—as much as they might sympathize with her desire to secure Anthony's safety—were likely to come down on his side of the argument when it came to a matter of gentlemanly honor.

As the ladies gathered round her, Jane felt comforted already. She explained the looming danger Lord Charles represented, and she told them how Anthony had been slandered by the three ladies society thought he had wronged. She was gratified by the sense of outrage that circled the room, but she had not realized the effect her news would have on Georgiana. The poor girl burst into tears, exclaiming how guilty she felt for ever having doubted her dear brother. Once she had calmed, each lady expressed frustration with how far off the mark Anthony's reputation in the *ton* was from the man that they knew, but none of them could think of a way to right the wrong that had been done to him.

"Oh, Jane," Letty exclaimed, "he is like a hero from a book! If only we could get someone like Lord Byron to tell his story in a poem, then everyone would know his virtues!"

Jane stared at her sister. "Oh, Letty, that is a brilliant idea!"

Letty looked quite startled. "Do you truly think so, dear sister? Byron has a devilish reputation with the ladies. I think perhaps you should approach him with the commission, for I do not think any of our husbands would countenance such a meeting!"

"No, Letty. I am not proposing that Byron craft a new tale for Anthony. I am proposing that *we* do it!"

"I do not know about that either, Jane. I am accorded a very fine storyteller, but I have never been able to spell at all, and I cannot form a proper rhyme to save my soul."

"Letty, do not be silly!" Maria exclaimed. "Jane is not proposing that we save Mr. Winston with a poem! She has a far superior idea in mind, don't you, my dear?"

Jane nodded.

"Then explain it," said Alex, "for I do not understand what you are getting at."

"Yes, Jane," said Georgiana. "I do not either, and I do not like feeling stupid!"

"My dears," Jane said, "when there is a great scandal flying about, what is the only thing that can drive it out of people's minds?"

"Oh, that is simple," said Letty. "An even greater scandal."

"Or," said Catherine, suddenly gazing at Jane with a look of comprehension, "a more compelling tale!"

"Exactly! We have to rewrite Anthony's story so that it is far more interesting and moving and even scandalous in its way than the rather commonplace and dull little tattle that Lady Darrow is casting about. As you say, Letty, there are certainly enough elements in the real story to make for a rousing tale."

"Oh, that is brilliant!" exclaimed Alex and Georgiana simultaneously.

Jane looked at Maria. "Do you think it can work?"

A martial light appeared in her sister's eye. "If it is properly planned out, I think it might. But it will take all our resources to achieve. We each will have to play our part. And we will have to leave the gentlemen completely out of it."

"Why ever so?" demanded Alex.

"Because our gentlemen are far too honorable to be of any use. They could never be as ruthless and cutthroat as we will need to be to succeed."

Alex led her three carefully selected friends into the garden where Mr. Winston was playing with the twins. She still was not comfortable with the role Maria had assigned her. She was loath to discuss her late brother-in-law's illegitimate child outside of the family. She felt no compunction about the small storm of scandal that would fall on the new baron when it became known that he had shirked his duty to his late brother's child, but Jane's late husband had shamed her, and Alex was uncomfortable revealing that shame to the world. However, if Jane did not mind it, it was not Alex's place to mind it for her.

It had been Jane's idea to have Mr. Winston present, playing with the children, when Alex confided the secret of little John to her friends, and as the ladies entered the garden, Alex could only marvel at her sister's wisdom. Mr. Winston had removed his coat and was racing about the garden with first one boy and then the other on his fine, broad back. He was grinning, and the boys were screaming with laughter, and he appeared more like a very large boy himself than a notorious rake. When he saw the ladies, he started and looked quite abashed and rushed to don his coat with gallant alacrity. And by the time the ladies had finished inspecting the newly-bloomed primroses which were the purported reason for their visit to the garden, Alex was satisfied that he had made a very positive impression indeed.

The ladies adjourned to the drawing room for tea, and Alex found

excuses to take first one and then the other aside to tell them the tale
of little John and of Mr. Winston's heroic assumption of responsibility
for the boy to save Jane from scandal. Letty had emphasized the
importance of telling each lady privately so that each thought she
was the one and only recipient of the confidence. "That way they will
spread the gossip faster and farther," Letty had insisted, "for they will
each think they have a tidbit of unique value."

Alex hoped her sister was right. She had picked these three friends,
because she had learned over the years never to entrust any of them
with information she truly wished to keep secret. She prayed fervently
that none of them had reformed her ways, for, thinking back to the
grinning man in her garden, Alex found that she very much wanted
to do anything she could to keep him safe.

Jane walked along the path by the lake with Lord Farleigh at her
side. His daughter ran ahead chasing after a flock of geese. "Beware,
Lizzie," he called to her. "They see out the sides of their heads, not the
front. They can nip you quite hard if you are not careful!"

Jane reflected that Lizzie seemed quite fleet of foot and adept at
keeping out of the reach of the geese, but once again she was touched
by his concern for his daughter. "It is very good of you to meet me,
sir—especially after the misadventure of last time."

"Do not fear," he said with twinkling eyes, "my chest has quite recovered."

"Sir, I was referring to Mr. Winston's rather impetuous appearance,"
she replied primly, "as well you know."

He made a great show of looking over his shoulder. "I admit I am
not eager to encounter him again when he is at such a fever pitch.
When he galloped up it gave me great sympathy for the French. Is he
safely stowed?"

"Yes, sir. He is in my sister's keeping for the rest of the afternoon."

"Good. Then I suppose we should get down to business—*Lizzie,
have a care!* Forgive me, Lady Jane. Where was I? Ah, yes, Lady
Henrietta is intrigued by your story and would like to be of assistance.
She has asked me to convey an invitation to you to attend a dinner
party at her house one week from tomorrow. May I tell her that you
will be there?"

"Of course, sir! Thank you very much. Do you think the gentleman you wrote to me about will be at this dinner party?"

"Mr. Hungerford? Yes, unless he is at death's door. Lady Henrietta is a favorite of his, and she has made it plain that she wishes him to attend that evening."

"And do you truly think he will be able to influence Lord Charles in the matter?"

He shrugged. "It is difficult to say. Lord Charles possesses a very mercurial temper. However, if anyone can influence him, it will be Hungerford."

"It is very kind of Lady Henrietta to assist me. To be honest, I am a little astonished that she is willing to be bothered. I have always heard that she has little use for other ladies, and prefers at all times the company of gentlemen."

"Henrietta has more the temperament of a gentleman than a lady. She does not tolerate fools gladly, and finds chatter about dresses and the latest *on-dits* and society in general to be intolerably boring."

"So do I much of the time," said Jane.

"Why does that not surprise me, my lady?"

"Sir, I am unsure whether to take that last comment as an insult or a compliment."

He laughed. "I think you and Lady Henrietta will rub along together very well."

They walked along companionably for a distance, and then Jane touched his arm. He turned to face her. "Sir, I do not know how to thank you for all your help in this matter. I had no right to expect such—" her voice caught, "such generosity of spirit from you, sir. I know how much you must feel I have cost you, and it is noble indeed of you to overlook the fact and assist me anyway." She held out her hand. "Thank you, sir. Thank you from the bottom of my heart."

He clasped her hand gravely, shook it, and then made her a little bow. "Lady Jane, is it possible that you and I have become friends?

She smiled at him. "Yes, sir. I believe we have."

"Well," he said with a chuckle, "I won't tell anyone, if you don't."

Maria led her small troop of ladies toward her husband's most precious sanctum, his billiards room. Normally, ladies were not allowed inside its hallowed walls, but after much pleading from her, Edward had finally agreed to make this one exception, since he was so proud of his new table from Mr. Thurston.

"Edward, my friends are all in a tumult to see an actual billiards game played, especially on the very type of table possessed by both Prinny and Wellington! Surely you do not want to deprive them of such a pleasure?"

"Oh, very well, my dear. I can deny you nothing." He offered her a very sweet kiss.

It had been luck, indeed, that Mr. Winston was such a proficient billiards player that Edward was mad to play him. Maria had arranged that the game would take place the day of her friends' visit. As she led the way toward the billiards room, she warned her friends that Edward had a strict rule against gentlemen playing billiards with their coats on, for he held it hampered proper movement. As she expected, the ladies were clearly more intrigued than put off by the notion of observing two gentlemen playing their game in a state of undress.

To Maria's surprise, billiards turned out to be a surprisingly intriguing and exhilarating game to watch, and Alex had been right. It had been very strategic indeed to introduce the ladies to Mr. Winston with his jacket off. He made a very impressive sight. He was also appealingly self-conscious about lacking his coat, and Edward reprimanded him in an undertone when he made as if to put it back on.

"They are not a group of green girls, sir. They will not swoon at the sight of your back. Let us continue with our game!"

Maria was not so sure her husband was correct about the swooning part, as several of the ladies were fanning themselves quite vigorously as they watched Mr. Winston play. She, herself, was quite enjoying seeing her husband without his coat, especially as he moved about the table. She realized she would enjoy seeing the sight more often.

As the gentlemen played, Maria began to whisper in an undertone about Mr. Winston. She told the ladies of his heroic service in the Peninsula and of his grievous injury at Busaco. She described in rather graphic detail the immense bayonet scar on his chest, and as Mr. Winston leaned towards them while concentrating hard on making a shot, Maria could see the ladies lean forward as well, clearly imagining that scar with great concentration.

Then she told them how he had been beaten and set upon by three ruffians with knives in an ambush and had still managed to fight back well enough to kill one of the scoundrels and mark the other two sufficiently that they were apprehended. Finally, she told the ladies how Mr. Winston had saved her dear sister from freezing to death in the snow. She saw her friends' eyes grow large in admiration for the manly hero before them. When the billiards game was finished, Edward was quite gratified by the ladies' open enthusiasm, and Maria was satisfied that the afternoon's entertainment had been extremely effective.

That evening, as she was lying in Edward's arms as they drifted off to sleep, she said softly, "You know, my dearest, I enjoyed having the opportunity to watch you play billiards today. It seems a very fine game. Do you think you would be willing to teach me to play?"

For a moment, Edward was quite silent. Then his arms tightened around her. "I think I would enjoy that, Maria. You are probably the only lady of my acquaintance I consider sensible enough to properly appreciate the game, and I must say it would be a pleasure . . ." He paused and flashed her one of those rare and precious grins he shared only with her. "It would be a pleasure watching you bend over to make your shots, my dear."

Catherine gazed at the lady being handed up into the coach by one of her husband's liveried footmen and felt a twinge of guilt. Then she thought of Jane and Mr. Winston and pushed the feeling away. Jane had approached the woman honestly and fairly. She had explained the seriousness of the situation and tried to make the woman see that this was a matter of life and death for Mr. Winston. Mrs. Brand, however, was one of those people who glide through life completely unaware and uncaring of the impact of their actions on other human beings.

Catherine did not often go out in her husband's formal coach. It was an impressive equipage. It was large and newly painted, and it bore the St. John family crest. It also required four horses to pull it. Most of the time Catherine found it pretentious. Today, however, it served a purpose. Jane had predicted it would do much to awe Mrs. Brand, as would being asked to go for a drive in the park by a marchioness. Looking at Mrs. Brand's excited face, Catherine realized that her sister-in-law had been right.

"Thank you, Mrs. Brand, for being so gracious as to join us this morning."

"It is an honor, my lady," Mrs. Brand said, her pale blue eyes quite wide.

"Please, Mrs. Brand, you may call me Catherine. Allow me to introduce my sister-in-law, Letty, and her friend Sally. My dears, this is Mrs. Brand—may we call you Susie?"

"Oh, of course ma'am. It would be a pleasure."

Catherine smiled at her. Jane had assured her the lady was rather stupid, which was an essential element of the plan, but Catherine had doubted she could be quite as dim as Jane had indicated. She had feared Jane was indulging in a bit of wishful thinking, but it was beginning to look as if the woman really was as simple-minded as Jane had claimed. Catherine had worried that this instant invitation to familiarity might put the woman on her guard, but she was apparently too foolish to realize the danger.

"I understand, Mrs. Brand," she said in her most sympathetic tones, "that you had a rather unpleasant visit from my sister-in-law, Jane, yesterday."

"Yes, ma'am."

"Catherine," she reminded her.

"Yes, Catherine."

"That is why I invited you to take this ride with us today. I fear our Jane has been taken in by her rogue of a fiancé and believes him innocent of these terrible crimes we have all heard of."

Mrs. Brand nodded. "She tried to get me to admit that Anthony—I mean, Mr. Winston—did not kidnap me at all!" Unobserved by Mrs. Brand, Letty and her friend exchanged a look.

"Yes, poor Jane is quite deluded, Susie. That is why I wish you to give me all the details of your horrific ordeal." Catherine spoke in a confiding undertone. "I feel that if I can share these details with my sister-in-law, she will at last understand the truth."

"All the details?" For the first time, Mrs. Brand sounded uneasy.

"Every last one, though I know it will require great bravery on your part. Let us begin at the beginning. How did Mr. Winston carry you away?"

"Carry me away, Catherine?"

"How did he transport you to the inn where your betrothed discovered you?"

"Oh! In a curricle, ma'am."

"A curricle," Catherine repeated, unable to entirely eliminate the tone of surprise in her voice. Letty and her friend exchanged another look.

"Yes, quite a fine yellow one with lovely green seats."

Catherine, unable to trust her voice, simply nodded. After a moment, she had herself enough under control to say, "And how did he force you into the vehicle?"

"Force me, Catherine?"

"Yes, my dear Susie. I assume he used some sort of force to get you into the curricle? After all, you were being kidnapped. You did not go with him willingly, I presume?"

"Oh, no, of course not! He—uh, he pointed a pistol at me and told me if I did not come with him at once, he would ... he would ... blow my brains out! Made me quite afraid for my life."

"Yes, I can see how that would. You poor dear! As he drove you away did he keep you at pistol point?"

"Oh, yes, Catherine, the whole long way. I almost swooned from fear."

"My dear Susie, how ghastly! One quick question. How did Mr. Winston handle the ribbons, if he kept the pistol in his hand?"

"Oh, he ... uh, now that I think upon it, he put the pistol down. Yes, that is it! He put it on the seat next to him. After all, I was already in the curricle, and I was not about to hop out again!" Mrs. Brand looked both relieved and pleased with herself at this excellent explanation.

"Yes, that makes perfect sense. By the way, on a totally unrelated note, someone told me that you are actually quite a good shot with a pistol yourself! Can that really be true?"

"Oh, yes, Catherine! My father taught me when I was just a girl. He says I am the best shot in the regiment!" She smiled proudly.

"What an impressive skill for a lady and so very useful. Tell me, my dear, if the pistol was next to Mr. Winston on the seat, was it not also next to you? It is a pity you did not grab it up and shoot him with it."

Mrs. Brand licked her lips nervously. "I tried to, but he twisted it out of my hands."

"Oh, goodness, my dear! How terrible! And how fortunate that the curricle did not overset."

"Overset, ma'am? Why should it do that?"

"Why? Because I presume that if Mr. Winston was struggling with you for the pistol, he could not have been driving the horses. I tell you, Susie, you had a very close call. It is as if you had a guardian angel watching over you. Now, when you reached the inn, what happened then?"

"Um, I went to my room."

Catherine's eyebrows rose.

"I mean the room Mr. Winston forced me to," Mrs. Brand corrected.

"And I suppose it was then that Mr. Brand arrived."

"Oh, no! He didn't arrive until the next morning."

"Of course. He still had to figure out where Mr. Winston had taken you, and that would have taken time."

"Exactly, my lady!"

"So how did Mr. Brand track you down, by the way?"

"Why Anthony left him a note, of course! I mean...he told Jack that he had taken me, and he planned to have his way with me, and Jack should just give up hope of ever seeing me again!"

"Well, that was very foolish of Mr. Winston, for then Mr. Brand knew where to find you. And the threat no doubt spurred him to come for you even more quickly." Mrs. Brand nodded eagerly. "A pity that Mr. Brand overset his carriage."

Mrs. Brand stared at her. "Overset his carriage?" she exclaimed in an outraged tone. "Jack is an excellent whip. He would never do such a thing!"

"Oh, forgive me. I misunderstood. Why then did it take him so very long to reach the inn?"

"He. . . um ... his horse went lame."

"He was riding, then—not driving a carriage?" This time Mrs. Brand's nod held less certainty. "But how did he plan to transport you away from Mr. Winston's clutches?"

Mrs. Brand stared mutely at Catherine for an excruciatingly long time. Then a relieved look finally crossed her face and she blurted out, "He planned to rent a post-chaise."

"How very practical of him! Now back at the inn, Mr. Winston had carried you off to a room to have his way with you. However in the world did you stop him?"

Catherine was beginning to feel quite sorry for Mrs. Brand. She was like a dazed sheep who does not know which way to run. "I ... um ... threw myself on his mercy."

"But, of course, he had none," Catherine remarked. "Oh, Susie, you poor creature! Did he tear your clothes from your body?"

"No, of course not!" Mrs. Brand exclaimed, her face turning quite red. "Anthony would never do such a thing!" Her hands came up to cover her mouth. "I mean, he was afraid of Jack, and knew Jack would punish him if he did!"

"But did he not tell your Jack that that was precisely what he meant to do? He is reputed to be such a fearsome rake, I am sure he must have terrified you with his debauched demands. Mr. Brand must have been anguished the next morning to find you no longer the pure maiden he fell in love with." Catherine gave her a sad smile. "He must be a very big-hearted fellow to marry you anyway."

"Now see here, my lady! Jack was lucky to get me! He knew he had nothing to worry about, not with Anthony watching over me. I mean, if Anthony had put one finger out of place, I would have—" Once again, her hand flew up to her mouth. But this time she did not even try to recover. Instead, she wailed, "Oh, ma'am! I'd like to get out now, please! I've had enough of riding around the park for one day!"

"Of course, Susie." Catherine signaled the coachman to stop, and Mrs. Brand scampered down the coach steps before the tiger could even get down to assist her.

After she had disappeared from sight, Letty said with a relieved sigh. "Sally, forgive us for this most tedious ride, but you see why we were in such desperate need of your help."

"Yes, dear Letty, I do see. I do, indeed. But the ride was not tedious at all. It was actually quite . . . enlightening."

Catherine smiled, and the nervous knot in her stomach began to uncurl. "Lady Jersey, would you like us to drive you home now?"

"Yes, Lady Ryde. That would be most kind."

Chapter 35

eorgiana relaxed against Matthew as he carried her to Lord Ryde's magnificent coach. He set her down on the seat and sat down next her, and, to her surprise, when she turned to look at him, he was silent and unsmiling.

The soirée had gone splendidly. Many gentlemen and even a few ladies had come to sit beside her during interludes in the music. She had been able to talk about Anthony and tell people what a wonderful brother he was and how glad she was he had found true love. It was amazing how many people suddenly wished to meet Anthony Winston's crippled sister. The idea stung, but she was happy to be helping her brother, and she could bear it.

Matthew was beside her always, which, of course, made everything bearable and even pleasant. It was wonderful to dress up in fine gowns and to have her hair done up in cunning styles and to feel pretty. And she did not fear the daunting, crowd-filled rooms, because he was there to carry her into them in his strong arms. He would stand beside her, so handsome and so devoted, and she would feel like a queen being paid court to instead of an object of pity being gawked at.

She sighed. She was tired—very, very tired. But now she could go home and sleep in her amazingly large bed—Lord Ryde did not seem to possess a small bed in any of his fine houses—and dream about the day she would be able to stand by Matthew's side in the pretty little church near Rosington as they were married. With another sigh, she nestled against him and tried to rest her head on his shoulder. But to her surprise and dismay, he slid away from her to the far end of the seat. The coach was so big and the seat so wide—did Lord Ryde possess *nothing* that was a normal size?—she could not even reach out and touch him.

"Matthew! Whatever is the matter? Did the evening tire you?"

"Of course it tired me!" he snapped, in a tone so unlike his usual calm, pleasant voice that she began to grow alarmed. She sniffed the air and realized it smelled of spirits. Her Matthew, who usually never drank more than a glass or two of wine, had been drinking in earnest tonight. He turned to look at her, and there was enough moonlight sliding in through the windows for her to see that his expression was blazing. "Of course I'm tired! I spent the whole damn evening watching a troop of men make up to you and flirt with you and try to steal you out from under my very nose, and I cannot even be angry with you, because you act like you do not even know that it is true!"

"Matthew, what in the world are you talking about? None of those gentlemen was flirting with me! We were simply talking—about Anthony! I spoke with several ladies, too, you know," she added in a voice that wavered.

"Oh, Georgiana, you are so cursed young and innocent! You've no notion when some man is lusting after you—no notion of how beautiful you are. I snapped you up before you had any chance to see the world, to see what your choices were, and now I cannot breathe for fear you will realize you have made the wrong one."

"Matthew, stop it! Stop it right now! Stop treating me like I am some idiot miss without a brain in my head!" To her mortification and chagrin, Georgiana's voice broke, and her eyes started to fill with tears. "You know quite well that every single gentleman who stopped to speak with me tonight did so as if I were a spectacle—a curiosity to go home and tell their friends about!"

Before she knew what was happening, he was back beside her and his strong arms were lifting her up onto his lap. "No, my sweet Georgiana, no!" he murmured, hugging her tight. "They came to speak with you because you were the most lovely woman in the room. Because in that green gown you looked like the most beautiful flower in the most beautiful garden in the whole wide world." He pressed his head against hers. "I spent the whole damn night so afraid one of those lofty, high-born gentlemen was going to snatch you away from me, I was not sure I was going to make it through to the end without planting someone a facer. But I realize now that I have been horribly selfish."

He began kissing her gloved fingers one by one. "You deserve a proper courtship," he said, his kisses skimming slowly along her gloved arm from wrist to forearm to elbow, "and the chance to be fought over," his warm lips were caressing the bare skin of her arm now, "and to see that there are—" his voice caught and his mouth withdrew, "other men who realize what a treasure you are."

Her chest began to ache. "I do not like the direction this conversation is going."

"My dear," he said, pressing a kiss against her hair. "I release you from your promise to me. You can consider our engagement at an end, if you wish."

"I do *not* wish!" she cried.

"But consider," he said, in an infuriatingly noble voice that tempted her to howl with frustration, "think of all the gentlemen who paid court to you tonight, who could offer you a richer and more comfortable life than I ever shall be able to!"

"Nobody paid court to me!" she insisted. "A few men came and looked at me and talked with me politely, but do you think any of them listened to me as you do, or made me feel safe and cared for as you do, or … called me a beautiful flower … or made me want to kiss them so much I feel as if … as if . . ."

"Yes?" he exclaimed, a sudden eager catch in his voice. "As if what?"

She seized his face with both hands and stared directly into his eyes. "As if—if you don't kiss me this very instant I shall break apart into a million painful pieces!" she gasped.

"Then I had better kiss you at once." His voice was so caressing she felt as if he were enfolding her in the finest, softest cashmere wrap. When the kiss was over, she snuggled close.

"Matthew?"

"Yes, my love."

"How soon could we be wed if we were married by special license?"

"I do not know for sure. Within a few days, I should think."

"That long?"

"Georgiana, my darling! Why so impatient?"

She felt suddenly shy.

But this is Matthew, she reminded herself. "This is so embarrassing," she whispered, "but, you see I feel as if … as if . . ."

"As if what?" he demanded again. This time his voice was impatient, even worried.

She continued in an embarrassed whisper, "As if I need to do something more than kiss you soon, or I shall begin to … to boil over like a teakettle!"

He stared at her, and then a surprisingly wicked gleam appeared in his eyes. "I shall go for the special license first thing in the morning," he assured her. "In the meantime —"

"Yes, Matthew?"

"We have a long carriage ride home." His fingers began undoing the fastenings of her pelisse. "Let me see if I can reduce you to a simmer."

Jane looked up at Lady Henrietta's fashionable residence and tried not to shudder. She was almost sick from nervousness. She had to handle tonight perfectly. Slowly she climbed the steps and lifted the knocker. It felt strange to be arriving at this house, alone and unaccompanied. It felt stranger still to enter the house and to be shown into a drawing room full of gentlemen. There was not another lady present except her hostess. Jane had never been any place where she had been so completely outnumbered. At first, she felt horribly uncomfortable and self-conscious. Then her hostess greeted her and made introductions, and some of the gentlemen began speaking with her, and Jane realized there was a certain exhilaration to be found in being in such an intoxicatingly masculine enclave that was still, somehow, ruled by a woman.

Lady Henrietta returned to Jane, an older gentleman at her side. "Lady Jane, allow me to introduce a dear friend to you. This is Mr. William Hungerford. Hungerford, this is Lady Jane Brawley, sister to the Marquess of Ryde." Jane and Mr. Hungerford murmured polite greetings to each other, but Jane noted gloomily how hostile the expression in the man's watchful eyes had grown at the sound of her name. "You must know, Hungerford. Farleigh has quite filled my ears with Lady Jane's praises."

"His generosity in doing so astonishes me, ma'am," Jane remarked quietly, "for he has every reason to do the opposite. I fear I cost him something quite dear to him." To Jane's surprise, Lady Henrietta flashed her a look that made it clear she knew exactly what Jane was alluding to. "As to the content of his praise—I find that even more difficult to fathom, for I am quite ordinary, ma'am, with the usual assortment of virtues and faults."

Lady Henrietta smiled. "He said you were an honest lass." There was a faint emphasis on the last two words, as she turned to the gentleman at her side. "Hungerford, escort me into dinner. Lady Jane, I shall send Sotherton to lead you in."

Sotherton turned out to be the Earl of Sotherton, a plain man with exceedingly handsome manners. He put Jane completely at her ease, which was a mercy, for her stomach was now churning so hard she was not sure how she was going to look at her dinner, let alone eat it. Perhaps sensing her nervousness, he told her several amusing stories that made her laugh. Then he distracted her from her whirling thoughts with interesting but comfortable small talk until she grew so calm she was able to take a few bites of Lady Henrietta's French chef's excellent cooking.

By the end of the first course, Jane was convinced that the earl was much more handsome than she had realized originally, and by the end of the second, she considered Anthony very lucky indeed that she was so single-mindedly devoted to him, for the earl might otherwise have turned her head.

They were beginning on the third course when Lady Henrietta—who was seated at the center of the table directly across from Jane—enquired in a surprisingly carrying voice, "Lady Jane, Farleigh tells me that you had a very eventful beginning to your year."

Jane took her cue and said as loudly and clearly as she could, "Yes, ma'am, the start of the year was indeed eventful for me, for I almost did not live to see the rest of it."

Suddenly the attention of a number of gentlemen shifted to her. The earl's gaze was quite fixed. Mr. Hungerford, however, continued to speak with the gentleman on his left.

"My goodness, Lady Jane!" exclaimed Lady Henrietta with a twinkle. "It sounds quite a tale. Will you share it with us?"

"Of course, ma'am, though I fear it does not shine a very flattering light on my good sense. I decided to take a walk, you see, in the bright January sunshine . . ."

She told them how she had walked deep in thought and had lost track of where she was. She described climbing up the stile and falling, wrenching her ankle. She tried to help them see her there in the field, unable to walk or even stand, with the snow beginning to fall.

"I had quite given up hope, ma'am," she said softly. She did not need to raise her voice now to be heard. No one else was talking. Even Mr. Hungerford was forced to listen, for the man at his side had abandoned speaking with him to fix his attention on her. "The snow was coming heavy and fast. I was blanketed in the stuff and had stopped feeling the cold. I began to say my final prayers. Then a man appeared out of the shadows and knelt before me. It was Mr. Anthony Winston. He had already been trudging through the snow for some time and was weary, but he lifted me up in his arms and carried me to shelter."

She described how they had made their slow progress toward Bagshot's cottage through the blowing wind and snow. She told them how Mr. Bagshot had been absent when they arrived at the dimly lit cottage, but how Anthony had gotten a fire going and provided them light. She had already decided that to be convincing she must be painfully honest in her story, so she told them of their sodden, icy clothing and of how she had been shivering so much she could not untie her own bonnet strings.

Taking a deep breath, she told them of Anthony helping her to remove her wet clothes. She sensed, rather than saw, the suppressed grins and bawdy glances many of the gentlemen exchanged at this portion of her narrative, but the earl was gazing at her with encouraging gravity, and Mr. Hungerford was finally paying her some heed. Cheeks burning, she described Anthony's cutting her boot from her swollen ankle and getting her settled in her chair and lying on the hard floor below her instead of upstairs in the bed so he could tend the fire and watch over her while she slept. She did not call him her knight errant, but tried to convey it in every word she spoke and every detail she gave.

"Then, in the morning, my brother and some men from the village found us, and Mr. Winston went to my brother and honorably offered to marry me." Several of the gentlemen inclined their heads approvingly. "We thought the storm safely past, but then—" Her voice caught. She had known that this would be the most difficult part of her story to tell, but had not been prepared for the raw feeling that suddenly filled her to bursting.

Lord Sotherton was urging his handkerchief on her. She took it and wiped her eyes quickly. She cleared her throat. "Forgive me, ma'am, I do not mean to be missish." She bit at her lip, and then launched in quickly, so as not to give her mind too much time to think. "Three local men decided that my honor needed to be avenged. They ambushed Mr. Winston and beat him within an inch of his life."

She paused and wiped at her eyes with the earl's handkerchief one more time. She told of how Anthony had fought valiantly against the three men with their knives and had driven them off before collapsing. She described how he had been so covered in wounds she had had to pat the blood off of him with wet strips of linen. The grinning, bawdy mood was gone. The gentlemen were somber. Mr. Hungerford watched her with less hostility.

"Fortunately," she said, "God was merciful, and Mr. Winston healed. However, we soon realized that those three scoundrels were not the only ones spreading lies about what had taken place in the cottage." Was she imagining it or did Mr. Hungerford almost look abashed? "In February, Mr. Winston—though still recovering from his wounds—escorted me on a short visit here to London so I could take care of some business of my late husband's." Again, several of the gentlemen nodded, finding this behavior quite seemly.

"One day, to cheer me after what proved a melancholy affair—" Several of the gentlemen gave a start of recognition. Had Alex succeeded in spreading the word about little John so quickly? "Mr. Winston took me for a ride in the park, and we had several unpleasant encounters. It became clear that rumors about our misadventures had preceded us to Town. Then we met the Marchioness of Darrow." No gentleman spoke, but they all shifted in their chairs and leaned forward, obviously curious to imagine such an encounter.

"Ma'am," Jane said, "I am sure you are aware of the rumors that have long circulated about Mr. Winston having kidnapped the marchioness?"

"Rumors, my dear?" Lady Henrietta said gently.

"Yes, I know. I believed them myself until quite recently, for Mr. Winston was too honorable to ever distress me by discussing the matter openly." Many of the gentlemen exchanged skeptical glances.

A few made dismissive sounds. Mr. Hungerford now openly scowled at her. "But I digress," Jane continued. "I was telling you of our visit to the park. In the distance, I saw a most beautiful lady approaching. She was driving a lovely phaeton with matched white horses. I did not recognize her, for I had never had the pleasure of making her acquaintance, but she obviously recognized Mr. Winston. She approached and hailed him by saying, "Why, Mr. Winston, is this your new whore?""

Several of the gentlemen openly gasped. The earl looked grim. Mr. Hungerford paled. Lady Henrietta regarded Jane sympathetically. "That must have been very painful for you, my dear."

Jane gave her a grateful smile. "It was, ma'am, though I thought I understood the bitterness behind the remark when I learned the lady's identity. You see, I still thought then that she was the injured party in the matter, rather than the other way around."

There was a stir of mutterings and expressions of disbelief. Mr. Hungerford became spokesman for the group. "Ma'am, in what possible way do you acquit Mr. Winston of the very serious harm he did that lady? Do you contend, as has been bandied about of late, that Mr. Winston only kidnapped the lady to prevent Lord Darrow from doing so?"

Jane shook her head vigorously. "Oh no, sir! That is a calumny against Wild Bill."

Her answer seemed to flummox Mr. Hungerford, and several hoots and snickers ricocheted around the room. Lady Henrietta remarked dryly, "My dear, I suspect that is the first time that those words have ever been spoken."

"Ma'am, if you reject that explanation of Mr. Winston's actions," Mr. Hungerford demanded angrily, "then how do you possibly excuse his abduction of the lady?"

"Sir, I do not excuse it. I say that it never happened."

Now the cacophony in the room became a roar.

"That is preposterous! That it *did* happen is a fact that all here are aware of!"

Jane's heart was pounding now, but she kept her voice calm and firm. "I fear, sir, that you are mistaken. The lady eloped with Mr. Winston and then sent word to Wild Bill that she had been kidnapped so he would chase after them and finally make an offer for her."

The room was silent, every man in the room staring at her. It was Lady Henrietta who gave Jane the courage to hold fast. She gave Jane a faint, silent nod as if to say that she, at least, believed her.

Mr. Hungerford's expression became almost pitying. "Ma'am, I regret to say that you have been fed a pack of lies by that scoundrel you are betrothed to."

"But sir, I did not learn the truth from his lips. I learned it from hers, when I overheard a rather heated discussion between Mr. Winston and Lady Darrow in my brother's drawing room, after she had the poor taste to pay me a call."

Mr. Hungerford's face was now a choleric red. "Are you telling me, ma'am, that the interview between Lady Darrow and Mr. Winston when he laid ungentle hands on her was *in your brother's drawing room*? He *proposed* to her in your brother's drawing room?"

"Pardon me, sir, but that report, too, is mistaken. After the unpleasantness in the park, Mr. Winston was understandably distressed at the thought of Lady Darrow's accosting me in my brother's house, so he went in to speak with her before I arrived. I was unaware of this, however, and I was about to enter the drawing room when I heard their raised voices." Jane paused. She could sense every man in the room teetering between belief and disbelief. She had to thread the needle exactly right.

"So you claim he did not propose to her?" Mr. Hungerford demanded.

Jane shook her head. "He did not. *She* proposed to *him*—a rather dishonorable proposal that he declined. Angry at his refusal, she raised her hand to him, and he seized it so that she could not slap him. As far as I know, that was the total extent of the violence between them, despite the provocation of her asserting that when she was done with me—forgive me, sir, I wish to get the words exactly right—I would have to 'aspire to the social standing of the lowest drab in Covent Garden.'"

Now the gasps slid all the way round the table, but Jane only had eyes for Mr. Hungerford. His expression had suddenly grown as shuttered as a closed-up house.

She had failed.

"Forgive me, ma'am," she said, suddenly sinking under a wave of despair. What did any of her sisters' efforts mean, if this one man remained unswayed? "I did not mean to mire your fine dinner party in all this unhappiness. Perhaps I may be excused?"

Lady Henrietta regarded her with kind sympathy across the table. "Of course, my dear. Of course."

As the butler summoned her carriage and a maid brought Jane her things, she was surprised to see Lord Sotherton enter the drawing room. The earl crossed to her. "Lady Jane, may I have a word with you before you go?"

"Yes, sir, of course."

"We gentleman have a tendency to see valor as a virtue unique to our sex, but I would like you to know that what I have observed here tonight was quite courageous. Your Mr. Winston is very fortunate indeed to have such a stalwart defender."

"But I failed, sir."

"Perhaps. But do not despair too soon. You have given *every* man in that room food for thought. However, some men do not like to wolf down their food in one bite. The results of your efforts may not be apparent for a while. Courage, my lady. You must continue to be brave."

"Thank you, sir. I will try."

Chapter 36

Anthony moved slowly up toward the ballroom, his hand tight on Jane's arm. She looked lovely in her new peach-colored gown, but it was not possessiveness that made him hold on to her so fiercely. It was fear. There was hectic color in her cheeks, and her heart was pumping so hard he could feel her pulse in her arm. For some reason, she was afraid, and that made him afraid. He did not want her swooning on this devilishly tall staircase.

He was still haunted by the memory of sitting on the floor in Ryde's drawing room, her bleeding head cradled against his chest. He had been terrified that she was dying—was dead already—because she had been so still. For a time, Anthony had felt Romeo's despair and had wondered how he would find the strength not to seek Romeo's remedy. Then Elton had come and assured him Jane still lived, and Anthony had dared to breathe again.

He looked up at Elton, toiling on the step above him, and smiled. Elton did not look as if he minded the effort it took to carry Georgiana all the way up this interminable staircase. Indeed, the sandy haired man looked happy and exceedingly well-pleased with himself, and who could blame him? Tomorrow was to be his wedding day. Anthony felt a pang of envy. When Elton and Georgiana had come to him to announce that they had decided not to wait and were going to marry by special license, he had been sorely tempted to join them and announce a double-wedding, but Ryde had said no, and Jane had refused to go against her brother. Anthony slanted a surreptitious glance at the swell of her breasts in that enticing gown. How much frustration was a man expected to bear?

Anthony began calculating the number of days it would take to have the banns read if they left for Rosington the day after tomorrow. He had promised Jane that they would leave London then, for she still feared that Regina's new fawning idiot meant to call him out. Anthony was eager to leave London, too, but not because he feared Lord Charles Burston. The man had been back in town for nearly three days now, and Anthony had not heard a peep from the fellow. No, he was eager to be headed home, because he begrudged each day—each hour—until they were wed and she was his. Why the devil did banns have to be read for three weeks in a row instead of two weeks—or, better yet, just once?

Yes, once would be quite sufficient.

They had finally reached the doors of the ballroom, but the crush was moving so slowly they still were not inside. Anthony glanced back and exchanged a look with Ryde, who was looking harried. Lady Ryde was decidedly pale. Anthony wondered if she was suffering one of her indispositions. Then she lifted her eyes, and Anthony realized she was not ill, but worried—for him? He felt a burst of irritation. His gaze shifted to Lady Charlotte. She, too, looked anxious. He could swear she was hopping from foot to foot. He looked past her to Lady Alex. That lady's eyes were large and mournful. His gaze flicked to Lady Maria. At least that lady could be counted on to maintain her calm, but to his shock, her eyes were shimmering with unshed tears. Confound them all! What the devil was the matter? He was taking his lady to a ball, not marching off to the guillotine!

Finally, they were inside the Duchess of Hereford's vast and beautiful ballroom. Despite the crush to enter, once inside there was a sense of space, and while the room was full of people, it was a comfortable fullness. One could look around and actually see who was present and move easily to the floor for dancing and move amongst the knots of people without jostling and unintentional rudeness. The ceiling soared high overhead, and one wall was covered in mirrors, giving the sense that the room went on and on.

Perhaps it was the feeling of space and comfort, perhaps he was just happy to be with Jane, but somehow Anthony sensed a difference in the crowd and its attitude toward him tonight. Somehow he did not feel so sharply an outcast. He passed one knot of people, and they recognized him and did not turn their backs. He passed another group, and one of the gentlemen actually made him a small bow. Startled, Anthony bowed back.

"Jane, do you notice something different about our reception this evening?"

But she was not listening to him. Her eyes were sweeping desperately to the left and right. He could see the nervous pulse beating along her throat. "My dearest," he whispered into her ear, "please! Calm yourself! It is difficult to see you so distressed. There is nothing to fear, I promise you. May I escort you onto the floor for a dance?"

She paid him no heed, just shook her head and kept looking about like a frightened rabbit terrified of spotting a hound. Anthony ground his teeth, then realized the other ladies were searching about as well, even Georgiana, who low as she was in her chair, could see nothing. Suddenly, Lady Charlotte went charging off in an entirely different direction from the rest of the family, dragging poor Crawford in her wake. Ryde came to a stop, settling on an open area large enough to encompass their entire party. Lady Ryde drew Jane away for a private word, and Anthony, his temper growing more and more uncertain, crossed to Ryde. "Do *you* know why the ladies are in such a frenzy?"

Ryde regarded him with a grave look. "Letty has heard a rumor that Lord Charles means to issue you his challenge this evening." Ryde spoke in his usual steady tone, but Anthony was irked to see that the other man's eyes were dark with worry, too.

Anthony said stiffly, "I hope that you, at least, have faith in my ability to handle such a challenge if it comes my way."

"Of course, of course! I would never bet against you in any fight."

"I am glad to hear it, sir."

Anthony spotted Lady Charlotte in the distance in a huddled conference with a very fine-looking lady in a turban adorned with a large peacock feather. With a shock, Anthony recognized the lady. "Ryde, your sister . . ." he said in an awestruck whisper. "Do your realize that your sister is talking intimately to ... *Lady Jersey!*"

"No doubt," Ryde replied, totally blasé about the fact. "The two of them are as thick as thieves."

Anthony had had no notion Lady Charlotte's friendships ranged quite so high. He felt a little queasy. No wonder she had seemed brittle to him of late. What had it cost her to be so closely associated with him? He crossed to Jane, suddenly in sore need of the reassurance of her touch. "My dear, may I *please* take you out on the floor for a dance?"

She reached out and gripped his hand tightly, but her glance was fixed on her sister. Suddenly that lady straightened from her talk with Lady Jersey and came hurtling back across the room towards them. Crawford was beginning to resemble a cart being dragged along by a runaway horse.

"Jane, please!"

"One moment, Anthony. I beg of you."

"Very well, my dear. But my patience is wearing thin."

Lady Charlotte was upon them. She tried to carry Jane off, but Anthony had had enough. He locked his grip on Jane's arm so she could not budge. Lady Charlotte flashed him a look of exasperation, but decided her message was too important to delay. "Jane, Jane! Sally says he is not here! No one has seen him all day. Is not that wonderful news!"

Quite certain he knew the identity of the mysterious gentleman she referred to, he was about to make a very biting remark when Jane's face lit up with the most radiant smile he had ever seen. Forgetting what he'd been about to say, he gaped at her, heartily wishing they were not in a crowded ballroom. He desperately wanted to kiss that smiling face.

"Anthony, I would very much enjoy that dance now."

A dance was not a kiss, but it would have to do. He led her out onto the floor.

The dance was pleasant, but it was not a waltz. He wanted it to be a waltz. He wanted to hold her and have exclusive rights to her. The exchange of partners as they moved down the line irked him. When the dance was finished, he went off to procure her some punch, but when he returned she was gone. Some gentleman had led her out to dance. *Where had their pariah status gone?*

When Jane's partner brought her back to him, Anthony offered her the punch he had secured for her. "My dearest," he murmured in a low voice, "do you have any notion what has happened to cause us to be treated in such a benign fashion?" But she had no chance to answer him. Before she could even open her mouth to speak, another gentleman swooped in to ask her to dance. Anthony crossed to Ryde.

"What in heaven's name has happened, sir? I have not been scowled at once this evening. Our ladies have not been slighted. The gentleman who was supposed to call me out has not appeared. And I cannot speak to my betrothed before she is stolen away for a dance. Has the world turned upside down?"

Ryde shrugged. "I am as astounded as you. Whatever has caused the change, I am grateful for it. I am not sure I could have tolerated another evening like the last. I had great trepidation about coming this evening, but I am glad I allowed Catherine to force me to it."

"Sir, when did your sister learn of the rumor that Lord Charles was to make an appearance tonight?"

"Oh, just this morning, I think. Why?"

"Jane, too, was most insistent we attend, but she changed her mind this morning. However, I had screwed up my courage to the sticking-place and was not about to be deterred." He smiled. "Good thing, too. Tonight has proven a marvelous surprise." He paused and added in a confiding tone, "I had begun to think Jane and I might have to spend the rest of our days in the country. I would not have minded, but I worried she might."

Just then Anthony saw Jane approaching and excused himself. "I believe this dance is mine, ma'am," he said sternly, leading her quickly to the floor before anyone could intercept them.

"Of course, sir. Though I must warn you that my next four dances are promised."

They had stepped into the line. *"Four!"* he exclaimed. The dancers to his left and right flashed him reproving glances. "But the next is to be a waltz!" He felt like a boy deprived of his treat.

"I am sorry," she said as he crossed her to the other side. "You did not fix your claim in time."

"You are enjoying this, aren't you?"

"Just a little, dearest. I do not want you growing complacent, do I?"

He did not reply, only scowled at her. She smiled.

When the dance was over, he remained fixedly at her side. He wanted to get a good look at the gentleman who had stolen his waltz. When the fellow arrived, Anthony was a little mollified. The man was tall, but not particularly handsome. However, his relief was short-lived, for Jane flashed the gentleman a far-too-warm smile and introduced him, and it turned out the damned beggar was a peer. Anthony's jaw clenched. He was heartily sick of being surrounded by the highborn. "Anthony, may I present the Earl of Sotherton. Lord Sotherton, this is Mr. Winston."

The other man made him a bow, and Anthony was forced to bow back.

"It is a pleasure to meet you, sir," said the earl. "Lady Jane has told me a great deal about you."

"Has she? I fear she has not told me a single thing about you."

For some reason, this comment, which Anthony had meant to be stinging, caused Jane and the earl to exchange amused glances. Anthony began to grind his teeth.

"That is, no doubt, because I figure so insignificantly in her thoughts compared to you," Sotherton replied with annoying graciousness.

"Indeed," Anthony growled, at a loss to think of anything else to say that would not soil his beloved's ears. The earl carried her off to his purloined waltz, and Anthony, deciding he did not really care to go through this three more times, headed off to the card room.

To his surprise, his benign treatment continued there. He actually had time to linger and watch the play without being chased from the room by people's scowls and disdain. He was immersed watching a game of faro, when a drunken fellow came listing up to him. Too late, Anthony recognized him. It was Jane's brother-in-law, the fellow who had so brazenly insulted her in the park. Anthony's eyes narrowed.

"You, sir, are a scoundrel!" said the drunken baron, taking a gloved finger and poking Anthony in the chest. "I do not care what fairy stories are—" his enunciation grew labored, "—cir-cu-lating about you." The man paused to haul himself upright. "You've soiled my sister-in-law and be-smirched my dead brother's honor. What the devil biz-ness is it of yours . . . if he fathered one bastard or a thousand?" His face was now alarmingly red. "How *dare* you pick that woman's by-blow out of the gutter and make us an object of ri-di-cule?" He leaned forward now, and Anthony flinched at his foul-smelling breath. "Someone should call you out!" He poked Anthony again for emphasis.

"Sir, remove your finger at once, or you shall be very sorry."

The man's eyes widened and his hand lowered. He fell back a step.

"As for a challenge," Anthony said, "am I to understand you are offering me one, sir?"

A deep voice drawled in his ear, "I do not think Lady Jane would appreciate the scandal that will result if you skewer her brother-in-law."

Anthony resisted the temptation to spin around and see who was offering him this unwanted advice. Instead, he kept his gaze fixed on the man before him. "Well, sir?"

The baron drew himself up, but he looked afraid. "I would not waste good steel on the likes of you!" he sneered. He turned his back on Anthony and lurched away.

Suddenly furious, Anthony made to follow him, but a hand shot out and seized his arm in a steely grip. "Unhand me," he snapped, whirling around. To his utter shock, the man holding him in place was Jane's dark-faced friend from the park, Lord Farleigh. *"You!"*

"Forgive me, sir, but I thought you might like a moment to cool your head."

Anthony was about to tell him what he could do with his unwarranted interference, when he realized the other man was right. He had been about to commit an unforgivable folly. Anthony was not quite sure why he was so very angry, except that the drunken baron resembled his dead brother in appearance, and—he suspected—in his condescension. "It has cooled," he said stiffly. Farleigh eyed him warily and released his arm.

"I apologize for interfering. I simply did not want you to throw away all the gains Lady Jane and her sisters have worked so hard to secure for you."

Anthony stared at the man. "What the devil are you talking about?"

Lord Farleigh's eyebrows rose. "You will have to ask Lady Jane about that. Speaking of your lady, I think it is time for me to go claim my dance from her." And with a provoking grin, he made Anthony a low bow and sauntered off.

When Anthony returned to the ballroom, he spotted Ryde's tall figure fixed in place, staring at the dancing. He felt a surge of fellow feeling for the man. Apparently he, too, had been robbed of his lady's company. Anthony crossed to stand by his future brother's side and realized it was not Lady Ryde and her partner that had so fixed Ryde's attention. He was staring at Jane and Lord Farleigh, and the look on his face erased any doubt that Jane had spoken the truth when she said Lord Farleigh was Lady Ryde's old love, not hers. Ryde's expression was so angry and so full of barely-leashed violence that Anthony feared he might have to seize the marquess bodily to keep him from striding to the dance floor and landing Farleigh a facer. "Sir?" he said, trying to rouse Ryde from his angry daze.

For the first time, Ryde noticed him standing there. He said hotly, "You should take better care, Winston, whom you allow to dance with my sister."

Fortunately, the dance was coming to an end. Lady Ryde was escorted back to her husband by her partner, but Ryde did not even look at her, and when she followed his gaze, she turned quite pale. Both of them stared fixedly at Farleigh as he led Jane back to them.

Farleigh made Jane a handsome bow. "Thank you, Lady Jane, for a most enjoyable dance." He turned to Anthony and made him a bow as well. "And thank you, Mr. Winston, for being willing to *share* her." Jane's cheeks went pink.

Anthony's mouth tightened. Was the man incredibly inartful or being purposely provoking? The latter it seemed. Farleigh rose from his bow with a challenging gleam in his blue eyes. It was clear, however, that he was trying to provoke Ryde not Anthony. The two men locked gazes, and Lady Ryde seized her husband's hand in a white-knuckled grip.

Anthony had to do something to defuse the situation. "Sir," he said, willing Farleigh to look at him and not Ryde, "consider it a return for the favor you did me in the card room."

After a long, heart-stopping moment, Farleigh's gaze swerved back to Anthony. With relief, he saw the glitter in the other man's eyes fade.

"Thank you," Farleigh murmured, giving himself a little shake. He stiffly inclined his head. "Ryde." Then he shot a short, yearning glance at Ryde's wife. "Catherine." The name came out a caress, and the man bowed almost to the floor. Without another word he turned and walked away.

"*Jane!*" Ryde exclaimed angrily. "What the devil were you doing—"

Anthony took Jane's hand and led her away. "Forgive me, sir, but they are starting up a waltz, and I have already been deprived of one. I do not wish to miss another."

Ryde flashed him a look that made it clear he was not pleased, but Lady Ryde pulled at his arm, signaling that he should let them go.

It felt splendid to have Jane in his arms again. Anthony knew he was holding her too close, but she was no debutante, and they were not at Almack's. He wanted her close enough to smell her hair and feel her breathe. For a while, he did not say a word, just enjoyed spinning her around, his body tingling with the beauty of the music, his blood pulsing with the rhythm of their movement. Finally, he murmured her name.

She gazed up at him, looking abashed. "Yes, Anthony?"

"You have clearly set the cat among the pigeons now. Why in heaven's name did you dance with Farleigh in front of your brother?"

"You are not angry about what he said to you?"

He shook his head. "He was not trying to make me angry."

Her shoulders relaxed, and she nodded glumly. "He usually behaves better than that, but he and Andrew have such an antagonism toward each other."

"You cannot blame your brother. If Farleigh had looked at you as he looked at Lady Ryde, I would have knocked him flat. Your brother showed great restraint. But you still have not answered my question. Why did you do it in the first place?"

"I was weary of feeling as if I were going behind Andrew's back to have dealings with Lord Farleigh. In any case, he has been a good friend to me. I owe him more than I can ever repay."

"You make me sorely regret my magnanimity," Anthony said sharply. "What the devil do you owe the fellow?"

"I will tell you after we are wed."

"I think I shall go after the fellow and force him to tell me."

"It is nothing shameful, I promise you. It is simply private. Please, let it rest. You obviously realize you have no cause for jealousy."

He nodded reluctantly. "No one with an eye in his head could see that look he flashed Lady Ryde and think he has room in his heart for anyone else—even you."

"So may we enjoy the rest of our dance in peace?"

"You are fortunate, ma'am, that I am too busy mooning over that first waltz we danced on Twelfth Night to stay angry with you."

"Oh, Anthony, it was splendid, was it not!"

"Yes, my lady with the broken heart, it was." His hand tightened on her waist. "I trust that your heart has mended?"

She smiled up at him. "Yes, and my reputed rake has turned out to be a most courteous knight in disguise."

The music stopped. He continued to hold her in his arms. "Do you still care what people might think?"

She shook her head. "Not a whit."

"Good." He kissed her. When he was done, he lifted his head and escorted her proudly off the floor, ignoring the startled looks of the people nearby.

"Anthony! By Jove, I was hoping I would see you here tonight!"

Thunderstruck, Anthony turned to his right. It was James Cosgrove, his dearest childhood friend, the man he had learned to ride and shoot and wench with. The man who had swung a drunken punch at him over Regina and who had once threatened—in a room very like this one—to call Anthony out if he ever addressed him in public again.

For a long time, Anthony could only stare at the hand James held out to him, too dazed to move, let alone speak. Then the hand began to fall back down to the other man's side. "I do not blame you for still being angry with me, Anthony. I should have realized you could never do the things they said you had. I was blinded by jealousy . . ." His voice trailed off, and he began to turn away.

"James!" Anthony cried. His friend turned back, and Anthony threw his arms about him and cuffed him fondly on the back. "My dear fellow! It is good to see you."

"It is good to see you, too, my friend!" James turned his gaze toward Jane. "I was hoping to have the chance to wish you happy."

Anthony introduced Jane to him, and to his delight James asked if he could attend the wedding. Anthony assured him of the invitation, and after they had said their goodbyes, he gazed after his friend as he moved off through the crowd. "Jane, do you know—I feel as if I have suddenly and unexpectedly been let out of prison." Jane's grip on his hand tightened, and she flashed him a wide smile.

Suddenly, Lady Charlotte came galloping up to them. She said breathlessly, "You must come—at once! Georgiana is about to unveil her surprise!"

As usual, Jane seemed to comprehend her sister's meaning, while he was left totally in the dark, but he allowed himself to be towed along. When they arrived back at Georgiana's chair, he was surprised to find Jane's sisters ranged on either side of her in a semi-circle with their husbands at their sides. Elton stood directly beside Georgiana, and a large space had been cleared before her, with a knot of people ranged in an semi-circle before her. Their attention was fixed on her seated in her chair.

Anthony knew how excruciating such scrutiny must feel to his shy sister, but she smiled reassuringly up at him. She did not seem to mind that all eyes were upon her. She called to him, "Anthony, I am glad you have come. I have something to show you." With one arm, she seized Elton's hand in what looked like an uncomfortably tight grip; with the other, she pushed down on the arm of her chair.

Then suddenly, swaying slightly, she rose slowly to her feet. A rustle of excitement rippled past him.

Anthony forgot to breathe.

She straightened. Elton pushed her chair back. Staring down at her feet, Georgiana put one foot forward and took a step, then put the other foot forward and took another, then a third, then a fourth before her strength finally gave way. She began to sway, and Anthony rushed forward, catching her in his arms and twirling her around in triumph. He realized, distantly, that the room had erupted in applause and cheering and wild hurrahs, but all he could do was look down into his sister's exultant face. Then he turned to Matthew Elton, who stood, eyes shining, watching her. "Elton, I cannot find the words . . ."

But the man just shook his head. He whispered something to Lady Charlotte, and she went charging off once again. Elton crossed to them and made Georgiana a deep bow. "My dearest, tomorrow is our wedding day, but I do not know if there will be an opportunity tomorrow, so may I have our promised dance tonight?"

She nodded and gave a contented sigh. Bewildered, Anthony surrendered her to Elton's outstretched arms. Her hands encircled Elton's neck, and he held her firmly to him. Humming softly, he began to spin her around, moving toward the center of the floor. The musicians began playing another waltz. Elton's movements sped up to match the music.

"Heavens!" exclaimed a woman standing behind Anthony. "I vow that is the most romantic thing I have ever witnessed!" She added in a slight tone of reproof. "Goodness, Mr. Winston. Are you going to just stand there and leave them on the floor by themselves?"

Anthony turned. The woman who had addressed him was Lady Jersey. He seized Jane's hand. "No, ma'am. Not at all." And he led Jane out to dance. Soon the floor was full around Georgiana and Elton. When the music stopped, the dancers did not immediately leave the floor, but instead moved aside to open up a corridor through which Elton carried Georgiana back to her chair, everyone applauding as they passed. Anthony thought his heart would burst.

Then suddenly the room grew abnormally quiet, and a different sort of mood seemed to ripple through the crowd. It was as if the sunshine that had just been shining in the room had suddenly been eclipsed by a vast, dark cloud.

Chapter 37

Anthony turned. Standing in the doorway to the ballroom was a barrel-chested man of middle height with bushy red hair and a bellicose face. He was surveying the room slowly, and his eyes settled on Anthony with the weight of a blow. Anthony knew who the man must be even before he heard the fluttering whispers of "Lord Charles! Lord Charles!"

Anthony looked around for Ryde, who quickly moved to his side. Crawford, Lord Godfrey, Sir Edward, and Elton all gathered round him as well. "Jane, go to your brother," he commanded, but she would not do as she was bidden, but instead affixed herself to him as if she were welded to his arm. "Jane!"

"*I will not go!*"

The pulse was beating so hard in her throat, he imagined he could hear her heart hammering in her chest. "Then let me hold you closer," he said, fearing she would sink to the floor at his feet. She loosened her hold on his arm, and he slid it round her waist. Then she clamped herself to his side to prevent him from pushing her away. He took comfort in the warmth of her pressed so close to him and turned his attention back to the man at the door.

Lord Charles was arguing with another gentleman now. Anthony had no idea who the man was, but the whispers in the crowd proclaimed him, "Hungerford." Anthony had no idea what they were arguing about, but Lord Charles shook his head violently, waved the other man off, and started shooting across the room towards Anthony. Halfway across the vast room, he paused by a small group of people clustered to one side. With a start, Anthony realized it was Regina with a much-diminished court about her. Lord Charles did not approach her, however, but instead swung wide and continued his barreling drive toward Anthony. Anthony drew himself up, ready for what was to come, but poignantly aware, as he gazed at Jane, how much he had to live for and how little he wanted to die.

Lord Charles thrust his bulldog face into Anthony's. "Sir, do you know who I am?"

"I have a fair notion."

"And do you know why I am here?"

"I have heard rumor."

Lord Charles made a disgusted sound. "Rumor is a distasteful word to me, sir. Do not soil my ears with it."

"Yet sometimes it is a necessary word when one is unacquainted with the facts of a matter and only has access to hearsay."

Lord Charles drew himself up as tall as his broad frame could go. "I judge only by *fact*, sir." His scowling glance suddenly swerved sideways and focused on Jane.

"Sir, your argument is with me, not the lady," Anthony said tensely.

"I am not so sure. I have heard reports . . ." He peered into Jane's face. "I have heard reports that this lady claims certain facts are not facts."

"Sir, I warn you, do not question the veracity of my lady. I have never heard her tell an untruth, and I will not allow you or any man to claim otherwise."

Lord Charles made a harrumphing sound. "Your lady, eh? Then why did you push so hard to take another lady as wife? Why did you propose to Lady Darrow?"

Anthony made sure the other man was looking directly at him before he spoke. "I did not, sir. I would have no cause to do so, for my heart is here."

The other man's face grew ruddy with agitation. "I suppose next you will deny abducting Lady Darrow, too, as this one claims!"

Anthony stared at him, then slowly turned and looked at Jane.

"Forgive me, Anthony, but you would not defend yourself. I had to do something!"

"Still contend she ain't a liar?"

"Sir, I have already warned you! " Anthony said sharply. "Do I need to call *you* out, to make the point? My lady does not lie."

The other man goggled at him, as if the possibility that a challenge might run the other direction had never occurred to him. "She claims what everyone else knows to be false. That is a lie in my book, sir!"

Anthony hesitated, reluctant to expose his stupidity when he was not going to be believed anyway. But Jane's honor was at stake now. He had to try. "What everyone knows, sir, is rumor. What my lady speaks is fact. I did *not* abduct Lady Darrow." An excited rustle swept through the crowd. "Lady Regina, as she was known then, willingly eloped with me. I thought she did it out of love, but it was a ploy to secure the title of marchioness. This imaginary abduction was the bait she used to hook Will Bill." The rustle became a roar.

Lord Charles's face was now beet red. "Wild Bill should have finished you off while he had the chance, sir! You did not deserve his mercy."

Anthony was so surprised he laughed. "Sir, *I* pinked Wild Bill, not the other way around. It was *he* who was carried off the field, and *he* who almost turned up his toes—not I! That, at least, is an undisputed fact. You can ask any of his seconds. They will tell you."

The other man's eyes narrowed and his mouth set in a furious line. Once more, his attention veered to Jane. "You, madam—your gentleman claims you are a truth-teller. If that is so, answer me this—"

Anthony's temper flared. "Sir, do not badger her! Address your remarks to me, or I *shall* call you out!"

Suddenly Jane pulled away, scrambling to be free of him. "No, Anthony, please! I am happy to answer the gentleman's questions. Sir, ask me anything! I will not demur."

"Jane, I will not have you laid bare before this throng. That is final. I am perfectly happy to fight the fellow." Behind and around him, Anthony could feel the approval and concurrence of the gentlemen of her family—his family.

But Jane was not done. Wildly she looked around, and then she seemed to calm. "Anthony, what if the gentleman questions me privately—"

"Never!"

"I mean, out of earshot," she amended. "Over there, in that corner." She gestured to a small alcove empty of people. "Anthony, it is reasonable for him to want to know if he can trust my word. Please, let me do this—for you."

Lord Charles kept watching the two of them, his attention flicking back and forth between them. Anthony tried to put the man out of his mind and focus on Jane. He wanted to refuse. Every instinct he had told him to refuse. But when he looked into her eyes, he could not. He wondered ruefully if he would ever be able to refuse her anything. "Oh, very well! But sir, do not cause my lady distress, or you will answer to me!"

Lord Charles made a dismissive gesture. "What good are your private assurances, ma'am? People can say anything when they do not fear public scrutiny!"

"Very well, sir. I give you permission to make public anything I say if—on your honor as a gentleman—you judge that what I have told you is false."

"On my honor as a gentleman?" he repeated uncertainly. With a silent chortle of appreciation, Anthony realized Jane had scored her first hit. Clearly Lord Charles was as unaccustomed to having a lady depend on his honor as Anthony had been that first night in Bagshot's cottage. "Very well, let us be off," he said gruffly as he offered Jane his arm.

Anthony watched her go with fierce pride. Whatever the outcome, he was determined. Ryde or no Ryde, banns or no banns, if he had to meet Lord Charles on the field of honor, he would do so as Jane's wedded husband. He had taken many risks in his life, but there was one he was now absolutely determined not to take. He was not about to die without making Jane completely, absolutely his.

Jane watched Lord Charles from behind her lashes, trying to get a sense of the man, trying to decide what tack she could take with him to convince him not to call Anthony out. They had arrived at their private corner, and she was waiting for his questions, but now—strangely—the man seemed hesitant to speak.

"Lord Charles, what is it you wish to ask me?"

The man gave her a considering look, and again, for a moment, he hesitated. "Ma'am before we begin, I must warn you. I have had a very full report of your character from Lady Darrow."

"Then you must think me a very depraved creature indeed."

His eyes narrowed. "Are you mocking me, ma'am?"

"Not at all, sir. I simply judge that Lady Darrow's opinion of me is every bit as severe as mine is of her."

He was intelligent enough to get the implication. He bristled, and once again his choleric face turned red. "Ma'am, I will thank you to keep your opinions to yourself!" He scowled at her. "Let us begin with the most salient point. Hungerford tells me you claim your gentleman did not assault Regina—Lady Darrow—when she refused his proposal. Can you state for a fact that he did not do so?"

Jane hesitated. This, indeed, was the crucial point. She had glossed over the difficulty with Mr. Hungerford, but now she felt as if she were walking on a narrow ledge above a roaring waterfall. One false step and she would go over—and drag Anthony with her. She thought of what he would do, and she made her choice. "Sir, I cannot."

He blinked in surprise.

"Unfortunately, I heard rather than saw the portion of the interview where he seized Lady Darrow's arm. I heard her demand to be released, and I assume he did so, because she did not protest further, but I have no proof to offer you that he did." Her voice wavered at the end, for she feared she had taken the wrong step. His expression had grown more fierce.

"Sir," she added desperately, "I know you have no use for my opinions, but if Mr. Winston *had* proposed to the lady—which he did not—he would never have reacted to her refusal with force. It is not in his character to force a woman to anything! Despite his reputation, he is a highly chivalrous man—the most chivalrous I have ever known."

For a moment, she thought he had actually been moved by this testimonial, but then he growled, "You are correct, ma'am. I am not interested in your opinions. You love the scoundrel. Your assessment is biased and unhelpful."

Jane pressed her lips together, for her lower one seemed determined to quiver. She was failing again, and she didn't know what to do to turn things in another direction.

"Lady Jane," Lord Charles said, his tone almost tentative. "Hungerford tells me something else."

"Yes, sir?"

"He says that you claim—" His broad, fierce face suddenly looked wary and oddly vulnerable. "That you claim Lady Darrow made an … improper suggestion to Mr. Winston. Is that true?" Now that he had spit the question out, he glowered at her, his expression baleful, daring her to confirm it.

Jane was reluctant to do so. "Sir, I have no desire to repeat something to you about your lady that can only cause you distress."

"Who said that she is *my* lady, ma'am?" he barked angrily.

"Forgive my clumsy assumption."

"You are stalling, ma'am. Admit that you are slandering her."

Again, Jane hesitated. Should she lie to placate him? Slowly she shook her head. "I am sorry, sir. I do not like to hurt you, but what I said is the truth. Lady Darrow insinuated to Mr. Winston that she desired an … intimate relationship with him and made it clear she thought he reciprocated her feelings on the matter. When he indicated that he did not, she took severe offense. I believe that is why she created this tale of a proposal."

"Again, ma'am—keep your damn opinions to yourself!" His voice was almost a shout. Over his shoulder, Jane could see Anthony starting toward them in alarm.

She held up a placating hand and said softly, "Sir, I am sorry. You are right. I cannot judge Lady Darrow fairly. I am too envious of her beauty and too jealous of the fact that Mr. Winston once loved her passionately. I promise—I will strive to be more restrained."

His voice lowered to a more normal volume. "See that you do so, madam. I am not here to evaluate Lady Darrow's character, but your own."

Anthony had stopped his advance but was eyeing Lord Charles with considerable antagonism. Jane knew she would have to proceed with care. Another outburst like that and all her efforts to avoid a confrontation between the two men would be in vain. Anthony would throw down the gauntlet himself.

"Sir, forgive me, but I do not see what significance my character is to the matter."

Lord Charles surveyed her with a look that made her glad that he had his back to Anthony, for her betrothed would have taken a swing at him for it. She tried not to show her discomfort with his scrutiny; Anthony was watching her like a hawk. Finally he said, "Your gentleman claims *you* hold his affection safe from any interest in Lady Darrow. However, your physical charms are inferior to that lady's, so

I am trying to determine if there is something in your character to balance the scales and make his claim credible."

Jane had absolutely no notion what to say to this. How was she to convince the man she was extraordinary, when she so clearly was not. She said weakly, "Sir, I make no claim to be worthy of his love, only grateful for it."

Lord Charles made a derisive noise. "That is foolish twaddle ma'am. Men may lust without reason, but their hearts usually demand some justification for their devotion, even if it is only the continued gratification of their lust." He paused, as if waiting for her scandalized reaction to his words. She, however, was much struck by what he had said.

"Sir, I am not sure that is true. I believe my late husband loved me—at least a little bit—but I now know that I did not satisfy his lust at all, and I am not sure I pleased him in any other way that was beyond what any other lady might have done. Certainly not as much as his mistress did. How do you explain *his* heart's devotion?"

Lord Charles was staring at her, open-mouthed. Jane wished she dared clap a hand to her own mouth in mortification, but Anthony was watching her. Oh, why had she chosen this moment for one of her misguided episodes of frank speaking?

"I have heard talk," Lord Charles said slowly, still looking a little dazed, "that you actually visited your husband's mistress in February. Is that true?"

Reluctantly, Jane nodded. "She was ill and badly in need of money."

"No doubt she threatened you with exposure of your late husband's bastard if you did not come?"

"No, sir!" Jane exclaimed. "Mrs. Chester was not that sort of woman!"

He goggled at her. "You defend your husband's mistress, ma'am?"

"You asked me to tell you the truth, sir. She—poor woman—is dead now and cannot defend herself. I will not stand here and slander her. She asked for my help, yes, but only because my late husband—" She hesitated.

His eyes narrowed. "Yes?"

Suddenly the bitterness poured out, "My late husband did not provide for her as he should have. While he lived, while he enjoyed the pleasures of her bed, he provided for her maintenance, but he made no provisions for her future or the future of his son. That was wrong of him, sir. That was very wrong of him." Jane added, more to herself than to him, for she was still haunted by the memory, "You would not believe the state we found her in."

But he seemed fixated on vilifying the poor woman. "So that is how she sugar-coated it, then? She told you she needed money for the boy. She tried to trade on that?"

Jane was starting to get angry now. "Sir, she did not even tell me there was a boy until the day I visited her poor, wretched room and found her ill—dying—lying in her own mess! I do not care who you are, sir, or what you threaten! That poor woman only told me about little John because she knew her time was up and she was desperate—" Her voice broke. She steadied it. "She was desperate to know he would be taken care of." She was dangerously near tears, but strangely Lord Charles looked as roiled as she.

"Then there was no blackmail? She did not extort the visit from you?" he exclaimed, staring at her. "Then why in the world did you go?"

"I have told you! She was ill and needed money. She was my responsibility!"

"Your responsibility!" he exclaimed, his voice indignant. "Your dead husband's whore, and he nearly two years in his grave!"

"Do not call her that, sir! She loved him in her way as much as I did, perhaps more. That day I visited her, when she had nothing and was dying—with no one to care for her and no dry place to lay her head—do you know what I found in the pocket of her soiled gown?" Jane's voice cracked and tears began to flow, but she could do nothing to stop them, so she just pressed on. "I found a locket, sir, a gold locket, worth a small fortune, but it held a portrait of my late husband and she could not bear to sell it—though it might have bought her food and comfort and a few days of p-proper c-c-care before she left this world."

Suddenly he was thrusting a large white handkerchief into her hands. "Here, madam," he said gruffly, "blow your nose."

Anthony was storming towards them. "Lord Charles—Mr. Winston, he is coming!"

Lord Charles swung around to meet him.

"Sir, that is enough!" Anthony shouted. "I will be happy to meet you at a time and place of your choosing, but you are to leave Lady Jane alone—*now!*"

"Calm yourself, sir. There is no need to be hasty. Your lady is fine and will compose herself shortly." Jane could not see Lord Charles's face, but his voice sounded remarkably mild. Jane felt a sudden buoyant hope.

"Sir, I thought you wished—that is—have you decided that you do not require satisfaction from me?" Anthony sounded baffled.

Lord Charles inclined his head. "I accept your statement that you did not propose to Lady Darrow," he said loftily.

"You do?" Anthony still sounded lost.

"Yes, it is obvious to me now why your affections are fixed elsewhere."

Anthony's eyes widened, as if he understood this strange comment. He exchanged a look with Lord Charles, but Jane could not see the other man's face, and she had no notion of what was passing unspoken between the two men. Then Anthony said cheerfully, "The difference is rather striking, isn't it? Thank you, sir."

Jane was sorely tempted to demand to know what the devil they were talking about, but bit her tongue. The important thing was that it seemed they were not going to fight. The truth of it suddenly hit her. Anthony was safe. Lord Charles was not going to kill him!

Her knees went quite weak. Her head began to spin. A roaring began in her ears. But she was so happy, she did not care.

"Oh, no you don't!" Anthony cried, rushing toward her. He slid his arm around her waist and ruthlessly pushed her head down almost to her knees.

She heard Lord Charles exclaim angrily, then the roar in her head shut out all sound. She enjoyed the dappled light swirling before her eyes, but it soon began to recede, and she could hear again and feel Anthony's warm arm tight against her stomach and see the polished floor of the ballroom in all its golden splendor. As she slowly lifted her head up, she was surprised whose face was peering anxiously down at her only inches from her own.

"Lady Jane, are you restored? Your face is still quite white!" His bulldog countenance was full of worry.

"Lord Charles, I am fine. I assure you. I am quite wonderfully, gloriously fine!"

Chapter 38

For some reason, Anthony insisted on an afternoon wedding, and Drew, who was the source of the vicar's living, persuaded the officiant to accommodate her irksome groom's eccentric wishes. Jane spent the morning of her wedding day with her stomach doing nervous circles. She had not slept well, and she was too agitated to eat. Even after she had bathed, and her maid had done her hair, and she had donned the extravagant gown Anthony had purchased for her, and she had put on the pearl earrings her brother had given her as a wedding gift, and she had double-checked and triple-checked that all was packed for her wedding journey, there were still hours to go until the appointed time.

Jane's agitation was not helped by the glances she kept darting at her mirror. Her sisters had come to wish her well, and each had assured her she looked pretty. Catherine had even declared that she looked beautiful. But Jane doubted. She looked well in her gown—her lovely, cream-colored gown embroidered in gold, which must have cost Anthony a fortune and which made her look like a queen. But what about tonight, when she took off the gown and was back to being only Jane—too short, too curvy, with eyes that were only an ordinary blue instead of emerald green and hair that was only plain brown instead of raven black? What would Anthony think of her then?

Finally, the hour arrived. Her brother escorted her downstairs and into the chapel. When she saw Anthony standing there so grave and handsome in his red uniform, his friend James Cosgrove by his side, she felt happy and calm for the first time that day. She watched him, hoping he would be pleased by how she looked. To her great relief and satisfaction, his eyes widened and he rocked back on his heels, so that his friend, James, actually shot out a hand to steady him. Then he smiled at her, a great beaming smile, and it was Jane's turn to sway. Her brother set her at Anthony's side before the vicar, and the wedding ceremony began.

When it was over, Anthony brushed her mouth with a light, chaste kiss that still managed to make her ache. He led her out of the chapel, and she could not stop smiling. They returned to the house for the wedding breakfast that was now a wedding supper.

The dining room was full of people. Anthony led her toward a group she did not recognize. The gentleman was almost as tall as Anthony and had the same broad shoulders, but he had brown, curling hair and somber gray eyes. "Jane, allow me to introduce my brother, Edwin. Edwin, this is my Jane." His brother gave her a friendly smile and made her a graceful bow, and went on to introduce Jane to his wife Cordelia and their three daughters. Jane liked him immediately. Despite the superficial difference in appearance, he seemed very like Anthony—he shared the same bright intelligence and gallant spirit.

Cordelia, on the other hand, turned out to be even more odious than Jane had expected from her treatment of Georgiana. She was a pretty woman full of her own importance, quick to find fault, and eager for attention. Jane's silk slippers were too thin and her mood too bright to carry out her threat to stomp on the woman's foot, but Jane had to bite her tongue as she watched the woman's treatment of her eldest daughter, who reminded Jane very strongly of Georgiana.

Matthew wheeled Georgiana over in her chair to greet them all. Edwin congratulated his sister upon her marriage and told Matthew how grateful he was to him for the work he was doing to rehabilitate her legs. Cordelia pointedly looked away, her disapproval plain. She had already expressed her opinion that the phrase "gentleman physician" was an oxymoron.

Jane had to choke back laughter at the expression on the woman's face when her eldest not only addressed Matthew as "Uncle," but expressed keen interest in the exercises he was employing to strengthen Georgiana's legs. Matthew, gratified by the girl's interest, began detailing his answer in blunt detail, and Anthony, perhaps sensing an eruption coming, bade his family goodbye and steered Jane toward their seats at the table of honor.

On the way, Jane was greeted and congratulated and fussed over and wished luck. She enjoyed everyone's good wishes, but she was eager to begin the wedding journey when she would have her new husband all to herself. The supper seemed to stretch on and on. "Anthony," she finally whispered to him, "when will be leaving? Surely it must be soon?"

"My dearest, you have not even touched your food. Eat up! You must fortify yourself for the night ahead." He winked at her.

Jane blushed. "Anthony!"

"Since you are so impatient, I will go check on the arrangements for our journey."

"You still have not told me where we are going!"

"It is a surprise, my love. Do you not like surprises?"

"Yes, but—"

"I will return soon."

She watched his retreating back, mooning over how handsome he looked in his fine red coat, but she felt no more inclined to eat than she had all day, so she simply sat there and waited for him to return. But she waited and waited in vain. Eventually, Jane grew so alarmed at his absence that she crossed to her brother. "Drew, I do not know where Anthony can have gotten to. He went to check on the carriage, but he has not returned, and I am beginning to fear something has happened."

"Janie, don't fret. I am sure he is simply speaking with someone too stupid or too drunk to realize they are delaying the groom from beginning his wedding journey. I will find him." He kissed her forehead and strode off.

"Jane, while you are waiting," Catherine suggested, "perhaps you should go change into your traveling clothes so you are ready to leave when Anthony returns."

Jane gave her a quick hug. "That is an excellent idea, dear sister! Thank you!"

She hurried from the room, practically skipping down the hall in her impatience, but as she exited the hall and made for the stairs, she saw a sudden shadow to her right. She was already in an agitated state of mind. She turned too forcefully and her lack of food and the sudden movement combined to set her head to spinning. A man loomed up, a man wearing a dark hat and scarf wound round his face and holding—amazingly—a pistol in his hand. He held the pistol up and motioned for her to move in his direction. Jane wanted to cry out in exasperation, but the spinning grew worse, and no sound emerged from her throat. She closed her eyes for a moment, trying to ease the dizziness, but somehow that only made it worse. She started tipping sideways.

"Damnation!" a voice called out above her.

She heard a woman's voice—shrieking.

She was seized, and her last memory before the darkness enveloped her was how indignant she was to be flung like a bag of potatoes over the man's hard shoulder.

"Jane, wake, my love! I did not mean to frighten you! I thought you would recognize me. *Jane!*"

Jane roused and looked up into Anthony's worried face. She was cradled in his arms, and they were in his carriage, trotting along as sedately as if they were out for a Sunday drive. "Of course, I recognized you!" she snapped irritably. "I fainted because I have not eaten all day, not because you frightened me. What sort of crazy start was that? You looked ridiculous in that silly hat and scarf!"

"Ridiculous! I was supposed to look mysterious and romantic! After all, this is my first proper abduction. I was trying to do it with style."

"And what about that infernal pistol? I hope the thing was not really loaded?"

He looked affronted. "Of course it was not loaded. Do you take me for an idiot?"

"I begin to wonder, sir! Who was the lady I heard shrieking?"

He grimaced. "Cordelia. That woman has an unholy knack for showing up in the wrong place at the wrong time. She arrived just as you started to swoon, so I had no choice but to grab you and run. I did not hurt you when I flung you over my shoulder, did I?"

"Are you telling me that this ridiculous playacting was observed? That my family—Andrew and my sisters—think I truly have been kidnapped? Anthony, you turn this carriage around right this instant!"

"Calm yourself, my fierce darling. All is well."

"No it is not! Andrew will be beside himself, as will all my brothers-in-law. They will come searching for us."

"No, they will not." He spoke with utter assurance.

Jane peered up at him in astonishment. "Do not tell me that Drew was in on this madcap scheme!"

"Of course not!"

"Then how—"

"Your sisters were my co-conspirators. Lady Ryde sent you to me at the right moment, and Lady Alex kept watch and waylaid your brother when he came looking for me. The scarf was Lady Charlotte's idea, and the pistol was Lady Maria's. I am sure by now they have informed everyone that all is well, and that it was only a joke."

"I do not believe it! Maria suggested the pistol? You're making that up!"

"Goodness, ma'am. Only married a few hours, and you are already questioning my veracity. I am not making it up! You should have seen the gleam in her eye when she did so. I think I shall have to drop a hint into Sir Edward's ear."

Jane tried to keep scowling, but a smile twitched at the corners of her mouth.

"It is too bad of you to complain, when I was trying so hard impress you." His tone was wheedling.

Now Jane did smile. She could not help it. She felt the arms holding her relax. She realized he truly had been worried that she was angry with him.

"May we kiss and make up?" he asked in a deeper tone.

She nodded, and he kissed her, but it was a very small kiss. It seemed a waste, when they had this nice long carriage ride ahead of them.

Suddenly Jane had an unpleasant thought. "You realize Drew is going to be furious! After all, what if one of our neighbors had witnessed the scene instead of Cordelia? What sort of honeymoon are we going to have when any moment he may knock on the door ready to ring a peal over our heads?"

"I am sure by now your brother has entirely forgotten we exist. Lady Ryde had just told him of her happy condition."

Jane's mouth fell open in awe. "Anthony!" she breathed. "That *was* masterful."

"Thank you, my love."

"But I do not understand. Why go to so much trouble? I am your wife. You do not need to kidnap me. I am yours already!"

He looked away. "I had to do something, my dear, to blot the memory of your last honeymoon out of your mind. I do not wish to spend this one competing with a ghost!"

"Oh, my dearest! There is no danger of that! Being with you is quite sufficient to knock everything else clean out of my head."

"That is very gratifying to hear." He flashed her a smile that made her stomach do a little flip. "And now may I present my wedding gift to you?"

"Wedding gift?"

He dropped a folded piece of parchment into her lap. She picked it up, unfolded it, and peered at it in the dim light of the carriage. It was a very official-looking thing, but she was too impatient to try to make out the script. "Anthony, what is it?"

"The deed for Rosington. I have purchased the place from your brother—actually from your sister-in-law. I thought it would make us a fine home. Do you like the notion of living there, Jane? You will be close to your brother, and I will be close to my sister."

She threw her arms around him and hugged him tight. "Oh, it is perfect!"

He smiled, pleased by her reaction. Then he looked out the window into the darkness. "I think we have arrived." The horses came to a sudden stop.

"But we cannot have had enough time to go anywhere!"

He didn't answer. He opened the carriage door, stepped down, and reached up to help her. When she made as if to step down, however, he swung her up into his arms as if he meant to carry her. He slammed the door shut, and the carriage rolled away. Anthony turned, showing her their destination.

They were standing in front of Bagshot's cottage.

"Welcome back, Mrs. Winston," he murmured in her ear.

Once again, the door was open, but this time Jane saw that the beloved room was warm and full of light, with a large fire going and candelabra distributed all about the room. The familiar chair was there, as was the makeshift Ottoman, but there was also now a bed—a bed that, while not large, seemed to fill the small room to bursting. The mattress was bare, and a neat pile of linens lay on one corner. Anthony set her on her feet, and Jane stared at the bed, unable to drag her eyes away from it.

"Took me three hours to maneuver that blasted thing down those tiny stairs," he remarked, "but it was worth it." He grinned at her. "I am sorry about its not being made up, but I was so worried you would learn the secret, I did not let anyone near the place, not even a maid." He took off his great coat and hung it on a hook by the door. He had changed out of his uniform and was wearing the clothes she remembered from the inn: the green coat, gold embroidered waistcoat and soft linen shirt.

"You did all this?" she said.

"Tom came by this evening to light the candles and the fire, but otherwise, yes."

"And where is Mr. Bagshot now?"

"Staying with a friend in the village. I have leased the place from him for a week."

"A week!" Jane squeaked.

"You think the time too short? Should I have made it two?"

She stared at him and then at the bed.

"I have no clothes, not even a nightgown," she said faintly.

His green eyes sparkled. "My shirt is quite dry tonight, and I will be happy to loan it to you so we need not plunder Mr. Bagshot's wardrobe. There are victuals in the kitchen if you are hungry, and Mrs. Rowick will bring us a very fine and very large breakfast in the morning." He added softly. "I plan to keep you in very good appetite."

Jane felt her eyes grow wide. The reality of what they were about to do sank in. "Anthony?"

"Yes, my love?"

She hesitated. How was she to ask him without seeming horribly gauche? "After we … after you … when we have been … together, you will stay with me, will you not?" He was gaping at her, looking as if he were trying hard not to laugh, and she cringed.

"Jane, as you well know, this is a tiny cottage. Where could I possibly go?"

Her throat felt tight. "I could not bear it if after we were done, you left me and went upstairs or somewhere else."

Suddenly, his face was all seriousness. "Jane, why in the world would I want to do that when I can be with you?"

"Even afterwards?"

"Especially afterwards," he said softly, gathering her up to him. "That will be the sweetest time to hold you in my arms." He gave her a gentle squeeze. "I promise you, I will not stir from your side."

His answer made her happy, but still she fretted. What if he found her lacking, as Bevin had found her lacking? He could swear to the Fairie Queen that she was enough for him, but he did not really know if it was true, and neither did she.

Suddenly in desperate need of occupation, she slipped out of his arms and picked up the pile of linens from the bed. Somehow holding them, experiencing the soft, cool feel of them, caused her to imagine she was already naked between them, waiting for him. Startled by how enticing and vivid the image was, she dropped the sheets abruptly on the chair. Gingerly, she picked up the first sheet and began making the bed—darting little glances at him as she worked. He hung up his green coat and perched himself on the makeshift Ottoman to watch her, his expression suddenly so intent she felt her skin prickle. Little waves of excitement danced and swirled in her chest.

"Jane, where did you learn to do that so expertly?" His voice was husky.

Jane tried to concentrate on the question, instead of the effect his tone of voice had on the warm feeling spreading down from her stomach. "When I was a girl of six, I grew angry with my mother and decided I should run off and be a maid. At the time, it seemed a clever scheme." She bent forward, lifting the mattress to tuck the corner. "One of the chambermaids—a girl named Violet—caught me trying to climb out my bedroom window. She let me follow her around each morning as she did her work even though I was probably a dreadful nuisance to her." Jane snuck a look at him, which was a mistake. His expression just made the warm feeling grow. She struggled to keep her voice light as she continued. "She told me I must learn the job before I could run off. She taught me to make a bed, and light a fire, and dust and clean. I had a wonderful time with her, and, of course, by the time I had learned it all, my interest in running away had completely disappeared." She tucked in the last corner and smoothed the sheet down nervously.

"Goodness, my dear, you never cease to amaze me."

Jane started, for he was no longer on the Ottoman. He spoke the words right next to her ear, his warm breath tingling against her neck. He had crossed to stand behind her and was now bent over her, as if he were spooning her standing up. His strong arms wrapped around her, his hands coming up to cup her breasts, and he pulled her tight against him. His chest was pressed hard and warm against her back, and she could feel his heart beating strongly. His long legs were tensed against her thighs, and against her bottom ... she was startled to feel that he was already aroused and ready.

Jane felt a brief moment of panic. The bed was not yet made. There were no covers to slip beneath and await him. If he wanted her now, it would happen plainly, in the open. The thought was overwhelming. Then she remembered his gentleness at the inn, and his patience, and his promise to remain with her afterwards, and she began to calm. And it occurred to her how pleasant it might be to actually see him as he had seen her.

He pulled her upright and kissed the back of her neck, which made her tremble. Then he began to undo the fastenings of her gown. Jane was reminded of the night he had stripped off her cold, wet things, and she felt a wave of tenderness. He slipped her gown off her shoulders, and it fell to the floor. She turned in the circle of his arms and boldly pulled his head towards her for a kiss. Her tenderness for him was growing—yet transforming into something more urgent and essential.

His hands were in constant motion now. Her breath quickened at his intoxicating touches, and with fingers made clumsy by her own increasing excitement, she struggled to undo the buttons of his waistcoat. Finally, she slipped it off. She stretched her arms to the utmost and got up on tiptoe to try to lift his shirt over his head, but she was not tall enough. Impatiently, he tugged it off for her. For a moment, she could only stare in awe at the beauty of his bare chest. Then feeling thoroughly wanton she placed both her hands on his warm skin and began caressing him with her fingers, her hands moving downwards until she was tickling the golden hairs that curled along the edge of his breeches. He gave a small groan, and the tender feeling flooded back. She placed a hand over his heart, treasuring the hard and increasingly jagged cadence it beat. Then she traced his terrible scar with her finger, bending down and kissing her way along it, beginning at his shoulder and moving all the way down to his ribs.

Now it was he who trembled.

He began tugging at the laces of her stays, and when they would not give way quickly enough, he tore the laces loose and flung the stays across the room. Then he jerked her shift up over her head in one desperate motion. "My beautiful Jane," he murmured, running his hands all over her naked skin. "I have dreamed of this."

He began caressing her with his mouth, his lips skimming downwards from her face to her neck to her breasts. Jane almost swooned at the pleasure of feeling his mouth there and clamped her lips shut so as not to allow the sounds out that were fighting to escape her throat. She must be thoroughly wicked to enjoy the sensation so much. Bevin had never liked her breasts; he considered them far too large and unseemly, but Jane was glad that Anthony seemed to feel differently, for she was sure she would not mind if he kissed her like this the whole night long.

Yet just as she had that thought, he pulled his mouth away, and restlessly pushed her down onto the bed while he remained standing. He seized her right foot and began peeling off her slipper and stocking. Then, to her shock, he began kissing his way from her bare toes all the way up her leg until she was completely on fire. He repeated the sweet caress up her left leg. To her great sadness, he did not linger.

Instead he straightened up, frenziedly tugging off his boots and pulling off his breeches. Then he gazed down at her imploringly. "Jane, I am sorry, I know I am rushing you, but I am quite desperate. May I, my love?"

She gazed up at him in wonder—her Saxon prince, no longer with his blanket, no longer fierce, just exquisitely handsome and staring down at her with such a look of yearning it took her breath away. What had she done to deserve such a look? She held out her arms to him, and he came to her, and when he eased inside her, it felt so very glorious, she had to hug him tight and tell him how very much she loved him.

Then he began to kiss her as he moved, and they began to dance, and the tempo kept quickening, and her longing for him kept deepening. She was back under the mistletoe that very first night, shooting up like a firework, higher and higher, until she finally exploded across the heavens in a blaze of glory.

Anthony gazed down at Jane, asleep in his arms. It frightened him a little, how precious she was to him now. He had not thought his heart capable of expanding any more; he had not thought any more affection could be crammed down into it. But somehow that frightening, exposed feeling was worse now—a hundred times worse. It was as if some part of him were now not just outside his body, worn on his sleeve with his feelings, but transferred entirely into her keeping—into her. How could one physical act give him such joy and yet create such havoc in his soul?

She made a small sound and nestled more closely against his chest. He tried to shift his arms without waking her. Her poor back was probably growing cold. He wished there were covers to pull over her, but he had been too impatient to let her even finish making the bed. The two blankets he had set with the sheets were on the chair just out of reach.

He had not meant to be so hurried. He had not meant to be so desperate and out of control. He had not wanted to be like her late idiot husband, thinking only of his own need, but from the moment they had stepped into the cottage, he had been beset by memories.

She had looked so lovely in the golden glow of the candles—so regal in her pretty wedding dress, but all he had been able to think of was her in Bagshot's shirt, her curves pushing it out in all the wrong places. He had enjoyed seeing her stare at the bed that he had struggled so hard and with so many oaths to get down into this tiny room, but it had been the sight of her near the chair that made him shiver with longing. Her eyes had opened wide when he had talked of giving her an appetite, but what had filled his chest to bursting was remembering her wide-eyed distress when he had told her of his scar and how close he had come to dying.

Then she had started unfolding the sheet and smoothing it over the mattress and bending over before him—so unconsciously provocative, her sweet behind beckoning to him—and he had been filled with wonder.

She is mine.

He had been overwhelmed with the need to prove it—to claim his prize and mark his ownership and stamp her as permanently, irrevocably his. In his urgency, he had been hasty and impetuous and graceless, doing little to ease her nervousness or prepare her for his intrusion. Yet she had welcomed him anyway. He had entered her, and she had hugged him and whispered the sweetest possible thing into his ear—that she loved him—and he had realized, too late, that it was not he who was doing the marking. With each beloved move of her hips, she had driven the stamp deeper, engraving herself upon his soul.

At the memory, he could not resist hugging her a little tighter. She moved restlessly, her head turning, and then her eyes opened. She gazed at him drowsily, her sky blue eyes heavy-lidded and enticing. Had he pleased her enough? Had he pleased her at all? Or did her late idiot husband still have precedence, because he was first?

"Jane, I——" He could not find the words to form the question that was uppermost in his thoughts.

She smiled at him, a great beaming smile that stopped the breath in his throat. "Anthony?"

"Yes, my love?" he prompted eagerly.

"I am so very *hungry!*" she cried, sitting up abruptly and giving him such a fine view of her womanly endowments that even her very dampening words were not sufficient to extinguish the flame she had just lit. He turned away and irritably seized one of the blankets from the chair.

"Then I shall fetch you something to eat," he snapped, tying the blanket round his waist and heading for the kitchen.

Behind him, she heaved a great sigh—he did not even want to consider what disappointing memory from their encounter had elicited it—and he fled to the kitchen in full retreat. He slammed a few drawers just for the satisfaction of slamming them, then slapped a mince beef and onion pie down on a plate and seized a knife and fork from the tray of cutlery he had brought from Rosington. When he returned to her, she had taken the other blanket and tied it neatly above her breasts, so that he was deprived even of his lovely view.

"Here," he said curtly, handing her the plate.

She took it and looked up at him, her blue eyes mournful. "Are you angry with me?" Her bottom lip actually quivered.

"No, of course not," he said brusquely.

"Will you sit with me?"

He dropped down on the mattress and folded his legs to sit next to her cross-legged. "Well," he said impatiently. "Start eating! It is about time you had something."

"I do not think I am hungry anymore," she said in a small voice, setting the plate aside, next to her on the bed.

"Jane!" In his disappointment and frustration, it came out an exasperated roar. She flinched. "My dear. I am sorry!" he apologized, instantly regretting his ill humor. He wanted to put his arms around her to show her just how very sorry he was, but he feared she would misinterpret his intentions.

"No, I am the one who is sorry," she said, that damn lip now vibrating steadily.

He didn't care if she misinterpreted his actions or not. He could not stand it. He pulled her onto his lap and held her tight. "Shhh. Don't cry, my Jane. Please! Don't cry." She burrowed her face against his neck and murmured something he could not make out.

"What, my love?"

She lifted her tear-streaked face. "I am sorry I did not satisfy you," she said in a choked voice. He stared at her, stunned into silence. "I fear the Faerie Queen was right. I do not have the ability to p-p-please in that way." She flashed him a beseeching look. "Do you think you might be able to teach me how to do it?"

"There is nothing whatsoever I can teach you!" he exclaimed fervently, the force of his feeling blinding him to how she might mistake his meaning until she tried to squirm off his lap. He tightened his hold on her. "No, Jane, wait! What I meant is that you already please me so very much, I cannot conceive how you could please me more!"

"Then I did satisfy you?"

"My innocent darling, I would think that fact was self-evident."

"I don't mean that!" she said dismissively. "Heavens, Bevin could accomplish that by himself!"

Anthony's cheeks were now burning. "Dearest, that is not a piece of information I had any need or desire to know."

"I am sorry. It is just—please, I must know—did I satisfy you? Was it pleasurable enough that you will not need to seek ... to look for ... satisfaction elsewhere?" The tremulous uncertainty in her voice made his stomach clench in anger at the bastard who had taught her to so doubt herself.

He drew back to make sure she could see the truth of what he said in his face. "Jane, I swear to you, if it had been any more pleasurable, I would have swooned dead away, and you would have feared that you had killed me."

Her eyes grew wide. "Truly, Anthony?"

He grinned at her. "Truly."

"Oh, that is so very wonderful!" she exclaimed. "I am so very glad! For that is precisely how I felt!"

Anthony's heart began pounding.

"Except, of course, I actually thought I *was* dying ... well, not dying exactly, for it felt so incredibly wonderful, but it was such a profoundly *intense* sensation that I did not know what to think, for I have never experienced anything like it in all my life!"

Feeling like a rooster desperate to crow, he longed to seize her in his arms and whirl her around in triumph.

"It was as if I were exploding and being wrapped in velvet and swallowing a great gulp of brandy and—"

He was extremely curious to hear what descriptions were going to follow this pronouncement, but his exultation was too great. He could not wait a moment longer. He interrupted the flow of words with his mouth. Then he tugged free her nuisance of a blanket with one hand and swept aside the plate with his other. The dish fell to the floor with a clatter as he paused his kissing long enough to let her catch her breath, but apparently she was not done talking. "The minute you slung that blanket round your hips," she murmured, "I was hoping . . ."

It was all the encouragement he needed. He pushed her down on the bed and in his most rakish tone said, "Ma'am, the gauntlet is now well and truly down. We shall see who shall make whom swoon this time around!" He yanked his blanket off with a flourish.

"Oh, Anthony!

Coming in 2015

REDEMPTION

~

LOVE'S LEGACY
BOOK 3

Chapter 1

Devon, October 1813

Phillip emerged from the trees and stared up at Parknam Hill. It was strange how different the place looked from down here. Last time he had seen it, he has been sitting at the top of the hill on his new bay horse, watching the woman he loved gallop toward him. She had been so lost in thought she had not even seen him until she had almost run him down, but he had seen her. Dear God, he had seen her. Even now, he could close his eyes and conjure up the image without effort: Catherine, with her usual exquisite seat, thundering up the hill like the goddess Diana setting out on a hunt—the power and speed of her ascent more rousing than a touch. To his delight, she had been riding astride, her skirts hitched up to reveal her shapely legs, and her lovely auburn hair had been loose and swirling about her face. He had wanted her so much in that moment, he thought if he could not have her, he would die.

But she had chosen someone else.

And he had not died, more's the pity.

Now Catherine was too heavy with another man's child to do any riding—up this hill or anywhere else.

Phillip wondered—not for the first time—what she looked like now that her time was drawing near. He tried to picture her with a rounded belly and full breasts and that strange, shuffling gait that would look silly if it did not denote so forcefully the awesome mystery to come. Yet though he dreamed of her almost nightly, he could not do it. Some part of his mind—whether awake or asleep—refused to conjure her up thus marked as Ryde's woman. When the nightmare part of the dream came, he was always too far away to really see her, let alone save her.

That was why he had come. He was determined to see her *and* save her.

Suddenly, Phillip realized it was too quiet. The birds trilled and the wind rustled the trees, but he heard no small, impatient footsteps, no restless chatter. He had been so intent on his reflections, he had totally lost track of where he was—and where his daughter Lizzie was not. She was not behind him anymore. He whirled around, searching for some sign of her.

"Lizzie!"

Nothing. No sudden appearance, no call in reply, no poorly-suppressed giggle to show that she was hiding. His heart began to hammer in his chest.

"Poppet! If you hear me, come this instant! I need to know where you are."

Silence.

He plunged back toward the trees, urgently retracing his steps. He called to her as he went, taking long pauses in between so he could listen—his ears straining for any sound of her. Then suddenly, in the far distance, he heard a small splash and a tiny cry. Panic rose up his throat, and he began frantically to run, trying to ignore the voice in his head that screamed he was too far away, that he would not arrive in time, that the one precious thing left to him in the world was about to be snatched away. He heard a much larger splash and wondered if she had pulled something in on top of herself.

Now he could see the river in the distance, but he was still too far away to see Lizzie. The trees had not yet shed their leaves, and they blocked his view. When he and Lizzie had walked past the river just a short time ago, it had looked benign and pretty, the swiftly moving water glistening in the late October sunlight. Now the glimpses he had of the dancing, dappled light were terrifying. It was like seeing the gleam of a dagger aimed straight at his heart.

Suddenly, Phillip thought he heard a voice, but it was not Lizzie's voice. Then he saw something in the water, something too large to be his Lizzie. As he broke free of the trees and approached the bank of the river, he realized there was a woman in the water, bobbing up and down, desperately trying to hold onto the large, exposed root of a toppled tree with one hand, while she gripped Lizzie tightly to her chest with the other. She was managing to keep his daughter's head above the water, but her face was white and strained, and he feared she was at the end of her strength.

"Hold on, I am coming!" he cried, as he jerked off his coat and plunged in toward her. He took Lizzie from her and fought his way back toward the bank. He laid his daughter safely on the dry ground. Then fearful the woman would not maintain her hold long enough for him to reach her a second time, he entered the icy water downstream and started toward her. He had been right. Her white knuckled grip gave way and the river sent her hurtling towards him. She slammed into him, and for a moment, they both went under. Then he managed to get his feet beneath him again and lock on to her with his arms. She sputtered and gasped, but he was able to haul her to shallower water where the current was not moving so fast. For a while, he dared not try to move more, just planted himself against the torrent and tried to give her some respite from the flowing water. Slowly, she managed to crawl up the bank and collapse on the ground. Legs trembling with fatigue, he followed, collapsing next to her. For a long time, all three of them lay on the ground, their heaving breaths gradually slowing. Finally, Phillip managed to sit up and check on Lizzie.

"Poppet, how do you feel?" he asked gently, pulling her onto his lap. She did not speak, just wrapped her arms around his neck and burrowed her face into his shoulder. He could feel her little heart still racing. "There, there, sweetheart. It is over. You are safe." She nodded, but clung to him even more tightly.

Phillip turned his attention to the woman. "Ma'am, what about you? I hope you have taken no serious harm?"

Slowly she shook her head. "Aside from feeling as if I had drunk half an ocean, I am fine."

"I am glad." He paused. "I cannot — " Feeling a sudden surge of emotion, he stopped and cleared his throat. Then he began again, "I cannot find words to express to you my heartfelt gratitude — "

She shook her head to stop him and gestured silently at Lizzie's bent head with her chin. "Your girl was very brave, sir. As soon as I came into the water for her, she reached for me and held on tightly.

There really was no danger after that, especially when you came so promptly to help us. Clearly, she has a cool head on her shoulders and knows what to do in a crisis. You should be very proud of her."

He frowned. "Of course I am, but — "

Slowly, Lizzie's head lifted from his shoulder. "Papa," she said tremulously, "I am sorry I went near the water."

He squeezed her. "It is all right, Poppet. I am just glad you are safe. Thanks to the lady, all is well."

Lizzie nodded gravely. She turned to the woman. "Thank you, ma'am."

The woman smiled. For a plain woman, she had an extraordinarily beautiful smile. "You are most welcome, my dear," she said softly. "We have had quite an adventure, have we not?"

Lizzie nodded again.

"But you are probably cold in those wet clothes. Sir, are you a guest of Squire Elton's?"

"No."

"Do you stay at Farthingsgate?"

"*No!*"

The violence of his denial clearly startled her, but she persevered politely. "Then perhaps you stay at Rosington?"

He shook his head. "We are staying with my aunt, Mrs. Montague, at Yew House on the other side of the village." At her surprised look he added, "We came this far on a whim. A farmer gave us a ride in his wagon." He did not add that he had been desperate for a look at Catherine's old home of Rosington and had even been considering venturing onto Farthingsgate land in the forlorn hope of glimpsing her.

She frowned. "That is much too far a distance for your daughter to walk in her wet things. I think you had best come home with me, and I will see what I can find for her to wear. My cottage is not far."

He thanked her, sorely regretting his wandering impulse of the morning.

Lizzie suddenly tugged at his sleeve. "Papa, we have not introduced ourselves." She struggled to her feet and made the lady an unsteady curtsy. "I am Miss Elizabeth Rawlingson. This is my Papa, the Viscount Farleigh." Phillip rose to his feet and made the woman a bow.

The woman stood up and replied with equal gravity, "It is a very great pleasure to meet you, Miss Rawlingson, and your father. "I am Constance, Lady Shelby."

Phillip regarded her in surprise. Even sopping wet, it was obvious her dress was cheap and old and out of style. And a lady who lived in a cottage? Clearly she had fallen on hard times. "How do you do, Lady Shelby. I suppose I will be apologizing to Lord Shelby for the drenching his lady took in the stream?"

"No, sir. That would be quite impossible. My husband is dead."

Phillip was not surprised by the news, for how else to explain the lady's straitened circumstances, but he was a little startled by the complete lack of emotion in her voice as she spoke the words. She did not sound sad or melancholy or even self-pitying; she sounded as if she had no feeling at all. "I am sorry to hear it, ma'am. I am a widower myself. How long have you been widowed?"

"Ten months, sir."

So soon? Had he been this devoid of feeling ten months after Lydia had died? As much as he reproached himself for his poor treatment of his late wife, he did not think he had been this cold to her memory. Lizzie, however, did not realize that the lady did not mourn. She charged forward and threw her arms around the lady's wet hips and hugged her tight. "I am sorry!"

Lady Shelby gave an odd little gasp and two small spots of color appeared in her cheeks. To his great surprise, she knelt down so that her face was level with Lizzie's own. "Thank you, my dear, you are very kind." Then she put her arms around Lizzie and hugged her back and put her mouth near Lizzie's ear and murmured softly, "And I am very sorry to hear about your mama." She stood up and held out her hand to his daughter. "Now let us go get dry and warm. Someone has given me some fine strawberry jam, and I think we should make some buttered toast and spread some on. What do you think?"

Lizzie nodded eagerly and took Lady Shelby's hand. They began walking together, and Phillip grabbed up his coat and followed. It was somehow an affecting sight to see his four-year-old daughter holding a lady's hand as she walked along.

Lydia had died giving birth to the child; he had never had the opportunity to see them together. And Catherine had never met Lizzie. The child had been a toddler when he had come so close to finally making Catherine his wife. It had not been until the dark days after she had married Ryde that Phillip—retreating home to lick his wounds—had paid any attention to the fact that he *had* a daughter.

Now she was the most precious thing in his life.

They had not gone far when it became clear how very tired his poor little girl was. Phillip swept Lizzie up into his arms and followed Lady Shelby as she led the way. He suspected the lady was tired, too, for the pretty sway of her walk kept slowing and slowing, but she was too polite to complain of her fatigue, and whenever he approached too hard on her heels, she would strive to speed her pace.

He tried to slow his strides to match her better, for he had no wish to press her, but he kept getting distracted from his pacing by the view of her as they walked. The lady's dress might be ugly and out of style, but sopping wet it had one advantage over many a dress of greater fashion and opulence; it showed the lady's figure to great advantage. It clung especially well to her generous hips, and Phillip was finding the undulating movement of those well-outlined curves a little too mesmerizing for comfort.

Fortunately, they soon reached Lady Shelby's cottage. It was smaller, even, than he had imagined it could be, and as she led them inside, Phillip noted that she seemed to draw herself up, as if determined to compensate for the meagerness of her home with the stateliness of her person. She courteously invited Phillip, who still held Lizzie in his arms, to be seated, but he was not about to ruin one of her few pieces of furniture with his sodden clothes, so she hurried off to find Lizzie something dry to wear.

She returned with a flannel nightgown and a long strip of cloth. The nightgown was obviously hers, and Phillip wondered how she thought the thing would possibly stay up on Lizzie's narrow shoulders, but he had underestimated Lady Shelby's ingenuity. She stripped off Lizzie's wet clothes and then slipped the nightgown over her head. As Phillip had expected, it drooped precariously, but Lady Shelby pulled the nightgown up so it was almost halved in length and wound and criss-crossed the strip of cloth so that the gown became a virtual kirtle on Lizzie's small frame.

"There," she said in satisfaction when she was done. She carefully rolled up one sleeve and then the other. "Now, my dear, doesn't it feel better to be dry? Sit down. You must be so tired."

Lizzie plopped down on the chair the lady indicated without a word.

"Now, sir," the lady said in a much more subdued voice, "I will see what I can find for you to wear." She abruptly left the room.

Phillip noted that Lizzie was drooping in her chair. There seemed to be no servant to ask, so hanging his dry coat on a hook by the door, he went in search of Lady Shelby to see if he could perhaps start the toast cooking on the hearth so Lizzie would have something to eat.

She was upstairs in her bedchamber, kneeling on the floor before a small chest of clothes. He came to a startled stop at the sight of her, for she was clutching a man's shirt to her face. Her eyes were closed, her nose was buried in the folds of the shirt as if she were smelling it, and her cheek was rubbing against the linen. He tried to retreat soundlessly, but a board creaked, and she looked up. She appeared as mortified as he felt, and he was chagrined to see her gray eyes shimmering with unshed tears.

"Lady Shelby, forgive me, I did not mean to intrude."

She shook her head wordlessly. She set the shirt carefully aside and pulled out another shirt and a pair of breeches from further down in the chest and handed them to him. "I will go be with your Elizabeth. You may change here." She hurried from the room.

Phillip looked down at the clothes in his hand ruefully. Her late husband's, no doubt. He grimaced to himself. So much for thinking she did not mourn him. He stared down at the folded shirt in the chest, feeling a pang. When he died, would there be anyone to grieve for him in such a fashion? Then Phillip heard a drip splash as it hit the floor, and he realized that if he stood there much longer in his wet things he was going to leave a puddle on her floor. He quickly stripped and put on the dry clothes, a little startled to find how very well they fit him.

He padded downstairs in his bare feet, holding his sodden boots and clothes at arms length. To his surprise, when he arrived in the tiny parlor, he found Lady Shelby down on her knees by Lizzie's chair. His daughter had fallen asleep on the chair and was perched very precariously. Lady Shelby was holding her in place with what must have been the last of her strength. Phillip hurried forward to set his dripping boots and clothes down on the bricks by the fireplace.

Lady Shelby turned to look at him, an expression of relief on her face. But that look suddenly turned to one of shock. Then her face was wiped clean of all emotion, and she said simply, "Can you take her, please? I did not want to lift her and get her all wet again."

Phillip went to Lizzie and scooped her up. She was so sleepy, she did not rouse at all but simply lay limp in his arms. He looked about him for some place to set her down, but there was no sofa, only another chair barely bigger than the one Lady Shelby had feared she would roll off of. "Perhaps you might put a blanket on the floor before the fire, ma'am, and I could lay her there?" he asked.

"Do not be ridiculous!" she snapped, warm, irate color suddenly flowing into her pale cheeks and animation into her face to replace that statue-like calm. "I may have little, sir, but I do have a bed! Take her up to my room and set her on it, please."

He was sorry to have hurt her pride, but preferred this irritated version of the lady to the emotionless one by far. He carried Lizzie upstairs, and Lady Shelby followed close behind him. Before he could lay Lizzie down, she pulled back the covers and then motioned him to set her down between the sheets. When he had done so, she pulled the covers up under Lizzie's chin and dropped a kiss on her forehead and gazed up at him with a challenging look as if she dared him to say a word.

He knew it would be wiser not to, but he felt compelled to speak anyway, "The bed might be a mistake, ma'am. She may sleep a good long time all cozy like that. I think her scare in the water took more out of her than I realized."

"Sir, she may have the use of the bed as long as she needs it."

"But I cannot walk her home in the dark, ma'am, and there are probably only three hours of daylight left. The walk home will take at least two."

She hesitated, then said tightly, "If need be, you are both welcome to stay the night."

He gazed at her. Damn, but he was regretting his stupid impulse to moon after Catherine the minute he arrived in the neighborhood. It had almost cost him Lizzie, and now he was becoming more and more indebted to this woman. "Do you have a servant that comes in the morning?"

She shook her head, avoiding his eye. "And you?" she asked. "Will your aunt worry if you do not return tonight?"

"No, she and my cousins have not yet returned from their shopping expedition to London. Lizzie and I were not expected until the end of the week." *I was just too damn impatient to catch a glimpse of Catherine to wait.*

"Then all should be well." She shivered.

For a minute, he was too stupid to realize she was cold. He thought she was just reacting to the thought of having him under her roof all night. Then she shivered again.

"You must change out of those wet clothes, ma'am. You have been so busy taking care of us, you have neglected yourself."

"If you will wait downstairs, I will put on some dry things now."

He nodded, but he was uneasy. She had no maid, and—he eyed her rather hideous brown dress—the fastenings looked to be behind her and were twisted up from the wet and their exertions in the stream. She was starting to shiver in earnest now. "You need no help, do you?"

Her eyes widened. "Sir, I believe I can manage."

He frowned. He was not quite convinced, but he had no desire to dig himself deeper. He made her a small bow and left the room.

Downstairs, he paced around the tiny parlor, suddenly restless. Considerable time passed, and still she had not come down. He moved into the small kitchen. He found a covered plate with some bread. He cut some slices and found a toasting fork and carried them back to the parlor. He had almost toasted two entire slices when Lady Shelby entered the room, still in her sodden dress, still shivering. Her face was calm, but her gray eyes were full of frustration. "Sir," she said, her voice wavering unsteadily, "I fear I do need assistance after all. Several of my ties are knotted. I have tried everything, but I have not the strength to rip them in two as I would sorely like. Can you please assist me?"

He set the toast on the plate and rose to his feet. "Of course, ma'am." He crossed to stand behind her, realizing suddenly that she had a great deal of hair. It was wet and tangled and looked a muddy blonde sort of color, but as he tried to lift it aside to see the back of her dress, there was something surprisingly appealing about the sheer weight of it in his hands and the texture of it against his skin. There was so much of it, that once he had managed to gather it all up, he could not simply set it aside on her shoulder and expect it to stay. He began to gently twist it round and round into a sort of plait.

Suddenly, she trembled and made a small sound.

"Lady Shelby, are you unwell?"

Mutely, she shook her head, which unfortunately pulled some of her hair free. Again he gathered it up and again he gently twisted it.

The sound was tinier this time, but it was there. He said nothing, just pushed her twined hair down her front where it would be out of the way. If in the process, his hand brushed along the soft skin above her bodice, he was not really being provocative, just curious. But her response left him in no doubt.

For a long moment, he was too distracted by the way she had quivered at his touch, to remember what he was supposed to be accomplishing. It had been far, far too long since he had been with a woman, and all he could think of was that he wanted to make her do it again. Then she shivered from cold, not longing, and he was recalled to the task at hand.

He began trying to untie the knotted laces on her dress—unfortunately, there were three—but they were too wet and too tight to be undone, and every time his fingers accidentally brushed her bare back she gave a little shudder that made it harder and harder for him to resist the impulse to simple rip the ties in two. Finally, he did give in to the urge to just tear at the things—for her soft breaths kept quickening and deepening in a way that was driving him a little mad—but the damned cloth ties would not rip. The wetness and the sturdiness of the fabric conspired to hold them fast, the knots only tightening with his exertion of force. Growing angry, he excused himself, returned to the kitchen, seized the knife he had used to slice the bread, and carried it back to the parlor.

"Lady Shelby, be very, very still. I'm going to cut your laces with a knife. Are you ready?"

Again she nodded mutely, which was just as well, for he feared the effect her voice would have on him just as he needed his hand to be steady.

He pulled the ties as far away from her back as he could and tried to pull the knife through them in one steady stroke, but again they proved too tough, and he had to saw at them back and forth. One finally was cut free, then the second. He continued sawing at the third and it began to shear. However, at the same moment the sodden weight of her dress shifted, and to his utter horror the fabric pulled at the knife, and he accidentally nicked her back.

She gave a small cry, and he dropped the knife with a clatter. A tiny line of scarlet appeared on her ivory skin, and filled with remorse, he pressed his mouth to it, trying to kiss it better as if it were one of Lizzie's scrapes.

"I am so terribly sorry," he murmured against her back, punctuating each word with another brush of his lips. Indeed, he was so contrite, that he did not, at first, notice how still and intent she had gone. Then he ran a finger lightly along the cut, checking to make sure it had stopped bleeding, and she gave a start. Fearful he had caused her more pain, he wrapped his arms around her to comfort her.

If before she had quivered, now her whole body shook.

Suddenly determined to see her face, he turned her in his arms. Her face wore its usual look of calm, but her lips were parted, and she would not meet his gaze. He tipped up her chin so she was forced to look at him. Her gray eyes were not calm at all. They were dark with longing and so full of tumultuous emotion he felt a stab of fear. Then she closed her eyes, as if determined to shut him out, and her lips clamped tightly together.

He felt bereft and unaccountably angry at her withdrawal. Without thinking, he kissed her, determined to get her mouth back open again. He coaxed her with his lips and teased her with his tongue and worried her mouth with his own until finally her lips parted and he could slide his tongue inside her. He felt a surge of triumph as he did so, but his triumph was short-lived.

Her face was cold and wet as he cradled it in his hands, but her mouth was warm and cozy and inviting, and he explored it with great delight. Then she began to return his kisses, softly at first, but then with a growing intensity that took his comfort away and set him on fire. Suddenly she was the one invading his mouth, and he wanted her there, needed her there with a desperation that frightened him even more than her emotion-filled eyes had.

His hands slid down from her face and inside the loose, wet folds of her dress. He caressed the swell of her breasts through her corset and her waist through her shift, and then he tugged up the sodden folds of her shift and dress so he could touch with trembling fingers the bare, round curve of her hips.

She moaned.

He was defeated. There was no turning back.

He looked into her face. She was almost panting, she was breathing so hard, but her eyes were still tightly closed. He grew angry again.

"Look at me!"

Slowly the gray eyes opened. At first, her gaze was unfocused, but eventually she seemed to actually see him. Feeling suddenly less certain, he said in a softer voice "I need you."

She stared up at him, and—to his great frustration—he had absolutely no idea what she was thinking.

He pulled her tightly against him, and he wanted to kiss her, but he couldn't stop staring into her eyes. "Do you understand me?" Now he was the one breathing hard. "I want to be with you. Right here. Right now. On this hard, detestable floor. Are you willing?"

She continued to stare up at him. Then in a tone full of despair, she said, "Yes, I am willing."

He wanted to shake her. Instead, he pulled her still tighter to him. "I do not want to make you sad. I want to make you happy."

She sighed. "I do not know if I can separate the two." She reached up and touched his cheek. "But I am willing to try. I think it would make me happy. I have been very lonely."

Then he did kiss her, and her arms came up to twine around his neck, and he began to feel happy himself.

Until suddenly—in the bedroom upstairs—Lizzie screamed.

www.ingramcontent.com/pod-product-compliance
Lightning Source LLC
Chambersburg PA
CBHW020228180626
46810CB00006B/2088